TEST OF FAITH

GIDEON RYKER
BOOK 2

JACK SLATER

Cover design by Damonza

Created with Vellum

ONE

"Papito," the boy cried, his features barely visible in the dark room and shadowed further by the shaky lens of the video camera. He was wearing a white vest and gray underwear. All other clothing had been torn from his body. Red welts covered his skin, and his crotch was stained dark. "Where is my daddy?"

A sicario wearing a mask emblazoned with a black-and-white skull leered at the camera, brandishing a pistol. His words were as crude as his rough country accent. "This is why you don't fuck with the Knights."

Then the gunshots rang out.

Eduardo Salazar shot upright in bed, the whites of his eyes visible through the gloom as the knock on the door faded into nothing. He reached automatically for the pistol on the chipped and battered bedside table of the seedy motel room. The weapon's safety was off, as it was every night. He leveled it at the glowing fire escape sign on the back of the door, his aim steady despite the racing of his heart.

Another knock sounded at the door, followed by a low whispered voice. "Sir, can you hear me? It's time."

Salazar didn't respond. His chest heaved, and he felt the clammy stickiness of the sweat drops that glistened on his skin and stained the T-shirt he'd worn to bed. He breathed out deeply, feeling his heart rate began to slow.

Just a false alarm. He glanced at the red display on the bedside clock. It was 3 a.m. His wake-up call was right on time.

His son's final words echoed in his ears as he climbed off the bed, which creaked and squeaked as it gratefully relinquished his weight. He heard them every night. He couldn't even remember how many times he'd watched that video. Hundreds?

Thousands?

He hadn't seen it since he first arrived at New Eden almost five years earlier as a broken man. Like the rest of his possessions, it had been taken from him. But he remembered every word. Every tremor of fear on his boy's face. He could practically smell the sweat and piss and fear in that cramped basement.

And then the blood. He would never again hold Mateo's warm hand. But he'd ensured that all those responsible for the boy's death had perished. And then he left his former life behind.

Salazar walked to the bathroom, set the pistol down on the porcelain counter, and splashed water on his face. He heard renewed knocking at the door and ignored it until he was washed and dressed in dark business-casual pants and a black shirt that he tucked in. He neatly folded the T-shirt he'd worn to sleep and left it on the freshly made bed.

He turned to leave, then stopped himself, slowly turning his head until his gaze stopped on the bedside table. The drawer was open a crack, not enough to see inside. He gritted his teeth and pulled it fully open, revealing a pair of dark orange pill bottles inside. The patient name section on both labels was blank.

What he was doing was forbidden, he knew. If the Brotherhood ever found out he was medicating himself, the consequences would be dire. It was against the Mandates.

And it was all that was keeping him sane.

He popped the cap on one bottle anyway, pulling out a pill that he swallowed dry. He closed the drawer, fully this time, and immediately felt a little more at ease.

And finally, he opened the door.

The man on the other side looked relieved and terrified in equal parts as Salazar appeared before him. He held up a black duffel bag, his hands only slightly trembling. "Your tools, sir."

Salazar nodded. He spoke in a gruff voice, when he spoke at all, little more cultured than the men in his dreams. He was a man of few words. "The targets?"

"Still there."

"Then take me to them."

The drive to the house in the desert was short, just half an hour. Salazar motioned for his driver to kill the lights, then slow to a crawl as they drove within a mile of the place. It took several minutes to close the last few hundred yards, during which time he pulled on a pair of thin tan work gloves.

The lights inside the house—really more of a shack—were dark. Only a faint glow emanated from inside. It flickered occasionally, indicating that it might be from a candle or an oil lamp. Salazar sat silently and watched the house for several minutes after his driver killed the engine, until he was satisfied that their approach hadn't been detected. The men inside were either asleep or unconscious.

"Wait here," Salazar grunted as he reached for the car's door handle. All the background noise in his mind began to fade away.

Was it the Prozac? Or his purpose?

"You're going in alone?" the man answered, his voice as nervous as it was hopeful.

"Wait here," he reiterated as he reached down for the duffel bag stored in the footwell.

He silently tugged the handle open and stepped out onto the dusty earth. The soil underneath his feet was soft and deadened the sound of his footsteps. He barely needed to move with his typical stealth and instead walked right up to the front door.

And knocked.

Nobody inside stirred until he knocked again and a third time for good measure. Finally there came a groan from inside, then the characteristic scrape of footsteps as someone rose and walked unsteadily to the door. A voice muttered something, but the words were indistinct and obscured by the walls of the shack.

Salazar tensed as he heard the familiar sound of the deadbolt sliding back. He waited until the door handle twisted from the other side and the door itself pulled back just an inch, then he kicked out with the heel of his foot and sent it flying backward, into whoever had opened it.

He strode into the candlelit one-room shack with his pistol raised, quickly casing the place with a single glance.

There were three men inside. Two slumped on threadbare couches by the far wall and one cowering on the floor clutching his bleeding face. The two on the couches were clearly under the influence. They barely stirred. Drug paraphernalia was everywhere and not limited to a single narcotic of choice, either. He saw a bong, a pipe for meth or heroin, and a scattering of small plastic baggies on the coffee table in the center of the room, along with a half-drunk bottle of cheap rum.

In addition to the drugs was a handful of weapons: a rusted

fighting knife, a dented Kalashnikov-style rifle, and a scattering of handguns. None were in easy reach of the man on the floor.

"Up," he growled, aiming his weapon at him. He dropped the duffel bag to his side and kneeled slowly, keeping his aim true and his attention fixed on all three potential dangers.

With his left hand, he unzipped the bag, reached inside, and felt for a bundle of cable ties. They were thick and unbreakable, as he'd requested. He stepped over to the man cowering in front of him and growled, "Can you stand?"

"What?"

Salazar pressed the pistol's muzzle against the man's bloodied temple. "Don't make me ask again."

"Yes," he whimpered, his eyes wide and white in the dark.

He pressed a bundle of the zip cuffs into the addict's grasp, feeling his emaciated frame as he did so. These three were barely men. He'd seen this progression before. Even without his assistance, they wouldn't last much longer.

"Tie up your friends," Salazar commanded.

He watched as the man did so, struggling to pull his friends' arms free from their slumped positions. When it was done, Salazar secured his assistant to a rickety wooden chair, then hauled the other two upright and settled them into seated positions on one of the couches.

This at last seemed to rouse the two men from their narcotic slumber. The one on the left, a sallow-faced sack of bones with teeth that were a riot of yellow and black, jerked awake with a start. Despite the pitiful physical condition of his body, his eyes were sharp.

"Who are you?" he asked in a raspy voice.

The last of the three, the one on the right, woke more slowly. Unlike his friend, he appeared to be more of a follower than a leader. He peered warily at Salazar but said nothing, his body language cringing.

"You're Chandler?" Salazar said instead.

"How do you know my name?"

"You stole something from my boss." Salazar paused. He leaned forward. "He wants it back."

"Get fucked!" Chandler said, jerking his head back and hiking up to fire a mouthful of spittle at Salazar, who dodged it easily.

This wasn't his first rodeo.

He stood up fully and looked over the interior of the shack. There was no electricity, but in addition to the sole burning candle on the coffee table, he found another half dozen or so scattered around the room. He lit a long, slender wick from the first, and in short order the shack was much better illuminated.

Salazar stood in the center of the room and turned slowly, his keen gaze taking in every detail. In addition to the drugs on the table, he noticed two large gray suitcases peeking out from behind the couch. If they'd attempted to hide them, it was a poor job.

He gathered all the weaponry, cleared rounds from chambers, and tossed the magazines out of the nearest window. Then he bent to the duffel bag on the floor and reached inside.

"What the fuck, man," one of the three addicts gasped at the sight of the blade he withdrew.

There was nothing fancy about it. It was a machete with a cheap wooden handle and a fifteen-inch blade that was sharpened to a vicious point. This one was new, but he'd carried many like it. Designed for hacking through thick brush, they made short work of human flesh and bone.

Chandler would have to die, he decided. He was clearly the ringleader of the three. It was probably his idea to steal the shipment. The addict with the bleeding face also had the air of a psychopath. It happened with men whose brains were rotted by drugs. Whatever vestiges of empathy and humanity they were born with were corroded away by the things they had to do to acquire their next fix.

Over and over it went. Until one day there was nothing left.

The quiet one, well.... He would have to see.

"Take them, for God's sake," Chandler whimpered as Salazar walked slowly toward him. "I couldn't resist. I know I did wrong, but..."

Salazar moved robotically, drawing the blade up above his head. He brought it down with the same brutal efficiency that he'd done dozens, maybe hundreds of times. All those years working for the cartels had drained the empathy from him. Corroded his own soul.

The machete bit into the upper part of Chandler's thigh, severing muscle and sinew and fat, not stopping until it hit bone, and even then, not fast. The instant the handle stopped vibrating, Salazar pulled it free, drew it back, and sliced again, hitting the same spot with practiced ease.

Again and again, he cut, somehow blocking out the sound of screams, his own, Chandler's, and the other two.

And then Chandler stopped screaming. He stopped breathing. And he was gone.

It took Salazar several seconds to realize that his victim was dead. He took a step back to survey his handiwork. The man's leg was almost completely severed. Arterial spray had soaked both the man to his left and the one to his right. Salazar himself was slick with sticky red blood.

"You're a fucking monster," the psychopath whimpered, his eyes wide and truly fearful for the first time.

Salazar just grunted. He pulled the machete free from Chandler's thigh bone, twisting to help loosen it, then turned to his second victim.

The man was even skinnier than Chandler. His body was

looking for a reason to give up. Salazar offered it one. There was less blood this time. It was as though the man's heart simply gave out.

Still, by the time he was done, Salazar was panting from the effort. He tried to pull the blade free but lost his grip on the handle. Everything was slippery from the blood. He was coated from head to toe. It would take hours in the shower before he was washed clean.

Of the blood, anyway.

"Please..." whispered the last remaining thief as he wrenched the blade free a second time, his eyes glassy with shock. "I just did what my brother said."

Salazar gestured at Chandler with the machete. "Him?"

The man nodded numbly.

Salazar stepped in front of him and rested the dripping blade on his shoulder. The man shrank away from it, but there was only so far he could go.

"What's your name?"

"Rick."

"Rick Weston?" he said, glancing sideways at the man's dead brother.

"Yes."

"You will live, Rick," he said in his thickly accented English. "But I want you to give your friends a message."

"Whatever you say."

Salazar leaned forward and pressed his forehead against his prisoner's. "Never steal from the Brotherhood. You understand?"

"I'll tell them," he gasped.

"Good."

Salazar wiped the machete's blade clean on the man's sweater, then used it to cut his cuffs free.

"You will wait here until it's light. I would advise against going to the cops."

Rick didn't move as Salazar gathered his things or as he pulled the suitcases out from behind the couch and checked the contents—two dozen plastic-wrapped bricks of pure heroin. Chandler Weston had taken the drugs on credit and failed to deliver a profit.

He'd paid for the mistake with his life.

Salazar grabbed the half-empty bottle of rum from the coffee table and placed it in the duffel bag before he zipped it up. He would need help sleeping tonight. He slung the duffel over his shoulder, then lifted a suitcase with each hand.

He walked to the car without a backward glance. The driver stared at him with wide eyes bulging from a pale complexion.

"Just drive," Salazar growled.

TWO

Gideon Ryker pulled at the straps of the backpack that rode high up on his shoulders, cinching it in place. It was weighed down with about thirty pounds of ballast—a combination of filled gallon milk cartons and rusted iron weight plates he'd found in the carport behind the cabin.

His brow was already speckled with droplets of sweat, his bare torso streaked where rivulets had coursed through the dust on his skin. He stared up at the winding road through the forested hill that led up to the cabin he was sharing with Zara Walker. His chest heaved as his lungs topped up on oxygen before the next climb.

The spot where he was standing was visible from the lookout window in the crook of the A-frame loft space. It was a strange room—barely six feet wide at its base and so short he had to double over at his waist to enter it.

But when you were lying on your belly, that was no concern. And that was how he spent most of his time up there, flat on the floor, his cheek pressed against a high-caliber hunting rifle. The distance was only about two hundred yards.

He'd zeroed the weapon's sights and tested his ability to fire half a dozen shots at that range in a matter of seconds.

Out of the corner of his eye, Gideon could also see the trees he'd attached security cameras to. They were battery-operated, on a wired network, and had thermal vision capability so they were able to pull double shifts at night. The sensors were paired with additional cameras scattered throughout the grounds and infrared trip wires hooked up to the same security system.

It's not paranoia if they really want to execute you in public.

A month earlier, he and Zara had barely survived their attempt to capture Senator Sheldon McKinney from his home in Middleburg, Virginia, along with a copy of the man's insurance policy—a file containing proof not just of his own crimes but also those of the mysterious cult known as the Brotherhood.

It was an organization that Gideon knew well.

Kind of.

His memory was still hazy from the effects of a poison called datura stramonium, an extract of a common weed that inflicted highly uncommon symptoms. Among these were delirium, psychosis, and amnesia. He'd been drugged with it during his capture and torture by a breakaway faction of the Brotherhood led by Senator McKinney.

Many of his memories had returned. Not all, but more with every passing day. It was as though his mind had tensed up like a hedgehog in the face of danger, and only now was it relaxing and giving up its secrets.

These days, his thoughts were relentlessly occupied by memories of his sister Julia. Somehow she'd been there that night in Middleburg. The Brotherhood had married her to Senator McKinney—though for what reason he had no idea. He'd given her the opportunity to escape with him and Zara.

But she didn't take it. He could see that she'd wanted to,

but she was too conflicted by her loyalty to the faith that exploited her. She'd taken McKinney back to the Brotherhood, ruining their plan to use the senator to reveal the cult's crimes to the public.

"What the hell were you thinking?" he muttered. He wasn't sure whether he was referring to his sister or himself.

He and Zara had escaped with McKinney's insurance policy—a thumb drive containing dozens of gigabytes of the senator's files on his own crimes and those of the Brotherhood. The problem was that they were encrypted.

Gideon's wristwatch—a cheap Casio—beeped, signaling that his allotted rest period was over. He welcomed the sound, if not the hardship it foretold. He tugged the backpack's straps one more time, then leaned forward, into the hill, and began to run.

The cabin was at the top of a wooded hill a few miles from the town of Clay, West Virginia. It was, for all intents and purposes, in the ass end of nowhere. And being that it was in the foothills of the Appalachian Mountains, it was also extremely steep.

He was panting heavily by the time he was a third of the way up the two-hundred-yard climb to the peak. By halfway, fresh streams of sweat poured down his temples, and spittle flecked at his lips like a prize horse at the end of a race.

Gideon wasn't trying to build an Instagram body. He cared little for the way he looked in the mirror, though in truth, the exercise regime he had begun was paying dividends in that regard. Though it might seem strange to an outsider, his regime was intended to maximize only one thing.

His lethality.

Excess muscle weighing him down was no better than having no muscle at all. Six-pack abs were a bug, not a feature—evidence that those showing them off didn't have enough body fat to sustain themselves through prolonged hardship. The same went for the ability to sprint, but not run for long distances, and the opposite.

Gideon was building himself a body capable of doing it all.

Or… *almost* capable.

The dirt road up to the cabin kinked to the right around a wooded knoll and grew even steeper on the final approach. It was only fifty yards, but with the weighted backpack pulling him backward with every step, it might as well have been the final assault on Everest.

Do it.

The picture at the corner of Gideon's vision began to fray and darken as his lungs struggled to provide enough oxygen to the muscles all over his body. His thighs and hamstrings felt heavy, his shoulders pinched, even his triceps were fatigued from the effort of pumping his arms up and down at his sides.

As he reached the top of the hill, about ten feet in front of a short set of wooden steps leading up to the porch of the cabin, Gideon doubled over and fell to his hands and knees on the ground.

Despite knowing what was coming, there was nothing he could do to prevent it. Leaving only his left palm flat on the ground to support his weight, he first retched violently and then vomited onto the dirt. The acid stung the tender flesh at the back of his throat, though Gideon couldn't even see the contents of his stomach for a few seconds until enough air flooded back into his lungs.

The stars and spots on his vision slowly faded, and he slumped back on his ass before lying flat on the ground, propped up only by the backpack. The sprint was his fifth. After making it to the top of the hill a fourth time, he'd known that it was playing with fire to attempt it again.

But he'd done it anyway.

His lungs slowly returned to their normal function, allowing him to roll onto his front and push himself upright. The puddle of vomit was thankfully clear—he'd consumed nothing but a few gulps of water since breakfast—and quickly seeped into the late-spring dirt.

Gideon glanced up at the porch, then checked the windows to see whether Zara was watching. A flicker of shame battled the heat of exertion on his cheeks.

"Some protector," he muttered, thankful that he couldn't make out anyone behind the glass.

He kicked up some earth and pushed it over the evidence before building up the courage to jog to the final task of his day's fitness plan. His muscles ached from exertion and the effects of the lactic acid that had to be building up within them. It would have been so easy to throw in the towel and head inside for a shower and a cold beer.

But that wasn't the way that Gideon was made.

And besides, he couldn't afford laziness. Not right now. Not with Zara inside the cabin, in danger merely because she'd associated herself with him. And certainly not with Julia still in the Brotherhood's clutches.

He puffed out his cheeks as his sister's tortured face once again filled his mind's eye. She appeared to him as clearly as she had that night, holding a gun on him.

Where is she now? He wondered. *And what are they doing with her?*

Around the back of the cabin was a carport. Their own vehicle wasn't stored back here—it was pointed nose down the hill in case they needed to make a quick getaway. The carport was used to store a variety of old furniture, bits of rusted machinery, and a huge stack of seasoned firewood.

Gideon pulled a heavy axe out of a thick wooden tree stump. Beside the stump were dozens of large sections of hardwood trees—some wider than he could stretch both his arms around. Beside that was a pile of already split logs, evidence of his hard work day after day.

They didn't need more wood. Despite the altitude, the daytime weather in Appalachia was a comfortable seventy-seven degrees. It dropped to the fifties at night, when they fired up the wood stove to cook with, but he'd split enough logs the very first day to last them weeks.

But that wasn't the point.

Before starting, he opened the backpack and pulled out one of the weighted gallon jugs of water that he used to swill his mouth clean before drinking deeply for several seconds.

And then he began.

As he manhandled one of the large sections of trunk onto the stump—it had to weigh a hundred, maybe a hundred-ten pounds—the sinews and muscles of his back strained and popped. His shoulders, already exhausted from supporting the weight of the bag, screamed for mercy.

"Come on," he grunted, and with one final push and a nudge from his knee, he managed to lift the heavy trunk section into place.

Unfortunately, that was only the start. He picked the axe back up, holding it in a double-handed grip, and brought it up over his head. He stood there for a second, his core tensed and the muscles of his arms popping from the effort of supporting the heavy axe. He almost resembled a Viking preparing to go into battle.

Gideon focused on a spot at the center of the log a couple of inches to the left of a knot that he definitely didn't want to hit. He inhaled deeply, then swung the axe down like a striking cobra, generating power from his thighs, back, and shoulders.

The head of the axe embedded itself deep into the surface of the wood. The handle vibrated slightly in his grip as the heavy tool came to an almost instant stop. Gideon didn't pause but gave the handle an upward push to free it, and brought it right back up.

He repeated the trick almost a dozen times, aiming the head of the axe a couple of inches to the side of the initial cut with each strike. It was even more exhausting than the sprint training on the hill had been, but before each cut, he pictured the face of an imagined enemy—Father Gabriel or a Chosen operative. Anyone he would have to scythe through to get to his sister. Rage at the reminder of her situation flowed through him, fueling his orgy of destruction.

Once the initial cut was deep enough, Gideon used the blade of the axe to make individual notches all around the circumference of the trunk section. They would be his logs.

And then he got to work, hoisting the axe high above his head and bringing it down on the first of those notches. The blade bit in, but the log failed to split. Over and over again, he brought down the axe, but each time the blade embedded without a satisfying crack.

Gideon's face reddened, both from the exertion of the chopping and his frustration that the log just wouldn't break. He brought the head of the axe down in a fury, beating out a tempo that somehow seemed in time with the beating of his heart.

As he snapped forward, he punctuated the strikes with curses: "You. Piece. Of. Shit."

On the last, two things happened at once. The blade of the axe finally drove in deep enough to cause the trunk section to split in two.

And the handle broke in half.

"Dammit," he said scornfully, tossing the smashed handle to the ground. Replacing it would require a trip to the hardware store in town. It wasn't as though anyone was looking for them in Clay, WV, but even so, he didn't like exposing himself to observation more than absolutely necessary.

A click behind him caused him to spin around. He saw Zara standing there, clapping slowly and ironically.

"I'm loving your Rocky arc," she said with a raised eyebrow. "But maybe you're taking it a little far?"

"Yeah, yeah," Gideon grumbled, sinking to his haunches and picking up the water jug. He lifted it to his lips and drained a dozen ounces of liquid.

He held it up to her. "Want some?"

"Thanks," she said with a mock-sweet smile. "But I heard you earlier. I'm good."

Gideon made a face. "Sorry about that. What's up?"

Zara grinned, her eyes sparkling. "It can wait—if you want to shower, that is."

"You didn't come here to get me in the shower," he fired back.

"Maybe I did, maybe I didn't," she said. "But you're right. My decryption program completed another batch. I think I found something."

THREE

Julia sat on the edge of her single bed, her back ramrod straight. The small cell in the nunnery had a locked window that was her only porthole to the world outside. It looked out onto a small yard hemmed in by a wooden fence. The space was neatly maintained and lushly planted.

But she'd been staring at it for over a month. Occasionally she saw some of the sisters working out there. They never met her gaze. They barely even acknowledged her presence.

She knew that they slept in rooms just like hers. There was just one difference. Theirs didn't have a bolt on the outside.

Her breakfast sat on a tray on the cell's small writing desk. Apart from the bed, that was the only other piece of furniture that the small space could accommodate. There were no books, other than the thin volume that contained the Mandates. She'd read that cover to cover more times than she could recall.

As she stared at her breakfast, her stomach twisted into knots, coalescing into a single hard ball that compressed and compressed until it exploded outward, a big bang of energy that flooded into her, compelling her to do something, anything, anywhere that wasn't here.

But of course, she couldn't.

Julia tipped her head back and let out a long, silent scream. A woman had taught that trick to her when she was just a child.

"Let it out, girl. Just don't let anyone hear."

Her head fell forward again of its own accord, and she sat panting for a few seconds to regain her breath. She was out of shape now. If she pinched the skin around her stomach, it felt soft and forgiving.

She wanted to run. To feel the wind in her hair and her legs stretching as they beat the ground.

But it was hopeless. No matter how often she begged to be allowed outside, the sisters refused.

"Be patient," they said. "Your time will come."

But when?

She stared wildly around the room, taking in the plain whitewashed walls for the thousandth time. There was nothing in here that could possibly distract her from her thoughts. That was the point. The Sisters believed that only by eliminating distraction and temptation could one truly understand her faith.

Maybe that was true. But in the absence of stimulation, Julia's mind had instead begun to creep into a different state.

Doubt.

Had she done the right thing coming back here? It seemed the only possible decision when she held that gun on Gideon—her own brother. She should have killed him. She knew that. But she had found herself unable to pull the trigger. She knew that family blood was thinner than that shared by the members of the Brotherhood.

And yet she couldn't kill him.

So she'd taken Senator McKinney back to New Eden to face his judgment. He'd betrayed the Brotherhood, that much was clear to her now. Worse than that, he'd betrayed Father Gabriel.

She'd been separated from McKinney—her husband—on arrival at New Eden. What happened to him? Was he already dead?

"Why do I care?" she whispered.

Julia stood, still suffused by the energy that had overcome her a few moments before. She pulled the simple white dress over her shoulders and lay it on the bed, standing in the center of the cell in just her underwear.

She couldn't run. But the sisters couldn't prevent her from exercising. Not in here.

Physical exertion was frowned upon for the women of the Brotherhood, though not forbidden. It was seen as being too close to men's work. Women were to cook, to clean, to bear children. *Always* to bear children so that the next generation could be born.

She dropped into a squat position and pushed herself back up, repeating the calisthenics routine twenty times before pausing to collect her breath.

Definitely unfit.

Gideon had always encouraged her to run when they played as kids. Before he was taken away to apprentice with the Chosen, anyway. And before her own preparation.

"Stop thinking of him!" Julia hissed.

She threw herself into the workout, pushing her body beyond what it was probably capable of. She had no way of telling time in the cell, at least not exactly. But the sun was setting overhead by the time she finished, her skin glistening with sweat. Every muscle in her body ached, and her heart pounded in her chest.

Julia stripped naked and walked to the small basin in the corner of the room. She wetted a small towel hanging on a hook on the wall and used it to clean herself up as best she could. Her left arm was pointing in the air so that she could dab her armpit clean when the telltale scrape of the bolt opening startled her.

She spun around as the door swung inward. It wasn't time for dinner. The thrice-daily deliveries of her meals were the only contact she had with the outside world, and the sisters didn't exactly make good conversation.

This was a break from the pattern.

"Lady," she gasped as the identity of her visitor became clear.

Lady Miranda was not only the head of the group of sisters who lived in this prayer house; she led the entire Order. Julia didn't know exactly how many of the Brotherhood's women had dedicated their lives to their faith—and forgone children in the process—but she was sure there had to be hundreds of them across New Eden.

Julia suddenly realized that she was still naked, and she reached hurriedly for the dress lying on the bed. Her skin was still spotted with water, and though she shrugged the dress over her shoulders, the fabric clung to her wet skin.

Lady Miranda was in her sixties. She was from the first generation of those who had founded New Eden, Julia knew, though she was only a child when her parents had brought her to the small ranch in Texas that was the seed for everything that followed. Her clothing was similar to Julia's—simple and white, though the cloth of her dress was thicker and fell all the way to the floor. Her eyes narrowed in her lined face at the sight in front of her.

"What is this?"

"I apologize, Lady," Julia said with a sharp bow of her head. "I was cleaning myself."

"Your hair is a mess," the Lady replied curtly. She pushed Julia toward and onto the bed, forcing her into a seated position, then began braiding her hair. The whole process took several minutes, during which time neither woman said a word.

When she was done, Julia said, "Thank you for visiting me."

"It's time," the Lady said, her face revealing nothing.

"For what?"

"Father Gabriel wishes to see you now."

LADY MIRANDA SWEPT Julia through empty corridors and past dozens of cell doors similar to her own. All were closed. Julia heard faint mumblings of prayer from inside and felt a flush of shame at her own recent absence. They walked in silence, as she had done on all previous supervised excursions to the communal bathrooms that all the sisters shared.

A black Suburban was waiting in the front driveway with a man behind the wheel. He jumped out instantly and hurried to open the rear door for Lady Miranda. Julia scurried in after, and he closed the door behind them.

They rode in silence for about half an hour. Julia pinned her nose to the window, grateful for the sight of anything that wasn't the convent's backyard. The ranch was in full bloom. They passed dozens of groundskeepers dressed in green overalls, carrying tools from the back of neatly maintained golf carts. As always, New Eden was a haven of peace and orderliness in a manic and dangerous world.

It was a sight that had brought joy to Julia's heart throughout her entire childhood and then all of her visits back to the ranch after she was sent to DC. But strangely, today it left her cold, despite the sun dappling through the canopies of the trees that lined either side of the road.

And I don't know why.

The roads inside the ranch were smooth, mostly freshly laid black asphalt as far as the eye could see. Potholes were filled almost before they had formed. The few vehicles on the roads pulled to the side to let the Suburban pass, something Julia barely even noticed.

The drive took half an hour, a silent reminder of New Eden's vast size. They only stopped once, at a guarded gate into a fenced compound just a minute or so before their final arrival. Men with guns and mirrors on long sticks checked the driver's credentials and examined the underside of the vehicle. When they opened the door to check who was riding in the back, they instantly bowed their heads in respect to Lady Miranda.

"Don't delay our work any longer," she chided.

The gate opened without further delay, and the Suburban slowed as it entered the lushly watered grounds of Father Gabriel's residence. Julia had only been here once before, the night she was summoned from her former life and told that she was to marry Senator McKinney.

A chill ran down her spine.

Did I fail him?

The Suburban slowed and braked to a halt in front of a water fountain in the center of the front driveway of the Tuscan-style villa. A woman in a white dress much like Julia's own—another sister of the Order—was waiting for them. The driver climbed out and rushed to open Lady Miranda's door.

"Come, girl," she commanded as she swept out of the car.

Julia followed, feeling like a leaf blowing in the wind. The sister waiting for them bowed her head as the Lady approached.

"I am to take you to Father," she said in a soft voice.

The sister led them through marble-tiled floors through the first floor of the villa. Occasionally Julia saw flashes of movement, mostly household staff cleaning various rooms or carrying supplies to the kitchen.

Despite her concerns about why she'd been brought here, part of her couldn't help but thrill to the fact that she was here at all. Most citizens of New Eden never saw Father Gabriel except during his sermons. He was above the rest of the community.

But not her.

The sister stopped in front of a pair of ornate double doors, bowed her head, and knocked. She waited for a beat, whether out of politeness or in response to some signal that Julia wasn't aware of, and then pulled the doors open and ushered them into a surprisingly small reception room that contained an L-shaped sofa facing a large flat-screen television.

Lady Miranda swept inside, her attitude indicating that this was nothing out of the ordinary for her. Julia scurried after her, customarily averting her gaze from the man seated on the sofa. All she saw of him were his shoes, tan desert boots, and the bottom of his slate-gray hiking pants.

"I've brought the girl, Father," Lady Miranda said in a voice designed to carry.

"Julia," Father Gabriel said, his voice warm and inviting. She watched as he patted the sofa beside him with a flat palm. "Come, sit with me. Miranda, you may go."

Julia almost felt the woman's dress crackle with fury at being so casually dismissed. There was a pause of no longer than a second or so— but noticeable regardless—before she curtly said, "Of course, Father."

And then Julia was left alone with the leader of the Brotherhood. She felt frozen, locked in place, not even daring to look up at him.

"Come here," he said, his voice slightly sharper and less inviting.

She did as she was requested, shuffling over with leaden feet, and sat a foot away from him. He inched closer to her.

"I apologize for leaving you waiting for so long," he said.

Julia blinked. Was he apologizing to *her?*

"Of course not," she said quickly. "I know you're busy."

"Even so. Look at me, Julia."

She raised her chin slowly, resisting the urge to bite her bottom lip. He was surprisingly slight for a man who exercised such power, though his wiry frame was clearly powerful for its size. More obvious than that, though, was the fact that he gave off a sense of vitality and complete self-assurance.

He studied her for twenty or thirty seconds without saying a word. His gaze was piercing. She felt as though she must be an open book to him, as though he could read her deepest secrets without her breathing a word of them.

"You did me a great service, Julia," he said at last. "Your faith in me is admirable."

"I did what anyone would do," she replied, her voice quivering.

"You went above and beyond," he said, never breaking eye contact. "Can I ask you something?"

"Anything."

"How do you feel knowing that your brother lives?"

Julia swallowed. In an instant, she replayed in her mind the moment she'd allowed him to escape. She could have pulled the trigger and still escaped with McKinney. And yet she'd been unable to do it.

"Ashamed," she whispered.

"Why?"

"I failed you."

Gabriel raised an eyebrow. "How?"

"I wasn't able to bring Gideon back to face punishment for his crimes. I wanted to. I just couldn't find a way."

But was that true? Had she really done everything possible —or had she made a choice?

"I'm not angry with you, girl," Gabriel said, his gaze so intensely probing she wondered whether he could read her thoughts. She struggled to keep her expression clear. "You did more than I could have asked of you."

Julia felt herself begin to shake with relief. "My husband betrayed you," she said. "I should have realized what he was up to sooner."

"Sheldon has—repented—for his crimes," Gabriel said.

"What—?" Julia began before tailing off. She cursed herself for forgetting her place.

"You want to know what will happen to him?" Gabriel asked. He seemed almost amused by her slip.

"Only if you wish me to," Julia said, averting her eyes.

"Sheldon betrayed me," Gabriel said. "But he also served this community well for decades. I have decided to spare his life. He will be placed under house arrest."

Julia's eyes widened. She'd heard nothing from her husband—Sheldon McKinney, the former Chairman of the Senate intelligence committee—in weeks. She'd half-assumed he was already dead.

But they can't kill him, can they?

For all she despised her husband, she knew better than almost anybody that he was viciously smart. And paranoid. He'd created a document containing the proof of his crimes—proof that also implicated the Brotherhood. It was leverage designed to prevent anybody killing him.

Sheldon must have used the threat of the evidence getting

out to save his life. Though even he hadn't been able to engineer his freedom.

"What are you thinking?" Gabriel asked, that strange, amused smile still on his lips.

"I trust in your wisdom, Father."

"Do you trust your husband?"

"If you believe he can be trusted, then yes."

"And what if I don't?"

"I'm not sure I understand," Julia said, her voice quivering.

"Why did I send you to live with Sheldon in the first place?"

"To watch over him," Julia said. "To report to Mr. Riley if he did anything suspicious."

"Do you love me, Julia?" Gabriel said, reaching out and touching the bottom of her chin. He stared directly into her eyes. The proximity was almost intoxicating. It was like he was staring into her soul.

"You know I do..." She whispered.

"I need you to return to your husband. I believe he's atoned for his sins. You will watch over him for me. Make sure there's no more evil in him. Can you do that?"

Julia flinched. She wanted to scream, to fight, to say that she'd rather die. Why did she deserve to be punished for her husband's crimes? She'd tried to stop him!

Instead, she nodded. Her eyes grew glassy as a wave of dizziness rocked her, and she answered almost automatically, her voice devoid of emotion. "Of course, Father. Anything for you."

FOUR

"Filenames..." Gideon said, mopping his brow with a cool, wet towel he'd left in the refrigerator before his workout. He didn't mean to sound disappointed, but he'd hoped that a month of concerted computational effort would have revealed more than that.

"Math is hard," Zara shrugged, not just unbothered by his tone but positively buzzing from her news. "And I'm not exactly working with a supercomputer in here."

That wasn't the way it looked to Gideon. They'd spent tens of thousands of dollars of their quickly diminishing resources on fitting out Zara's decryption computer. He had no idea that high-end computer chips were so expensive, let alone the server racks, cooling systems, and power assemblies that were required to make the damn things function.

"How long will it take to find out what's inside?" he asked, guzzling another few ounces of water.

His pores still hadn't stopped streaming. The cabin's lack of air-conditioning didn't help dissipate the body heat his exercise had generated, but the worst culprit for his present sweating was the heat the computers were putting out.

"No idea," Zara replied gaily. She tapped the screen of her computer monitor. "But look."

Gideon did so. When Zara had first started building her decryption computer, he'd expected it to look like something out of the Matrix—vertical green lines of code washing down the screen like raindrops on a window. The reality was much more mundane. The picture on the screen was of an ordinary file system browser window. Inside the primary folder—the one they'd taken from McKinney's computer—were dozens, maybe hundreds of subfolders.

"Ankara, Bogotá, Cannes, DC, Faithless, London, Paris..."

His forehead wrinkled as he read the folder names out loud. About half of them were locations—mostly capital cities. He drummed his fingers on Zara's desk as his gaze returned to the third name he'd read out.

"Faithless," he repeated. "What the hell is that?"

"Hell if I know," Zara replied. "But I have a theory on the city names."

"Shoot..." Gideon said, spreading his palms as he stared at the folder labeled *Faithless*.

"We know that McKinney headed up the Brotherhood's presence in DC. Same for Mariella Tilley in Cannes."

"Yeah. They called themselves the Brotherhood's 'ambassadors'."

"Well, it stands to reason the cult might need to exercise influence and keep an eye on events in more than just the two cities we stumbled across."

"So you think the Brotherhood have an operation in each one of these cities?" Gideon asked, his eyebrows rising as he reached for the mouse and began to scroll through the long list himself. Dozens of cities were listed before he reached the bottom.

"It's just an idea. But I'm not ruling it out," Zara nodded, reaching for the mouse and pushing his fingers aside. She wrinkled her nose and gave the air a long, exaggerated sniff. "I'm not pointing fingers, but one of us really needs a shower."

"I was on my way before you distracted me," Gideon replied tartly.

"I thought you'd be interested," Zara said with mock anguish in her voice. "Okay, if this isn't enough to float your boat, maybe I can up the ante."

She scrolled down almost to the bottom of the list and double-clicked a folder labeled "Problems."

"This folder is the smallest," she said. "The program has made more progress decrypting its contents."

He wrinkled his forehead and peered at the screen. Inside the folder were just three files. Two of them had names that were just incomprehensible alphanumeric strings, indicating that their names hadn't yet been decrypted. The last was titled "Mark Rainier."

"Who's that?" Gideon asked. Try as he might, he didn't recognize the name.

"I'd never heard of him either." Zara opened an Internet browser. An archive news report was already brought up on screen. The image just underneath the headline was of a totaled passenger car—maybe a Jeep—that had clearly been in a terrible accident.

"Brookland resident and *Guardian* journalist Mark Rainier, 37, was pronounced dead at the scene of a fatal car accident a little after three this morning," Gideon read out loud, his eyes flicking to the date at the top of the article. March 15, 2002. "Emergency services responded to reports of the accident but were too late to extinguish the fire that consumed the vehicle."

"He was a journalist," Zara explained. "He worked the culture beat for the *Washington Guardian*. The paper went under a few years ago, so I was lucky to find an archived copy of the article."

"Were there any indications of foul play?"

"None that anybody reported on at the time. But it's suspicious, right?"

"No kidding," Gideon mused. "What do you do with problems?"

"You try and solve them."

"Yeah," Gideon said, his eyes fixed on the image of the burnt-out truck. "It looks like this guy got solved good and hard."

"Yeah," Zara replied, her excitement entirely at odds with the gravity of the situation they were discussing. "And if this is anything to go by, then the rest of this hard drive could be damning evidence. If we can decrypt the entire thing, then we might have all the evidence we need to bring the Brotherhood down."

"We need to move faster," Gideon said in a low voice. He looked at the list of cities on screen and imagined Brotherhood operatives destroying evidence in every single one of them. With every day that passed, the likelihood of their evidence being worth a damn diminished even further.

"I know," Zara said solemnly. "I have an idea to help with that. But I don't think you're going to like it."

"HIS NAME IS ETHAN RHODES," Zara explained later that afternoon as Gideon fired up the cabin's brick barbecue.

As the flames crackled through the blackened iron grate, long-ignored deposits of fat sputtered and burst into flame.

Gideon unhooked the steel brush hanging off the side of the barbecue and worked it up and down the grill grates. Shards of blackened food remnants coursed off and fell into the pit of coals underneath. The pyre of white smoke turned a stormy gray until the flames burned through the detritus.

Gideon took a step backward and leaned back to avoid choking down a lungful of the thick fumes. He hooked the brush back onto the side of the grill and dusted his hands off before turning back to where Zara was leaning against the cabin's outside table.

"And he's the key to unlocking this?"

"He's *a* key," Zara nodded. "There are a few dozen living cryptographers who could probably break the encryption on the drive on the kind of timescale we need. But almost every one of them is either directly employed by an intelligence agency or works for a high-dollar security contractor."

"I'm guessing that's just a way of sidestepping federal pay grades?"

"You got it."

"But Ethan is a lone ranger?"

"He was fired from the National Security Agency about five years ago. Ever since then, he's worked for whoever pays the best. Sometimes that's the government, when they need something done that they can later deny. More often it's not."

Gideon raised an eyebrow. "Fired why?"

Zara made a face. "He's a piece of work. He has some kind of personality disorder. He used NSA tools to stalk his ex-girlfriend. Got her fired from her job, called SWAT teams to raid her house, you name it. Settling the suit cost the Agency over a million bucks. Most of that was in return for her keeping silent about what he did."

"Oh, great," Gideon said, tipping his head back and groaning. He walked over to the cooler by the table, lifted the lid, and pulled out a beer. It was a twist top, so he pulled the cap off and tossed it into a nearby trash can.

"Beggars can't be choosers," Zara said. She reached out and beckoned for him to share the bottle.

"You want one?" he asked as he handed it over.

She shook her head. "I just want some of yours."

"I'm not sure I like it," Gideon said, rubbing his chin. "You know what they say, lie down with dogs, get up with fleas."

"I agree with you. But we're not exactly overflowing with good options. If we keep doing it my way, it's going to take months to decrypt the whole drive. And we probably don't have that long. My mom might not, either. I want to be able to see her one last time, before she passes. To say goodbye."

Gideon stared into the barbecue's flames. The coals were beginning to glow red, jacketed by tiny tongues of flame that occasionally erupted in an explosion of sparks. But he didn't really see the fire. Like so often, he saw his sister's face staring back at him, as she had that night in Middleburg.

He'd failed Julia that night. And if it was up to him, he would go meet this Ethan Rhodes character right now, no matter the risks. If losing his own life to save his sister's was the trade the devil offered, then he would make the bargain.

But it wasn't just his life on the line, was it? It was Zara's too.

"I'm sorry you got wrapped up in this," he said at last, clutching the neck of the bottle tight in his fist and grimacing unconsciously. "It's not your fight."

"It is now."

"Well, it shouldn't be."

Zara let out a short, humorless laugh. "I made my bed. I didn't know it would end up like this, but I didn't have to accept McKinney's offer either. Two men died because I called to let him know where you were."

"You were doing your job."

"Bullshit," she fired back, standing so fast she knocked the wooden chair out from behind her. It fell backward and stacked itself away in the process. She walked over to the ice cooler and pulled out a bottle of her own, twisting off the cap and lifting it to her lips in one sudden, frustrated movement.

"We don't have to have this talk," Gideon offered, wishing he hadn't brought it up. He'd been stewing over Julia for days. Weeks, actually. He realized now that he probably hadn't been great company to be around.

Worse, he'd let Zara chew over her own demons alone.

"Yes, we do," she said. "I wanted to save my career. I told myself that the Agency was better off with me than without. But that was a lie. Not because I'm bad at my job. I am—was—a damn good case officer. But I know dozens who are better. I lied to myself to protect my own ego. Ninety-nine percent of the time you do that and nobody gets hurt."

"And sometimes they do," Gideon whispered.

"Their names were Marwan and Florian," Zara said, now staring into the coals herself. "Marwan has a son. He's one year old. That little boy is never going to know his daddy, and it's my fault. So don't go protecting me out of some misplaced sense of guilt, Gideon. This is my journey too. My path to redemption. And I'll walk it with or without you."

Gideon got the message. He'd been around Zara long enough to know that her mind wasn't for changing.

"Okay. How do we get in touch with this Ethan character?"

"I already did. We're going to Pittsburgh."

FIVE

Father Gabriel drummed his fingers against the conference table. He sat at the head with two members of his core team on either side. Before seizing the leadership of the Brotherhood, he hadn't anticipated how much of his life would be swallowed up by the mundane bureaucracy of keeping a community of almost thirty thousand people running. A few moments earlier, he'd dismissed his wider leadership team and left only these four behind.

To his left was Morgan Baker, the leader of the Brotherhood's paramilitary force—the Chosen—and Lady Miranda, who ran the Order of the Sisters. Facing Morgan was Trent Riley, who headed up Internal Security, and Bradley Stone who controlled the group's finances.

Morgan and Trent couldn't have been more opposite characters. The former was six foot three, Black, and, despite being in his early forties, had the naturally athletic physique of a football wide receiver. By contrast, Trent barely reached Morgan's armpit. He had a narrow, almost ratlike face and an entirely disagreeable personality. He was, however, an excellent reader of human emotion.

Bradley usually spoke little. He was a certified accountant and had once served as the CFO of a billion-dollar company before finding his way to the Brotherhood via a prolonged battle with opioid addiction. Miranda was the memory of the group. She was two decades senior to Gabriel and had been at New Eden since its inception. She was the exception to the unspoken rule that women were to be seen and not heard.

"We need more recruits," Morgan stated. "We've lost too many men. I need an increase in the training budget, but most of all, I need people."

"And whose fault is that?" Trent asked snidely.

"Can it," Gabriel snapped.

The deaths the previous month of some of the Chosen's best operatives was still a sore subject. Gabriel had commanded some of those men personally, and the Brotherhood had invested hundreds of thousands of dollars in their training. They weren't irreplaceable, but neither could they be switched out for spare parts. Every military-aged male in the Brotherhood was either an active member of the Chosen or served in the reserves—refreshing their training a weekend a month.

But the reality was that most of the weekend warriors weren't cut out for combat. Those with the highest aptitude for military work were selected before their teens for military training. The best of the best of those were selected to apprentice for the Chosen.

"How much?" Gabriel asked, flicking his gaze in Bradley's direction.

"Five million," Morgan replied without consulting the folder on the table in front of him. "We'll reactivate two dozen retirees and with your permission double the intake of nomads for this year's Trial."

"That might cause unrest," Trent warned. "People want to believe we are at peace. All these deaths have them worried. We know we have a Faithless problem already. This could make it worse."

"And whose fault is that?" Morgan asked, his booming, deep voice no less snarky than Trent's had been.

"I said, *can it*," Gabriel growled. "Request approved. We need the numbers. Focus your attention on increasing the size of the standing force."

Morgan bowed his head respectfully. At his side, Miranda took in everything but said nothing. She rarely spoke in the sessions, preferring to converse with Gabriel in private. The others preferred it that way too. Little about life in New Eden had prepared them to deal with a woman with opinions.

In truth, Gabriel wished he could dispense with her sharp words in his ear. But even as a living messiah, his power wasn't absolute.

Gabriel snorted to himself. More and more these days, he saw his role as being like that of a medieval king: balancing rival factions and power bases against one another. He was in charge as long as none of the other factions banded together.

Especially the military.

In truth, the Chosen was the only outfit that could really threaten his power. But that was what Trent was for. His people in internal security had the group thoroughly penetrated. They could barely think too loud without it ending up in a file on his desk.

So long as Trent doesn't make a deal behind my back...

"Can we afford it?" Gabriel asked, turning his attention to Bradley.

The accountant adjusted his thick-rimmed rectangular spectacles. They were a surprisingly stylish touch for a man with such a dull personality.

"Our finances are strong," he confirmed. "Liquid assets are touching six hundred. With interest rates as high as they are, I have most of that in treasuries. It's a nice little earner. But on the revenue side the Albanians are getting restless. I spoke with our contact this week. He was," Bradley coughed and reached for the glass of water on the table as if to buy himself some time to think, "concerned by our recent security problems."

"What about the Mexicans?" Trent asked.

After touching his spectacles once again—a nervous tic, Gabriel thought, Bradley shrugged. "They are less squeamish about public displays of violence."

"Inform our friends that we are cleaning house," Gabriel instructed. "The product will keep flowing so long as they keep paying."

"I will reiterate the message," Bradley said, inclining his head respectfully.

"They'll keep getting concerned if we don't change strategy," Trent said, sending a fiery glance in Morgan's direction. "This is a job for a scalpel, not a sledgehammer."

"Is that what the Chosen are?" Gabriel said, the calmness of his voice belying the fire that ignited in his chest. "Just brutish door-kickers?"

Trent averted his gaze. "Of course not, Father. I was merely pointing out that they failed to catch him twice now. He's still out there with that woman. Who knows what they are plotting?"

"This is a different league to snatching old gossipers off the street, Trent," Morgan growled. "Women and children don't fight back."

"Enough!" Gabriel snapped, slamming his palm down on the table. "I've heard all this before. Morgan, you will put an end to this. Or I will find someone who can."

SIX

"All right," Zara said as the journey time on the screen in the center of the dashboard ticked below one hour remaining.

They'd been forced to get rid of the Wrangler—though Zara had parked it in a lockup in the hope of actually rebuilding it if they were lucky enough to survive their feud with the Brotherhood.

For now, though, it was too recognizable. Gideon had replaced it with a nondescript black Ford F-150 pickup truck. It was a 2017 model, with its engine and transmission in perfect condition. The cargo bed was tied down with a black tarpaulin underneath which Gideon had secured the tools of his trade: everything from several thousand rounds of small-arms ammunition to the marksman rifle he had previously use to cover the road up to the cabin.

"Ethan sent the meeting location?"

"No," Zara replied. "He sent five."

"Are we supposed to clone ourselves?"

Zara masked a smile at his acid tone. "It's good tradecraft. He sends over five locations, we get to pick one of them."

"That way neither side is able to set up a proper ambush," Gideon mused out loud. "Smart."

"It's not a guarantee that he isn't setting us up, but it's a little bit of insurance at least. It would be hard for the FBI to set up surveillance in five separate locations across the city. And I doubt the Brotherhood has enough resources in Pittsburgh on this short notice. We're a long way from Texas."

"What are we looking at?"

Zara listed them on her fingers. "Market Square, the UPMC Children's Hospital, the Carnegie Museum of Art, something called Rivers of Steel and the National Aviary. They are all within a few miles of each other, some closer."

"What the hell's Rivers of Steel?"

She typed the query into her cell phone and waited for the search results to populate. After a few seconds, she said, "Looks like an old steel mill on the Monongahela River."

"They still produce steel down here?"

Zara shook her head. "I don't think so. It's a museum. They're doing tours between 1 and 3 p.m."

"When does he need an answer?"

"Sixty minutes before we meet."

"Take a look at spots we can leave the truck, plus multiple ingress and exit routes."

"For all of them?"

Gideon checked each of his mirrors for the thousandth time, only responding when he was certain that they were still not being followed. "Let's rule out the kid's hospital. If this goes sideways, I don't want children getting caught in the crossfire."

"Got it."

Zara went silent for about half an hour before deciding that the Rivers of Steel—otherwise known as the Carrie Blast Furnaces—was their best option. Though it was bracketed on one side by the river, the Rankin Bridge was nearby and offered routes into Pittsburgh or over the river through Whitaker and out of the city. The other locations risked plunging innocent bystanders into danger, which they both agreed was out of the question.

"How are we looking for time?" she asked.

Gideon shrugged. "Traffic looks fine. I'd say we could be there in twenty minutes. We don't have to send Ethan our choice of location for another couple of hours."

Zara glanced over at him. "Should we go scope it out?"

THE OLD STEEL mill was housed in a hulking brick building right on the edge of the river. Decades earlier, huge pipes had sucked vast amounts of water to quench both the new steel and the factory's insatiable demand for power. It was surrounded by a chain-link fence topped with barbed wire—more of a speed bump for any potential vandals than a real obstacle to a concerted effort at entry.

When Zara and Gideon arrived just after 10 a.m., the front gate was still closed. He could see a couple of cars parked inside, but no obvious human activity. An enormous circular logo at one end of the building read "USS," which Gideon guessed stood for United States Steel.

It was less of a museum, he realized, and more of a living monument to Pittsburgh's past. For decades, the city had been home to much of America's steel industry. Once, dozens of similar furnaces had lined the banks of the river. Now there were just two: Carrie furnaces six and seven. The rusting steel cylinders jutted into the sky like teeth.

"It's kind of sad," Zara said as they climbed out of the truck.

Gideon was wearing an oversized black Houston Texans jersey, mostly to conceal the pistol holstered at his waist. He readjusted the weapon as he joined her on the passenger side. They both leaned against the truck as they studied the old mill. Other than a woman walking her dog along the riverbank in the distance, they were alone.

"What is?"

"I don't know. I'm supposed to be in the CIA, right? At least, I was."

"Yeah."

"That should be one of the most exciting jobs you can imagine. But the truth is, before I met you I spent most of my time behind a computer screen running down leads and eating my lunch at my desk. Just like any other corporate drone."

"Doesn't sound so bad now, does it?"

"Then you look at this," Zara said, ignoring him as she gestured at the mill, which was now bathed in sunlight. "We used to make things in this country. Cars and ships and tanks. Real, physical things. Now, even in the factories we have left, robots do most of the work. And all that's left are a couple of rusting blast furnaces."

"I guess so," Gideon said slowly. "But forty years ago, the sky was black and half the male population of the city had premature arthritis or had lost a limb to an industrial accident."

"But at least they went out with a bang," Zara said mournfully. "These days, people get disability for typing at their computers too long. Hell, I almost gave myself carpal tunnel. Wounded in the line of duty."

She laughed out loud. "Sorry. You're right. You see that guy fishing?"

Gideon squinted, shielding his eyes from the sun. There was a man sitting on a folding chair on the opposite side of the river. It was a small distance away, but he was pretty sure he was holding a can of beer despite the early hour. "Yeah."

"I doubt he could have done that fifty years ago. This river would've been black with pollution. You could probably swim in it now without getting sick."

"Let's hope we don't have to," Gideon said.

He spent the next few minutes taking in as much detail of his surroundings as possible. He was about as certain as he could be that the location wasn't under surveillance. There were no marksmen stationed high up in the machinery or cars parked on the road leading up to the mill. A short walk to the edge of the river—or at least as far as the fence allowed—confirmed that there was no watercraft close enough to be within visual range.

"Looks clean," he finally said. "Maybe it's time we called our friend."

THE PLAN WAS to wait for the tour to start at 1 p.m. So that is exactly what they did. A nearby McDonald's provided calories if not sustenance. Though it was still relatively early in the day, the long drive from West Virginia had stiffened Gideon's body, so before hopping back in the truck to return to Carrie Furnaces, he performed a short routine of stretches and gentle calisthenics in the parking lot by the drive-through lane. They weren't intense enough to tire him out, just enough to get his heart rate up and loosen his posture.

"They were watching you like you were some kind of zoo animal," Zara commented, gesturing toward the line of cars waiting for their takeout orders.

Gideon put the truck into drive and glanced out of the window. "To them, I guess I might as well be."

The only photo of Ethan Rhodes that Zara had been able to acquire was low-resolution and somewhat blurry—a blown-up social media profile pic from a long-deleted account. For some reason, this particular image hadn't been scoured from the Internet. He was African American, roughly five foot eight, and had curly light brown hair. In the picture, he wore dark blocky spectacles.

They paid close attention to the drivers of the cars heading down the dusty lane that led toward the steel mill. Nobody immediately jumped out as Rhodes, but between tinted windows, baseball caps, and hooded sweatshirts, it was impossible to be sure.

"No sign of trouble," Gideon said as he tucked the truck into the parking lot.

Even so, he was prepared for it. In addition to the pistol at his waist, he carried a compact Brügger & Thomet MP9 submachine gun that hung from a sling around his neck. Despite the heat, he was wearing a black workwear jacket with a sheepskin lining—wide and boxy enough to disguise the evidence of the weapon. At only fifteen inches in length without the stock extended, it was easy to conceal on his muscular frame.

Let's hope I don't have to use it, he thought as his boots crunched against the dusty gravel parking lot.

They'd paid for their tickets online, like the rest of the day's tour group, so they headed for the rough gaggle of sightseers and checked in with a woman wearing a lanyard. The entire time, Gideon's gaze flicked in every direction. He was careful never to let Zara out of his sight. Nothing about this smelled wrong—yet, but past results were no guide to future performance.

"Looks like we've got a couple stragglers," the tour guide said in a Midwestern accent after consulting a clipboard. "We'll wait a couple minutes and then get started."

"Where is he?" Gideon said in a low voice out of the side of his mouth. Nobody here looked like Ethan Rhodes was supposed to look.

"Not sure," Zara said with an equally uncertain look on her face. She gestured at a gleaming BMW 7 Series that was inching down the potholed road toward the steel mill. "Maybe that's him."

Gideon blocked out the inane chatter of the waiting tour group and fixed his attention on the approaching BMW. The sun was shining directly on the windshield, so it was impossible to make out the sex, age, or ethnicity of the driver.

At least, it was till he parked and stepped out.

"It's him," Zara said, relief mixing with certainty in her tone.

Rhodes wore a red baseball cap, but his hair was thick enough that tufts of it catapulted out in every direction. He walked with a strange swagger, plenty of shoulder movement and a strangely rigid back. Gideon couldn't work out whether the motion was affected or if he had simply never grown into his body.

They were careful not to pay too much attention as Rhodes approached the tour guide. From this distance, it was difficult to make out his words, but he was visibly apologetic for his lateness.

As the guide whistled for the group to close in around her, Gideon performed one last check of their surroundings. There was still no movement on any of the rusted machinery. The hulking steel mill blocked his view of the river behind it, but no watercraft had approached from the direction he could see. Most of the other group members looked like they were retired, and one man had a cast on his leg and a visibly pregnant wife. None of them were likely to pose much of a threat.

Gideon sighed. Maybe this was exactly what it was supposed to be.

You're getting paranoid.

SEVEN

"As we enter the site," the tour guide began, "you'll immediately notice a pair of immense blast furnaces dominating the landscape. Constructed from steel and brick, these enormous structures are engineering marvels of Pittsburgh's industrial past. The two furnaces in front of you are known as Carrie Furnaces 6 and 7. Each stands over ninety feet tall and has a classic curved stone design..."

She continued with visible and apparently genuine enthusiasm. Gideon kind of wished he could listen. The truth was that the industrial site was fascinating. All around him was an intricate latticework of brick and metalwork that was so complex it seemed difficult to believe it could have been built over one hundred years earlier.

He shook off the thought. Maybe once this was all over, he could come back and do the tour for real. Right now he needed to concentrate. The weight of the MP9 submachine gun bounced comfortingly against his chest, reinforcing the point.

"Let's go," Zara said, tugging at his wrist.

As the group of about thirty sightseers had begun walking,

they'd been separated from Ethan Rhodes, who was now on the opposite side of the pack. As the tour guide explained that the reddish-brown color on the brick furnaces was a result of heat staining over decades of operation, Gideon stared up at them to make their path across the crowd a little less obvious.

We're just like you, he thought, glancing around at the sea of lined faces, cargo shorts, and sun visors.

"Shit, I hope not," he mouthed.

"Huh?"

"Nothing."

Ethan had his hands shoved into his jacket pockets as he followed the tour guide. He glanced back at Zara and Gideon several times, his movements jerky, but he made no effort to slow down.

"Over to your right you can see the remains of the cast house..." the guide continued. Above them, wind whistled through the metal scaffolding creating an eerie howl. It was surprisingly cool in the shade of the vast furnaces despite the early-afternoon heat.

"What's he playing at?" Gideon muttered. Zara increased her pace, and he did the same so as not to be left behind. The two of them maneuvered through the crowd.

Finally they caught up with the cryptographer. In person, he was slight of frame. Gideon reached out and tapped him on the shoulder and said in a voice that was slightly raised but designed to carry only few feet: "Mark, buddy. Is that you?"

Ethan turned, though the motion felt somehow reluctant. Gideon brought the man in for a hug the second he was certain that he matched the blurry profile pic. He used the opportunity to subtly pat him down. As far as he could tell, he was unarmed, though there were a couple of hard objects in pockets around his body. Probably a cell phone, maybe a headphone case. Things like that.

The crowd around them gave them only a few mostly disinterested glances before returning their attention to the tour guide, whose excitement about reading out a clearly well-rehearsed patter hadn't diminished. She moved on to extolling the virtues of the workers who had contributed their blood, sweat, and tears to Pittsburgh's historic empire of steel.

"We going to do this or not?" Gideon growled in a low voice that was for Ethan's ears only.

"Don't touch me again," Ethan replied curtly. His posture still had that strange rigidity Gideon had noticed before. "I didn't consent to that."

"I didn't ask," Gideon fired back.

"Boys," Zara interjected in a warning tone. She turned away from Gideon and focused her attention on the man they'd come to see. "Thank you for coming."

The three of them were now at the back of the small tour group. To the right was a stack of rusted pig iron ingots. Gideon wondered whether they had really been left behind when the plant closed or whether they were merely props. He took a step back and let Zara do the talking, recognizing that him towering over their contact probably wasn't conducive to striking a mutually beneficial deal.

Instead he allowed his eyes to rove around the old steel mill. Nobody in the group was paying them a bit of attention. In the distance he heard a car engine, but this close to the water, it could have carried a long way. Other than that, Gideon heard only the whistle of the wind, the scraping of footsteps, and the chatter of conversation as some of the older members of the tour group dispensed with listening in favor of discussing time-critical topics such as their grandkids' grades.

"$200,000. Cash," he heard Ethan say from upfront. The man appeared nervous. Maybe he wasn't used to dealing with customers face-to-face. Or maybe he'd felt Gideon's submachine gun press against his chest when they'd embraced.

"I can do half that. Fifty now, fifty when you deliver," Zara countered.

In the distance, another sound joined the background hum. The low beat of helicopter rotors somewhere over the river. Gideon guess the aircraft was miles away, probably too far to be visible, but he craned his neck up to the sky anyway.

No dice.

He was only half-listening to the negotiation in front of him, expecting it would take several more rounds before Zara struck a price. As a result, he was surprised when Ethan agreed to Zara's first counter.

Gideon stiffened as Ethan reached into his pocket, and his own hand moved surreptitiously toward the pistol at his waist. He tensed for an instant as the cryptographer withdrew his hand, then relaxed when he saw only a small scrap of paper or maybe a business card in his hand.

Zara glanced at whatever was written on the paper before putting it in her pocket. She nodded and glanced toward Gideon to signal that the deal was done.

My turn.

He knew that Zara was uncomfortable with this part of his plan, but he'd insisted anyway. Ethan had to know there would be consequences for his actions. In the right hands, the contents of McKinney's files could be far more valuable than a mere hundred grand.

Gideon took a step toward Ethan, who was already turning away from the group as if ready to walk back to his car. The sound of the helicopter grew louder, though he guessed it was probably coming from the other side of the mill.

"You live in Buffalo," he said in a low, pleasant voice after stepping in front of the cryptographer. The man's face was drawn. "819 Potomac Avenue."

"You don't need to threaten me," Ethan replied, attempting to brush past him. "I always deliver for my clients."

The clatter of rotors bounced off the furnaces and echoed around the old mill. Gideon's stomach knotted with worry. Something about this definitely didn't feel right. He squeezed Ethan's upper arm. The man was wiry but lacking in any bodily strength. He tried to wriggle away but failed.

Gideon narrowed his gaze and studied the man's face intently. His eyes were wide, his breathing seemed slightly labored. Was it just from the effort of attempting to escape his grasp?

"Let me go," Ethan hissed, his voice high-pitched. Gideon wasn't sure how he knew, but something clicked in his mind.

They weren't Ethan's client. Somebody else was.

As the head of the group disappeared around some hulking piece of metal in the center of the multistory brick warehouse, Gideon dragged Ethan back and pushed him up against the wall. He drew his pistol, ignoring the sharp intake of breath from Zara as he did so.

"How much did they pay you?" he said, jamming the muzzle against Ethan's ribs.

"I don't—"

"You don't want to lie to me," Gideon said in a cold voice. Despite the fury in his tone, internally he was wracked by fear. Not for himself, but for Zara.

And Julia.

Most of the tour group was out of sight now, but out of the corner of his eye, Gideon saw a few of them craning their necks up at the sky in search of the helicopter, which now had to be just a few hundred yards away. His own chest was heaving now as his fight-or-flight reaction kicked in.

Ethan attempted to twist away once again. His foot skidded out from underneath him and sent him tumbling backward against the wall. If it hadn't been for Gideon's hold on his arm, he might have knocked himself out. Even so, his head made a dull thud against the brick.

As he groaned, Gideon shoved him roughly against the wall. The movement pushed his head against the brick and elicited a sharp intake of breath.

"What are you doing?" Zara hissed.

"Getting answers," Gideon replied roughly. He jabbed the pistol into Ethan's side once again. "Tell me now. Don't make me figure it out on my own."

With his free hand, Gideon patted Ethan's clothes and frame with careful, practiced intensity. He pulled a cell phone out of his right jacket pocket and tossed it without looking behind him to Zara.

"Open this up," he said, pulling the cap off Ethan's head. He noticed a smear of blood in the inside lining before he tossed it onto the floor. Turning back to his captive, he growled, "Smile for the camera."

Despite her obvious hesitation at his tactics, Zara didn't argue. She held the cell phone up in front of Ethan's face so that the device unlocked. Gideon idly wondered whether Apple had ever considered this particular fail case when designing the phone's security protocol.

There was nothing in the other jacket pocket, so Gideon dropped to his haunches with the weapon still pressed up into Ethan's flesh. The man appeared to be struck dumb, his eyes flickering from side to side and sweat beading on his temples. Gideon squeezed each ankle and worked his palm around his calves and thighs to check he wasn't packing a hidden weapon.

"You don't understand," Ethan mumbled.

Gideon pushed himself back upright as his hand squeezed

Ethan's right pants pocket. It brushed against the hard object he had felt earlier and classified as a potential headphone case.

"Pull that out," he ordered.

From behind him, Zara said, "You need to see this."

Her voice was tense. Worse still, she had to raise it to be heard over the sound of the incoming helicopter. Gideon knew that he didn't have time to burn. He was also under no illusions that they could run from a chopper. Even if they made it back to the truck, anyone inside that aircraft could pick them off from the sky. There would be nothing they could do about it.

It was a death sentence.

Ethan reached into his pocket with trembling fingers. He closed his eyes as he pulled out the object, which he held in his clenched fist.

Gideon didn't wait for him to play ball but roughly twisted his wrist around and tore open his fingers. Finally he saw it in Ethan's open palm.

A tracking device.

EIGHT

"What was the play?" he snarled, his hot breath bouncing off Ethan's face as he pressed closer to him. "Confirm we were here, activate the beacon then get the fuck out?"

It would explain the disgraced ex-NSA employee's desire to get away.

Gideon decided he didn't have time to listen to the man's explanation.

"He sold us out," Zara said numbly from behind. "It's all right here in his email. He didn't even encrypt them!"

That last plaintive complaint seemed to cut her the deepest. Gideon momentarily closed his eyes as he ran through every conceivable scenario for how the next few seconds—or even minutes—would play out. He settled on a plan before he finished his next exhale.

He took a step back and unzipped his jacket, freeing the submachine gun. With his next movement, he handed the pistol to Zara along with a spare magazine.

Keeping his peripheral vision on Ethan, who was now

slumped against the wall and appeared to pose no imminent threat, Gideon stared up at the eaves of the huge brick steel mill. It was difficult to make out which direction the helicopter was coming from. What he was certain about was that it was close.

"Okay," he said, fixing the grip of the MP9 in his palm. He cast one look at the remainder of the tour group, which was deep inside the main building they were currently standing in. "We need to get out of here so these folks don't turn into collateral damage."

Zara seemed to take comfort from his decisiveness—little knowing that Gideon felt some of the same panic she did. He was just better at hiding it. She nodded, still holding Ethan's cell phone in one hand. "What's the plan?"

"Working on it," Gideon said, reaching out and grabbing the tracker from Ethan's hand. He pocketed it, then took a firm grip of the man's collar and walked him out in front. "Ditch the phone."

He heard a crunch as Zara followed his instructions. The black rectangle skittered across the dusty concrete floor. How far away was the helicopter now—half a mile?

It took about thirty seconds to frog march Ethan back to the entrance of the old steel mill, retracing their earlier path. Gideon took comfort from the thickness of the brick walls as well as the hulking magnitude of the furnace machinery. If this went volcanic, there was plenty of heavy shit to hide behind.

Gideon pressed himself behind the entrance, concealing his profile from the outside as he peered out toward the parking lot. He could see the truck they'd driven here in, sunlight glinting off its dark hood. It was about eighty yards away.

"Do we make a run for it?"

"It's too far," Gideon said softly.

He knew the river was to the right, though it was impossible to see it from this angle. He turned to Zara and gestured at their captive. "I'm going out to take a look. If he gives you any trouble, put a bullet through his skull."

The warning was more for Ethan's sake than Zara's. He trusted her implicitly. Even if he was the expert, she was no stranger to combat. She was more than capable of handling this sniveling traitor.

With one firm hand on the weapon that rested on a sling around his neck, Gideon sprinted to his right, following the short-sided front of the warehouse until he reached the corner of the long wall that led in the direction of the water.

The sun reflected back off the surface of the Monongahela River. The guy was still fishing on the other bank, indifferent to the coming battle even as the chopper arced into view. It was flying low over the surface of the water, probably only thirty or forty feet above the drink. There were three doors on either side—one for the pilot's cabin and two for the passenger compartment. Gideon guessed it probably had capacity for six of those.

"Shit."

As he watched, the helicopter banked to the left, one side of the spinning rotors dipping toward the bank, the other soaring toward the sky. It seemed to turn on a dime as it swung toward the mill. The pilot was clearly no slouch.

Which meant there was definitely no chance of outrunning it.

Gideon cursed himself for underestimating the Brotherhood's resources yet again. But he didn't allow himself to flounder in the quicksand of regret for more than a couple of seconds. He sprinted back to where he'd left Zara, knowing every second he waited to do so would make it more likely that he would be spotted. As he skidded to a halt, he reached into the pocket where he'd left the GPS tracker.

"It's definitely them," he said curtly.

"What's the plan?"

Instead of answering, Gideon pushed Ethan up against the wall, intentionally roughing up the weedy cryptographer a little bit so that he didn't feel the small black device being slipped into his jacket pocket. It wasn't much of a ruse, but it was the only hope they had.

"What are you doing?" Ethan moaned. "I told you the truth!"

Gideon ignored him. He waved the business end of the MP9 menacingly in his captive's face. "Ever seen one of these before?"

Ethan shook his head, eyes wide with terror.

"It's accurate to two hundred yards," Gideon lied, knowing that once the action started cycling, he would be lucky to put more than the first handful on a moving target within fifty. At least with hot lead pinging the other way.

He was banking on Ethan not being a gun guy. And judging by the sick look on the man's face, he was correct to do so.

Gideon gestured in the direction of the river. "You're going to run that way as fast as you can. Don't stop until you reach the water. Got it?"

"What if they shoot me?"

"You should've thought of that before you sold us out," Gideon replied unsympathetically. "Here's the thing. The guys in the chopper might or might not gun you down. But I definitely will. And I won't lose a wink of sleep over it. Understood?"

In truth, Gideon wasn't planning on shooting an unarmed

man in the back—not even one who had been willing to see both him and Zara either captured or murdered. And if he had to do so, he probably wouldn't sleep right for the rest of his life.

But that wasn't the kind of thing you said to your bait.

Ethan was blinking rapidly. "What do I do if they open fire?"

"Find cover." Gideon pushed him out of the exit and leveled the barrel of the submachine gun at his back. "What are you waiting for? Run!"

The cryptographer stumbled at first. It almost looked like he would topple over. But his left foot kicked out at the last second and stabilized his ungainly running—shuffling—style. His arms pumped by his sides, flying excessively high in the air with each revolution. It didn't look pretty, but it worked.

"What are you doing?" Zara hissed as Ethan's silhouette disappeared into the distance.

Gideon reached into his jacket and pulled out the keys to the Ford. He pressed them into Zara's free hand. "When I say so, you make a break for the car, okay? Get the engine running and be ready to gun it."

"What about you?"

He grinned broadly, masking the nervousness he really felt. "I'll be right behind you."

Judging by the look on Zara's face, she didn't fully buy the act. At least she was polite enough not to say it. He took a couple steps out of the entrance to the mill and kept his gaze trained on Ethan's sprinting form.

"He's faster than I figured," he muttered in surprise. Only a few seconds had passed, but the cryptographer had made it farther than he expected.

The helicopter appeared from behind the rusting blast furnaces. It arrowed toward Ethan, who was about sixty or seventy feet away now, its nose down. The grass on the field behind it rippled away in the downdraft. The aircraft was now just twenty or thirty feet off the ground and losing altitude with every passing second.

Gideon turned back to Zara as he thumbed the submachine gun's fire selector to full automatic. "Count three, then go!"

He took a deep breath, then ran in the direction of the chopper, keeping his grip firm on his weapon. The rushing of blood, rotor noise, and his own panting filled his ears.

One.

Two.

Three.

Ethan's speed might have surprised Gideon, but he still wasn't quick. As the cryptographer skidded to a halt up ahead, protecting his face with his raised arm from the downdraft hitting him from every direction, Gideon made up twenty or thirty feet of the distance between them.

He didn't have time to check whether Zara was on the move, but he trusted that she would follow his instructions. Ahead of him it was obvious that someone in the chopper had noticed the flash of movement from his direction. The nose angle jerked up. But not quickly enough.

Gideon steadied the submachine gun against his sling, creating as solid a firing position as he was able to. He stared down the tritium sights, lining up the cabin of the helicopter as the pilot recognized what he was planning to do. Slowly, the chopper began to rotate—now paying for sacrificing speed and altitude.

Too slowly.

Gideon depressed the trigger, firing bursts of half a dozen rounds before letting off the pressure. Any more than that, and the nose of the weapon bucked up, sending rounds flying downrange miles from the target.

The first burst missed completely as the nose of the chopper swung away from Gideon. The second didn't.

He was close enough to see several cracks shatter the helicopter's windshield. He squeezed the trigger a third time, knowing his aim was true now and sent most of the burst whistling into the helicopter even as the pilot desperately attempted to wheel away, offering up the belly of the flying machine to shield himself. Either the sun glinted off the spinning rotors or a bullet sparked against steel before clouds of shimmering exhaust blocked them from view .

Gideon emptied the rest of the magazine with the trigger fully depressed, the gun bucking against its sling. He was already turning before he knew whether any of those rounds had hit. He didn't wait to perform a damage assessment.

There was no time.

He kept hold of the submachine gun with one hand as he sprinted for the truck so that it didn't bash against his chest. He saw that Zara was almost at the vehicle already. Behind him, he heard the helicopter's engine squeal as the pilot attempted to increase power.

As he ran, Gideon dumped the expended magazine and reached for a spare, which he pressed home. It was more for peace of mind than in any expectation that he had a chance of pumping the chopper with lead a second time. That was the kind of trick you only got to pull once.

A strange groan split the air behind him. Gideon chanced a look over his shoulder as his left arm pumped at his side. The movement made his gait unbalanced, but relief flooded over him at what he saw. The chopper was losing altitude, using engine power to soften what was undoubtedly going to be a hard landing instead of gaining altitude and coming hunting for him. He didn't know what he'd hit.

He didn't care. With the chopper out of the fight, they had a fighting chance.

Gideon didn't slow down. In a matter of seconds, he made it to the parking lot, catching a glimpse of the silver-haired tour group that was now crowded by the entrance to the furnace hall—gawping at the combat enfolding in front of them instead of taking even basic precautions for their own safety.

I guess they had a good run.

Zara was already inside the pickup truck, the driver's side door slammed closed. The engine roared and tiny pieces of stone spat out of the rear wheels as they skidded before finding purchase. As always, Gideon had parked it with the nose facing out. You never knew when you might need to beat a hasty retreat.

She gunned the engine and accelerated toward Gideon, braking just in time to avoid knocking him to the ground. He pulled open the door and dove inside.

"You mind if I drive?" she asked, white-knuckling the steering wheel and already pressing her foot against the gas pedal. The momentum pushed Gideon back against his seat.

"Maybe just this once," he panted.

He buckled his seat belt just to silence the infernal beeping and peered out of the window at the apparently crippled chopper. It wasn't smoking and there was no visible sign of damage. Either he'd hit the hydraulics, the control system, or the pilot.

Maybe all three.

Gideon returned his attention to the windshield and the road ahead of him as Zara rocketed toward the exit. He jerked his neck back and slammed his head against the headrest behind him. "You have got to be kidding."

A large Suburban was accelerating toward them. About a hundred yards behind it, another vehicle swung into view from around the corner. As he watched, eyes wide with shock at this new threat, the SUV's driver slammed on the brakes and skewed it across the road, blocking their only escape. Before the enormous black vehicle had even drawn fully to a halt, several doors swung open and men in black masks jumped out.

Armed men in black masks.

Zara braked to a stop, panting heavily, her face pale with fear. Her voice was pinched as she said, "What now?"

NINE

Gideon aimed his MP9 through the windshield. The three men were now spread out along the length of the Suburban. He was pretty sure the SUV's driver was also armed. None of them had yet opened fire.

But it was only a matter of time.

"Shit," he cursed. "Shit, shit, shit."

"So you've got it all under control, right?" Zara asked in a voice that was just barely under control. "Everything's going according to plan?"

Gideon nodded, switching his aim left and right so each of the Chosen operatives—at least, that's who he presumed they were—in front of him knew that he was armed and had the ability to take them out.

The problem was clear: he could probably take one of them down before returning fire turned him into a pincushion. Maybe two. But that was it. The math was definitely not in their favor.

Zara slowly reached down, careful not to make any sudden movement. Out of the corner of his eye, Gideon saw that she was reaching for the pistol he'd given her, which she'd stashed underneath her thigh. Not exactly a safe place to keep a loaded weapon, but maybe he'd keep that thought to himself for now.

"What are we going to do, Gideon?" she said, her voice shaky.

"I have no idea," he said honestly. The truth was, despite facing supposedly insurmountable odds on multiple occasions only to come out on top over the previous few weeks, he wasn't John Wick, and this wasn't the movies. Sometimes you came up against an immovable object and found out that no, you weren't an unstoppable force.

At least it was a sunny afternoon. There was something unspeakably grim about the prospect of meeting your maker in the pissing rain.

"Throw your weapons out of the truck," the man on the left yelled in a booming voice. "We ain't fucking around."

"Shit," Gideon repeated for good measure. He grimaced, then decided he was done wallowing in fear. He rolled down his side window and said, "Okay, Zara, can you reach the mirror controls without being too obvious about it?"

"Yeah, I guess so."

"We're fine right here," Gideon yelled through the now-open window. "None of us need to die today."

In a lower voice he whispered, "Select the one on my side. Move it out until I tell you to stop."

A slight exhale told him that she had no idea why he wanted her to do it, but Zara complied. There was a slight mechanical whirring before Gideon said, "That's good."

In a bid to buy time, he raised his voice again. "What guarantees do we have you won't just kill us?"

"You're testing my patience," the same man called out.

Out of the corner of his eye, Gideon focused on the now-widened field of view in the passenger side mirror. It gave him the ability to see the scene behind him without having to turn his head and give the gunmen the opportunity to open fire while he was distracted.

Importantly, it gave him a view of the field to the side of the mill where the chopper had put down. Its engine noise was now almost inaudible—meaning that the pilot was probably alive enough to manage the shutdown procedure. Since he hadn't heard any explosions or the screaming of rending metal as the rotor blades dug into the earth and ripped out of their housing, he deduced that the helicopter certainly hadn't met a more permanent fate.

His view of the chopper itself was slightly blocked by the presence of the chain-link fence that surrounded Carrie Furnaces, but in the distance, he saw another half dozen armed men running toward their current position.

That explained why the three gunmen from the SUV hadn't yet opened fire. They knew help was on the way. They only had to delay a couple of minutes before the truck would be surrounded. There would be no way out.

"Gideon," Zara said in a warning tone.

"One second," he replied, focusing on the incoming Brotherhood operatives as he tried to estimate how long before they were surrounded.

"Nope," she said, raising her voice. "You really need to see this. Like, now."

He looked up but didn't see what had attracted Zara's attention. The same three men were arranged in front of them aiming loaded weapons at the truck. The Suburban was still parked in the same place, slewed diagonally across the road as a makeshift roadblock.

The only thing that was out of place was a strange growling sound.

An engine.

A powerful one.

Gideon didn't see it until it was almost too late. The vehicle he'd seen farther back down the road leading to the steel mill just thirty seconds earlier was now almost upon them. It had to be going at seventy or eighty miles an hour, kicking out a thick cloud of dust behind its rear wheels. It was only fifty feet from the Suburban.

And it wasn't stopping.

"Hold on!" Gideon yelled, reaching out and pinning his left forearm across Zara's chest. Like him, she was buckled in, but he held tight as he waited for the inevitable impact.

Three heads turned in unison just a second before a black truck barreled into the dark Suburban. The two vehicles were roughly the same size and weight. But only one of them was traveling flat out. In the final seconds before impact, its driver seemed to adjust the steering a little—as if aiming for the SUV's rear bumper.

It smashed into the Suburban, the front bumper collapsing into the engine block. The last image that imprinted on Gideon's retinas before the black truck exploded into a shower of metal and glass was a pair of airbags popping in its front seats.

The force of the impact shunted the Suburban forward and pushed it off to the side of the road. By the time it came to rest, Gideon was pretty sure it was totaled.

Two of the three Brotherhood gunmen had jumped out of the way of the careering vehicles at the last moment. The third had been hit and knocked to the ground, his rifle lying on the road several feet from him. He wasn't moving, but didn't appear to be visibly injured. Maybe a head injury.

Gideon blinked. The world seemed to slow. His palms felt sweaty against the grip of the submachine gun. It took a few seconds for the realization to hit home.

This was it. The only chance they were going to get.

He pulled his hand free of Zara's chest and reached across his body to unclip himself. He pulled open the passenger door and jumped out, sidestepping a few feet to open up his fields of fire. The other two Brotherhood gunmen were on their feet but were visibly stunned by the unexpected collision.

But they were still armed.

And they were in the way.

Gideon didn't hesitate before squeezing the trigger. Two bursts of three rounds spat out of the barrel, followed a second later by a wisp of smoke that quickly dissipated. The two gunmen fell back against the road, blood quickly forming a puddle underneath them.

Before he had a chance to switch his aim to the last of the shooters, a man in tan cargo pants and a black denim jacket staggered into view. He held a black pistol in his right hand and was clutching his bleeding forehead with the other. At a guess, Gideon would have placed him at around fifty, with long but thick gray hair that fell to about chin length.

Who the hell are you?

The barrel of Gideon's MP9 dropped a couple of inches as he tried to process what he was seeing. Was this guy a threat? It seemed unlikely, seeing as how he'd just crashed his own car into the Brotherhood Suburban. The fact that he was carrying also indicated that this wasn't an extremely coincidental car accident. But the entire scene was so chaotically out of place, it was hard to believe it was really happening.

The loss of focus only lasted for a couple of seconds. But it was long enough for the third and final living Brotherhood shooter to twitch back into consciousness. He was lying flat on his back, his rifle loose on the ground a few feet away from him. His fingers jerked before he inhaled a deep, gasping breath and rolled his neck wildly as he attempted to regain situational awareness.

Behind him, the Suburban and the other SUV were both smoking. Gideon could smell gas. It was possible that any second now, both vehicles would go up in flames.

"Gun!"

Gideon yelled the word automatically as he watched the Brotherhood operative reach for the pistol holstered on his thigh. But right as he wrenched his weapon toward the man and moved his finger to the trigger, the gray-haired man stepped into his field of fire.

"Fuck," Gideon muttered, sidestepping in an attempt to get a clear shot. The other man moved calmly despite both the chaos all around him and a now heavily-bleeding head wound. He seemed to pause to watch as the Brotherhood shooter drew his pistol from its holster.

In the blink of an eye, he coiled his body and unleashed a fearsome kick that sent the pistol flying out of sight and that was accompanied by a sharp crack. The shooter's wrist snapping, Gideon knew.

The man didn't stop. He crouched down in front of the now-screaming operative and slid a fighting knife off a sheath attached to the same thigh rig as the holster. He worked with an economy of movement and said nothing as he reached forward and, without pausing for breath, slashed the blade of the knife across the shooter's throat.

He tossed the bloodied weapon onto the man's chest and turned away. Gideon noticed for the first time that he was wearing gloves.

The conclusion was obvious: *He knew all this was going to go down.*

The unknown man jogged toward where Gideon was standing a couple of feet away from the truck. Gideon halfheartedly brought his submachine gun to bear. But he didn't pull the trigger, not even as the guy reached for the rear door handle, tugged it open, and climbed inside.

Gideon followed. The thickness of the scent of smoke and gasoline in the air was only obvious once his door slammed closed. He twisted to stare at the man in the back seat, now pulling off his gloves and tossing them beside him.

"Who the hell are you?"

"Lachlan," the man replied in a gruff, deep voice. He stared back at Zara and Gideon as though he was dealing with idiots. "What are you waiting for? Drive!"

TEN

Gideon shook off the sense of unreality that was assaulting him. The guy in the rear was armed, bleeding, and had just executed a man in cold blood. On the other hand, it seemed unlikely that he would go to all these lengths to get into the truck just to kill them. He could work out the details later.

"Do it," he called to Zara.

Apparently, she'd already come to the same conclusion because the wheels of the truck were spinning by the time the words were fully out of his mouth. He blinked a couple times as he tried to figure out what to do next. The Ford pickup truck began moving at five, ten, then fifteen miles an hour, its powerful engine struggling to get its equally vast bulk up to speed.

Zara jerked the wheel left and right as she tried to dodge shards of glass and metal and even bodies on the ground. Her face was pale, and she looked like she wanted to throw up, but she struggled manfully through the shock.

Gideon spun around as a bullet cracked into the rear windshield. In the chaos, he'd forgotten there was another party of Brotherhood shooters coming for them—the ones who'd arrived in the chopper.

"Shit," he said, first twisting in his seat and aiming out of the window before just as quickly discarding the idea in favor of a better option.

He glanced up to the roof and touched the button just above the rear mirror that operated the sunroof. Another couple of bullets impacted the rear of the truck as Zara finally cleared the debris field left behind from the crash. She floored the accelerator just as the sunroof slid open wide enough to accommodate Gideon's frame.

Their uninvited guest apparently had a similar idea. He rolled down the rear window and aimed his pistol toward the crowd of men chasing after the truck. He fired without pausing to take aim.

Gideon grunted as the edge of the sunroof dug into his pelvis. He was standing on the passenger seat, his body diagonal inside the cabin. He reached out and held one of the cargo bars for support as he brought his MP9 back up into a firing position.

He squeezed the trigger the second his aim was in the right zip code. The weapon bucked from the recoil as he depressed it on full automatic, burning through the remainder of his magazine in a matter of a couple of heartbeats. As Zara accelerated, dodging potholes on the dirt road leading up to the steel mill, he swung back and forth despite his grip on the bar, sending the last couple rounds miles wide.

Every single round missed. But half a dozen puffs of dust rose from the road about fifteen feet ahead of the black-clad Brotherhood shooters, causing a couple of them to duck and roll away to find cover.

The submachine gun ran dry with a click that was audible

over the rushing of the wind in Gideon's ears. The truck had to have hit fifty miles an hour by now. He knew there was almost no chance of scoring a hit at this range and with his firing platform so unsteady. But he dumped the empty magazine and slid in his last remaining stack of rounds regardless.

The half dozen shooters at the other end of the road appeared to have realized that pursuit was hopeless. But that didn't mean they'd given up. They brought their weapons up into firing positions as if reacting as one to an unheard command. About half of them crouched to one knee, the others remained standing but braced their rifles against their shoulders.

The play was clear: if you couldn't chase them, kill them.

Gideon racked a round into the chamber. He exhaled and held the weapon as steady as he could in his grip. He just needed to buy a few seconds, and then they would be completely out of range. The bend in the road he knew had to be just a few yards away now would swallow them into its protective embrace.

He squeezed. He saw puffs of smoke from the barrels of the weapons aimed toward him and imagined he heard the whips and cracks of rounds zipping past his ear.

And then the men in black were gone. He slumped back down into the truck, his weapon dry for the second time. He sat there panting for a long time, his heart racing as his body tried to deal with the consequences of the adrenaline flooding his system. His palms were slick with sweat and his face felt covered in dust. It was still hard to comprehend how quickly everything had just turned to shit.

"Hey, buddy," a male voice inquired from the back seat, speaking louder over the sound of chiming. "You planning on clipping in? That bonging isn't doing my hangover any good."

Gideon wiped his palms against his face. It was hard to

believe what he was hearing. Still, he obediently reached for the seat belt and clicked it in. "Who the hell are you?"

"I already told you. Name's Lachlan."

Zara braked hard as she navigated a rapid series of turns as the road left the steel mill complex before passing under Rankin Bridge. Sirens were now clearly audible in the background. "Guys. Hate to interrupt, but maybe we can save the introductions for later. Where the hell do I go now?"

Gideon gritted his teeth, cursing himself for failing to anticipate that this whole thing might have been a setup. He closed his eyes and tried to think.

Lachlan got there first. "Take this left," he said, for once speaking in quick, commanding tones. "Up onto the bridge and over the river."

"Where to?"

"You'll see."

Zara puffed out her cheeks but apparently decided they didn't have much choice other than to trust this bleeding killer who appeared to have fallen from the sky. She spun the steering wheel to the left and accelerated hard onto the ramp that led up to the bridge. She stopped dead for a couple of seconds at the top, waiting for a gap in traffic, then punched the accelerator once again.

Gideon realized he was still holding the submachine gun in a firing position. The truck was high off the ground, but it was not the biggest vehicle on the roads. The last thing they needed was for a concerned driver to give 911 their license plate and a description of the pickup truck they were riding in.

"Idiot," he cursed, unclipping the weapon from its sling. He clicked the safety back into place and tossed it into the footwell.

A police cruiser rocketed past in the other direction not a second later. Gideon held his breath until the flashing lights disappeared from sight, counting to three before he turned in his seat to watch it disappear into the distance. His eyes widened as he saw the spiderweb patchwork of cracks in the rear window. He had little doubt that the rear of the truck was pockmarked with bullet holes.

Not good.

"What's the plan, Lachlan?" Zara called from the driver's seat. They were almost at the end of the bridge.

"Take a right, then the next right after that. It'll take you down to the riverside. Drive nice and easy. Don't speed. Don't do anything to attract attention."

A couple of minutes passed in silence as they first hit the set of lights at the end of the bridge. Luckily, traffic was light at this time of day. No car rolled up behind them until the lights turned green—probably not long enough for the driver of the car behind to realize that the marks on the back of the truck were anything other than crash damage.

Most people weren't looking out for bullet holes.

I hope.

Another police car sped past on the other side of the road. As so many times before over the last few weeks, Gideon knew that before long, the police would put a cordon around this entire area. They needed to be out of here before that happened.

Preferably in a different vehicle.

Zara followed the second right past a storage facility on the left and a large warehouse on the right. The road brought them under another metal bridge that probably dated from around the same time as the steel mill. Gideon guessed that if he'd paid attention to the tour, he would probably know for sure. After that, it opened up into a mall complex.

"What are we doing here, Lachlan?" he said.

"Just keep driving along the front. I'll tell you when to turn."

Another minute passed. Gideon's breath had returned to normal now, but he felt completely exhausted from the burst of activity in the near brush with death.

Again.

"Here," Lachlan said. "Take this right."

Zara almost didn't comply. "Are you serious?"

As Gideon glanced out the window, it took him a few seconds to process the fact that he really was looking at a giant red crab bolted to the wall just above a sign that advertised the Storming Crab Cajun restaurant.

"I have a car," Lachlan explained. "We can't leave here in this thing."

Zara reluctantly complied. Gideon felt the same sensation in his chest. It felt insane not to floor the gas pedal and get as far away from the steel mill as possible. It was bound to be the scene of an enormous counterterrorism operation drawing in a massive number of three-letter government agencies within minutes.

"Park there," Lachlan said.

Zara backed the car into the last space at the far side of the parking lot. It was unlikely anyone would walk around the back of the truck in an attempt to access their own. Not here. That meant they might have a little time before the vehicle was discovered. Once a description got out into the press, then all bets were off.

But that would take time.

"Here," Gideon said, reaching into the glove compartment and bringing out a pack of disinfectant wipes he'd stored for precisely this purpose. He handed half a dozen or so to Lachlan, then the same to Zara. "Wipe it down."

The three of them got to work in silence. The question of who the hell Lachlan was still hung over Gideon and Zara, but that was for later. It took no more than ninety seconds to clean every exposed surface of the truck. It probably wasn't a perfect job, but perfect was the enemy of the good. As with the bullet damage on the back, they only had to slow the cops down. There was a big difference between a forensic tech finding a print on their first run through the truck and digging a partial off the inside of the glove compartment three days later.

Once the job was done, they quickly stowed their weapons into a duffel bag on the back seat. Gideon had no doubt that Lachlan had a backup piece, since he had the same. He grabbed the bag and gave it to Zara.

"Which one's yours?" Gideon said to Lachlan when they were standing in the lot. "We have a few things in the back. Weapons, mostly. I'd prefer not to leave them behind."

"That one," Lachlan said, gesturing toward a vehicle a few spots over. Gideon idly realized that he'd taken a couple of seconds to wipe most of the blood off his face.

He turned to look in the direction Lachlan had pointed out. Then he blinked. "You're not serious?"

"Doesn't exactly scream 'getaway car,' does it?" Lachlan grinned as he strolled languidly toward a fire-truck-red Porsche Cayenne SUV. "That's kind of the point. And don't worry, it's electric."

The three of them turned as one when a booming explosion rolled across the water. It was chased a few seconds later by a pyre of black smoke curling into the sky.

"I guess they rigged the chopper to blow," Lachlan said quietly. "Probably stacked the bodies inside before they set the charges. Easier to get rid of the evidence that way."

Gideon stared directly at the man, raking his line-weathered face with a piercing stare. "Enough messing about. We need to know who you are—and how you know all this."

"I'll tell you everything," Lachlan said, reaching into his pocket and opening up the Cayenne, which beeped and flashed behind them. "And I can keep you safe, too. But you have to trust me. Can you do that?"

ELEVEN

"Again, Morgan?" Father Gabriel said, his voice grating like steel against stone.

The leader of the Chosen stood on the opposite side of Gabriel's desk, his ordinarily confident posture shrunken by failure. A couple of steps behind him, Trent, the head of the Brotherhood's internal security department, looked on with scarcely concealed glee. The two men were fierce rivals in the system that Gabriel had constructed around him. He balanced the power of each against the other.

It led to a lot of wasted effort. But it was a key pillar of ensuring his own continued survival. When no faction could be confident of defeating its rival, stasis was the obvious outcome. And stasis benefits the guy at the top.

"This can't go on," Trent said, shaking his head with disappointment from the back of the room. "Give me a chance, Father. I can bring Gideon to heel."

"You and what army?" Morgan said dismissively. "Gideon had help. My team had him and the CIA woman surrounded until they were stabbed in the back."

"By who?" Gabriel said. "He has allies now?"

"I'm guessing Faithless," Morgan shrugged. He jerked his thumb behind him without bothering to look around. "And that's Trent's department."

Gabriel looked between the two men and found himself growing frustrated by their obvious animosity toward each other. If they just worked together...

I'd be out of a job.

"You going to say anything for yourself?" Morgan grunted, finally twisting his body to stab a furious glance in Trent's direction. "I hear we had two defectors just last week. Eight last month. When are you planning to get a handle on it, Trent?"

Gabriel raised his eyebrow and stayed silent.

"Perhaps we should continue this topic in private," Trent said, his voice an octave higher than before.

Gabriel considered the suggestion for a moment. Annoyed as he was by the failure of both men, Morgan's fuck-up rankled more in the present moment. Another half dozen Chosen were dead or critically injured. Worse, the brazenness of the daylight helicopter attack in a major American city was bound to draw both media attention and FBI interest.

It would cost a lot of money, time, and political capital to remedy the situation.

"Out," he said, stabbing his finger at the door. "Not you, Trent. You stay."

Morgan left without another word, though his posture crackled with renewed energy as he walked out the door. Gabriel made a note to keep an eye on him. Some animals were perfectly harmless when they were allowed to run free.

It's another story when they're backed into a corner.

Trent closed the door off to Morgan. His face was wiped clean of glee by the time he walked over to Gabriel's desk. He might have taken a little flak in getting it, but access to the king was the ultimate prize. And right now, he had it.

"You had better have a plan," Gabriel said. "This needs to end. Quickly."

"I do," Trent nodded. "Morgan wasted too much time chasing Gideon. He should have realized after the escape at the airport that it was never going to work."

"I don't follow."

"We need him to come to us," Trent said.

"How?"

"His sister. We make an example of her. Force him to come to her aid and close the trap on him when he takes the bait."

"I made McKinney a promise. He gets to keep her."

"He betrayed us," Trent pointed out.

"The situation is delicate," Gabriel said, his tone final. "We don't touch her. Not yet, at least."

"Then there is one other way," he suggested.

"Don't keep me waiting."

"The woman from the CIA. We know they are working together."

"She has family?"

"A mother in an assisted-living facility in Saratoga Springs. I already had one of my people test security.

"I want your best people on this, Trent," Gabriel instructed. "Don't make me regret this decision."

"I sent word to the Mexican. He'll handle this personally."

Gabriel nodded slowly. The Mexican—Salazar—had been of great service to the Brotherhood. His time as an enforcer for one of that country's most feared cartels had sanded away the innate human morality that held back even the most devout of the Chosen's operatives. He would get the job done. There was no doubt about it.

"It's a good plan, Trent."

"There's one other thing," Trent added, trying not to show off his pleasure at the compliment. "The Faithless threat is real. Treachery is like a virus. We need to deny it the conditions it needs to replicate, or everything we've built might turn to dust."

"Go on."

"Father, it's time you made a statement."

TWELVE

"What is this place?" Zara asked as Lachlan turned off the main road onto a dirt lane through the trees. The GPS on the dashboard indicated that they were somewhere south of Ebensburg, Pennsylvania.

Wherever that was.

Gideon rolled his eyes from the back seat. He'd long since given up asking where they were going since Lachlan had steadfastly refused to answer questions the entire journey. He just kept saying that patience was a virtue.

It was infuriating.

The woodlands to both left and right of the dirt track were fenced off. Every couple of hundred feet, signs suggested variously that this was private property or that trespassers would be shot. Sometimes both.

The trees were so closely spaced that barely any light got through despite the fact that it wasn't yet dark. The expensive SUV's headlights automatically flicked on to illuminate the potholed, dusty road ahead of them.

"A temporary stopover," Lachlan said. "Somewhere we all can rest up and decide how to proceed."

He slowed as a vehicle gateway came into view on the right. In addition to the warning about being shot was a sign that indicated the property was guarded by dogs. It looked a bit like the entranceway to an out of the way cabin in a horror movie.

Gideon brushed his fingers against the duffel bag on the seat next to him. His pistol was still holstered at his waist, but there was something comforting about the highly inaccurate MP9 submachine gun. He'd never felt upset about being able to fire twenty-five rounds downrange in less time than it took to say the word *elephant*.

The gate rolled open automatically as the Cayenne turned in and stopped in front of it. It took about thirty seconds to open fully, revealing another dirt lane behind it. This time, a single-story house was visible in the distance, along with a large barn just to its right. Despite the gloom, no electric light leaked from the windows.

It looked empty.

"That doesn't exactly answer the question," Gideon commented.

Lachlan chuckled and gently tapped the gas pedal—electric pedal, Gideon thought—and the motors smoothly whisked the vehicle forward.

"What's the battery like on this thing?" Gideon tried next. "You sure you're not going to run out of juice out here in the sticks?"

The older man guided the Cayenne along the bumpy road, slowing as he reached the barn. To Gideon's surprise—and concern—as they slowed within a few feet of it the doors swung open and two armed men stepped out.

They were both wearing jeans, baseball caps, and dark balaclavas, along with AR-type rifles clipped to their chest harnesses. The rifles hung loosely, and both men had their hands at their sides. But they looked alert.

Gideon drew his own pistol in a flash and aimed it at the back of Lachlan's head. "What the fuck is this?"

"Easy, Gideon," Lachlan said, breathing slowly and keeping both hands on the steering wheel in front of him.

I never gave my name, Gideon realized. Judging from the way Zara stiffened from the passenger seat up front, she had realized exactly the same thing.

"That's right, I know your name. Both your names," he clarified. "I told you that I would tell you everything, and I will. But I also asked you to trust me."

"Driving us out to a murder shack in the middle of nowhere to meet a couple of armed killers doesn't exactly set the conditions for trust," Gideon fired back.

Lachlan inhaled sharply through his teeth. "I admit the optics aren't great. But our organization has been forced to take certain precautions to stay alive. This is one of them."

"Who are you?" Gideon growled, enunciating each word in turn.

Glancing up to meet his stare in the rearview mirror, Lachlan said, "We're the Faithless."

The cabin filled with silence for several seconds. Gideon shifted his gaze from Lachlan's eyes in the mirror to the men with guns outside and then to the back of Zara's head. His mind was suddenly blank. He was sure he'd heard that term before.

But when?

"Put the gun down, Gideon," Zara said in a strained but authoritative voice. "Lachlan could've killed us a dozen times already. Or just left us to be murdered by the Brotherhood back in Pittsburgh. Let's hear what he has to say."

Gideon frowned as the memory came to him. Faithless was

one of the filenames in McKinney's encrypted drive. He slowly lowered the weapon.

"Thank you, Zara. You too, Gideon. My head's been through enough trauma today as it is."

"What now?" Gideon muttered uncharitably.

"The two men out there are going to pat you down. It's protocol."

"Whose protocol?"

"We'll come to that."

Gideon reluctantly released his grip on the pistol, safetied it, and set it on the seat beside him. Lachlan released his grip on the steering wheel a second later and opened the door. "Shall we?"

The two anonymous armed men stepped toward Zara and Gideon as they climbed out of the Cayenne after him. Zara must have left her pistol in the car because her search proceeded quickly. She only protested once, when the guard lifted the USB drive containing McKinney's encrypted files from her pocket.

"Hey!"

The man flashed the tiny black thumb drive at Lachlan, who shrugged and said, "Let her keep it."

"Spread your arms," the other guard said to Gideon.

Gideon eyed the man for several long seconds. He was on edge, his system still vibrating from the aftereffects of the adrenaline and cortisol that had pumped through his veins a few hours earlier. No doubt his brain was digging deep into near-exhausted reserves to dump some of those same chemicals into him now.

The man's rifle was clipped to a sling on his chest with what looked like a plastic carabiner. It was an amateur, homegrown solution. And a stupid one at that. One quick, powerful tug, and he could probably rip the weapon free of his grasp.

But to what end? Lachlan had asked for trust. And Gideon had survived enough gunfights by the skin of his teeth in the last few weeks that he had no intention of provoking another. Besides, their attempt to enlist help to decrypt McKinney's files had met with catastrophic failure.

What choice do we have?

The shooter patted him down slowly and thoroughly. He found nothing more dangerous than a penknife in one of his pockets and a couple of loaded pistol magazines that Gideon hadn't found the opportunity to use.

"He's clean," the man reported to Lachlan, who was clearly in charge.

Lachlan tossed the keys to the Cayenne to the man who'd searched Zara. Gideon noticed for the first time that a couple of other—significantly more discreet—vehicles were parked inside the barn. A large Chevrolet truck and a couple of other vehicles that he couldn't make out behind it.

Gideon relaxed his shoulders but filed away every detail for later reference. He trusted that Lachlan didn't intend to kill them—but that was as far as it went. Whoever the Faithless were, they were clearly a professional outfit.

He glanced at the plastic carabiner once again. *Mostly.*

But the fact that Lachlan had a backup vehicle in place proved it. In fact, it proved that there had almost certainly been another, unseen operative working in Pittsburgh. It was the only explanation that fit. After all, Lachlan couldn't have driven two cars at the same time. Especially not on such short notice.

But one extremely large question remained: How had the Faithless known where he and Zara were going to be?

Lachlan led them up to the porch in front of the house as Gideon turned these questions over in his mind. The other armed guard filed in behind him and Zara. Lachlan pushed the front door open, and the hinge turned without protest. The property was old and needed a lick of paint, but up close it was apparently otherwise in fine condition.

That judgment was only reinforced when the lock clicked without protest and the hinges swung silently inward. The house's outward disrepair was intentional, he decided. The internals worked just fine.

And apparently that included electric light. The glow just wasn't visible outside due to the boarded-up windows.

"Don't worry about taking off your shoes," Lachlan said airily as he led them into a well-lit hallway. Outside, the tires of the Porsche crunched on the gravel beneath it. "We're not fussy."

The walls were paneled with a deep red wood that mellowed some of the harshness of the overhead light. The first two doors—one to the right, the other left—were closed, but the one at the end of the hallway was open. It appeared to lead into a living room.

"You must be Gideon," a woman said in a kindly voice as they entered. She was about Lachlan's age, her hair darker than his but not much longer.

Gideon glanced around the room. A few more doors led into the large house. One was a couple of inches ajar, and he heard the rustling of activity behind it. He squinted without making it obvious that he was trying to take a better look. He thought he saw computer screens, but that was it before the door clicked shut.

"And Zara," she continued. "We've heard so much about you both."

"I wish we could say the same," Zara replied evenly.

"Oh, I know, the secrecy," she said, gesturing toward the dining table, which was laid for four. "It grates on me as well.

But I always say it's better than being dismembered and having my body parts dissolved in a barrel of acid."

Gideon blinked at the statement.

"Don't mind Harriet," Lachlan laughed. "Most people don't get her sense of humor. It's a little dry. Are you hungry?"

"Why don't you tell us who you are first," Gideon said, despite the rumbling in his stomach. He glanced at the pot on the stove and found it difficult to tear his gaze away. "It's not that we don't appreciate the hospitality—"

"But you've been stumbling around in the dark for months and you just want some god damn answers," Harriet laughed. "I get it. Lachlan, put them out of their misery. Tell him everything."

Lachlan stared longingly at the stove himself before sighing. "That's fair, I guess. Where do you want me to begin?"

Before either of them had a chance to answer, Harriet did it for them. "Where else? The start."

THIRTEEN

Julia placed her breakfast plate under a stream of steaming water in the sink while she wiped down the table. Long experience had taught her that congealed egg yolk was almost impossible to shift without a little soaking. Two more eggs sizzled on a pan on the stove. Sheldon liked them sunny-side up.

The toaster pinged just as she was wringing out the cloth. She set it down on the side of the sink and walked back to the stove. A quick glance at the clock on the wall told her that it was 8:55.

She needed to hurry.

Despite wearing an apron to protect her pristine Monday-best white dress, Julia was careful as she scooped the two eggs out of the pan and placed them on a plate that was already laid out with cutlery on a silver tray. In addition to the knife and fork was a small butter plate, salt-and-pepper shakers, and a small glass of freshly squeezed orange juice. She'd already cleaned out the juicer and tossed the pressed fruit into the garbage.

She picked two pieces of perfectly toasted bread out of the

toaster and put them on the plate to the side of the eggs. Using a paper cloth she tore from a roll, she cleaned the plate as she'd been taught years before—brushing away crumbs and condensed steam.

Before picking up the tray, Julia reached around to her back and undid the apron straps so that she could lift the garment off her neck. She pinned it up then smoothed down her dress, allowing a smile of pleasure for managing to keep it clean while she cooked and ate her own breakfast.

That's the problem with white.

She picked up the tray and walked it upstairs. Her smile faded with every step she took. She hesitated on the top step. Maybe she could just leave it here and avoid seeing him. Sun was streaming in through the windows of the opulent villa and up until now, her mood had been the best she could remember. For the first time in days, she was going to be able to stretch her legs and see another human face beyond her husband's— and her own in the mirror.

Apparently hearing her approach, Sheldon McKinney called out gruffly, "Julia? What's keeping you?"

Julia sighed quietly.

This is your path, she reminded herself. Everyone had to sacrifice for the Brotherhood. That was the deal. This was hers.

Sheldon glowered at her as she entered his bedroom. Her side of the bed was conspicuously undisturbed. She'd pledged Father Gabriel that she would continue to care for her husband. But she no longer loved him. He'd betrayed their community. He'd betrayed *her*. She'd taken to sleeping in the guest bedroom. It was almost identical to the master, save the en suite.

The worst of Sheldon's bruises were fading, she observed as she set the tray on the bed in front of him. The juice rippled in the glass but didn't spill. His lip was still split and the left side of his face remained swollen, but he was healing day by day.

Maybe it would be better if he hadn't survived. Julia grimaced as a sensation of shame shot through her at the indecent thought. Sheldon was still her husband. She'd made a commitment to him, to Father Gabriel, and to the Brotherhood to stand by his side. That had to mean something.

"What are you wearing that for?" Sheldon said suspiciously as he reached for the cutlery.

"It's Monday," she replied simply.

"So what?" he said, spitting crumbs as he shoveled a forkful of egg and toast into his mouth. The pain hadn't stopped his appetite. "Oh. Service. You have to be kidding me."

"Father Gabriel gave me permission," Julia said, turning and walking toward the door to avoid an argument.

"You don't honestly still believe that shit, do you?" Sheldon snorted as he slurped from his glass of juice. "I thought you were smart."

"No," Julia answered too softly for him to hear as she stepped out of the master bedroom. "You thought I was naive."

The doorbell chimed a moment later. Julia wasn't wearing a watch, but she guessed that it was exactly 9 a.m. She opened the door to reveal a girl in her mid-teens with blonde hair pinned back in a bun and wearing a chaste gray dress.

A novice.

"I'm here to escort you to Service," the girl said. "I'm Rae. Lady Miranda sent me."

For a moment, Julia was unable to speak. A wave of unbidden memory washed over her. She saw herself at Rae's age. Before her Mission and her marriage and before all that youthful hope crumbled into dust.

"Then we should get going," Julia said when she recovered

her composure. She shot the girl a slight smile. "We wouldn't want to be late."

Rae led her to a car parked out front. The driver was waiting for them in the front seat. Julia hid a frown. The Service Hall wasn't more than a fifteen-minute walk from the villa that Senator McKinney had been assigned several decades earlier, before the Brotherhood's population had grown to require satellite villages and towns all over New Eden.

Julia thought about suggesting that they walk. In the distance she could see dozens of other members of the community streaming in the direction of the Service hall in their Monday best. And then she realized that mingling with her people wasn't an option. She was being kept apart from them deliberately.

"Tell me about yourself, Rae," she said after climbing into the rear of the car and realizing that the novice's gaze was fixed on her, eyes wide with admiration.

"I don't think there's much to tell," Rae squeaked.

"Everyone has a story."

"Not like yours," Rae answered as the car engine started and the vehicle began rolling forward. "You're Ambassador McKinney's wife! He's a hero. You're so lucky."

Julia swallowed and glanced out the window at a family— husband and wife and two young children— walking hand-in-hand to buy herself a moment to respond.

"Lucky," she whispered eventually. "I suppose I am."

"I didn't mean to suggest you didn't earn it," Rae added hurriedly. "I pray every day that I get selected to go on a Mission."

"Is that what you want?" Julia replied evenly.

"Of course! New Eden is my home. I'd do anything to protect it. We all have to do our part."

The car pulled into a reserved lot right in front of the entrance to the service hall. Julia supposed she ought to feel honored, but instead, Rae's words kept echoing in her mind. Had she been like that once? So full of hope and expectation and duty? So...

Naive.

She shook off the feeling for a short while as she climbed out of the car. Rae led her through the crowd into the hall. The building was built a bit like a theater, with seating in a semicircle around the stage. On the walls on the left and right were boxes, each with space for two or three people. They were reserved for dignitaries and important figures within the Brotherhood. There was one with her surname on the door.

At least, there used to be...

There was space for almost a thousand worshippers in here, she knew. She caught occasional glimpses of people she remembered from her childhood or functions from her time as Sheldon's wife as she passed through the crowd and exchanged a smile or a wave with some of them even as she knew that for both their sakes and hers, that was as far as things could go.

To her surprise, Rae led her up the stairwell to the same box she always sat in. The McKinney name was still on the door. There was even a little bottle of water on the seat waiting for her. Julia twisted it and drank gratefully. She didn't know if it was the morning heat or just the effort of walking to her seat after several weeks confined first to a cell and then the villa, but she was feeling a little flushed.

Julia sat and watched the Service hall fill up. Almost all the seats were now occupied. As was customary, families with young children sat in the middle section, separating unmarried women from unmarried men. A low murmur of conversation filled the hall. She frowned, sensing something strange about it. Almost tense.

"Sit with me, Rae," she said after noticing that the novice was still standing behind her at the rear of the box.

Rae slipped into the seat beside her just as the lights in the hall dimmed and the entire space quieted as one.

Julia inhaled as Father Gabriel stepped onto the stage. As always in public, he was dressed in olive-green military fatigues that signaled his past life as the commander of the Chosen, and a purple sash around his neck. Her heart couldn't help but fill at the sight of him. Behind him sat a circle of the Sisters as always, with Lady Miranda at the center. They were the most devout believers in the entire Brotherhood. They sat there to inspire every little girl. As they had Julia, long ago.

"Congregation," he said as he stepped in front of the microphone, spreading his arms and holding onto each side of the lectern. "These are dark days."

Julia stiffened in her seat and sensed the hush of the crowd all around her. If it had been quiet before, now it was almost silent. The lights in the room darkened further until it was plunged almost into blackness—save a single overhead spotlight that focused on the lectern.

"Our enemies have sought to crush our faith for years. But decade after decade, we have persisted through the power of faith."

A murmur of support greeted his statement.

"As all of you know, before I was chosen to succeed Father Ezra I was honored to lead the Chosen."

Julia inhaled at the mention of her father. She hadn't known the man personally, only that she was his offspring. Beyond that, she was treated like any other girl. But Father Gabriel rarely mentioned his predecessor.

"Those brave men defend us night after night. I know their dedication to protecting us all because I was one of them." Father Gabriel bowed his head slightly. "I am troubled to tell you that several of our Chosen soldiers gave their lives in our service this week. They died protecting those they loved. They died to save us all."

A pronounced gasp of horror rang out in the silence of the service hall. A few seconds later, a muffled sob could be heard. Julia wondered whether the families of the dead had already been informed of their loss.

A moment later, she flinched at the sensation of something touching her hand before realizing that Rae had reached out and was now holding onto it. The young novice was entranced by Father Gabriel's words. Her face was etched with pity. Julia supposed she should feel the same way, but in truth she felt only emptiness within her. She'd seen with her own eyes how casually the lives of the Chosen were spent.

And for what purpose.

Julia shook off the thought, gritting her teeth at the cognitive dissonance it caused within her.

"Thankfully, I can report that the immediate threat has been contained. Our Brotherhood remains strong. We will defend our lives and our homes to the end."

Cheers of support echoed all around the hall.

"But we have been lied to," Father Gabriel said harshly, slamming his open palm down on the lectern. The crack that resulted was amplified by the microphone and burst from the speakers. "There are informers among us. Traitors sent by our enemies who wish nothing more than to destroy our faith. They know that we are the holders of the torch. The protectors of the light. And they want to extinguish it."

Silence once again returned to the hall. Julia barely felt able to breathe, conscious of the sound of every inhale. She glanced to her right and saw horror and fury mixed in equal parts on Rae's face.

"These people want us all dead. They want your children dead. They want to sow our fields with salt and burn our homes and desecrate all that we hold dear." He spread his arms wide. "Will we let them?"

"No!" a single resounding cry rang out. At the same exact moment, every light in the hall turned on. It took Julia's eyes a moment to react to the sudden glow.

She gasped once her vision refocused. A dozen men in Chosen uniforms had appeared behind Father Gabriel and the sisters on the stage. Their weapons weren't aimed, but their presence was enough to silence the crowd. A bang echoed at the rear of the hall as the doors swung open violently.

"What's happening?" Rae whispered, still squeezing her hand. The earlier exultant anger on the girl's face had been replaced by fear.

"Quiet," Julia whispered. She made her face a mask. Her heart pounded uncontrollably in her chest.

She craned her neck and looked around the room, realizing for the first time that three more columns of armed men were filing into the hall—one down the center aisle and the others along the aisles that bordered the outer wall. They stopped and spread out in pairs that were arrayed all around the hall.

"Fear not," Father Gabriel bellowed. "Because we know their names. In some cases, we have been watching them for years. Waiting for them to slip up. Waiting to *punish them*."

He glanced at the small group of armed men behind him and must somehow have silently signaled to them, for one hurried to the lectern and handed him a sheet of paper. He laid it on the front of the lectern and smoothed it flat.

"Brenden Kent," Father Gabriel hissed, stabbing his finger in the direction of the watching, spellbound crowd.

With the speed of a striking cobra, a pair of Chosen soldiers darted into the crowd and dragged out a slim man that Julia realized must be Brenden. They slammed him onto the floor of the aisle and secured his hands behind his back with zip cuffs.

"I didn't do anything!" Brenden screamed, his voice choked with fear. "I swear, Father—"

Whatever he was about to say was silenced by a swift and vicious punch to his kidneys. He bent over and was hauled out of the room with his toes dragging along the floor.

"Eliza Lyles." Father Gabriel said without visible emotion. He gestured to his men.

Just as with Brenden, it happened quickly. The woman said nothing, just shrieked and tried to defend herself. Compared to the men arresting her, she was tiny and quickly secured. The two young children sitting by her side screamed with fear and tried to reach out to her. A man whom Julia reasoned must be her husband simply sat rigid with shock and did nothing to defend his wife.

Father Gabriel's mouth curled into a vindictive snarl. "*Michael* Lyles."

Another squad of Chosen soldiers who had been lurking nearby pulled Eliza's husband to his feet. He seemed too stunned to resist as they secured his wrists behind his back and dragged him down the aisle, leaving his children weeping and alone.

"Traitor!" a lone voice yelled from somewhere in the crowd.

The cry momentarily hung alone in the air. It was as though a thousand people held their breath at once. And then it was swallowed by a swell of voices all shouting in unison. "Traitor! Traitor! Traitor!"

Julia was shaken by the sudden explosion of sound. It beat against her breast like a physical assault. Rae squeezed her hand so tight it almost brought a tear to her eye. But instead of jerking it back, she savored the pain as though it was a rope tying her down to sanity. Her gaze danced from face to face, all torn in rictuses of fury. Scowls and sneers were etched into skin like gargoyles into stone. There was blackness in the eyes and hearts of people Julia had known her entire life.

"Traitor!" Rae called out beside her. But the expression on the young girl's face wasn't anger but confusion. And behind that: fear.

Everybody's afraid, Julia realized as she returned her gaze to the crowd. Every time Father Gabriel read out another name, the intensity of the chanting and the cries of anger and hatred and the stabbing of fingers and the spitting increased by an order of magnitude. They might have been crying "traitor," but they were thinking "*Please, not me. And not my family.*"

Nothing on this scale had ever happened before at New Eden. It had never needed to. Everybody knew the consequences of stepping out of line. The Mandates didn't spell out the consequences of doing so. But they were obeyed nonetheless. Occasionally a familiar face disappeared. Perhaps they had indiscreetly said the wrong thing or were too inquisitive.

The message was clear: stay in line, and everything will be all right.

But this was different. This was a statement. And as Julia watched Father Gabriel read out more than fifty names, and as husbands denounced wives and wives husbands and children their parents, all in a mad scramble not to be on that list, and as men in masks dragged terrified faces from the crowd, she knew that after today, nothing would ever be the same.

Father Gabriel wasn't saddened by what was happening. He was exulting in it. She saw that now more clearly than she'd ever seen anything before. His face was alive with hunger for the chaos unfolding around him.

"They will be punished!" he roared as he reached the end

of the list. "They betrayed you and they betrayed me and they betrayed our mission. Should we forgive them?"

Hundreds of voices cried out in unison. "No!"

Julia stayed seated as a wave of nausea rose up from her stomach. She kept sitting as Father Gabriel left the room and as the remaining Chosen personnel filed after him. It took almost half an hour before the great hall emptied entirely, as if nobody wanted to be the first to leave.

"Ma'am?" Rae ventured after she had been staring at the stage for so long it had begun to blur. "Shall I take you home?"

Julia shook herself back to life. The worst of the nausea seemed to have faded, but she felt bloated and heavy. She grasped the arm of the chair and pushed herself upright, but the instant she was on her feet, the world started to spin. The wave of nausea returned with a vengeance, crashing over her with a fury that threatened to topple her.

"Are you okay?" Rae blurted out.

"Bathroom!" Julia muttered through a hand that was now firmly clenched over her mouth.

She sprinted out of the box and down the stairs to the nearest bathroom. It was an austere row of gray-walled cubicles, but the decor mattered little to her as she pushed her way into the first stall and bent over the toilet. She started retching the instant she reached it and didn't stop until her stomach had purged itself of every ounce of her morning's breakfast.

"Should I get a doctor?" Ray said nervously once a minute or so had passed since Julia's last bout of vomiting.

Julia shook her head. She rose unsteadily to her feet. She still felt ill, but there was nothing left to bring up. She flushed the toilet and turned to face the girl, her face ashen.

"I'm fine," she lied. "Must not have cooked my eggs properly this morning. I just need to lie down. Can you take me back?"

Acid burned the tender flesh of the back of her throat as she followed the young novice to the waiting car. She barely heard the girl's attempts at conversation on the return journey. A single question echoed over and over in her mind.

When was my last period?

FOURTEEN

"The Brotherhood didn't start out as what it is now," Lachlan explained. "Back in the late sixties, half the country was going crazy. The Vietnam War was kicking off, everybody was afraid of Soviet nukes raining down on American cities, and you could buy patches of LSD cheaper than a hamburger at McDonald's."

He grinned and sank into one of the chairs around the dining table, beckoning the others to follow suit. "Or so I hear. I wasn't born until a couple years later."

"Jamie, take off that mask," Harriet interrupted, frowning at the armed man who had followed the three of them into the house. "You know it makes me uncomfortable."

"Yes, ma'am," Jamie said, sounding a little embarrassed to be chided in front of the group. His shoulders folded forward a couple of inches as he reached up and pulled the balaclava over the back of his head to reveal a floppy-haired blond kid who couldn't have been much more than nineteen or twenty years old. He had startling blue eyes.

"Check on the pot for me, will you?" Harriet said. "I'm worried I added too much salt."

Jamie nodded and hurried to the stove. He looked relieved to be dismissed from the center of attention.

Gideon returned his own to Lachlan. "You were saying?"

"I was born in New Eden. My parents were a pair of dreadlocked beatniks. Dad got a draft notice and tried to cross the border into Canada only to be turned back because he didn't have a passport. Somehow they ended up in Texas where a group of like-minded hippies were setting up a commune modeled on a kind of Israeli kibbutz. They were rejecting capitalist materialism and processed food and the anti-commie propaganda they watched every night on the evening news."

Gideon glanced at Zara, and they both took seats around the table. It felt like this might be a long story.

"They weren't the first members of the commune, but they were early. Probably among the first hundred or so to move to the ranch. Back then it was only a twentieth of the size it is today. Still big, but no bigger than any of the other neighboring properties. They didn't even call themselves the Brotherhood back then. That came later."

There was a clink of metal on the stove as Jamie adjusted the lid of the Dutch oven and dipped a spoon into the liquid inside.

"The initial patch of land was arid and almost impossible to farm. Rocky soil, no water source. It was a hard life. They grew pot to supplement the meager income the farm generated and struck a deal with a local biker gang to distribute it. No different from dozens of other similar groups across the country. It was too small for the cops to bother investigating."

Jamie shot Harriet a thumbs-up, then held up both hands with fingers splayed to indicate the dish probably needed another ten minutes or so of cooking time. Harriet smiled warmly in response.

"Things really started to accelerate in the mid-seventies. People joined all the time before that, but most of them left within a few months. The idea of living on a commune and smoking marijuana all day is much more compelling than doing ten hours of backbreaking manual labor in a field under the Texas sun, seven days a week."

"So what changed?" Zara asked.

"Money," Lachlan shrugged. "The neighboring ranch was enormous. One of the largest acreages in Texas. It was bought up by some oil tycoon back in the nineteen twenties. He didn't even really farm it. But the land was much more fertile than the original New Eden. He died and left only a wife, no kids. She must have been in her eighties by then."

He flashed an open palm. "Mind you, I wasn't much more than a bundle of cells in my mom's belly at this point. I pieced most of this together secondhand through my parents' recollections before they passed and obscure county property records."

"This old lady came into money?"

"Liliana Hoffer," Lachlan nodded. "She lived alone on this enormous ranch with only a few farmhands for company. I guess somebody at New Eden looked over the fence and saw an opportunity. The community started doing errands for her. Then started farming the land for free. Long story short, she left the place and most of her fortune to them. It was like the Big Bang."

"How did she die?"

"The operative question is *when* did she die?" Harriet said, now taking a seat herself. "And the answer is: about six months after signing the latest version of her will. As far as we know, she was old but otherwise in good health. The death certificate says she died of a massive heart attack. Out of the blue."

"Right," Zara said skeptically.

"I said somebody looked over the fence," Lachlan said, fixing his gaze on Gideon. "But that's not exactly correct. That somebody was Ezra Richter."

Zara screwed up her face. "Who?"

Gideon gritted his teeth. He turned his head away so he didn't have to make eye contact with Lachlan or anyone else but found instead that Jamie was staring at him with a strange intensity. He sighed and turned back to Zara. "My dad."

Her lips spelled out "Oh," even if she didn't say it aloud.

"Ezra was like my parents—not one of the founders of New Eden, but pretty early. The way I heard it, he was always spiritual in that 1960s kind of way."

"You mean experimental," Gideon murmured.

His childhood hadn't been normal by any stretch of the imagination. Until he was a teenager, he'd barely seen his father. But later on, he'd been close enough to observe the man on any number of psychedelic drugs.

"In every sense of the word. But again, this wasn't exactly unusual for that group. They were building a free love, free drugs society. Everybody smoked pot and shared each other's wives. LSD, mushrooms, and other psychedelics were part of the furniture. They were all high all of the time. Ezra convinced himself that he was chosen by the universe as some kind of messiah. He gathered a group around him who believed he was touched by the divine. Not the Abrahamic kind, nothing to do with Christianity, even if he took on some of the trappings of the religions that came before it."

"That's why everybody called him Father?"

"Exactly. Anyway, it was about that time he was going around saying that the universe wanted to bestow a gift on the community."

"The old lady's inheritance."

"Yeah. I was too young back then to know whether Ezra really believed the story he was weaving or if he just liked the attention it got him. Either way, by that point the community probably numbered three hundred or so. Some of the early members, like my parents, had kids and were raising them in conditions that weren't much above abject poverty. A bit of comfort sounded appealing."

"So my dad killed her?"

"He made friends with her. His close circle of believers were the ones who helped out on her ranch. And a few months later, she was dead and the inheritance was made out in his name."

"How much?" Zara asked.

"The ranch was almost three hundred thousand acres. She had another fifty million bucks or so in investments."

Gideon narrowed his gaze. "How the hell was she managing a ranch that size with just a handful of farmhands?"

"Much of the land was leased out at the time to various local farmers. It took over a decade before the last of the existing leases ran out and the land came under the Brotherhood's control. But enough of it remained to easily feed a few hundred people."

"And it was Dad's land, not the community's."

Lachlan nodded. "He used his access to money to secure his power over the rest of the commune. A few left or were forced out, but mostly people were just happy to be comfortable after so many years scratching a living out of the dirt. And if they had to go along with Ezra's ravings, then it seemed like a small price to pay."

"We'll be here all night, Lachlan," Harriet said, gesturing at him to hurry up.

"From the mid-seventies, the population of the commune took off like a rocket ship. There was money to build housing and land to feed the residents. Ezra sent his favorites out into the wider world to recruit more and more people to the cause. Mostly they were the kind of folks who had been chewed up and spat out by the rest of society. Addicts and depressives and runaway kids. The kind of people who nobody misses."

"Us kids—the first generation—we started to grow up," Harriet continued. "We didn't know anything different other than the faith. It's a bit like a frog being boiled alive. You don't realize how hot the water's getting until it's too late. At the start, it was just a kooky new-age belief in the rhythms of the universe, that kind of thing. By the time I was in my teens, Ezra was convinced that the world was going to end and that only we would survive. After so long hearing that day after day, I guess you don't question it."

"It started getting real bad after Waco. That's when my parents started to have doubts. Ezra was convinced that the federal government was going to come after us next. He went out and found military trainers—special forces vets from Vietnam, that kind of thing—to build a security force he called the Chosen. It was a personal bodyguard at first. But it wasn't long before he was recruiting child soldiers to ensure the people protecting him were devoted to him."

"So you left?" Gideon asked, gritting his teeth as memories of his childhood began to bubble up. He ran his hand over his mouth, subconsciously tracing the line of the scar on his bottom lip that had been left after a scrap during martial arts training when he was only a child of eleven or twelve.

Lachlan laughed out loud. "No. My parents were institutionalized by that point. They didn't have a penny to their names—they'd been living on a commune for almost two decades. No family on the outside either. And you have to understand that by the time you were born in 1994, New Eden was almost like a police state. Saying the wrong thing had consequences. You didn't even want to think them too loudly. Just in case."

Harriet reached out and took Lachlan's hand. She squeezed it fondly. "We left because we loved each other."

"Still do," Lachlan grunted, raising his eyebrows.

"Somehow," Harriet smiled. "I was told *Father* Ezra had a purpose for me. He needed me to go out into the world and protect the Brotherhood—my friends and family—from the forces of evil that wanted to do us harm."

"Protect it how?" Zara asked with a frown.

Gideon closed his eyes and did the math in his head. In the mid-1990s, Harriet and Lachlan would have been teenagers. Probably around fifteen or sixteen years old. He started to get a sickening feeling in his stomach.

"The videos," he said softly as he opened his eyes.

Lachlan's gaze flashed with anger. "My parents loved Harriet like a daughter. They had suspicions about what happened to all the girls who were being sent away. When she was picked, they made a stand."

"And it cost them their lives," Harriet whispered, her eyes growing shiny. "But we managed to escape. We've spent the best part of the last thirty years honoring their memory and trying to expose the Brotherhood for what it is."

Zara sought out Gideon's gaze, her eyes wide.

"I know what you're thinking," Lachlan laughed, the humor on his face belying the hardness in his eyes. "We haven't had much success. Maybe not in bringing the whole edifice crashing down. But we've helped hundreds escape and build new lives. It's a start."

"Okay," Gideon said slowly. "But what do you want from us?"

FIFTEEN

"What are you doing in there?" Sheldon McKinney yelled, his ill-tempered voice only somewhat muffled by the locked door to Julia's bedroom.

She didn't answer. The reason was that she was curled up in the fetal position on top of the bed, the crisply made hospital corners undisturbed beneath her. She stared out of empty eyes and saw nothing at all. Her mind was elsewhere. It had been that way for hours.

This can't be happening.

But couldn't it? She'd been back at New Eden for over a month, and the box of tampons under the shared bathroom sink at the nunnery been undisturbed for that entire time.

"I've been stressed," she whispered to herself over and over. That could disturb a woman's cycle, couldn't it?

It didn't cause nausea, though. And enough time had passed that Julia was certain she wasn't sick. Her body wasn't purging itself of a contaminated meal. She wasn't waking up soaked in sweat, shivering, and popping a Tylenol every couple of hours.

It was worse than that. She simply couldn't stomach the smell of food.

The suddenness with which the morning sickness—if that really was what it was—had swept over her still stunned Julia. Yesterday she was fine. Today her stomach ached from the cramping and her throat was tender from repeated trips to the bathroom.

The problem was that the dates matched up. Just.

This. Can't. Be. Happening.

And yet it was. Julia ran her fingers through her hair, pulling the fine strands away from their roots. The pain briefly edged out the waves of nausea that made her feel like she was constantly standing on a tiny boat on an endless choppy sea.

Sheldon had only deigned to sleep with her once in months, and even then only after she had pleaded with him over and over again. It was just a couple of days before the attack on the Middleburg house and her hand being forced by Gideon's return into her life. The only possible way out of her situation had been to capture her husband and return him to New Eden to face Father Gabriel's justice.

"Gideon..." Julia whispered.

His face—his grown face, not his boyish features—had rarely been far from the edges of her thoughts over the past few weeks. But every single time she thought of him, she concentrated on something else. The thought of him was too dissonant, too painful to contemplate.

The problem was that, even if she wasn't yet ready to admit it to herself, Julia knew deep down that she'd made a mistake by returning to New Eden. She'd expected—well, she didn't know what she'd expected, but it wasn't this.

Sheldon wasn't supposed to live.

"Dammit, Julia, answer me," he shouted, slamming what

sounded like a closed fist against the bedroom door. "You can't lock yourself away in there forever."

He was out of bed now. Day by day, he was recovering from the beatings he'd experienced at the hands of the Brotherhood's interrogators. She didn't know why Father Gabriel had let him live. He had betrayed their family. And somehow *she* was suffering for it.

Sheldon stopped right in the midst of a stream of curses. She heard his footsteps thudding away from the door, then the creak of the third step on the way down to the first floor. She didn't know what had caught his attention and she didn't care. She just wanted to be left alone.

The reprieve didn't last. Thirty seconds later, she heard footsteps—his footsteps—thundering back upstairs. If anything, he sounded more frustrated than he had before.

"Open up, dammit," he yelled, fruitlessly twisting the door handle before thumping against the wood once again. "Someone's at the door for you."

The idea was so fanciful that Julia first assumed it was just a ploy. She wasn't permitted visitors. Neither was her husband. They were essentially under house arrest, barring the single trip to Service she was allowed once a week. And since the horrific arrests the previous day, she wasn't sure she wanted to go back.

"Hurry!" Sheldon snapped. She could hear him panting through the door. There was a note of tension in his voice now. "A man from Internal Security is with her."

Her?

Julia considered pulling the pillow over her head and attempting to smother herself. Her entire body felt heavy. She didn't want to go anywhere. She didn't want to do anything. She barely had the energy to think.

Could it be Rae?

"Who is she?" Julia called out, her voice raw from the aftereffects of the nausea. Out of nowhere a spark of excitement ran through her at the idea of being able to talk to someone, anyone who wasn't her husband. Especially a woman.

Not that she could come clean about her situation. Not yet.

"Oh, she speaks," Sheldon said scornfully.

"Answer the question or I won't come out," Julia said, delighting in the brief ability to exercise power over the husband she now realized she hated with every fiber of her being. The act of resistance would doubtless cost her later, but she didn't care. It let her feel something that wasn't pain.

"I don't know. Some novice."

So it was Rae. Julia puzzled over the presence of the Division—internal security—agent but figured he was probably a driver like the day before.

Could she share her worries about her pregnancy with the young girl? Hiding something like that had to be against the Mandates, didn't it? The highest ambition for a woman in the Brotherhood was to give birth to the next generation. That had been drilled into her since she was barely out of diapers.

No. She couldn't say a word.

Julia climbed off the bed and walked to the door. Her legs felt unsteady beneath her but improved with every step. She unlocked the door to see her husband's bruised face twisted with anger.

"Well, don't keep them waiting!"

He seemed smaller now, Julia observed as she followed him down the staircase to the first floor. It was more than that: he actually *was* smaller. He walked with a stunted gait as if cringing with every step.

It was as though she saw him through a completely different set of eyes than the young girl he married had possessed. Back then he had seemed impossibly wise and important.

Now she saw the truth. He was just a man.

And not a particularly impressive one, either.

The front door was open, and Rae was standing on the threshold in her gray novice's dress. Her face lit up at the sight of Julia. She was still capable of girlish joy. It wasn't long before her expression molded into a frown.

"Are you okay? I told them you were sick, but..."

"I'm fine," Julia said, self-consciously fixing her hair as she noticed the man standing behind the novice. "It's passing. What's this about?"

Rae shrugged and half-glanced behind her. "I don't honestly know. I was asked to escort you."

"Where are you taking my wife?" Sheldon said in a quiet voice that was more grouchy than angry. He seemed to think he had to defend Julia's honor, but he was only going through the motions.

"Official business," the man from Internal Security said. "Don't stand in my way."

THIS TIME the car was a minivan with blacked-out windows. The interior light stayed on the entire time, and its cold electronic rays washed out what little color there was on Rae's face. She held her knees as the van pulled away, her knuckles white.

"What's going on?" Julia said softly before immediately regretting saying a word. Was it possible the back of the van could be bugged?

"Actually," she added hurriedly, "it doesn't matter. We'll find out when we get there."

The drive was about half an hour. The first two thirds must

have taken place on the ranch's main roads because the ride was smooth. For the last ten minutes, Julia and Rae held onto their seats to avoid being bucked around like corn in the microwave.

"Out," the driver said after the door slid open and locked in with a *thunk*. He gestured at Julia. "Only you."

Julia smiled at Rae as she unclipped her seat belt and clambered awkwardly past the young novice to get out of the back of the van. She didn't say anything. Was she in some kind of trouble? If so, she didn't want to risk attaching her stink to Rae.

The heat of the day greeted her as she climbed out. Before she could say goodbye, the driver slammed the door closed once again. They were in a parking lot to the front of what looked like an office building. She'd never been here before; she was certain of it. Several dozen other nondescript vehicles were parked out front, but she couldn't see anyone.

"Are you leaving her in there?" Julia said sharply.

The man blinked as if unused to being questioned. "What's it to you?"

"Leave the engine running so the AC works. Otherwise she'll cook."

"She'll be fine..." he snorted.

Julia dug in her heels. "Do it. Or I'm not going anywhere."

The parade of emotions that swept across her chaperone's face was almost impressive. Before, the rage that was predominant among them might have frightened Julia into submission. But those days were over. It was almost as though the scales had been cleansed from her eyes.

They stood facing off against each other for several long seconds. She watched him debating what to do. His thoughts were so transparent she could almost narrate them.

He was afraid. It was obvious now that she knew what to

look for. In his daily life, he was top dog. But there was always a bigger beast to fight. He dared not risk his bosses' wrath.

In the end, he turned away, his heel scraping against the asphalt as he yanked the driver's side door open with excessive force. As he turned the van on, he muttered something that sounded a lot like "Dumb bitch."

Julia hid her smile as he led her inside, but she felt lighter after her display of power. The feeling faded despite the cool interior climate of the office building. She didn't recognize the man behind the reception desk, but he had a cold, lifeless face. Everybody she saw did.

I'm in the heart of evil.

It was obvious where she was now: the headquarters of the Division, the colloquial name for the Brotherhood's Internal Security Division. She didn't know anyone who'd been here before.

Maybe they never came out.

Julia's hand unconsciously tapped her belly, but she snapped it down by her side before anyone could notice. Nobody could know. Not yet.

Her nervousness built to a crescendo as the driver led her to a bank of elevators and tapped the button that led down to the second basement level. The elevator didn't move until he swiped his identity card. She saw him studying her face with a sick pleasure, as if daring her to ask where they were going, but she resolved not to give him the satisfaction.

The answer became clear the second the elevator doors slid open. Unlike the cool, clean office aesthetic aboveground, the basement was dark and the floor was bare concrete. The space was lit by bare bulbs. And the smell that assaulted her the second the doors opened was the worst feature of all.

It was the scent of human fear.

SIXTEEN

"It's true what we heard about your amnesia?" Lachlan asked.

Gideon nodded. "I lost everything for a while. Most of it is coming back, though not always in the right order."

"You wouldn't remember this anyway," Harriet said. "It happened after you left."

"What did?"

"You became a symbol to some people. You weren't forgotten. Even as Gabriel took power, cracked down and formalized his—*teachings*—in a pamphlet he called his 'Mandates', others looked to you instead. Cast you as a symbol of hope."

"Me?" Gideon said in a disbelieving tone. "Why? I didn't do anything."

"You didn't need to. It's not about what you did, but who you are. Or more precisely, who your father was."

"You're saying I have, what...fans?"

"A better word would be believers. A lot of people in New Eden are scared. They don't know what to believe; they just know that the life they are living is *wrong*. It was far from perfect when Ezra was in charge, but at least it was their choice. Nobody can leave, not anymore."

"Sounds like East Berlin," Zara said.

"That's a closer analogy than you would believe."

"How do you know all this? You all left a long time ago."

Lachlan nodded slowly. The wrinkles on his face grew more pronounced as shadows and light passed across them. "We did. But Jamie didn't. And we've helped others over the years. There are hundreds of us now."

Gideon glanced at the younger man near the stove. Jamie looked away, perhaps too embarrassed by the attention to meet his gaze.

Or too overwhelmed...

He shook his head and leaned away from the table, subconsciously trying to put distance between himself and what Lachlan was suggesting. He didn't want to be a symbol. He didn't want any of this.

"Then what do you want with *us*?" Gideon repeated, his temper rising. He felt Zara's hand on his as she gave him a surreptitious but comforting squeeze under the table.

"For years we've been able to get people out one, maybe two at a time. Each extraction takes weeks of planning and they don't always succeed. It takes enormous resources, but we think it's worth it."

"Recently we've been losing people," Harriet said, her tone at once more comforting and sadder than her husband's. "Not during the extraction process, but before."

Gideon almost automatically glanced around the room. "Could you have been compromised?"

"It's possible," Lachlan said, nodding slowly. "But there's no pattern to the extractions that fail. We use different personnel, different routes. There is no correlation that we can point to."

"So how do you explain it?" Zara asked, leaning forward slightly. Gideon smiled at the familiar look of intrigue gleaming behind her eyes. The last few weeks had taught him that there was nothing she liked more than solving a puzzle.

Lachlan sighed. "Informers. Zara, earlier you compared New Eden to East Berlin under the Soviet regime. Back then one in three East German citizens was informing for the Stasi. Sometimes husbands informed on their wives and wives their husbands and neither knew what the other was doing."

"In the early days," Harriet continued, "the Brotherhood's Internal Security arm—the Division—was more of an aspiration. It existed in name only. Even after Gabriel put more resources into it, it wasn't a professional outfit."

"We ran rings around them," Lachlan grinned. "But it couldn't last."

"A few years back, Gabriel placed a man called Trent Riley in charge of the Division. He has no formal counterintelligence training, but he has a gift for sniffing out leaks. And he pairs that with an utter lack of conscience," Harriet said with a look of disgust on her face. "Torture, execution, murder, nothing's beyond the pale for him."

"Under his influence, Gabriel has spent the last five years preaching to the community that they have a responsibility to inform on their friends and family. To protect them, of course." Lachlan wrinkled his nose. "The more you hear a message like that, the deeper it gets drilled into your skull. We don't think our extractions are failing because *our* network is penetrated."

"No," Zara said slowly. "But before, your chances of accidentally contacting an informer were like pulling a needle out of a haystack. Trent's flipped that calculation on its head."

Lachlan nodded. "Exactly. These days, every time we recruit someone on the inside, it's like flipping a coin. Either they're compromised, or their closest friend is. Their wife.

Husband. It's an equation that simply doesn't work. We're losing too many good people."

"And worse," Harriet said, her lips pursed, "we're losing our contacts on the inside. We paused all extraction operations for the time being. It's too risky."

Gideon drummed his fingertips against the table. "I still don't get how we feature in all this. You put a lot on the line to come rescue us. You must have had a reason."

Harriet and Lachlan exchanged a long glance before she turned back to face him. "We do. You see, even in East Germany, most people weren't informing because they were true believers in communism. They were just scared. They wanted to protect themselves and their families. Maybe one in ten is a fanatic. The rest just want to get by."

Lachlan leaned forward. He had a fierce intensity in his gaze now. An energy practically crackled off his skin. "I know you didn't have a normal childhood, Gideon, but you must've seen pictures of the Berlin Wall coming down?"

"Yeah," he shrugged. "After I got out, I got Netflix like everybody else. I watched a documentary."

"Well, one day nobody in the Soviet Union imagined that it could ever fall. And the next day ordinary people took sledgehammers to it, and brick by brick they tore it down. Most people knew that their lives were different—worse, much worse—than their neighbors on the other side of the wall. They were just too scared to take the next step. Until they weren't."

Zara's eyes widened. "You want to use Gideon as a symbol, don't you? You want to turn him into a...a hero."

"I've spent years thinking about this," Lachlan said, practically vibrating with intensity. "If the federal government learns what's happening in New Eden and takes action, it'll be a bloodbath."

"Why? You don't think they learned from Waco?"

"I'm sure they did. But so did Ezra. And sure as shit Gabriel did too. He's spent years telling people that they should choose death instead of surrendering to the government. It's his ultimate trump card—a last-ditch way of staying out of jail if the walls ever start closing in. They stashed weapons caches all over New Eden. Likely poison, too. If it comes to it..." he spread his hands wide.

Zara nodded thoughtfully. "You're right. Even if ten percent of the Brotherhood pull the trigger—," she winced at the thoughtlessness of her metaphor, "—you're looking at a 9/11 worth of casualties. If it's more than that...no way the government intervenes."

Gideon slammed his hand down on the table a little harder than he intended. "But what do you want with me? How does making me a symbol help?"

"We can get messages into New Eden. Information, too. Surprisingly there's a thriving black market of contraband films and books inside the ranch. We'll start with an information operation. Call it propaganda if you like. We'll spread the word that you are alive, that you are Father Ezra's true heir—and that you're coming back."

"A lot of people thought that it should've been you who succeeded Ezra, not Gabriel," Harriet said. "They still do, even if they don't talk about it. We've interviewed every single defector we've ever gotten out, and most say the same thing. Most of them follow Gabriel because he controls the guns and the pulpit. Not because they love him."

"Yeah..." Gideon said. "But he's still there. He's still in charge. And he's still the one who controls the guns."

"Oh," Lachlan said, a tight, malicious smile spreading across his lips. "But what if he wasn't?"

Zara tilted her head to one side. She spoke softly, but

Gideon could see in her eyes that the puzzle pieces had fallen into place. "You want to cut the head off the snake, don't you? You want to mount a coup."

"WHAT TOOK SO LONG?" Trent snapped as Julia approached. She was about to open her mouth to reply when she saw that the question was directed at the man who'd driven her here.

"Sorry, boss," came the subdued reply.

"Fuck off and make yourself useful."

The driver shot Julia a hateful glance as he scurried off. It bounced off her. Her cup was too full to deal with someone else's troubles. It was all she could do to hold herself together right now. Her teeth were clamped shut as her mouth pooled with saliva. The urge to vomit was almost overwhelming.

Not here. Anywhere else.

As Trent turned his attention on to her, the hairs on Julia's arms stood to attention. She fought the urge to shrink, and instead straightened her back. Despite Trent's slender frame, there was something chilling about his narrow, ratlike face. The only benefit of her building anxiety was that it was quenching the worst of her nausea—if only to a level where she wouldn't actually be sick.

"What am I doing here?" she asked, hating the sound of the tremor in her voice.

"Father Gabriel assures me that you are reliable," Trent said, his gaze drilling into her face. "Is he right?"

"Of course!" Julia said automatically. "I'm honored he says so."

Trent observed her for several seconds longer before he

continued. He turned a few inches away from her as if losing interest. "Good. We have more guests than usual. You will help us manage them."

He strode away without offering any further information on what she would be required to do.

Julia soon found that nobody really knew. The basement contained approximately two dozen cells, like you might find in any jail. Each one held a single bed, washbasin, and toilet, although there were at least two prisoners to a cell. Some held as many as five.

The holding cells were only a small part of the overall subterranean complex, Julia quickly decided. An electronically locked doorway at the opposite end of the room from the similarly secured door leading to the elevators was in frequent use. Armed guards would walk to one of the cells, pull out a prisoner—often screaming their innocence or soiling themselves—and drag them through the doorway.

After that, she heard only silence.

And, of course, the constant background noise of quiet weeping, moans of pain, and occasional bouts of terrified, almost hysterical prayer. Julia simply stood at the center of it for several minutes with her entire frame shaking as she tried to process the unhinged depravity of it all. Nothing in her life had prepared her to cope with sheer evil on this scale.

You have to help them!

Julia's mind instinctively turned to ways she could help the prisoners escape. As she looked around, she saw familiar faces—some of them people she'd known her entire life. Not just kind people but folks she knew to be innocent in every sense of the word. Individuals who were as pure of heart and soul as anyone she'd ever known.

Only two guards remained in the holding area continuously. Their job appeared to be to open the cells when the interrogators came to collect a fresh victim or deposit someone they'd already worked over. The cells had physical keys—all seemed to be opened by the same master key. In addition, there were a handful of orderlies in medical scrubs. They all had hollow eyes and avoided Julia's gaze at every opportunity.

In total, there were half a dozen people around her at all times. It was quickly apparent to Julia that she had no hope of engineering any kind of mass escape. Even if she could somehow subdue one of the guards—both men who had at least fifty pounds on her—what then? There would still be another to take her down, along with plenty of others to raise the alarm.

"Water," a voice nearby said. The words came out in a low rattle. The speaker sounded as though he might expire at any moment. "Please..."

Julia started. The voice shocked her back into the present. She looked around, her eyes wide, heart racing, and located the source of the voice: a man naked to the waist lying on the single bed in his cell. Two other sets of eyes stared dully back out at her, their owners covered in bruises and contusions.

She looked around and chided herself for slipping into a fantasy of escape that did nothing but salve her own guilt at allowing such a horror to continue. The orderlies were clearly supposed to care for the wounded and the sick, but they performed their duties mechanically rather than with any real eagerness.

Do something!

Noticing a stack of medical supplies and other items in the center of the room that appeared to have been dumped and mostly forgotten, Julia hurried over and grabbed a first-aid kit and several bottles of water. She beckoned one of the guards over to the cell and made him open it. He stood back and watched but said nothing.

Julia handed a water bottle to the other two prisoners. They accepted the offering gratefully but slunk back to the far end of the cell, as far away from the guards as physically possible. One of them shrank back behind the toilet in his quest for safety.

She kneeled by the side of the bed, twisted the cap off the remaining water bottle, and gently tipped it to the prisoner's lips. She didn't know his name. He stared sightlessly at the ceiling but turned his head toward the tiny trickle of water that spilled over his lips and down the side of his neck.

"Thank you..." he whispered when she was done.

Julia shivered at the sound of his voice. It was so weak she feared the cause was much greater than simple dehydration. She turned her head and began to examine his body. She was no doctor, but she didn't need to be to see the dinner plate–sized bruise that had swallowed his stomach. It was already a nasty purple. Other welts and scrapes covered his entire frame.

She unzipped the first-aid kit and flicked through the contents before pulling out a packet of antibacterial wipes. They seemed an impossibly meager treatment in the face of his wounds, but they were all she had. He winced as she ripped open the packet and began to clean his cuts and scrapes, but he bore the pain without complaint.

"Closer," he whispered when she was done.

Julia frowned, wondering whether she'd misheard him. But there was a longing in his eyes as he looked up at her that made her lean forward. He repeated the request until she pressed her ears against his lips.

"Tell me your name," she said softly.

"It's Brenden," he coughed. There was a fierce light in his eyes, but also a weakness. He looked as though he could pass out at any moment. He raised his head off the thin mattress and spoke so quietly even she could barely hear him. "You're Gideon's sister, aren't you?"

The unexpected mention of her brother's name caused Julia to flinch, but before she had the chance to pull away, he reached out and gripped her arm, speaking with such a longing intensity she didn't dare abandon him. "Tell me. Please. Is he coming back?"

SEVENTEEN

On a busy Friday or Saturday night, Caroline Street in Saratoga Springs drew drinkers like moths to a flame. This Tuesday it was dead.

Eduardo Salazar hung back as a police cruiser turned onto Maple Avenue and pretended to tie his shoelace until the vehicle was out of sight. He spoke decent English despite his Mexican origins and carried a California driver's license. His background story was well constructed and clean as a whistle. Even so, there was no sense tempting fate. It was better to practice good habits at all times. You never knew when they might save your life.

A bell on the door tingled as he stepped into a sports bar that described itself as a pub. A row of large-screen televisions started near the glass windows and ran all the way to the back. There were only a handful of customers in evidence, most seated alone nursing a drink.

Salazar's eyes roamed around the space from beneath the baseball cap pulled down over his brow. He was wearing a brown thrift store tweed jacket that was unlike his usual style, cheap tan loafers, and dark corduroy trousers. He looked a decade older than he really was.

It didn't take him long to confirm that his intelligence was correct. Carl Johnson was a man of habit. He visited this same bar almost every night, usually only for an hour or two judging by his bank statements, before heading home.

The visits had started a couple of years earlier, a few months after his wife's obituary appeared in the local paper. Wanda Johnson was the same age as her widowed husband when she passed. The article didn't say why exactly she died, but Salazar figured it was probably cancer. It usually was.

"Get you a drink?" the bartender said in a gruff voice. He was only half-looking at Salazar, the rest of his attention consumed by the reflection of a Yankees game on a mirror that faced the bar.

"Bud," Salazar said. He slid a banknote across the bar and waved away the offer of change.

Carl was an African American man in his mid-sixties. He looked older than the ID image in his employee file. His remaining hair still had speckles of pepper when it was taken, but it was now completely salted over. He was sitting on the barstool at the end of the bar, beneath a four-piece Bud Light poster that covered a false window at the back of the bar. Behind him was the hallway that led to the bathrooms.

He was staring up at the row of screens but with the glassy expression of a man who wasn't really watching. It wasn't much of a life, Salazar thought. Just a way of passing time until the Grim Reaper came knocking. He walked over to the man slowly, so as not to seem too eager.

"Mind if I keep you company?"

Carl started and looked around. His eyes took a second to

refocus on Salazar's face. They were slightly milky—at least cataracts-adjacent if not a full-blown example of the condition.

"Do I know you?" he asked in a hoarse voice.

Salazar placed his beer on the bar to Carl's left. The glass landed with a satisfying and somehow final thud. "Nah. I'm in town for work. Didn't have no place to go and figured this was better than drinking alone."

Carl gestured at the stool next to him, which Salazar was already leaning against. "Be my guest."

Close up, Carl looked even older than he had from a distance. The knuckles of his index and middle fingers were swollen and crooked—more so on the right hand than the left. When he picked up his beer, he did so with difficulty. The backs of his hands were sun-blotched and the pigmentation was patchy, but his face was surprisingly free of wrinkles.

"What's your name, friend?" Salazar asked, extending a hand. "You can call me Bob. I grew up as Roberto, but it never really stuck."

"Nice to meet you, Bob," Carl said as he shook the offered hand. "I'm Carl. Always have been."

Salazar grinned broadly in response. One of the skills that had served him best in his career was the ability to draw up charisma on command. People couldn't usually tell the difference between a fake and the real thing. Perhaps it was easier for people to believe that they were funnier and more interesting than they really were. Or maybe it was just nice to have someone listen to you from time to time.

"Watching the game?" he said, jerking his chin at the row of television screens.

"Nah. More of a football fan," Carl replied. "You?"

"Basketball. I'm a Bucks guy, for my sins."

"Hard luck," Carl said as he lifted his glass to his lips and took the tiniest of sips. "So, what brings you to Saratoga Springs? Can't be the glamour or the ladies."

"I'm an elevator technician," Salazar lied. "My company sends me wherever one needs fixing. I'm working on a job down at the hospital. Control board shorted out. I replaced it easy enough, but it's pinging out error messages like you wouldn't believe. It's like fighting a wildfire. Every time I put one out, another springs up in its place. Got to seven and I decided I was done for the night."

"You get overtime?"

Salazar raised his glass in a mock salute. "And a per diem. According to the Bureau of Labor Statistics, guys like me are an endangered species. I guess a bunch of us retired after the pandemic. Those that are left get to make hay while the sun shines."

"Guess you won't mind buying me a drink then?" Carl said with a raised eyebrow and a twinkle in his milky eyes.

Salazar shrugged. "Company's paying and they don't ask for receipts." He drained the second half of his beer and lifted it over the bar before flashing two fingers at the bartender. "What you drinking?"

"I was only kidding," Carl said, sounding mildly embarrassed.

"No worries. It's nice to have somebody to talk to."

"In that case, whatever you're having."

In short order, two fresh Budweisers appeared on the wooden bar in front of them. Salazar and Carl clinked glasses and fell silent for a moment as each took a sip.

"What about you, Carl?" Salazar asked when his own glass thumped against the wood. "You retired?"

"I've got three years to kill before my full Social Security kicks in. In the meantime, I work in an old people's home mopping floors at night." He laughed out loud. "Ain't much younger than some of them. It's a nice place. Must be thousands of dollars a month."

"They got a bed waiting for you?"

"I wish. They'll bury me in a plain pine box. But I don't mind it. Keeps me busy. I ain't got a wife at home, not anymore. Nights are the worst ever since Wanda died. Find myself staring at the ceiling watching shadows."

"I'm sorry about that."

"You didn't kill her," Carl laughed mirthlessly. "But I appreciate that, man. And thanks for the beer."

"No worries. You got kids?"

"We tried. Never happened for us. I see my brother's grandkids every Christmas and Thanksgiving. That's enough."

"They live close?" Salazar asked.

"Florida. Keep telling me I should move down, but," he shrugged, "I'm comfortable here. I don't have much but it's home."

"And it's where your wife lived."

"There's that," Carl agreed, lifting his beer to his lips and drinking deeply.

Salazar raised his eyebrow and asked a question he already knew the answer to. "I guess you're not working tonight?"

"Not until Friday. Middle of the week's usually quiet. Then you get visitors on Friday and over the weekend and that gets our guests—that's what management calls them—overexcited sometimes. Can't always control themselves, you know?"

"I hope I go out quick," Salazar grunted.

Carl spread his hands. "It isn't so bad. They love and are loved. That's all any of us can ask for."

Salazar's fingers clenched on his glass, and he found himself unable to answer for a few seconds. When he finally gathered himself again, he glanced sideways at Carl to check whether his lapse was noticed. Thankfully the older man's attention was focused in a half-hearted manner on the television screens above the bar.

They chatted about nothing in particular for a little longer while both drained their glasses.

"Can I get you one more?" Carl asked as Salazar's empty glass landed on the bar top.

He shook his head. "Two's my limit or I don't sleep. In fact, I better be going."

"Join the club," Carl said. "In that case, thanks for the beer. I should probably be off as well. I have a steak in the fridge that won't grill itself."

He began laboriously climbing off his stool. The process took several seconds and was punctuated by several grimaces of discomfort. Still, the light in the older man's eyes was undimmed by the failings of his body. He seemed genuinely grateful for the conversation.

"You coming?" he asked when he was finally upright.

"I gotta use the bathroom," Salazar said. "Nice to meet you."

"Likewise."

Salazar walked down the hallway to the male restroom and relieved himself in the urinal. He washed his hands with soap, rinsed them, then dried them with towels from the dispenser on the wall. The count in his head was background noise but accurate to the second. He kept facing the sink in case anybody else entered, but nobody did. When the count hit a minute, he pulled the door open and exited the bar.

The space in the parking lot the next block over that had previously accommodated Carl's gray Tacoma was now empty. Salazar had checked it out before entering the bar. He climbed into his own vehicle—a nondescript Japanese sedan—and followed Maple Avenue north until turning onto Route 29.

Another left turn put him on Route 9 out of town. It was familiar only because he'd driven it once earlier that day.

It was fully dark by the time Salazar arrived at his destination. He killed his lights two houses before the one he was looking for and crept into the space behind the gray Tacoma pickup truck with his engine revs barely off the floor. He reached into his glove compartment and pulled out a loaded pistol before pushing the door open. He pressed it into his waistband the second he was upright.

As he passed Carl's truck, he heard a series of low popping and hissing noises as it cooled, a little like the sound made by Cocoa Krispies upon meeting milk.

His house was a single-story ranch home on a decent-sized plot. The houses along the street were about a hundred feet apart from each other. Many, though not this one, had been extended or completely rebuilt over time. Overall, though, it was a nice middle-class neighborhood—the kind of place a man like Carl had probably lived his entire life.

Salazar noted approvingly that there was a simple electric doorbell on the right side of the frame. He didn't have to knock and risk alerting the neighbors of his presence or, worse still, leave evidence on a cloud-linked doorbell camera. He pushed it and a quiet chime rang out.

It took Carl almost thirty seconds to answer the door. Salazar was pretty sure he heard a toilet flushing inside before footsteps approached. The door clicked open, and a familiar face peered out, squinting so hard to make out the face of his visitor in the darkness that it almost looked like he was closing his eyes.

"Hey, Carl," he said quickly. "You forgot your wallet at the bar. Figured I could save you a journey back to town."

"Oh, Bob," Carl said haltingly as his brain slowly processed what his ears were telling him. "Thanks. Wait. Did I say where I lived? My wallet?"

"Yeah," Salazar said firmly, leaning on his years of experience in situations like this that told him people reacted to confidence and purpose even when their lizard brains sensed that something was horribly wrong. "Let me grab it."

He reached down as if to pull something out of his pocket but drew the pistol and took a step forward into the door in the same movement instead, his superior strength easily brushing the older man aside. He grabbed him by the shoulder and pressed the muzzle of the pistol against his belly button as he maneuvered him into the hallway.

"What is this?" Carl said frantically as he backpedaled.

Salazar kicked the door closed behind them. He pushed Carl a couple of steps forward but kept the pistol raised so that the man knew not to do anything stupid. He shook his head slowly. "I'm sorry. I wish I didn't have to do this."

"Do what?" Carl said, blinking almost manically as he finally clocked how much danger he was really in. "You don't have to do anything. I won't tell anybody about this, I swear!"

Salazar glanced left and right. The house was almost completely dark. Beyond the fact that only Carl's truck—and now his—were parked in the driveway, he was certain that the old janitor was alone.

He took his time reversing the pistol in his hand. The safety was on, and he hadn't chambered a round. He held it by the barrel and paused for a second.

Carl must've realized what was about to happen because he raised his hand and tried to stop it. But too late. Salazar brought the weapon up high and smashed it down against the old man's skull with all the force he could muster. The crack of the impact bounced back against all three walls and the floor.

It was followed a moment later by a dull thud as Carl's inert body collapsed to the floor.

Salazar looked down at him for several long seconds as he wiped the blood off the butt of the pistol. He'd told the man the truth: he didn't want to do this.

But he was also a professional. And sometimes hard men had to do hard things.

EIGHTEEN

Gideon switched his attention between Lachlan and Harriet several times, studying both intently for any sign that they were joking. When he finally reached the conclusion that they were completely serious, he shook his head in disbelief. "You've lost your fucking minds."

"Possible," Lachlan conceded. "But we've spent half our lives thinking about this. It's the only way."

"You want to make me a king..." Gideon replied before trailing off. He squeezed his eyes shut in an attempt to hide from the insanity of it all.

"For a day," Lachlan said. "That's all. Just long enough to take the wind out of the sails of the fanatics and give the fence-sitters a reason to lay down their arms."

"And how are you proposing to go about this?" Gideon looked around theatrically. "Do you have some kind of crack SEAL team hiding somewhere that I can't see?"

"As a matter of fact...yes. I'm not saying we're Team Six, but there are enough of us Faithless who are willing to lay down our lives for this cause. We have family inside too. Friends and husbands and wives and lovers. Even children."

"It takes more than a willingness to die," Gideon said.

"And we know that," Lachlan said, his tone hardening. "Or did you forget who saved your asses this morning?"

Gideon felt Zara's calming touch on his forearm and forced himself to expel some of the tension that had gripped him. He exhaled slowly. "Point taken."

"We didn't say it was going to be easy. But we aren't planning on fast-roping down from Blackhawks in the middle of the night Bin Laden–style, either."

"So what is the plan?"

Lachlan made an apologetic face. "That's need to know. Before we tell you, *we* need to know whether you're in or out."

Gideon puffed out his cheeks. He was certain that Lachlan was telling the truth—he had a plan, and he believed in it. But equally what he was proposing was insane. And even worse, it posed a huge risk to Julia's safety. Pulling off Father Gabriel's assassination—because that's what they were talking about—would take the resources of the entire organization. If there was any chance at all that the Faithless had a leak, then his involvement in this operation risked her life.

Even if they were buttoned-down tight, the plan called for spreading propaganda, presumably for weeks or months in advance. If the Brotherhood were even halfway competent, they would have her under lockdown. Or worse, make an example of her. He'd abandoned her once before and carried that guilt with him ever since.

Doing it a second time simply wasn't a choice he was prepared to make.

Lachlan held up his hand. "Before you make your decision, there's one sweetener. We know where they are keeping your sister. And we're prepared to get her out."

Gideon blinked. The proposal spiked his immediate arguments against. He suspected that it was far from an accident. There was a lot they didn't know about Lachlan, and Harriet, and the entire Faithless organization. But it was already clear they were well-organized, dedicated, and, most of all, smart.

"How?"

One of the doors that led into the dining room clicked and then opened. A woman they hadn't yet been introduced to walked out. Gideon caught a glimpse of what appeared to be a communications hub—although that was a fancy description for a room with just an assortment of computer monitors and networking hardware—before the door closed behind her.

Lachlan glanced over at the new arrival. The woman said nothing, but some unspoken signal appeared to pass between them. Gideon guessed from the stiffness in her posture that whatever it was, it wasn't good news.

"We can discuss that later," he said, rising slowly and gesturing for Harriet to follow. "Right now I have a matter that I need to attend to. I'll have you shown to your rooms."

Zara said, "One's fine."

Lachlan nodded. "As you wish."

Harriet smiled as she also stood up and followed her husband into the communications center. There was a murmur of conversation before the door closed behind them and silenced it once more.

Gideon and Zara looked at each other with wide eyes.

Zara brushed her hair back from her eyes. "Huh," she said. "I gotta admit, I didn't see this coming."

"Me neither."

Right now Gideon wasn't sure what else there was to say. The news that there were other people fighting against the Brotherhood was a lot to process. They'd spent the last month—

and he'd been on the run for years before that—thinking they were alone in the world.

After a couple of minutes, Jamie appeared. He seemed a shy kid. He didn't say much, but Gideon felt Jamie's gaze on him when he thought he wasn't looking.

"It's really you, isn't it?" he finally said as he stopped in front of the open door to a modest but comfortable double bedroom.

Gideon's lips tightened. Jamie's response reminded him of the drone operator at the airport ambush a few weeks earlier who'd almost treated him like royalty. There was a hunger in his eyes.

It can't be healthy, he thought.

"I'm just a person," he replied awkwardly. "No different to you."

"Yeah. Sorry." Jamie flushed. "We moved your things from the car, and there are toiletries and towels in the bathroom."

Gideon raised an eyebrow. "And the guns?"

"I'm sorry," Jamie replied, his voice catching. "I don't know anything about that."

"I guess not," Gideon replied before the kid practically ran off.

He followed Zara into the bedroom and was halfway through opening his mouth when he saw her touch her index finger to her lips. He frowned but cut himself short.

Zara paced around the room, lifting up the lights from the bedside tables, unscrewing bulbs and checking power sockets. The whole process took ten or fifteen minutes before she seemed satisfied that the room was clean. Gideon tried to help but soon realized he wasn't exactly sure what he was looking for, so he gave up.

"Paranoid, much?" he asked when she was done.

She shrugged. She didn't look repentant. She walked into

the small but well-equipped bathroom and turned on the shower full blast before beckoning him to join her. She angled the showerhead so that it bounced against the plastic shower curtain. The sound was like hail falling on a tin roof.

"You think they might be listening to us?" Gideon asked in a low voice, though he suspected the sound of the shower would wash out the audio feed of any bug in the bedroom.

"I think they didn't survive this long by being stupid."

"You're probably right," he agreed. "Can we trust them?"

"Probably," she answered after a second's consideration. "Just as long as our goals align with theirs. We can't just trust them just because they saved our lives."

"Nah," Gideon said, reaching for her hand and giving it a squeeze. "That never works out."

"I don't get bad vibes from either of them. But people with a mission in life make sacrifices. And we don't want to be one of those."

"So we leave," Gideon said. "Do things our way."

Zara looked intently into his eyes. She reached his other hand and faced him head-on. "And what about Julia?"

"We'll find some other way of getting her out."

She exhaled slowly. "It'll take time. Maybe years. Even if we break the encryption on McKinney's files, we can't bank on releasing them now. Not if the outcome leads to hundreds of deaths. And we sure as hell can't just walk into New Eden without being recognized. Not anymore. If they are telling the truth, then the Faithless have a way in."

Gideon grimaced. "I don't like it."

"Me neither," Zara admitted. "But my mom's dying in a nursing home without me. I'd like to see her before...it's too late."

NINETEEN

Eduardo Salazar molded his hands around a paper cup of coffee. The liquid was as black as the gloom outside the windows of the dented Ford transit van that was his chosen vehicle for the night's operation. He'd never seen the stringer who'd arranged it.

He made a face as he took another swig from the steaming coffee cup. The drink tasted like battery acid. He'd found the instant granules in Carl's kitchen, along with the thermos flask now lying on the passenger seat.

An image of the old man briefly flashed across his mind's eye. He'd left him lying in the bathtub with enough cold water running to keep the body cool without flooding the bathroom. Combined with leaving the air conditioning at full blast—the dust on the remote control indicated that Carl preferred doing without rather than running up his electricity bill—the cold water would probably slow the rate of decomposition by several days.

They'll start looking for him sooner than that, Salazar thought. But it didn't matter. He would be long gone by the time they did. He tossed the dregs of the coffee down his throat, wincing as the hot liquid singed the tender flesh, then crumpled the cup and tossed it into the passenger footwell.

He glanced at his watch. It was almost midnight. He was sitting at the far end of the parking lot outside the Saratoga Heights assisted living facility. Only a dozen or so other cars were parked in a space that could accommodate at least five times that. It looked like the night shift was as sparse as he had hoped.

It's time.

Salazar opened his door and climbed out before closing it silently. He didn't bother locking it. If everything went well, he'd be back here in a few minutes. And if it didn't, he wouldn't be back at all.

He walked casually toward Saratoga Heights but avoided the main entrance and went around the back, where he found a set of double emergency doors with a black key fob receiver to one side. He was wearing Carl's uniform—a dark work jacket and pants—and had the dead man's ID badge clipped to his left breast pocket. The outfit was overly padded on his lean, muscular frame but fit well enough—and had the added benefit of disguising the pistol currently nestled in an interior pocket. He'd kept his Yankees cap, figuring it was unlikely to attract attention in this part of the state.

He reached for the badge and tapped it against the reader. A green LED flashed, and the locking mechanism clicked quietly. It was that simple.

The motion-activated overhead lights flickered on in the hallway behind him as he stepped inside and closed the doors silently. A sales video on YouTube had given him a rough idea of the facility's layout. You could find anything on the Internet these days. This utility hallway hadn't been featured, but the goods elevator was right in front of Salazar. Just to the left of it was a doorway marked PRIVATE.

Acting on impulse, Salazar walked over to the door and tapped his borrowed identity badge on the reader. Again the light went green and the lock released. He pulled the door open to find a small cupboard full of janitorial supplies—endless rolls of blue paper towel, chemical sprays, a mop and cart, and various other products. He wheeled the cart out and stared at it for a couple of seconds before deciding that it fit well with his disguise. He should have thought to bring his own, just in case.

Salazar shrugged it off. He pushed the cupboard door closed and called for the elevator. He only had to wait a couple of seconds before it arrived with a muted ping and the doors slid smoothly open in front of him. There were four above-ground floor buttons, along with a basement level, which he guessed was probably used for storage and the kitchens.

And probably a makeshift morgue...

He pushed the button for the third floor and waited in silence as the doors closed and the elevator whisked him to his destination. He knew which ward his target was in and even her room number. He didn't know how the details had been acquired, and he hadn't bothered asking. His Division handlers were fastidious in their attention to detail.

Another ping—louder in the dented and scratched goods elevator car—signaled his arrival. The doors opened in a central lobby. Hallways spread out in all four directions around a reception desk.

A *manned* reception desk.

Salazar took in the mid- to late-twenties blonde woman in pink scrubs sitting behind half a dozen computer monitors with one efficient glance. She had music playing quietly in the background and was reading what looked like a romance novel. He didn't break stride and simply pushed his cart out of the elevator, hoping that she would either not notice his presence or be the kind who didn't notice the janitorial staff.

Unfortunately, that wasn't the case. She stood up and peered out at him, cocking her head slightly when she saw his face. "Where's Carl?"

He stopped. So did the cart's squeaky wheel. "Hurt his back," he lied. "I'm filling in."

"Nobody told me," the nurse said, putting her book down on the lip of the reception desk.

Bad sign.

Salazar shrugged. "I just go where they tell me."

"What are you doing up here, anyway? I didn't call for help."

He blinked slowly. This was a complication, but he had his instructions. He changed course and pushed the cart toward the desk, pretending to limp as he did so. He needed the woman at ease, and despite the fact that she was in her own workplace, it was late at night and he was an unfamiliar male. Salazar was aware that there was probably an emergency button on the desk beside her that she could use to call for assistance if one of the residents required it.

Things would get messy if that happened.

"I don't know what to tell you," he said as he brought the cart to a stop in front of the desk. He patted his thigh pocket, then the ones on the front of his jacket as if searching for something. "I just go where the work order tells me."

He reached inside the jacket, rolling his eyes. "Always the last place you look."

"Don't I know—"

The nurse's eyes widened, and she took an involuntary step back at the sight of the pistol barrel that emerged from Salazar's borrowed jacket.

"Keep your hands where I can see them," he said. "I'm not here to hurt you."

The woman's mouth bobbed open and shut several times as if she couldn't believe what she was seeing. It was an understandable reaction. Who the hell robbed an old person's home?

"We don't have money, if that's what you're looking for," she said, her voice growing higher and higher in pitch with every word.

"It's not," Salazar said, gesturing at her to move out from behind the desk with the pistol. He quickly and efficiently frisked her, running his hands over every inch of her body. He had no doubt that she would consider the act a violation, but there was nothing sexual about it for him.

It was just business.

"Then what do you want?"

He pulled the cell phone from the left pocket of her scrubs pants and powered it down before setting it on the desk. Next, he stepped back and pointed at the Apple Watch on her wrist. "Take that off."

A muscle flickered on her face as she complied with his instruction. Salazar idly wondered whether she'd only just realized she could've used the device to call for help.

Too late for that.

He glanced around and found the sign pointing to the ward he was looking for—the Washington Lounge. He ordered the nurse—Karina, according to her name badge—to push the cart to the wall so that it would attract less attention if anybody passed by.

"This way," he said, gesturing at the door on the other side of the desk.

Karina's expression grew more and more befuddled as she shuffled ahead of him in her Crocs. The rubber shoes squeaked on the tile floor. They passed through the doorway using her identity badge. The other side was quiet, save for a guttural snoring coming from one of the resident's rooms.

"Show me where Hillary Walker sleeps."

"I won't help you kill her," Karina said, her voice shaky but defiant nonetheless. "I don't know who you are, but this is nuts. If you leave now I swear I won't call the cops."

"Yes, you will," Salazar said evenly. He drew the slide of the pistol back and chambered a round. "This will go easier if you don't lie to me."

Karina visibly swallowed. "Okay. I'll give you a head start."

"Kind of you to offer," Salazar said without any hint of emotion in his voice. "Do you have kids, Karina?"

She suddenly froze before shaking her head violently from side to side in a manner that told him that she did.

"I don't hurt children," Salazar said, his voice growing harder for a second before he shook off the feeling. "But yours need a mother."

She exhaled slowly as the implicit threat hit home. "What do you want with Hillary? She has dementia. You can't scam her, if that's what this is about. She's basically nonverbal."

"I don't want to scam her. And I don't want to hurt her."

The second part of his statement appeared to give Karina permission to help—or perhaps enough plausible deniability to salve her conscience.

"This way," she said, briefly squeezing her eyes shut.

She led him past half a dozen glass doors. They were shut but mostly lit by green emergency lights and the flickering LEDs on medical assistance machines despite the nighttime darkness. She stopped at the seventh and opened it.

"What do you want with her?" she whispered.

Salazar's gaze narrowed as he saw the frail elderly woman lying underneath the covers on the single bed on the other side of the room. She was wearing an oxygen mask. He'd seen no respiratory condition on her medical charts.

"What's with the breathing apparatus?"

"She had the flu last week," Karina said, continuing to speak in a hushed tone. "She's better now, but she needs the air still."

He saw a wheelchair against the wall, just next to the window. He jerked his chin at it. "Get her into that."

"What?"

"Do it," he said, punctuating the point with his weapon.

"Don't you understand? She can't go anywhere. If you take that mask off her, she won't last the day."

Salazar's eyes turned black. It was a look he deployed rarely but usually to great effect. He spoke in a low growl. "Then you better find a tank."

TWENTY

Gideon was startled back to wakefulness by the sound of heavy footsteps in the hallway outside. He didn't remember falling asleep, only his eyelids beginning to droop and Zara nestling her head in the crook of his shoulder, and a warm, happy feeling overcoming him.

"What's going on?" Zara murmured sleepily.

He sat upright, eyes glancing left and right in their sockets but mostly as a matter of habit. There was nothing to see in this bedroom that they hadn't already. The curtains were drawn, and it was pitch black beyond them anyway—the true darkness that you only found this far away from a city.

"I'm not sure," he whispered. Despite the low pitch of his voice, it sounded unnatural in his ears—his hearing had ramped up to a sensitivity that was many times greater than normal.

Another series of thumps confirmed it. It wasn't just footsteps he was hearing—it was someone running. And Gideon wasn't a crack intelligence analyst like the woman lying at his side, but some things a man just knew.

People don't run inside. Not unless something's very wrong.

The more intently he listened, the more sure Gideon grew. The isolated house was suddenly alive with activity. Doors opened and shut, the reverberations and squealing of hinges echoing throughout the building. Thuds—and also hushed voices—carried through the hallways.

Zara climbed off the bed. They were both still fully clothed. A quick glance at Gideon's wristwatch revealed that they couldn't have slept more than half an hour. The stresses of the day had simply caught up with them.

"Where are you going?"

"To find out what's happening," she replied.

Shafts of light stabbed through the gaps in the curtains and were followed an instant later by the growling of a vehicle's engines.

More than one.

Gideon jumped to his feet. Whatever was happening, it was clearly out of the ordinary, otherwise Lachlan or Harriet would have flagged it to them.

"There's a fire drill at 9 p.m. It's resistance group policy. Happens every week..."

He smiled to himself at the thought, but the momentary humor quickly faded and was replaced by a sense of unease. He hurried to join Zara at the door, and they exited together. Lachlan turned a corner and stopped a few feet away from them.

"What's happening?" Zara asked directly.

The man's expression was drawn. His weathered face looked somehow more tired than he had just an hour earlier. Older, too. "I was coming to warn you. There is a situation that requires my attention."

Gideon's hand twitched. It felt empty without a weapon in his grasp. He instinctively glanced around the room in search of danger.

"Here?" he asked sharply. He had to raise his voice to be heard over the growl of car engines outside.

Lachlan shook his head. "Not...here. I have to go. Harriet too. We'll be back as soon as possible. You will be perfectly safe here. There's food—"

Zara interrupted even as Gideon's mouth was opening to do the same. "No dice," she said firmly. "We're grateful for what you did. But we're not staying here. And we sure as hell aren't staying while you keep us in the dark. For all we know this situation of yours could blow back on us."

Lachlan frowned. "I don't have time for this."

"Make time," Zara said immediately.

Her tone wasn't cutting, but it was firm. Lachlan clearly saw that he wasn't going to be able to stonewall his way through this one. A rictus of irritation flickered on his jaw as he glanced toward the window through which headlights streamed into the bedroom, then back at Zara.

"Fine," he sighed. "Shit's hitting the fan in New Eden. I just got word from our people inside that dozens of people have been arrested and are being held—tortured—by the Division."

"Are they Faithless?" Gideon asked.

"Some," Lachlan nodded. "But not more than a handful. Many are innocent, probably plucked at random from the street. Others are Chosen officers and family members. It's a show of force from Gabriel. He's demonstrating that nobody can stand against him."

"What will they do with them?" Zara asked.

Lachlan shrugged. "We don't know for sure. But I have my suspicions. This is all being driven by Trent Riley, Gabriel's security chief. He's been battling for influence for years. After the Chosen's failure in apprehending you guys, it seems he has the upper hand. This is his demonstration of that. A lot of innocent people are going to get hurt."

Zara frowned. She had an almost disbelieving expression on her face. "You think they'll kill them?"

"I can't rule it out. I don't have any solid information saying that's the plan. But I can't see Trent releasing them either. He's drawing a line in the sand. The top ranks of the Brotherhood are a dangerous place to be. Crudely, he's demonstrating to the others that he isn't to be fucked with."

Gideon turned and grabbed one of the bags that Jamie and the other Faithless guard had placed in the corner. Neither he nor Zara had even opened them yet, let alone unpacked. He shouldered it, then stooped to pick up the other.

"What are you doing?" Lachlan asked.

"We're coming with you," Gideon said.

"YOU'LL RIDE WITH JAMIE," Lachlan said as half a dozen people that Gideon hadn't even realized were in the isolated house hustled outside carrying suitcases, duffel bags, or computer equipment. Most of the supplies were being loaded into the first of two black SUVs. The third appeared to be their ride.

The red Porsche was nowhere to be seen.

"Where are we going?" Zara asked.

Lachlan glanced toward where Harriet was directing the chaos all around her—seemingly unaffected by it as though she was standing in the eye of the storm. "I'm not sure yet."

A minute later, Gideon and Zara were settled in the rear seats. Most of the bags were in the trunk of the SUV, but they'd removed some of their personal effects, which now rode in the rear with them. Gideon had insisted on being given a weapon, and Lachlan acceded to this demand without complaint.

Gideon peered out of the windshield and watched as the

Faithless operatives piled into the front two SUVs. Lachlan was the last to climb in, surrounded by a cloud of dust illuminated by headlights. The car door thunked closed, and before the sound had finished echoing around the woodland clearing they were in, the first SUV was on the move.

"You think they have a mole?" Gideon said, quietly voicing a suspicion that had been growing inside him for the last few minutes. "Could just be coincidence that some of their assets got rolled up with these arrests. But then again, it might not be."

Instead of an answer, Zara jabbed him in the ribs with her elbow. When he turned to find out why, rubbing his side, she shot the back of Jamie's head a meaningful look. The message was clear. *He's listening.*

"I have no idea," Zara said after half a beat. "But something spooked them, all right."

They drove for about half an hour before reaching the highway. It was only then that Zara reached into the backpack between her knees and pulled out her cell phone. It was a cheap Android model on a burner SIM card—just useful for making and receiving phone calls and having access to the Internet.

The screen lit up as she powered the device up. The flash of light must've caught Jamie's attention, because he glanced at them in the rear mirror, his eyebrows furrowed. "Please don't use that."

Zara peeled a piece of tape from the back cover. Stuck to the underside was a new SIM card and a metal pin for popping open the tray. She held the card up long enough for Jamie to clock what it was, then explained that it was a virgin number. "Even if somebody could trace it, they don't know what they're looking for."

"I'll have to ask Lachlan about that."

"I understand," Zara said, smiling in a kind of Southern manner that indicated she was going to do what she damn well pleased.

Gideon concealed his own smile. He hadn't known Zara for long in the grand scheme of things. But it only took a few hours in her company to understand that there was no sense in standing in her way. She was going to do what she wanted, and there was nothing anyone could do about it.

"What's up?" he asked as Jamie scrabbled in the storage compartment in the door for something that sounded hard.

"Just wanted to see if there was anything from the rat bastard who sold us out in Pittsburgh," Zara said with her lips pursed. She gestured around them and then lowered her voice. "If this collaboration doesn't work out then at least we have a lead of our own to track down."

"You make it sound like a fashion line," Gideon said. "Zara x Rat Bastard. In stores Friday."

It was a weak joke, but it didn't seem as though Zara had even heard him. Her fingers flew over the phone screen as she furiously navigated through a variety of apps and web pages.

"Rear to lead," Jamie radioed—Gideon now realized that he had been reaching for a handset all this time.

He turned back to Zara, raising an eyebrow to see how she would respond to this development. He suspected that Lachlan would have to physically clamber into the SUV and tear the device out of the hands before she would stop.

And even then, he didn't fancy the man's chances of success.

He watched with a mild expression of amusement on his face and waited for Zara to say something. He realized weeks ago that nothing got through to her when she was locked in like this. You just had to wait it out.

"Lead to rear," the radio crackled upfront. "What's up?"

The reflection of the phone screen glinted back as Zara's eyes widened and she suddenly stopped typing. Her expression was drained of color.

Gideon leaned forward and tried to make out what she was looking at, but the screen was turned away from him. "What is it?"

"It's my mom..." Zara whispered. "She's missing."

TWENTY-ONE

The convoy of SUVs skidded to a halt in a twenty-four-hour roadside diner's parking lot halfway to Punxsutawney. The three vehicles were similar in style but were from different model ranges and production years, so they didn't attract any obvious attention from either the customers inside or the trickle of truckers who climbed in and out of their vehicles.

"What the hell's going on?" Lachlan asked, joining Gideon and Zara, who were huddled on the far side of the SUV they had been assigned to. The driver, Jamie, was still sitting in the front seat with the window rolled down.

"We have a problem," Gideon said when Zara didn't answer. She was glued to the cell phone, rapidly typing in queries and pausing for only seconds to peer at the screen before she was on to the next.

"I gathered," Lachlan said, thin-lipped. He seemed to catch a glimpse of Jamie in the front seat and rapped his knuckles on the SUV's body. "Get out and form a perimeter."

Gideon looked around for the first time and saw that the rest of the Faithless personnel had fanned out to cover the entire parking lot. They did so in an unobtrusive manner—leaning against vehicles, pretending to smoke or talk on the phone—but it was clear that they were well trained.

"I think Zara's mom's been kidnapped," Gideon said.

Lachlan didn't even blink. "Why?"

Zara finally joined the conversation. She flashed the cell phone's screen at Lachlan. "You see this?"

"What am I looking at?"

"My mom has early-onset Alzheimer's. The last three years she's been a full-time patient at Saratoga Heights, an assisted living facility in upstate New York. She can't function without round-the-clock care. A couple of years ago, she went missing for about thirty-six hours. Hitchhiked halfway to Albany before the police found her. Ever since then she's worn a bracelet with a small tracking device in it, just in case."

"And I'm guessing there's no reason for her to be in Vermont?"

Zara shook her head emphatically. Her complexion was pale, but otherwise she was handling the stress of her mom's disappearance well. "She doesn't leave Saratoga Heights. Not ever. I told you, she needs full-time assistance."

"Could she have been transferred without your knowledge?"

"No way," Zara said. "Her insurance pays the bills directly, but I'm the one who has power of attorney. They can't move her without my approval."

"When did this happen?"

"Two hours ago," Zara said immediately. "The bracelet's set up to notify me via email if it leaves the grounds of the facility. That happened about half past midnight."

"Okay. What's your mom's name?"

"Hillary. Hillary Walker."

Lachlan held up a finger and reached into his jacket pocket

for a cell phone. It was powered down, so the three of them waited in silence as the screen flashed into life and the operating system loaded.

Finally he dialed a number from memory. Whoever was on the other end answered within a single ring. Lachlan wasted no time with pleasantries. "I need you to look into something for me," he said. "I'm looking for a resident of a nursing home called Saratoga Heights. Her name is Hillary Walker. She might've been kidnapped. I need an answer fast."

With that he hung up the phone.

"Is the tracker still active?" he asked.

Zara nodded. She turned the screen back around so that Gideon and Lachlan could see it. A blue dot hovered over a road marked Route 315. At the bottom of the screen, a readout indicated that the tracking device had last called home seven minutes and twenty-seven seconds ago. "It pings the satellite every fifteen minutes to save battery. I can turn it fully active, but it's down to twenty percent charge already. That'll last a couple days easy, but less than an hour on active."

"Keep it like it is," Lachlan nodded.

Gideon made and released a fist several times. He tracked a truck driver climbing out of his cab, his boots kicking up a puff of dust as they hit the dirt surface of the parking lot. The man glanced toward the array of parked SUVs and seemed to study them for several seconds before turning toward the diner.

He forced himself to breathe out slowly. He was on edge, but worse, he felt impotent to help Zara. They were almost five hundred miles away from Vermont. It would take hours to drive that far. By then it might be too late.

"What are our options?" he said to Lachlan. "Do you have a team that way?"

"We're not the FBI," Lachlan replied with a curt shake of his head.

"Then we better get moving," Gideon said, pivoting toward the SUV. This time he had no intention of sitting in the back. "We're wasting time here."

Lachlan opened his mouth—seemingly to argue—but was cut off by the harsh screech of his phone's ringtone. He cut it off instantly and lifted it toward his ear before changing his mind and putting the phone on speaker.

"All right boss, there's definitely something up here," a businesslike female voice said without pausing for pleasantries. "Saratoga Springs dispatch was called an hour ago by the nursing home. A nurse was held at gunpoint before being tied up and left in this woman's bed. The patient was abducted by a Hispanic man in his thirties or forties, just under six foot tall, spoke good English with an accent. He was wearing the night janitor's uniform. Buzzed into the building with the guy's ID."

"Where did he get it?"

"Saratoga County Sheriff's Office just rolled up to the janitor's house. I don't have details, but they also put a radio call out for a medical examiner."

"Shit," Lachlan muttered. "Homicide?"

"Looks that way."

"I want footage from inside Saratoga Heights," Lachlan ordered. "I don't care what you have to do to get it. Make it fast."

"Strong copy," the voice on the phone said before hanging up without another word.

"Homicide?" Zara repeated in a low murmur. She blinked slowly.

"Zara, get in the car," Gideon said in a firm voice. "We need to get rolling."

"Let the police handle this," Lachlan said, before directing his next question at Zara. "Does Saratoga Heights have access to the GPS tracker?"

"I can give them access" she said. She seemed slightly in shock from what she'd heard.

"Then—" Lachlan started before stopping himself. "How obvious is this thing?"

"The tracker? It looks a bit like a wristwatch, but it doesn't have a screen," she answered, more fluent when concentrating on precise details. "But you wouldn't know what it was supposed to do if you saw it."

Lachlan closed his eyes. His eyelids flickered with movement before they snapped back open. "No way the Brotherhood sends an amateur for this. Whoever it is, they've left the bracelet running on purpose."

"What are you saying?" Zara asked.

Gideon answered before Lachlan could. "They want us to know where she is. It's a trap."

TWENTY-TWO

A scream echoed throughout the basement prison, at first high-pitched before its guttural death bounced off the walls and into Julia's ears. She gritted her teeth as a surge of saliva pooled in her mouth to forestall the urge to vomit. It took several seconds of deep breathing before the desire faded and she was able to swallow again.

A deep silence followed the cry. It was as if every prisoner inmate was holding their breath, hoping—praying—that they wouldn't be next.

"How long is this going to take?" the guard at the cell door asked. "She looks fine."

"Just a few more seconds," Julia said, wiping the sweat off her brow with the underside of her forearm.

Her mouth was already bone dry again. She'd been working down here in the gloom amid the smell of urine and blood and sweat for hours without a break. Her knees ached from kneeling on the bare concrete, and her lower back kept spasming from the strain of crouching over the beaten prisoners who were crammed into every spare inch of the overflowing cells.

The prisoner she was working on needed a hospital. At the very least she needed a doctor. She was about Julia's age, though judging by the thick calluses on her hands and the deep tan on her face and arms, she likely worked a manual job outdoors. Probably on one of the farms.

She was unconscious. Had been that way ever since the guards dragged her out of the locked interrogation rooms at the far end of the basement twenty minutes ago. Julia hadn't glimpsed much more than flashes of what lay behind the thick metal door. Just more bare concrete and locked doors, and brief interludes when the screams weren't so muffled.

Julia tore open another disinfectant wipe and added the packaging to the small pile on the floor to the right of her patient. She'd already attended to the wounds on the woman's palms. They were shallow but bled profusely. The cuts themselves were fine, perhaps inflicted by a razor blade or sharp knife. They'd been slashed in the shape of a T.

For Traitor?

She wiped another gash on the woman's cheek, wincing as she guided black debris out of the wound despite the fact that the patient didn't react at all. She should've felt that, shouldn't she?

"This woman needs a doctor," Julia called out without looking at the guard behind her. Satisfied that she'd cleaned all of the visible wounds, she picked up all of the discarded medical litter and added it to a small white trash-can sack.

"She ain't getting one," the guard grunted with no real emotion in his voice. "Hurry up. I need a piss."

Julia looked up and caught the gaze of one of the other inmates, another woman in her late forties or early fifties. She had a matronly air and dimples on her cheeks that must've been carved in by decades of warm smiles.

All that was gone. In its place was a pleading look in the woman's eyes, an expression of rank desperation on her face.

After fishing a bottle of water out of her makeshift bag of medical supplies, Julia handed it to the woman. "Can you make sure she gets fluids? Dribble it into her lips a few drops at a time. I'll be back when I can."

The woman nodded quickly, jerkily, but said nothing. Julia didn't blame her. Speaking up attracted attention. And attention was a dangerous commodity in a place like this.

"Okay, I'm done," Julia said.

She zipped up her bag, grasped the sack of trash, and pushed herself back upright. Her knees groaned after being in one position for so long. As she straightened, her head spun slightly from the sudden change in blood pressure. She reached out and gripped one of the bags as the edges of her vision faded to black.

Don't faint, she thought desperately as she tried to hold onto her consciousness. The last thing she needed was a visit to the doctor. He—always a he—would quickly uncover her secret.

"What's wrong with you?" the guard asked.

"Just hungry," Julia lied after snatching a shallow breath. Her grip tightened around the cell bars before she pushed herself away. "Been a long day."

It was the truth. She had no way of telling the time down here, but she had to have been here for hours in a place whose bleakness made every second feel like a minute and every minute a day.

"Get out of the cell," the guard said without interest. Julia hobbled out, fighting her aching muscles and exhausted frame just in time to avoid the cell door crashing shut behind her.

Another scream ripped through the basement. Julia flinched but steeled herself not to look. She couldn't face seeing another broken body being dragged from interrogation.

"I need help down here," Julia said to the guard. "There are too many of them."

Before he could answer, a whistle split the air between them. Surprised by the unusual sound, Julia turned. At the far end of the basement, she saw Trent had just emerged from the interrogation wing. He beckoned toward her.

"Come here," he called.

Julia glanced over her shoulder, assuming he was talking to somebody else. But the guard gestured at her to follow. She walked slowly over to the Division's chief, dreading the need to talk to him. As far as she was concerned, Trent Riley was the personification of pure evil. Something about his mere presence felt wrong, like the scent of dead flesh.

"What is it?" she asked as she stopped in front of him. Her eyes widened as she saw that his hands and forearms were speckled and smeared with blood.

"I need your help," he said before turning on the balls of his feet and striding into the interrogation wing. He stopped on the other side of the door and waited impatiently for her.

For a moment Julia just remained where she was. She didn't know if she wanted to follow. But she was certain she didn't have a choice.

She walked across the threshold with leaden feet. It was colder on the other side of the door. So cold she felt the hair on the back of her arms standing at attention.

Trent swung the heavy door closed. The metal clanged as it sank into the frame. Julia heard a click and realized that the door had locked automatically. There was no getting through it without a key—and the only one she could see was clipped to a belt loop on the waistband of Trent's pants.

Julia inhaled and momentarily panicked that there was no air to breathe. The interrogation wing was darker and colder and more soulless even than the cells on the other side of the door.

"He's in here," Trent said, pointing at one of the metal doors. It was marked with a 3. There were three almost identical doorways on either side of the hallway. He pulled out the keychain, flicked through the keys, and selected the correct one, which he inserted into the lock before twisting.

"Who?"

Trent didn't answer as he pushed the door open. The space behind was pitch black until he reached inside and flicked on a light switch.

Julia gasped and stumbled backward, her hand closing on her mouth. The flash of a naked man was imprinted on her retinas. He was slumped on his knees with blood dripping from slashes and cuts all over his body. His arms were raised above his shoulders and hung from chains attached at one end to a hook on the ceiling and the other to blood-soaked manacles that had bitten into his wrists.

But of all his injuries, it was the enormous bruise that swallowed his stomach that caught Julia's attention. She realized she'd met him before. His name was Brenden. He'd asked whether Gideon was returning, before passing out completely. That was the last time she'd seen him.

Trent jabbed his index finger at the man. "Wake him up. He's no use to me unconscious."

"What did he do?" Julia whispered, briefly forgetting her senses. Rule number one in a place like this was to never ask questions.

"He's a spy," Trent replied in a bored tone. "Or he's not. That's what I'm trying to find out. You have an hour. Make sure he's conscious when I get back."

TWENTY-THREE

"We split up," Lachlan said, snapping his finger against his thumb before pointing at Gideon and Zara in turn. "You two go with Harriet. I'll take a couple of my guys. We'll get her mom back, and reconnect at the training camp in Georgia."

"Hell no," Zara replied. "I'm going. She's my family, not yours."

"Too risky. If you put yourself in danger, you're playing into their hands. I believe you could help. But you're also emotionally invested and that's a bad frame of mind for something like this."

"I didn't ask for your opinion," Zara snapped. She was leaning forward, her gaze furious, her fists clenched.

Gideon winced. He closed his eyes briefly, then said, "Lachlan's right."

"What?" she said, spinning to face him. "We can't hide like children while they take care of business for us."

"We're not hiding," Gideon said firmly. "And I won't let them handle this alone. I'll go. But this is definitely a trap, and we need to be coolheaded about how we go about this. It's going to be dangerous, and a second's hesitation could get you hurt. It could get your mom killed. You don't want that, right?"

"Who said you could come?" Lachlan said with a frown.

"I don't remember asking for permission," Gideon said, flashing a smile to keep tensions from simmering over.

"*You* are what they want," Lachlan reiterated. "Not Zara, and sure as hell not her mom. You can't seriously be proposing that you just give them exactly what they want?"

"I'm not planning on getting caught," Gideon said, matching Lachlan's disbelieving stare without blinking. "You can either get out of my way—or you can help me."

Lachlan chose the second option. In truth, it was the only one open to him, and both men knew it. As much as he hated it, Gideon had come to accept that he was important—if only to mistaken people for the wrong reasons. But so long as he had status, he might as well put it to work.

Gideon and Zara embraced before she climbed into Harriet's SUV. To his obvious dismay, their driver Jamie was now tasked with taking the two women to wherever the Faithless operated from along with another armed shooter for security.

Zara's posture was stiff with frustration even as she hugged him. It was obvious to Gideon that she was furious with him for taking sides with Lachlan, even if she was resigned to the outcome.

"You better come back," she said before they parted.

"Is that supposed to sound like a threat?" Gideon joked to ease the strain between them.

Zara jumped up into the rear seat of the SUV and reached out for the door handle. Harriet turned away, conspicuously demonstrating she wasn't eavesdropping. "Take it however you want."

She slammed the door closed. Barely a couple of seconds later, the engine fired up and the SUV was moving again.

Gideon turned to see Lachlan conferring with three other men that he'd only seen in passing. He was thin-lipped, clearly irritated that he'd been forced into taking Gideon along with him.

But it was the only way, Gideon knew. Zara would have refused to let the Faithless handle her business any other way. And she would have been right to do so. He felt the same.

"Theo, Evan, you ride together," Lachlan said. "Francis, you and Gideon with me. I'll drive."

For the first leg, Gideon and Francis sat together in the back.

"I don't recognize you," Gideon said, realizing they were about the same age. "Did you live on one of the farms?"

"I've never been to New Eden."

"Not sure I understand."

Francis grinned, though the smile was tinged with regret. "I was never in the Brotherhood. My big sister ran away when I was fourteen. She was two years older. My parents didn't hear a peep from her for years after she disappeared. Dad ate a shotgun before we found out she was in Texas. Mom passed from cancer, but I think it was grief that really did her in."

"Shit, man, that's heavy," Gideon muttered, his own thoughts drifting to what Julia was doing right now and whether she was even still alive.

"I joined the Marines at eighteen. Wasn't nothing left for me in civilian life. Government paid for my therapy by letting me throw a shit ton of lead downrange."

"No beating it," Gideon agreed from experience.

Francis's expression tightened. "Sis turned up in a ditch thirty miles from New Eden six months before my four years were out. Local cops said it was a suicide. Nothing about it smelled right to me. I had a little saved after I got discharged, so I started investigating. One thing led to another, and I found my way to the Faithless."

"What are you here for?" Gideon asked quietly, already knowing the answer.

"You know," Francis replied, his expression dark. "Revenge."

They switched drivers whenever they needed to stop for gas and only stopped long enough to fill up the two SUVs and purchase gas station snacks and energy drinks. The GPS tracker stabilized in a single location just a couple of hours into their seven-hour odyssey.

"What is it?" Gideon asked, flicking his gaze up to the rearview mirror to see Lachlan with a laptop computer perched on his knees, the glow from the screen lighting up his face.

"Looks like an old Catholic convent, at least according to Wikipedia. Shut down in the sixties. It's been empty ever since."

"Could be a Brotherhood safe house," Francis suggested.

"Mmm," Lachlan murmured.

"You don't sound convinced," Gideon said.

"Google Maps satellite photos aren't exactly military reconnaissance grade," Lachlan said as he tapped the laptop screen, "but these were last updated only six months ago. The place looks overgrown. Doesn't look like anybody's visited it for years. And I have a pretty good working knowledge of the Brotherhood's network of safe houses and staging posts. As far as I know, there isn't a single one in the whole of Vermont."

"We're three hours out," Gideon replied, quickly glancing at the screen on the center console. "We've got enough gas to drive straight through to the convent. We do that, we'll arrive a half hour before dawn."

"And then what?" Lachlan asked.

"No sense waiting around," Gideon said, clenching his fingers around the steering wheel. "We hit them fast and we hit them hard."

TWENTY-FOUR

"There's only one road up to the convent," Lachlan said, raising his voice to be heard over the drumming of a furious rainstorm that had come on suddenly about fifteen minutes earlier. He held up the screen so that Gideon was able to catch a flash of it in the rearview mirror.

The brief glimpse told him little.

"And there's this track through the forest," he continued. In the half-second that Gideon allowed himself to look away from the road, given the conditions, he saw Lachlan make a face. "Leads from the viewing station at the top of this hill right through the trees."

"How far is it?"

"About a mile," Lachlan answered. "Problem is we have no idea what the conditions will be like. Could be a flat dirt track, could be locked up with timber. No way of knowing from here."

"What are you thinking?" Gideon asked.

He had a pretty good idea what he would do—send one of the SUVs right up the main road to the convent and have another team sneak down the dirt track. On foot if necessary. Even weighed down with a rifle and ammunition—and in sneakers rather than boots—he was sure he could make the mile sprint in under twenty minutes no matter the terrain.

Well, he thought he could do it faster than that. But they needed to hit the X at the same time to maximize their only advantage: the enemy's uncertainty as to their precise time of arrival.

It was a slim chance at best. The enemy had picked the terrain. They had baited the trap. And they were waiting for Gideon to stumble into it.

He didn't even know how many men he was facing. For all they knew, it could be an army.

But what choice did they have?

"Two teams," Lachlan said, confirming that he was thinking on the same track. "One goes straight down the road up to the convent. The other tackles the track. Probably three in the first, two in the second in case the forest's thicker than it looks."

"I'll take the track," Gideon said.

He glanced at the map screen on the dashboard. They were just twenty minutes out from the target. They would need to stop and gear up any moment now. Between the lashing rain and the darkness of night, it was still black as coal outside. True dawn would come a little later up here in the foothills of the Taconic Mountains, delayed by the thickly forested mountainsides. But the first glimmerings of light weren't too distant.

"I'll go with you," Lachlan replied.

Gideon spared a look up at the rearview mirror and matched the older man's gaze. "No offense, but I'd rather take Francis."

"Why?"

"He's a leatherneck. The terrain's going to be tough. He can handle it."

He looked back at the road, but not before glimpsing Francis squirming beside Lachlan.

"You're saying I'm too old."

"I'm—"

"—right," Lachlan said, finishing his sentence for him. "I'd slow you down."

Both vehicles pulled up at the side of the road ten miles out from the target, just before the road separated and led both ways around the base of a hill. A hundred yards ahead, a large structure—an outdoor supply store, according to the map—loomed out of the darkness. There were no lights on inside.

All five men jumped out of the two SUVs and were instantly soaked to the skin by the lashing rain.

Lachlan popped the trunk of the second SUV. Several large weapons cases and other various bags were piled inside.

"We weren't exactly geared up for a hostage rescue operation," he yelled over the pounding rain. "Guns and ammo we got plenty. We'll have to make do with everything else."

"Could have fooled me," Gideon said, eyes widening at the sight of the makeshift armory.

He picked out an M4 carbine and half a dozen magazines, plus a pistol. There was no holster, so he pushed the sidearm into his belt loop and secreted the rifle magazines in every spare pocket. In a capacious tan duffel bag, he found a thigh rig for a fighting knife, which he strapped around his right leg.

"No grenades?" he asked.

Francis chuckled. "No grenades."

Gideon shook his head and made a joke to mask his growing nervousness—mostly from himself. "And here I thought you guys came to party."

"These are the only radios we got," Lachlan said, waving at

the handset that the three SUVs had used earlier to communicate. He pulled out his cell phone but winced at what he saw on screen. "No signal."

The five men geared up, then huddled underneath one of the trunk lids for the protection against the rain it offered. Lachlan set up his laptop in the dry space and pulled up the satellite map of the area.

"We're here," he said, tapping a spot on the screen and leaving a droplet of rainwater behind. "The drive up to the viewing point will take ten, maybe twelve minutes. You have to find the track in the dark, so add five. Then twenty for the last mile."

He glanced at the clock on the bottom right of the laptop screen. "That takes us to 5:15 a.m. Just after dawn."

Gideon pulled a face. It was later than he would've liked. It would be lighter. On the flip side, they only had one thermal scope between the five of them and no other night vision aids. Between the smothering clouds and the rainstorm that was still beating down with no sign of abating, they had no hope of operating underneath the moonlight. The sprint down the forest track would be fraught with risk—though more from a fall or stumble than enemy action.

So after dawn it was.

"Radio check at 5:10," he said, meeting each man's gaze in turn. "No matter what happens, we hit the target at quarter past. Understood?"

Even Lachlan nodded his agreement. Gideon felt a flush of excitement—even pride—at once again leading men into combat. But he'd never prepared for something like this. It had been different in the Legion. Foot patrols in IED-infested terrain were hours of numbing monotony punctuated by brief interludes of adrenaline-soaked terror.

This was a planned assault. And a woman's life was on the line if he failed.

He checked his watch. It was 4:35 a.m. The darkness all around made a mockery of the arrival of dawn. "Then let's move."

Unlike the team of Lachlan, Theo, and Evan, who were to approach the abandoned convent directly, he and Francis were making an end run around the backside of the next hill over. It meant that as Gideon gunned the SUV's powerful engine, sending waves of displaced rainwater surging away from every puddle he hit, he was able to keep the vehicle's headlights on high.

It was a lucky break.

The road up to the viewpoint was narrow and steep, with several switchbacks through the thick forest, around each of which the hillside plunged away. If they'd been forced to do it in the dark, Gideon had little doubt they would either have arrived an hour late or fallen to their deaths in the process.

"What was your sister's name?" he said, glancing at Francis once the road straightened out.

"Holly," Francis replied quietly, gripping his rifle as he stared out into the narrow strips of light thrown by the headlights. "Her name was Holly."

Gideon pushed the gas pedal down until the speedometer hit sixty miles an hour and held it there. The wiper motor screamed with the effort of clearing the endless rivers of rain that were now falling.

"Thanks for doing this," Gideon said as they finally reached the parking lot in front of the viewpoint. "I know you didn't have to."

"That's where you're wrong," Francis said, briefly catching his eye. The Marine's gaze was breathtaking in its intensity. "I read the autopsy report. The police advised me not to, but I made them give it to me anyway. Holly was abused. I don't know how the hell she survived what I read in those pages. And I'm not gonna stop until every last one of those psychopathic fucks is six feet deep. No matter what it costs me. You understand?"

"Yeah," Gideon said, feeling a calm descend over him now that the action was about to start. "I think I do."

He reached for the door handle with his left hand and prepared to kill the engine with his right, but Francis pointed into the darkness. "See that? I think it's where the track begins."

Gideon narrowed his gaze and stared down the hill into the edge of the forest. The trees swallowed every last ray of light. "I'll take your word for it."

"It's drivable. Least the first part is. How do you feel about saving some time?

TWENTY-FIVE

Gideon killed the SUV's headlights and briefly slowed the heavy vehicle as he approached the grass shoulder at the edge of the parking lot. The seat jolted underneath him as the front tires kicked up over the drenched long grass.

"Hold on," he warned, tightening his grip on the steering wheel. He took a deep breath, then gingerly tapped the gas pedal. "This could get bumpy."

It was a hell of an understatement. Even before they hit the dirt track, they had to negotiate several hundred feet of long grass. Despite the power the engine provided, he was forced to select the lowest gear setting to stop the tires spinning out on the slick surface.

It wasn't a complete success. The terrain sloped down to the edge of the forest, and as the gradient grew steeper, Gideon realized that he wasn't really in control of their speed anymore.

"I'm not kidding," he warned, his voice pinched as the SUV began to slide toward the wall of trees. He could barely see twenty feet ahead of them, but he knew enough to know he was pushing thirty miles an hour heading into some very thick trees.

It took all of Gideon's willpower to resist the urge to steer away from the skid. Instead, he trusted in physics that he didn't fully understand and leaned in. He regained control of the careering SUV just in time.

"Dammit, that was close," Francis said, inhaling sharply as a branch slapped against the driver's side door, scything the wing mirror clean off.

"I told you I wasn't kidding," Gideon said, finding himself panting rapidly as his mind came to terms with how badly that maneuver could have gone.

The slope toward the edge of the forest leveled out, allowing Gideon to regain control over the vehicle's speed. He dropped it to about ten miles an hour—still significantly faster than they would have been able to cover on foot. It was as fast as he could go with the limited visibility.

"Pothole right," Francis said, unclipping his belt so that he could lean closer to the windshield.

Gideon trusted the Marine's eyesight and jerked the steering wheel left. The warning had been given just in time because the rear right wheel clipped an obstruction that was more a canyon than a pothole. "Good call."

From level, the gradient began to creep upward again as they surmounted a rib on the side of the low mountain. The dirt track they were following was about two cars-width across, but only in theory. In practice, there were two rutted tire tracks at the very center of the road. To either side was a swamp. He clipped the thick mud several times, and on each occasion feared that they wouldn't escape it.

"We got time," Francis assured him as branches rattled the roof of the vehicle and a spray of mud kicked up the door and coated the rear windows—already too blackened to look through even if there was anything to see. "Pothole left."

"I see it," Gideon said.

Once again it wasn't so much a pothole as a mine shaft. He steered away from the obstruction—and right into another even larger hole. The SUV tipped forward, and Gideon felt his stomach flip underneath him. He gave the car a little more gas, but it was in vain. The tires spun hopelessly against the mud without finding purchase.

"That's the end of the line," he muttered, already unbuckling his seat belt.

It would take heavy machinery to pull the SUV out of its current predicament. A very surprised park ranger would probably find the car in a couple of days when the rain stopped and the track dried out enough to pass.

But that wasn't his problem.

Gideon jumped out of the SUV, landing ankle-deep in a thick, black, sucking mud that made him immediately grateful for the fact that they'd covered half the distance through the trees in the car. Running through this would suck the strength out of a seasoned trail runner's legs.

He grabbed his rifle from the rear seat and slung it over his back, tightening the strap to secure it in place. He quickly bent to undo then retie each shoelace in turn, lashing the shoes to his feet as tightly as possible. When he was done, he stood and ran through a couple of light stretches while he waited for Francis to finish doing the same. Finally, he crouched and grabbed a handful of the sticky mud from underfoot and daubed it over his face, skin, and clothes.

When the other man straightened up, Gideon caught his eye. He had to shout to be heard over the fury of the storm. "Ready?"

"As I'll ever be," Francis yelled back. His light brown hair was already soaked through and stuck to his forehead. He quickly dipped to smear his own face in mud. The rain cut rivulets through the black camouflage almost before he was done.

The two men took off at a steady pace. Within a minute, Gideon realized that the SUV had made it almost as far as it was going to in any case. A pyramid of stacked tree trunks blocked half the track about sixty yards up from where they'd abandoned the vehicle. To the right of it was a morass of sludge and standing water that looked too deep to cross.

Gideon hopped up onto the lowest of the trunks and jogged across, gritting his teeth as the rifle banged against his spine. Realizing that the pistol was about to come out from his waistband, he reached back, grabbed it, and ran with it in his right hand.

He jumped back to waterlogged earth, and fat droplets of dirt splashed all the way up to his upper thigh. Already he was soaked to the skin, water pouring down his back, his sneakers sodden.

A piercing white flash briefly lit the trees all around. They stood like gaunt statues for just a second before the crackle of thunder signaled the return of darkness. And Gideon and Francis just ran side by side through the sucking mud and the orchestra of the raging storm that drowned out any chance of communication.

Francis tripped on an exposed tree stump and fell forward. Before he hit the ground, Gideon grabbed his left arm and pulled him back upright. The two men continued without a word of thanks.

After ten hard minutes of running, another flash of lightning lit the sky and revealed the end of the dirt track. The two men slowed, now covered in splotches of dirt and water running freely down their frames. They crept toward the asphalt road that led to the convent itself.

"It's 5:01," Francis whispered. "Let's take this nice and slow."

Gideon nodded his agreement. They had time. He thought he could see the first suggestions of dawn on the horizon, but it might have been his mind playing tricks on him. The cloud overhead had to be as thick as molasses.

The convent was still a few hundred yards to their left down the road. If his recollection of the map was correct, then it was still blocked from view by tree cover.

"I don't see anything," Gideon said softly. "You?"

Francis shook his head.

As the two men reached the edge of the forest, Gideon pulled the thermal scope from an inside pocket. He held his breath as he flicked the switch on the side, hoping that the waterproofing was as good as the box it came in promised. He lifted up the lens cap and exhaled with relief at the grayscale image that greeted his right eye. It worked.

He slowly guided the scope down the road toward his left. It was lit up in a pale gray. Darker splotches signaled heat, but there were few of those.

"It's clean," he said, before quickly checking to their right as well.

He hated wasting time, but it was possible that the enemy had somebody stationed out in these woods for an occasion just like this. His heart raced from the exertion of the headlong sprint down the track, but he knew that this was only the beginning.

Once satisfied that nobody was lying in wait for them, the two men began jogging down the road toward the convent. They stopped every fifty yards to scan through the thermal scope, each time coming up dry.

"Two minutes till radio check," Francis whispered as they

reached the final bend in the road that kinked toward the abandoned convent.

Gideon flashed a thumbs-up sign in response. He gestured toward the bend, and Francis nodded his assent. The two men dropped to their bellies and crawled down the grass shoulder at the side of the road, their soaked clothing squelching against the earth. They stopped at almost the same time, as if reaching some telepathic agreement. Gideon raised the scope once again.

"I see it," he mouthed.

The building, like the road, was a ghostly light gray. It was an ugly structure that appeared to be made out of concrete slabs. The main building was two stories, and single-story spurs stretched out in all four directions of the compass. He guessed they had once served as living quarters for the nuns.

He started moving the viewfinder over the first of these spurs but shifted it up as something caught his eye. A window at the center of the second story of the main structure glowed dark—meaning a heat signature.

"Someone's definitely home."

He handed the scope to Francis and squinted, using just his own Mark I human eyeball. Now that he knew where to look, he realized that there was actually a faint glow of light emanating from the window in question. Only a crack, perhaps escaping from a set of curtains drawn over the opening.

Francis glanced at his watch. He reached for the radio clipped to his waistband and squeezed the transmit button twice to clear the line before lifting the handset to his lips. "This is Francis. We're in position. Possible target location on the second floor."

"Copy that," Lachlan radioed back. "Good luck."

TWENTY-SIX

Eduardo Salazar's eyes flickered open. He'd neither been asleep nor awake but somewhere in between. It was a state he was practiced at entering and swifter at exiting. He had to be. Man was the most dangerous prey. A hunter had to be well rested when he came to face such a creature.

Or more than one.

But rest wasn't the only reason for his meditation. At times like these, his heart rate dropped to below twenty beats per minute. Some men wouldn't survive a pulse that low. But Salazar had found that these trancelike states allowed him to endure hardships that few men were capable of facing.

Tonight's work was more of a discomfort than a true test. The rain pelting down on the makeshift shelter was intense and hadn't relented for several hours, but it was warm enough to survive. He was covered by a tented tarpaulin that he'd camouflaged with branches and half-disintegrated leaves that had dropped from the trees above during the previous fall until he was certain that someone could walk right up to him without ever noticing. Even his shooting position was reasonably comfortable—raised a few inches off the sodden ground using a wooden pallet he'd discovered inside the convent.

Salazar's nostrils flared. He breathed in deeply, savoring the scents of the rain and the forest.

And fuel.

It was impossible to hear the sound of an engine over the drumming of the storm on his hide. By rights he shouldn't even have been able to smell its exhaust. Not through the rain and the wind.

And yet he did.

Salazar inhaled slowly and deeply, filling his lungs to the brim with air and flooding his bloodstream with oxygen. He looked down at the tools of his trade in front of him: a loaded pistol on the right-hand side of the bolt-action rifle whose scope was fixed on the front of the convent, and a machete on the left. He was more than comfortable using all three weapons, but something about the blade called to him.

A rifle bullet was no true death for a man. And there was no honor in killing with one.

"Honor..." Salazar grunted softly, snorting at the ridiculousness of the thought. What did he know of such a thing?

And yet he did. Because despite the fact that Eduardo Salazar had grown up in abject poverty in a society shaped by violence and the whims of violent men, he also had a code. He had no problem killing men. He didn't mind shooting them. He just liked to be close enough to look them in the eyes when he did so. To give them a fighting chance.

Salazar slewed the rifle slowly to the right, moving smoothly an inch at a time to ensure the movement didn't attract attention. He rested his cheek against the stock of the well-worn weapon and looked through the scope, tracing it down the main road that led up to the abandoned convent.

"I know you're there," he whispered.

There was a faint glimmering of light on the horizon now. Barely enough to see fifty yards with the naked eye, but the powerful scope gathered what there was together and granted him the power of a god.

He saw it.

Salazar fixed the viewpoint on the dark SUV that had just crept into view at the most distant point of the road he could see from his shooting position. He wondered how his enemy would choose to attack.

Stealth?

The SUV stopped dead. He fixed his scope on the windshield despite the fact that it was black to him at this distance. He could make this shot easily. The driver would be dead before he saw the glass splintering in front of him.

Salazar smiled. He sensed the driver's choice an instant before it happened. "No. *Speed.*"

The driver of the SUV punched the gas. The vehicle's hood rose a few inches as the power of hundreds of horses hauled it from a standing start to fifty or sixty miles an hour in a matter of seconds. At the exact same moment, the full-beam headlights flicked on, momentarily blinding Salazar.

The assassin lifted his head from the rifle. His dark eyes gleamed from his hiding place, his pupils relaxing now that the headlights were no longer being concentrated into his retinas.

He watched as the SUV swallowed the distance between its starting point and the convent in under twenty seconds. Its driver waited until the very last instant before braking and spinning the vehicle to the left, stopping the SUV side-on barely a couple of feet from the convent's main entrance.

The rear right door opened first. In the reflected glow of the headlights against the walls, Salazar saw a man with a rifle emerge, followed an instant later by another man. A couple of seconds later, the front passenger door was kicked open—enough time for the driver to scramble across.

A slow smile stretched across Salazar's face as he watched the way the men moved. They were well trained. They moved like killers.

They'll make fine prey.

The main door was open. He knew that. His quarry found out a moment later. It was only when all three men were inside that Salazar finally moved, rolling out from under the tarpaulin and crouching outside just long enough to reach for the pistol and the machete. The first weapon he holstered on his thigh.

The second he gripped tight.

It was time.

TWENTY-SEVEN

Gideon's shoulder thudded against the side of one of the convent's accommodation spurs with a painful thump. He ignored it, instantly pivoting to his left as Francis converged on the first-floor window from the right. They spotted it from a distance—it was an open scar on the building's side.

"Got you," Francis called out in a low, urgent tone.

Without hesitating, Gideon hopped up onto the ledge and thrust himself inside the building. It was almost pitch black inside and he had no night vision aids. Not even a flashlight. But after more than half an hour operating in the dark of the storm, the combination of the faint glow that reached the side of the convent from the headlights of Lachlan's SUV and the quickening dawn was like having stadium floodlights beating down.

"Clear," he whispered, grimacing as he wished the Faithless had proper radio comms. They had no idea where their other team was. And he had never operated with either of them before. He had no idea what their usual tactics and procedures were, let alone their skill level.

Head in the game.

He cleared his mind as Francis clambered into the long room. It was just a wide hallway leading to the main building. There were a couple of rusted camp beds stacked by the opposite wall, and the floor was covered in rusted beer cans and smashed glass, but otherwise there was no sign of human presence.

The two men jogged forward, avoiding the worst of the patches of smashed glass but otherwise heading straight for the door into the main building at the end of the convent's wing.

"Blueprints would be good," Francis muttered as they reached it.

"No kidding," he whispered in return, glancing to his right to check that the Marine was covering him as he reached for the door handle. The metal was extensively corroded, and fragments of rust flaked away in his hand as he twisted. Whether the mechanism simply broke or whether it was unlocked, he wasn't sure, but the door swung open regardless.

Francis piled through and Gideon followed, pivoting to cover the black space to the left as Francis spun to the right. They worked as a surprisingly well-oiled team. They had entered another empty room, much larger than the wing they'd left. There was nothing in here, either. And it was darker.

Gideon's heart raced as he confirmed that it, too, was empty. The two men headed for the door on the other end—the only other exit. As he moved through the dark, Gideon stepped on an old can and the sound of the crushing metal rang out in the open space, bouncing off the walls and causing him to wince.

A second later, the thought was swept from his mind as gunfire rang out on the other side of the building, barely muffled by the thick concrete walls. Three shots, then another three, then several weapons firing at once.

"What the hell was that?" Francis hissed.

In brief snatches between the now almost unbroken stretches of gunfire rippling out on the other side of the building, muffled shouts were audible, if not the exact words. Then yet more gunshots. There was no way of knowing for sure, but the fight sounded harried and desperate.

"Let's move," Gideon muttered. It took every fiber of his willpower to resist the urge to sprint toward the action. The convent wasn't huge, and the first floor seemed mainly to be composed of large, open rooms rather than a rabbit warren of tiny cells. It would have been easy to run.

And also potentially fatal.

Instead Gideon and Francis hopscotched across rooms and through doorways, silently clearing the spaces behind them with a fierce but controlled urgency. They passed what had to be the main staircase up to the second floor, which Gideon covered with the muzzle of his rifle until they were safely clear. He hated the idea of leaving potential enemies behind, but he had no choice. Barely twenty seconds after it began, the noise of the raging battle died away and was replaced by silence once again.

Their senses were sharpened, magnifying every tiny scrape of a boot and distant tinkling of a rolling round casing as the two men approached what Gideon guessed was likely the final doorway between them and the location of the action. The door was metal, and the side facing them was dented and scratched. It was impossible to say whether any of the damage had been sustained in the gunfight.

Francis held up a closed fist and indicated for Gideon to cover the closed doorway. When he nodded his confirmation, Francis reached for the radio and twisted the volume knob all the way down to its lowest setting.

"You guys okay?" he whispered, lifting the device to his lips.

As he waited for a response, Gideon's peripheral vision was attracted to a strange splotch on the floor. It almost glistened in the first shafts of daylight now testing the convent's shuttered windows. With his rifle still covering the door, he dropped slowly into a crouch and reached toward the mark.

The second he touched it, he knew exactly what it was.

"Blood," he whispered.

At exactly the same time, the radio in Francis's hand crackled. "Theo's dead," Lachlan radioed, the words coming out between snatched, heaving breaths. "And Evan's cut up pretty bad. He came out of nowhere. *Shit.*"

Gideon spun violently, bringing his rifle up to cover the rear of the room. Francis looked up sharply and brought his own weapon to bear on the doorway to ensure they were covered on all sides.

"What is it?" he hissed.

His eyes widening, Gideon's gaze started at a point just a few feet ahead of where he was standing and followed a trail of bloody footprints back to the door they'd just come through. "I'm guessing those aren't Lachlan's," he said, gesturing at the marks.

"What's your status, Lachlan?" Francis radioed urgently.

"Moving back to the SUV," Lachlan replied between pants. "Need to get pressure on Evan's wounds. Had to leave Theo back there. Dammit, he followed us in! Wasn't expecting to be attacked from behind..."

"How many guys came at you?"

"Just—one," Lachlan radioed. "He had a fucking, I don't know—machete or sword or something. Cut Theo down before we knew he was in the room."

Gideon's face set into a snarl. Another innocent life had

been lost because of him. If Francis was anything to judge by, then Theo would have given his life gladly to bring the Brotherhood to justice.

But another man was dead even so.

"Let's go," he snapped, gesturing with two fingers toward the door.

Francis nodded and let Lachlan know that they were moving again before silencing the radio and shoving it into a pocket.

The bloody footprints grew fainter with every step. They were almost impossible to make out by the time they reached the door. But there was only one place the killer could have gone without running into them already.

"Upstairs."

Gideon paused by the open doorway for Francis to catch up. He then stepped through and swept his weapon to the left as his partner did the same, covering his right. "Clear."

The staircase loomed out of the darkness at the center of the room. At one point, it must have been a key feature of the building. To Gideon's dismay, it had a split design—a wider base at the bottom bifurcating into two smaller staircases that led to opposite sides of a balcony that wrapped around the second floor.

In short it was a kill box. An enemy shooter could stand almost anywhere above them and pick both him and Francis off before they were in a position to return fire. On the other hand, they didn't exactly have a choice.

"Covering fire," he murmured, holding up three fingers as he crept toward the base of the staircase, angling his head from side to side and holding his breath in an attempt to better listen for danger.

Two fingers. He pressed the butt of his rifle into his

shoulder and brought the barrel higher, picking out a random spot on the balcony.

"One," he whispered, waiting a beat before he depressed his own trigger and fired.

Three rounds rang out in a fraction of a second, followed an instant later by a burst from Francis's weapon. Gideon squeezed his trigger again. In the instant after the last muzzle flash erupted, he sprinted up to the landing where the staircase split into two and thumped against the back banister. The impact stole the breath from his lungs but didn't stop him from bringing his rifle up again.

"Go," he yelled with his last mouthful of air.

He started coughing again from the lack of oxygen and the dust kicked up by his flight up the stairs. He sucked in a breath and fired short bursts along the length of the balcony, hoping that the shots were angled high enough up that there was no risk of hitting Zara's mom.

The second Francis reached his side, Gideon muttered, "I'm going right. Cover me."

Panting, Francis flashed a thumbs-up. Gideon inhaled deeply and offered up a prayer to anyone listening. And he sprinted. Muzzle flashes from Francis's rifle lit up the space behind him, and his sneakers crunched plaster that must've fallen from the ceiling years before.

He didn't feel the strain of the effort as he ran. Not until he reached the final stair and crested the staircase and felt the effects of the adrenaline coursing through his system. His pulse ragged, he swept his rifle across the entire balcony as Francis emptied the rest of his magazine on the landing below.

Before his partner's weapon ran dry, Gideon ejected his own magazine and slammed a fresh one home, then released the bolt and heard a click as a new round was stripped from the magazine and fed into the carbine's chamber. For a brief instant, all he could hear was the cells dying in his ears and the panting of his breath.

Francis looked up at him, and Gideon shot him a thumbs-up in return. Both men knew better than to audibly signal what was about to happen in case their enemy heard. This time, he held his fire as Francis sprinted up the opposite staircase, his footsteps ringing out in the cavernous room.

Gideon breathed a sigh of relief as his partner reached the top unhurt. He finally allowed himself to examine the second floor in greater detail now that two guns were covering the space rather than just his own. There were four closed doors on the sides of the balcony that both he and Francis was standing by, and just two on the others.

"Where the fuck are you?" he whispered.

A memory of the view through the thermal scope came to him. The room with the heat source had been in the middle right in a bank of four windows on the second floor. After a second's thought, he realized that the orientation of the convent meant that it was on the side he was now standing on.

"Stay there," he called in a low voice to Francis, indicating for the Marine to cover him. The danger of their position was that there were only two of them to monitor ten separate doorways. If they tried to clear each of them in turn as a pair, then their enemy could easily ambush them from the rear.

Game over, he thought.

Then again, there was a simple description for a one-man room clearance operation. And he had to clear ten of them back-to-back.

Suicide.

But that was exactly what he was going to have to do.

TWENTY-EIGHT

Gideon stood at the center of the balcony, two doors to his left and two to his right. His heart still raced, but his breathing was mostly under control now. He knew the brief interlude wouldn't last.

The first door to his right was the one that had showed up on the thermal scope. What was the right play here: to walk straight into a potential trap?

Why the hell not?

He signaled his plan to Francis using hand gestures, then braced himself just to the right of the door. It was wooden and had once been painted white, though what remained of the paint had peeled into a patchwork texture that resembled a choppy sea. The handle was on the right, indicating that it opened to the left. The faintest strip of light escaped from underneath the door.

Gideon lowered his rifle and reached for the pistol that he'd once again stowed in his waistband after reaching the convent. It was a better close-quarters weapon than the long gun. He clicked the safety off and brought it up with his right hand, which remained tight to his body. He closed his left around the handle.

"Here we go," he muttered, breathing in deeply, then twisting the handle and kicking the door inward. He braced his body against the right side of the frame so that half of him was behind some form of cover—even up here, the walls were concrete and might provide some protection.

With the door open, there was nothing to protect his widened pupils from the assault of electric light. Gideon squinted as they contracted sharply, but he was almost blinded for several critical seconds.

It's empty.

Almost empty. As Gideon's vision returned to normal, he realized he was looking at a rusted camp bed, like the ones he'd seen on the first floor. Unlike those whose wires and springs had been in full view, this one was covered with a thin layer of white blankets. They looked clean, practically brand-new. An electric heater was attached to a large battery and pointed toward the bed.

"She was here," Gideon muttered.

He was just stepping into the room to examine it more closely when a metallic scrape caught his attention from behind. As he turned, he saw a door behind Francis swinging inward. He tried to call out a warning, but it was too late.

A dark silhouette surged out of the room with a large blade raised over his head. Francis was late reacting to the threat, but he raised his rifle just in time to parry the first strike—intercepting a blow that would likely have split his skull into fragments otherwise. The clang of metal on metal rang out in the open space.

"Fuck," Gideon yelled, bringing his pistol up even as he realized that he didn't have a shot. Francis and the man with the knife—the machete, he realized—were circling each other tightly. The Brotherhood killer was slashing the blade down, pinning Francis back with a fury of strikes so that he couldn't raise his own weapon and fire.

Gideon quickly came to the conclusion that there was nothing he could do from this distance. He had to get closer. But it might already be too late for Francis.

He sprinted around the landing, pistol in hand. Twice he paused, thinking he had a shot, only for the moment to die.

"I can't—" Francis yelled, only for whatever he wanted to say next to be swallowed by the need to preserve his life.

Hold out much longer, Gideon guessed he wanted to say.

The assailant drove Francis back toward the staircase, wielding the machete with vicious, practiced strikes that didn't allow the Marine to separate even for a second. Gideon was only twenty feet away now. He ran with the pistol raised, but the attacker must have realized what he was planning to do and twisted around Francis as they reached the stairs so that their frames were practically entwined.

Ten feet.

Five.

Gideon fired a trio of warning shots, hoping to distract the assailant, but the man was clearly far too experienced to be thrown off his game. He barely even flinched at the bullets that tore splinters of wood from the floorboards around his feet.

"Dammit," Gideon muttered, realizing what he had to do. He reached for his knife with his left hand, not flicking his pistol's safety—which he engaged mainly so he didn't shoot himself in the ass—until the weapon was raised. He kept closing, until he and the killer were only separated by a couple of feet.

And at that precise moment, Francis tripped and fell out of the man's grasp, tumbling backward down the staircase and clearing his field of fire.

Too late.

The man with the machete spun faster than Gideon would have believed possible. All he saw in the darkness was that the attacker was wearing a dark baseball cap pulled backward. And then it was Gideon's turn to be driven backward by a twenty-inch blade.

As he backpedaled, he had a moment of pure clarity. Time seemed to slow, and he observed himself as though watching in third person.

There was nothing quite like the pure adrenaline of a knife fight. Gunfire, explosions, car bombs, artillery, they all induced terror that could shake a man's brain and change him for life. But nothing felt as immediate as facing another man with a blade in his hand. A single slip could end everything.

You know what they say about knife fights. Always bring the bigger blade.

Gideon skipped backward and cast a single quick glance at his own fighting knife. It paled in comparison to the machete wielded by the other man. It was five or six inches long, barely a third of the size of the machete.

He grunted as he dodged yet another strike. Just keeping out of his assailant's much longer reach was tiring enough. Despite the adrenaline flooding his system, his core was beginning to tire from the constant ducking and weaving, and his soaked-through clothing was weighing him down. The longer this went on, the greater his opponent's advantage would be.

"You're a real man, huh?" he spat, watching the man's eyes and timing his moment to strike. He didn't just have to be lucky —he had to be perfect. One mistake, and the machete would split him apart. "Kidnapping an old lady like that."

To his horror, when his opponent spoke, he barely sounded out of breath despite the added weight of his much larger weapon. He didn't look particularly athletic—there was a little padding around his waist and his dark features were soft rather than angular, but he nevertheless moved with an easy grace.

"Just doing a job," the man said. He definitely wasn't a native English speaker, though he spoke the language well.

Gideon took in his opponent's features for the first time. He looked Latin, with thick eyebrows but no obvious hair underneath his baseball cap. He had a pistol holstered at his waist, but at no point had he made any move for it.

He studied the man's face and eyes, searching for any tic or sign that he might take advantage of. But he never telegraphed his strikes with the blade. He held the machete close to his body, then lashed out with no warning at all.

"Shit," Gideon hissed, ducking a downward strike that missed slashing his cheek by only a fraction of an inch. If he hadn't stepped back in time, the blade would've kept going through his collarbone and into his shoulder.

Game over.

"Where is she, big guy?" Gideon taunted, wishing Francis would appear behind his assailant but seeing no sign of movement from the staircase. "You killed her already?"

There was no emotion on the man's expressionless face. It seemed that Gideon's verbal weapons were just as ineffective as the blade in his hand. He breathed in deeply, waiting for the next machete strike.

It came right on cue, and this time Gideon dodged it easily. He still hadn't even gotten in a strike of his own. It was too dangerous; the added reach of the machete could cut him apart while his arm was extended.

But now Gideon saw something different. His opponent really was tiring. It took him just half a second longer to retract his own blade. Barely an opening.

And yet it would have to be enough.

He took another step back, keeping his fighting knife raised to about chest height, his arms tight to his body, and his torso tensed. He weaved slightly left and right, always moving, always ready to dodge the next blow.

Now.

The man's right arm lashed out and down, slashing across Gideon's body. He ducked back, and the blade missed his right shoulder by a few inches. And then it hung there, pointing toward the ground as though this was a fencing competition.

Gideon's face screwed up as his tensed body uncoiled. He drove his own steel out and down in a vicious, twisting slash that cut into the fighter's forearm and sent droplets of blood spurting out onto the floor.

As he charged forward to take advantage of the cut, his face twisted into a snarl, the toe of Gideon's left sneaker caught an exposed floorboard and his attack turned into a stumble at precisely the wrong moment. To avoid tumbling to the floor, he turned on the afterburners and practically sprinted toward the man with the machete. He recovered just in time to remain upright.

But not quickly enough to lose the advantage.

His opponent tried to raise the machete one last time, but as he did so the strength in his fingers gave way and the machete clattered against the floorboards. He reacted without hesitation, smashing his arm against Gideon's still outstretched right blade-hand. The force of the blow was almost impossible to comprehend. Gideon's muscular, tensed forearm was slapped down to his side as if he was no stronger than a child.

Before he had a chance to react, the assailant wrapped him in a bear hug and began charging forward, dipping his shoulders so that both men collapsed to the ground.

Gideon grunted as the force of the impact drove all of the air from his lungs. A blackness began to coil around the edges of his vision as the man—how the hell was he so strong—

continued to squeeze. It was like having a python wrapped around his torso.

Surely you couldn't kill another man like this?

But Gideon wouldn't want to bet on it.

He tried ramming his knee into the man's groin, but it was hopeless. The other guy was lying on him, and the difference in weight made it impossible to move. He was going to die. There was no way out. Unless...

The knife.

The second he realized he was still holding the knife, despite the fact his arms were pinned to his sides, Gideon understood he had a chance. Somehow his body had known to keep holding on even when his mind was stunned. His arms were pinned, but his wrists and hands were free to move.

Gideon pivoted the tip of the blade and drove it up into the heavier man's thigh with all the force he was able to generate from his pinned position. It wasn't much. The knife probably only cut an inch or two into his assailant's flesh.

But it was enough.

The force crushing his lungs relinquished long enough for Gideon to suck in a breath of air, to slash the knife across the man's thigh once again, and then to wriggle out from underneath him, the slick blood adding to the weight of his drenched clothing.

Once again, he pedaled backward—this time kicking out with his back on the floor and the rifle bouncing against his chest. He kept scrambling back until there was ten feet between the two men, enough space for him to drop the knife and bring the rifle up and aim it.

Too late.

As his finger grazed the rifle's trigger and his core musculature ached with the strain of lifting his upper back off the ground to give him enough of an angle to fire, Gideon realized that he wasn't the only person who'd brought a gun to a knife fight.

The other guy had too.

"You're good," the man said as he leveled his pistol at Gideon's forehead, his eyes flashing with emotion for the first time. Blood dripped down his forearms, but his aim was steady.

"Where is she?" Gideon spat, realizing that somehow his opponent's blood had seeped into his own mouth. It tasted coppery and acrid. He was at a disadvantage. He couldn't shoot. Not if this man was the only person who knew where Hillary was. Killing him would doom her.

Despite the streams of blood coursing from several wounds, the man spoke as calmly as if he was out for a Sunday stroll. "Alive. For now."

"What do you mean?"

"In about half an hour, her oxygen will run out. If you want to save her, you don't have long."

"Bullshit."

"I disconnected her oxygen concentrator from the battery. It has a backup tank. It won't last."

"What do you want?"

For the first time, the man smiled. "A rematch."

"What?"

"We both walk out of here. Alive. If you don't shoot, I won't either."

"Why would you do that?"

The man bared his teeth. "I haven't felt this alive in years. I don't want it to end. Call it the thrill of the chase."

TWENTY-NINE

"I'm sorry," Julia whispered over and over as tears stung her cheeks. "Please forgive me."

She tilted Brenden's head back. One of the guards had helped her lower him to the ground so that he was now lying on his back—his hands still manacled. She was certain that his left shoulder was dislocated; the way it was twisted looked completely unnatural.

But it was the least of his problems. She wasn't sure he would survive the night.

She poured a steady stream of water from one of the plastic bottles onto a length of bandage she scrunched up in her right hand, soaking it completely, then moved it over the man's lips and squeezed just a little. Enough for a couple of droplets to form, fall, and bead on his lips before slipping into his mouth.

Forgive me.

Julia was alone in the locked interrogation room with Brenden. Unlike the rest of the holding facility there were no cameras in here. At least, none she could see. She feared that there would be microphones, however, so when she whispered, she barely let the words escape her lips.

On the other side of the room was a metal toolbox. She didn't like to look at it. The implements inside were responsible for most of the man's injuries. The lid was streaked with his blood.

She squeezed a little more water into his mouth, and for the first time in what felt like hours his tongue darted out in search of more. Though her knees ached from so much time in this position, she leaned forward on them and gently dribbled more water until she saw his body relax against the stark, blood-stained concrete.

"It's okay," she crooned.

A rattle of air escaped his lips, and for a moment she thought his soul was signaling its departure. Her eyes widened with horror just as his opened for the first time. They were bloodshot, and it appeared difficult for him to focus on her.

"Are you thirsty?" she said softly, stroking his cheek and showing him the bundle of bandage. "There's plenty more."

"No," he muttered, his head rolling from side to side on the concrete. The movement caused his mouth to screw up in a grimace. Julia realized that he was trying to shake it, and she cupped her hand around his cheek to prevent him from moving any further.

"Don't," she murmured, leaning over him so that her long hair brushed his face. She blinked away the salt left behind from tears now that she had no more to give. "You might hurt yourself."

His lips kinked into a smile, and he seemed to try to laugh, but the motion only wracked his body with coughs. He lay back against the concrete, his gaze finally focused on her. He was smiling, she saw. A real one, his eyes full of humor.

"It's too late for that," he coughed.

Julia just nodded. He was right, and she didn't know what else to say.

"I can't forgive you," he said, still speaking in a voice that was barely over a whisper. A muffled scream rang out from one of the other interrogation rooms, almost drowning out his words.

"That's okay," Julia said, continuing to stroke his cheek. "Just rest."

"No," Brenden said, his expression hardening. His eyes filled with an energy that she wouldn't have believed, and he tried to sit up until she pressed her palm against his chest to stop him doing any more damage to himself. His chains rattled against the concrete as he lay back, the brief surge of defiant energy already fading. "I can't forgive you because you didn't do this to me. They did."

"I'm part of it," Julia whispered, and tears flowed freely from her eyes now, falling like rain against his face.

"They'll do this to all of us," he said, no longer staring at her but somewhere else. His tone had turned fatalistic. "And it won't stop there."

"I wish I could help you," Julia said.

"You can," the man said, his gaze once again sharpening. "Do you know where they are holding us?"

Julia nodded, dislodging another tear that ran down her cheek. A wave of nausea cut through her, but she found she didn't have the energy to even feel it. There was just an emptiness where the sickness should have been.

"You're Gideon's sister, aren't you?"

It was the same question he'd asked before.

"I was..." Julia replied, her voice cracking. She saw her brother's face crystallized in her mind's eye. The look of surprise, then horror as she told him she wasn't going with him. "Now, I don't know."

"You know what's happening is wrong, don't you?"

She nodded slowly. She did, truly. The things that Trent and the others were doing down here were more horrifying than she could ever have imagined. Nothing justified this.

"I believe you," he replied. His voice was difficult to hear now. It seemed as though the energy was draining from his body. "There's somebody you need to find. A man. Tell him where we are. He'll know what to do after that."

"Who?"

"His name is Marcus Bennett."

"I don't know him."

Brenden coughed, and blood came up, frothing in his mouth before dribbling down his cheek. "Find him. Please."

Brenden's head rolled to the side, and his eyes fixed—fixated—on the toolbox full of the implements of torture that had marked his body. He seemed to lose himself for a long while, then turned back to Julia. He beckoned for her to come closer.

"I need you to do something for me," he whispered.

"Anything."

"I'm going to kill myself."

"No!" Julia said automatically.

"I have to," he said, his voice raw. "You don't understand, do you? I don't trust myself not to break!"

Julia rocked back. She understood what he was saying. He was going to sacrifice himself.

"I will help," she said shakily.

Brenden shook his head. "I have to do this. But you will suffer the consequences. You know that, don't you?"

She looked down at the heavy manacles that surrounded his wrists. "Maybe not," she said, eyes widening as a thought rocked her. "Maybe there's a way."

Several minutes later, she helped him into a seated position, speaking loudly for the benefit of any hidden microphones. She kept her tone harsh, as if she was disgusted by what she was being forced to do. "That's enough. You're awake. I'm going to call for them."

"No!" the man yelled. He lifted the manacles and sideswiped her hard. The blow was real. It knocked her backward. She felt a trickle of blood stream down her cheek from a cut on her left temple.

Julia lay on the floor watching through a teary blur as he crawled across the room toward the toolbox. He reached inside and pulled out something that looked like a scalpel. The blade was dark, not shiny. He rolled onto his back.

And then he drew the blade across his throat.

THIRTY

Gideon raced out the convent's main entrance with Francis slung over his right shoulder in a fireman's carry and the stock of his rifle thudding painfully against his hip bone. He stopped sharply as he stared down the barrel of yet another weapon, only to breathe a sigh of relief as he realized Lachlan was the one holding it.

"What happened in there?" the older man asked hoarsely. Blood streaked his face and hands.

"Is Evan alive?" Gideon said, ignoring the question.

Lachlan nodded. "He's stable. I just finished bandaging him up. Clotting agent's stopped the bleeding for now, and I got an IV line into him."

"Help me," Gideon grunted as he lowered Francis off his shoulder. The Marine moaned with pain, the first sign since Gideon had picked him up that he was coming around.

The two men maneuvered the Marine into the back seat where Evan was already strapped in, slumped against the right door with an IV bag taped to the handrest over the window. He was conscious, but barely. Blood was everywhere in the vehicle, soaking into the seats and smeared on the inside of the windows.

Gideon's heart stopped after he clicked the seat belt into place around Francis's waist. He glanced to the right and saw a face poking up above the headrests. Theo's face. His body was unceremoniously squashed into the SUV's trunk area, lying on ammunition crates and bags of various other types of equipment.

"Shit," he muttered, grimacing as he extricated his body from the back seat, checked that none of Francis's limbs were extended, then slammed the rear door closed. He gestured at the driver's seat. "Get in!"

"What happened?" Lachlan repeated, though his feet numbly began obeying Gideon's command.

"Drive," Gideon said, so amped up on adrenaline he could barely focus on anything other than the main goal in his mind. "We don't have long."

"For what?"

"Hillary. She's alive."

He jumped into the passenger seat and pointed through the windshield for emphasis. Lachlan finally seemed to understand the need for urgency and put the SUV into drive. Gideon twisted in his seat and stared through the rear window searching for a muzzle flash that never came.

When Lachlan finally accelerated out of sight of the decaying convent, Gideon slumped against the seat back. The knife-wielding psychopath had kept his word. Whoever he was, the man had promised not to shoot Gideon in the back as he escaped. More than that, he'd told Gideon where to find Hillary Walker.

Unless he was lying.

But Gideon didn't believe so. He couldn't put his finger on

exactly why, except for the strange look of messianic certainty in the man's eyes that their fight wasn't over.

That it was only round one.

After about a mile, Gideon's energy fired back up. He leaned forward against the seat belt and probed the early-morning gloom for the location the man had told him about.

"Where am I going?" Lachlan snapped. A sideways glance at the man revealed that he was under immense stress.

"Not much farther," Gideon promised, scanning the darkness for anything that resembled a manmade structure. Finally, the headlights revealed what he was looking for: a narrow dirt road going off to the left. He jabbed his finger at it. "Come off here."

The two injured men in the back moaned as Lachlan took the turn and the SUV jolted over the uneven terrain. Gideon grimaced, but there was nothing he could do for them.

"We need to get them to a doctor," Lachlan said, speaking through gritted teeth. "If this is some fool's errand—"

The headlights bounced up off a decrepit wooden cabin at the end of the track. It was almost consumed by encroaching forest. Gideon breathed a sigh of relief. "It's not."

He barely waited for the SUV to stop before he unbuckled his belt and jumped out. He didn't bother with a weapon. He probably should have, but his instincts didn't warn him of danger.

Gideon slowed as he approached the cabin's only door. Window frames to the left and right were shuttered, though the planks blocking the gaps were rotted and falling. There was no obvious lock. A crack between the door and its frame revealed that it was open. He pushed it.

As soon as it opened, he heard an insistent beeping sound. It took his eyes a moment to adjust to the murky shadows inside the cabin.

And then he saw her. An old woman in a wheelchair. Her eyes were closed. He couldn't see any movement of her chest. But she had an oxygen mask clamped over her lips. Droplets of moisture beaded the inside of the clear plastic. Gideon rushed toward her, kneeling to examine her.

He lifted an impossibly frail left wrist and squeezed it gently. Between his own panic and his still-racing heart, it took him several seconds to locate her pulse. It was weak but steady.

She's alive!

Gideon didn't allow himself to exult in that fact. He quickly traced the clear tubing down from the mask to where it plugged into a squat device—part oxygen concentrator, part backup tank. He squinted at a gray digital readout on top.

WARNING: 11% REMAINING.

His already-racing pulse ticked up another eleven notches. How long would a tenth of the tank last her? They were at least half an hour from the nearest medical facility. Probably longer than that. The tank was probably nothing more than an emergency reserve.

Would she die immediately once it ran out?

"I'm going to help you, okay, Hillary?" Gideon said softly. He hoped it wasn't a lie.

Still crouching, he picked up the cylindrical oxygen concentrator and began to examine it. The tank was on the back half. It was about a foot and a half tall, painted green, and attached to a wheeled contraption that also harbored the suitcase-like concentrator.

"Come on," he hissed as he studied the device.

When he saw it, he cursed himself for not figuring it out quicker. There was a simple switch on the top with two options: AUX on top and MAIN underneath. The switch was flicked down, meaning that all the operating lights on the front of the concentrator were blank. Only the presumably battery-powered digital screen remained operational.

Gideon reached out and flicked the switch. For an instant nothing happened. Then a green light flickered into life on the front of the concentrator. Did that mean it was working? He turned his head and cupped his ear toward the device but immediately realized he couldn't hear anything above his own labored breath. He gritted his teeth together and clamped his lips shut and listened.

There it was. The tiniest mechanical hum. He closed his eyes and mumbled an incoherent prayer of relief. It was working.

It took both him and Lachlan working together to safely carry Hillary out of her wheelchair and into the SUV. To make enough space for the portable concentrator, they had to move Francis—now conscious, mostly—to the front seat. Hillary went in the back with the tank strapped into the middle.

"You sure you're up to this?" Lachlan asked when the consequences of this decision finally hit home to him.

Gideon popped the trunk. It was equipped with an auto-open function, so it rose slowly through the air, revealing Theo's prone corpse inch by inch. When the trunk was fully open, Gideon nodded. "Yeah. I am."

He climbed in and Lachlan closed it back up behind him. It took Gideon several minutes to create enough space to graduate from squashed to merely cramped. And when he was finally done, he was left face-to-face with Theo's sightless eyes.

He reached out and gently closed the man's lids. He felt helpless doing so. He'd cost this man his life. He hadn't seen Evan's injuries, but they'd caused enough blood loss that he wouldn't walk away from them easily. And then there was Francis. Thankfully, he'd only hit his head when he tumbled back down the staircase. He would be okay. He might not be doing algebra in his old age, but it was a fair trade.

Hillary had survived. But at what cost?

And what kind of psychopath does that to an old lady?

Gideon's face contorted into a silent snarl as the SUV jolted over an obstruction he couldn't see. He barely needed another reason to take the fight to the Brotherhood. But they'd given him one anyway.

Because that was what they were. Evil. And they had to be stopped.

THIRTY-ONE

Father Gabriel stirred at the sound of the bedroom door clicking open. His head pounded from the previous night's overindulgence, though all physical evidence had been cleaned away while he slept.

All except the girl lying in the bed to his left.

As always, he snapped instantly from sleep into wakefulness. Men in his position couldn't afford to be groggy. His right hand slipped down the side of the bed until his fingertips brushed the pistol he stored there, and he raised his upper back half an inch off the pillows as he scanned to see the source of the disturbance.

"Father?"

Gabriel slumped back into the soft bedsheets, relaxing as he recognized the anxious face of one of his aides standing near the threshold to the bedroom. The girl at his side mumbled a few indistinct words in her sleep but didn't wake. A single bedsheet covered most of her otherwise naked form, though his movement tugged it down her body, revealing a bare chest marked with evidence of his excitement the previous night. The red blotches had already turned purple.

"What is it?" he grumbled.

"You have a visitor, sir."

"Who?" Gabriel frowned. "There's nothing on my schedule."

"Lady Miranda, sir. She was insistent."

Gabriel squeezed his eyes closed and massaged his temples. The pressure briefly relieved his budding headache, but it returned full force the moment he stopped.

"Get rid of the girl," he ordered without opening his eyes. "Then show her in."

He climbed out of the bed, caring little for his modesty as the previous night's entertainment was ushered from his bedroom. She was a favorite. She would be back, he decided.

He shivered as his feet touched the marble floor, chilled by the AC, then strode toward the en suite bathroom. Five minutes in the shower had his skin a fire truck red. He wrapped a thick Egyptian cotton towel around his waist and walked casually back into the bedroom.

"Miranda," he said in greeting, deliberately dropping her honorific. "To what do I owe the pleasure?"

Lady Miranda's eyes raked his bare torso. She sat primly on the right-hand of a pair of plush couches that faced each other over a low coffee table at the other end of the room. Not even a flicker of emotion displayed on her icy face, though somehow Gabriel sensed she was displeased by the sight. It felt like an Arctic wind scouring the back of his neck.

"I can step out while you dress," she said, phrasing the question more as a statement.

"No need," he shrugged, casually sauntering toward her, though the movement was anything but. His nostrils flickered with irritation as he realized it rang false. He was trying too hard to— not quite impress her, exactly, but to demonstrate his power.

He relaxed into the couch opposite her. "What's up?"

"What is to become of the prisoners?"

He shrugged. "The traitors will be punished. The specifics I will leave to Trent."

It wasn't exactly true. Their fates were preordained. But it didn't look right for him to be seen bothering with the details.

"Some of my girls were taken," Lady Miranda said.

Gabriel looked around for something to drink. His tongue was like sandpaper. He gave up in frustration when he saw the nearest bottle of water was on his bedside table and returned his attention to his guest.

"Rats burrow deep," he said. "You should keep a closer watch on your girls, Miranda."

"I do," she said, seemingly with supreme self-confidence. No fear for her own position. "They can be trusted."

"Apparently not."

She fixed him with a stare, almost daring him to look away. He refused to do so, but the moment reminded him of why he resented this woman so much. She had been Father Ezra's closest sounding board when his predecessor built the Brotherhood. The rank-and-file loved her as much as they had him. They saw her as they would never see *him.*

Finally, she relented. "I see. Then I apologize for failing you."

"None of us is perfect," Gabriel said magnanimously.

"May I offer a piece of advice?"

He narrowed his gaze but gestured for her to continue.

"I'm hearing whispers of... discontent. Your people are worried. You should offer them a vision of the future, not just fear of the unknown."

Gabriel's voice took on a dangerous tinge. "More traitors? You should take their names to Trent."

Lady Miranda shook her head. The expression on her face was resolute. She stood, slowly, without asking for permission to leave. "Remember, Father: an oak can lean into a gale long after termites have eaten away its roots. Even withstand storms that by all rights should tear it down. But one day the wind will shift. It always does."

THIRTY-TWO

Rae's hands twisted anxiously into her novice's dress the entire way home. She barely took her eyes off Julia. Perhaps that was no surprise.

Julia had tried to wash herself as best she could in the holding facility's small restroom—the one the guards used—but there was only so much you could do to clean blood from your skin. It stained the cracks of her fingers and the lines on her face. She must look like a creature from a horror movie. She knew she should say something to put the girl's mind at ease.

But what could she say?

Certainly not the truth: not with the driver from Internal Security up front to overhear what she really thought.

And Rae clearly knew better than to ask. Because they all did. Especially the Brotherhood's women. They learned at a young age to keep the community's secrets. To stand by their men. To carry the truth about what happened after dark to their graves.

Julia's thoughts were consumed by memories that she'd repressed over the years. Memories of things she'd seen and done and squashed into a deep, dark part of herself never to think of again. The journey back to the villa she shared with her husband passed before she knew it.

"We're here," the driver announced. He twisted in his seat to fix Julia with a hard stare. "Get inside quickly. Keep what you saw to yourself."

She nodded quickly. Rae looked at her with wide, terrified eyes, and before she climbed out of the car, Julia reached out and squeezed the young novice's hand. She didn't tell her that everything would be okay. She couldn't. It never would be again.

The door to their house was unlocked. That was one of the ironies of New Eden. There was no petty crime here. No burglary, no vandalism, no murder, or rape.

Except when Father Gabriel orders it.

Even with her husband Sheldon under house arrest, there was no need for him to be locked inside. He was far too recognizable within the Brotherhood to go anywhere without being seen. Even if he could make it to the fence that surrounded the enormous ranch, he couldn't cross it without help. The razor wire at the top prevented it from being climbed, and the cameras and sensors ensured that anyone who tried to do so would be spotted and quickly dealt with.

Julia stepped inside. Sheldon appeared almost immediately, as if he'd been waiting for her to return all day. His fists were bunched, his face was consumed by anger, and his beady eyes were in the process of being swallowed by thick eyebrows.

"Where the fuck have you been?" he snapped.

She didn't have the strength to answer. But after Julia pushed the door closed behind her and turned toward the bathroom, her husband stepped across her path. "I'm still your husband. Answer me."

He reached out and grabbed her by the forearm, squeezing

tight so that she couldn't pull herself free. The force of the grip would have brought a tear to Julia's eye if there were any left to cry. A stabbing pain from her twisted skin momentarily shocked her out of the numb horror she'd sunk into on the car ride home.

"Get off me," she hissed.

"What have you been doing? Where are you going? Has he got you sleeping with someone else?"

With that last question, a feeling of release swept over Julia. All this time she'd been hanging onto her responsibilities, her duties, everything she owed to the Brotherhood. They had shaped her entire life: stealing her childhood from her, foisting on her a husband she had no say in choosing.

And what had they given her in return?

Julia unconsciously placed her free hand on her belly. She stared up at him, crackling with fury. "Who? Say his name."

Sheldon appeared taken aback by the dark anger that flashed at him. He wasn't used to his placid wife flipping his own script on him. "Gabriel. What does he have you doing?"

"Look at me," she said, her words slow and furious. "Really look at me, for once in your life."

Her husband flinched. "You can't speak to me like that."

"Look at me!" Julia screamed. The ferocity of it tore at her throat. It would doubtless have been audible from the other side of the front door.

Sheldon released his grip on her arm—his expression almost embarrassed—and took a step back. His gaze swept over her. "Blood. You're covered in blood. What happened?"

"I don't owe you an answer," Julia snapped, her own fists now clenched. "I don't owe you anything. Not anymore. Now get out of my way!"

He did as she instructed, seemingly stunned by the force of her rage, and stepped aside without another word. Julia's eyes finally filled with tears as she stumbled into her bedroom and slammed the door behind her. She tore at her bloodied clothes, not caring if they ripped as she pulled them over her shoulders and tossed them onto the floor.

She climbed into the shower without waiting for it to run hot. The first, icy blast of water caused her to flinch, but she didn't duck it. It was only a faint echo of the pain she'd witnessed in the holding cells and interrogation rooms.

The water heated as she stood under its flow. She didn't start scrubbing until the small bathroom was filled with a fog of steam that was so thick she could barely see the tiles in front of her. Even as her skin reddened, she reached for the temperature control and turned it all the way up until the water scalded her skin and she could barely stand under it.

You deserve this, she repeated in her head over and over again.

It was the truth. She wasn't just a victim. Her own choices had led her to where she now stood. Perhaps she would have chosen another husband if one had been offered; she had never wanted to marry a man twice her age. But despite Sheldon's coldness, his obvious dislike for her, she'd settled easily into the comfort of his life before that night in Middleburg. He was a wealthy man. He could afford the finest foods, the best wines, luxurious clothes, and opulent homes. And she'd taken advantage of all of it.

And then that night with Gideon she'd had a choice. She could have gone with him and left this horrific life behind.

She still didn't understand why she'd taken the other path.

"I'm done," she whispered as she finally reached out and turned off the flow of water overhead. The last few droplets hung suspended in midair for the briefest of instants before the pattering of the shower faded and left only silence behind.

She couldn't change any of those past choices. They were

set in stone. But she could change what happened now. She could refuse to be a part of any more of this violence and torture.

"I have to."

And now she had a way to do something about it. The man Brenden had told her about, Marcus Bennett. He could get a message out. After that, who knew what would happen.

But at least she wouldn't just sit by and let it.

THIRTY-THREE

Every step lashed Salazar's thigh with a stabbing pain. His pants were soaked with his own blood, and he could barely make a fist due to the deep cut in his forearm. None of it was fatal. But though he'd suffered much worse, any ordinary man would have been laid low by the accumulation of injuries.

In truth, he would have been too. But today was different.

Because Salazar had found a worthy adversary.

It took almost forty-five minutes to limp from the convent to the spot in the forest where Salazar had stashed his van—a different model than he'd used to abduct Hillary Walker. And almost the entire way, his mind was filled not with thoughts of his pain but an image of Gideon Ryker's face.

He reached into his right pants pocket and pulled out the van's keys, then squeezed the unlock button. The vehicle's lights flashed once as the locks clicked open. He opened the side panel door and climbed inside, dripping blood the entire way. He reached for the first aid kit that was velcroed to one of the walls and pulled it down to the floor by his side.

Once unzipped, the contents revealed themselves to be

completely different than what might be found in a normal work van. This kit was designed to his specifications and contained sachets of clotting factors for serious wounds, battlefield tourniquets, IV bags, chest decompression needles...the list went on.

Salazar didn't require most of the kit's more esoteric components. The forearm cut was deep and had probably damaged a tendon, but it was at least clean and had been made with a sharp, fresh blade. He washed it out, applied disinfectant and sutures, then bandaged it before turning to the shallower, somehow more painful slashes to his leg.

He taped the final bandage, then paused for a moment to survey his handiwork. There were a couple of streaks of blood on the dressings, but they would hold. The forearm cut would probably inhibit some fine motor control for a few weeks. He would have to adapt.

Finally, Salazar climbed out of the van's cargo compartment and into the front seat. He reached into a storage compartment underneath the dashboard and pulled out a fresh burner phone. He powered it up, then typed in a number from memory.

"He was here," he said without introduction.

"I take it by your use of the past tense that he got away?" Trent Riley replied.

"Correct. He's good. I didn't expect that."

"Clearly. The senior?"

Salazar shrugged. "I have no idea," he said. "I assume they found her."

"What am I going to tell the boss?" Trent asked, a hint of desperation in his voice.

"I will find him," Salazar said with complete confidence. "And when I do, I will end it."

"You didn't this time."

Salazar grinned to himself. Birds had begun chirping in the trees all around, heedless of the intrusion into their forest. "I didn't know how good he was. And now I do. He didn't come alone."

"The daughter?"

"No. Men. I killed one, maybe two. There were others. You didn't say he had help."

There was a short pause before Trent answered. "It seems so. Somehow, he found his way to the Faithless."

"That's a problem," Salazar said, though the creeping smile on his face gave lie to the words. He needed a challenge. The emptiness of the last few months had been almost overwhelming. But now it seemed he'd found one.

"Perhaps not."

Salazar frowned. "I don't understand."

"Keep your phone on. I'll be in touch."

THIRTY-FOUR

Since flying commercial was most definitely out of the question, Gideon, Lachlan, and Francis were forced to tackle the thousand-mile journey to the Faithless base in Georgia on four wheels. They stopped only twice, except for gas.

First, they dropped Evan—still unconscious, though his vitals were now stable—with a contact of Lachlan's just outside of Harrisburg, Pennsylvania. Gideon stayed in the vehicle, waiting for Francis to wake up and praying that neither his condition nor Hillary's unraveled before they could get the medical attention they so desperately required.

They left Zara's mom on a bench outside the Western Maryland Hospital Center, a nursing home on the north side of Hagerstown, and waited just long to ensure that she was in safe hands before continuing their journey. They placed calls to both the nursing home and the authorities in Saratoga Springs to inform both where the former's newest patient had disappeared from—along with a warning that police protection was nonnegotiable.

Only then could they complete their journey. Francis woke up about six hours in. He was a little dizzy from the blow to his head and probably required a CT scan, but he point-blank refused.

"We don't have the time," he insisted. And he was probably right.

Twelve hours in, Gideon cleaned himself up to the best of his ability in a coin-operated truck stop shower that left him feeling dirtier on his way out than his way in, despite no longer being stained with the blood of friend and foe alike.

Lachlan tossed him a meatball sub as he climbed back in the SUV—front seat now that their passenger count had been whittled down to just two.

"Sure you don't want me to drive?" Gideon asked. His stomach started doing backflips the moment the aroma of the sandwich hit his nostrils. "You look like you could use the rest."

Lachlan shook his head. "Maybe later. Need to keep my mind off what happened."

Gideon shrugged, correctly deducing that the man wanted to chew over his thoughts for a while. He unwrapped the sub and devoured it with the enthusiasm of a crippled hyena stumbling into an abattoir. He barely tasted the marinara and cheese before he came to his last bite. He eyed it sadly, hoping there was more but knowing there wasn't.

"There's a soda in the bag by your feet," Lachlan said. "You ever thought about etiquette lessons?"

"No."

The older man snorted, and a smile crossed his lips. "Yeah. Didn't think so."

"Who the hell was that guy?" Gideon said, finally asking the question that had gripped him ever since they escaped from the convent. "He's better than anybody the Brotherhood's thrown my way before now. I'm not saying the Chosen guys aren't good. I've damn near lost my life to half a dozen of them."

"But he was different," Lachlan interrupted in a knowing tone. "Not so...mechanical."

"Exactly!" Gideon said, twisting in his seat to get a better view of Lachlan. "This guy was a street fighter. He was brutal. Nothing fazed him. Don't get me wrong; there were technical flaws with the way he fought, but..."

"This is real life. Technique takes you a long way. But nothing beats a little improvisation."

Gideon nodded. "You know him, don't you."

"They call him the Butcher," Lachlan said, glancing quickly up at the rearview mirror before returning his eyes to the road. The SUV hit a pothole deep enough to jolt all three men out of their seats and elicit a moan from Francis in the back.

"Great," Gideon muttered.

"We don't know much about him. He was a sicario for a cartel south of the border. The kind of guy the head honchos turned to when they had a job that would turn the stomachs of their ordinary footsoldiers. How he ended up with the Brotherhood we don't exactly know. But it's a common path."

"Why?"

"Violence without a cause is corrosive to the soul. It's bad enough when you know what you're fighting for." Lachlan shrugged. "But just money? Women? Guys like that burn like fireworks. It's a fast life and a quicker death."

"So he tried to get out of the game," Gideon mused. "Found himself something to believe in."

"And unfortunately for all of us, that thing was the Brotherhood. He got a reason to fight, and they received a ready-made hitman in return. The only other thing we know about him is that he reports directly to Trent Riley, the Brotherhood's spy chief. This hit came all the way from the top."

Gideon closed his eyes, and almost immediately his mind started replaying scenes from his scrap with the Butcher. His blood pressure spiked, and a hit of adrenaline dumped into his system.

I had no business surviving that. He was faster. Stronger...

He tried opening his eyelids once again but found they were weighed down. They flickered wide enough that he caught a couple of glimpses of motion before closing shut. He was tired, both from lack of sleep and the physical exertion of his brush with death. It was easier to point to body parts that didn't hurt than those that did.

He had been lucky to walk away from that fight, Gideon knew. If it happened again, in his current state, there was no telling what the outcome would be.

The next time he opened his eyes, they had already crossed the border into North Carolina, which meant he'd missed the entire state of Virginia. And Francis was in the driver's seat.

"You definitely shouldn't be driving" were the first words that came out of his mouth.

"A good day to you, too," Francis replied cheerily.

Gideon inhaled deeply and brushed the sleep out of his eyes. "Can you even see straight?"

"Does that sign say Arlington in 1212 miles?"

"Twelve miles," Gideon said, knowing he was walking into Francis's joke.

"Well damn, you got me."

"Asshole," Gideon muttered through a grin as he rummaged through a landfill of fast-food wrappers around his feet for a bottle of water. "How long was I out?"

"'Bout six hours," Francis replied, holding out his hand for the water.

Gideon glanced over his shoulder as he handed it over and saw that Lachlan was comatose on the back seat—his lanky frame held in place with two sets of seat belts, his knees dropping off the edge of the seat to the floor.

"You should've woken me up."

"Oh, we tried," Francis grinned. "You were out for the count."

"Seriously?"

"Nah. I already got a few hours in the back. My head felt fine so I took over. That was about three hours ago."

Gideon tipped a little bit of water into his palms after Francis handed the bottle back and splashed it on his face. It did little to wash away the accumulated layers of sweat and fast-food grease, but it did at least wake him up.

"My turn," he said.

"I'm good."

"Don't be a hero."

"No danger of that," Francis said softly.

Gideon almost didn't hear him. It took a couple of seconds for the comment to process in his mind. "Don't give me that," he said. "That guy was an animal."

"I let him get the jump on me," Francis said, his face knotted with shame. "If it wasn't for you..."

"That's how this shit works," Gideon said. "Last night you, next time me. None of us have a divine right to survive. Every single fight's a crapshoot. A mad desperate struggle to avoid death. There is no honor in battle. Just fear and panic and rage and doing whatever it takes to survive. That's all."

"Geez," Francis muttered when he was done. "Thanks, I guess. But don't ever go into motivational speaking. Not sure it's really your vibe."

Gideon nodded slowly. "Yeah. Maybe not."

Despite the feedback, Francis's mood noticeably lifted over

the next few minutes. They stopped once again to fill up the tank, and Gideon slipped into the driver's seat. Francis fell asleep within twenty minutes—either his parents lulled him to sleep as an infant by taking him out for a drive, or his head still wasn't quite right.

Gideon didn't mind that he was the only one left awake. The hot North Carolina sun was beating down on the SUV's dark hood and the AC was just barely managing to keep the internal temperature comfortable. He drove a couple of miles an hour under the speed limit down Interstate 77 into Columbia before switching onto the 20. Traffic was light and they made good time as they crossed into Georgia.

Both Francis and Lachlan woke up when they were a couple of minutes out from Augusta. Patchwork clouds speckled the horizon now, though the day's fierce heat was in full swing. Gideon guessed he could probably fry an egg on top of the SUV. The thought made his stomach rumble. He'd give a lot for a hot meal right now.

"One of you's going to have to tell me where we're ending up," he said, raising his voice and eyeing Lachlan in the rearview mirror. "Because right now I'm driving blind."

Lachlan grunted as he stretched from his cramped position in the back seat. Gideon watched him with a hint of jealousy. His lower back was setting faster than concrete. If this drive lasted much longer, he wasn't sure whether he'd be capable of crawling out of his seat, let alone walking.

"Technically I should have you wearing a blindfold," Lachlan finally said. "But given who you are and what happened last night, I guess we can probably cut you some slack."

"Do what you have to do."

"It's okay. If *you're* a Brotherhood mole, then we're all screwed anyway."

They swapped drivers one last time, only stopping long enough for Gideon's fingers to tickle his toes before they were on the road again. The brief stretch didn't do much to relieve the tension in his body, but he was grateful for the rest nonetheless.

The Faithless nerve center, it seemed, was an old paintball center and gun range just west of the town of Rhine, a settlement with a few hundred residents in Dodge County. The signage out front was tied to a brand-new eight-foot chain-link fence topped with razor wire and surveilled with multiple security cameras.

"Corporate team-building events only," Gideon read off the sign. "Fully booked through July 2027."

He glanced at Lachlan in the driver's seat, who chuckled.

"There's a phone number. Anybody rings, they get quoted three times the price of our competitors. Most people don't bother reading any further once they find out they won't get a slot for three years."

"And it explains the sound of gunfire?"

"Something like that. The guy who built this place figured he could turn it into an adult summer camp. Get corporate types to come down from Atlanta and hole up in cabins for a few days drinking and shooting, and get a tax dodge to boot. The business never worked out. But it was perfect for us."

"Smart," Gideon said, nodding slowly. And it was. A paintball center would be perfectly set up as a quasi-military training facility. And the fact that the locals already knew that there was a gun range on-site excused the rattle of gunfire.

Not that anybody's gonna care out here.

The sun was dropping in the sky by the time Lachlan eased off the gas and let the SUV roll to a stop outside the center's front gate. Like the safe house they'd departed almost a full day earlier, the presence of any buildings on-site was obscured by a thick wall of trees, mostly loblolly pine and river birch.

Lachlan put the SUV into park and popped the door. He stepped out and stared directly at a camera on a pole just behind the gate before flashing the lens a thumbs-up.

A moment later, the gate rolled open and he climbed back in. "We're home."

THIRTY-FIVE

Zara sprinted out of the largest of the cabins, an L-shaped single-story structure that sat on the northeast corner of a space that reminded Gideon of a parade ground. The Faithless camp really was just like an adult summer camp.

Except for all of the guys with guns.

"She's okay," he said, holding up his palms face-out as Zara skidded to a halt in front of him. Her cheeks were dry, but her eyes were red and puffy from crying. She looked as though she hadn't slept the previous night.

Zara wrapped her arms around him and buried her head into his shoulder. Gideon was a little taken aback as warm tears hissed down the side of his neck. He'd never seen her like this. She was one tough cookie when it came to managing her emotions.

Family hits different.

"She's really alive?" Zara whispered, her voice hoarse with emotion. "They didn't...hurt her?"

The slight break in Zara's voice drove a blade into Gideon's heart. She sounded like she was barely holding herself together.

"Your mom's really okay," he insisted.

"She wasn't even there where—" he stopped himself before finishing with *"where the killing went down."*

"She wasn't in any danger," he said instead, squeezing Zara warmly and drinking in the scent of her hair. Despite her emotional state, she was at least clean, which made him grimace at his own distinctly more agricultural condition. "When we left her at the nursing home, she was fine. I watched a nurse come out and check her vitals myself."

He pulled back and squeezed Zara's shoulders. "You can believe me, Zara. She's going to be okay."

Zara sniffed and wiped away a fresh streak of tears with the back of her forearm. "I don't know why it hit me like this," she said through teeth gritted against the prospect of another round of sobs. "I've been preparing for her to pass for years. She barely recognizes me these days. But not like that."

"It's okay," Gideon whispered, pulling her close once again. She sank into his embrace, not crying, not upset, just breathing slowly and deeply as though in a meditative trance. He felt the tension fade from her body and willingly absorbed it from her. "It's natural."

After about a minute, Zara pulled away, but her hand trailed down and wrapped around his.

"Thank you," she whispered softly. "You put yourself in a lot of danger. I heard what happened. Is the other guy going to be okay?"

"Evan," Gideon replied. "He'll be fine. It might hurt to laugh for a couple of months, but he got lucky."

"A man died because of me, Gideon," she said, her expression pale. "And when I heard that somebody else was hurt, you know what I did?"

He looked her in the eye and shook his head.

"I prayed that it wasn't you. What does that say about me?"

"That you are human," he said. He twisted his fingers away from hers and gripped her hand tight. "It doesn't make you a bad person. Anybody would do the same in your position."

"I don't know..."

Gideon squeezed tighter. "Did you wish harm on Evan?"

"Of course not."

"Then don't beat yourself up. We did what we had to. And I bet you any money that he doesn't regret it. Theo wouldn't either. None of us do. It's not every day you get to save an old lady. Next stop's pulling a cat out of a tree."

Zara's eyes closed for a second, and it seemed to Gideon as though she was centering herself. When they snapped back open, she was back to her usual self. Her lips kinked into a tired smile. "Maybe. Thank you anyway, Gideon. I owe you one."

"Forget about it."

Harriet emerged as the two turned toward the large cabin. She was carrying a hot cup of coffee and something wrapped in aluminum foil. She pressed each into Gideon's hands. "You must be hungry."

Despite the fact that he was practically running on gas station java, Gideon lifted the cup to his lips and drank deeply.

"Either that's the best coffee I've ever tasted," he announced. "Or I got hit over the head and I don't remember it."

"I grind it myself," Harriet said with a smile before gesturing at the wrapped sandwich. "And eat. You need it."

Gideon tore open the aluminum foil to discover a cream cheese and smoked salmon bagel. He raised a dubious eyebrow.

"What, never been to New York?" Zara asked teasingly. Her voice was still strained, but she was breathing easier now.

"Nope. I guess I was busy."

He took a bite. Then another. Before he knew it, the entire

bagel was gone and he was staring hopefully at Harriet's back as she handed another over to Francis.

"Do we need to plan a trip?" Zara asked, clearly noticing his expression.

"When this is all over?" he asked.

"Yeah."

"Let's make it a month."

"I think we deserve it," Zara agreed, squeezing his hand as he finished the coffee.

"So, what's the latest?" Gideon asked as the calories began hitting his system. He gestured around the encampment. "Doesn't exactly feel like action stations around here."

Zara's lightness faded immediately, causing him to regret just as quickly having asked the question. She grimaced and gestured at the main cabin. "Harriet's been in there ever since we arrived. It's not good news. But we can discuss it later. After you rest."

"Can't sleep," Gideon said gruffly. Though that wasn't exactly true. He was exhausted. Despite the six hours he'd caught awkwardly scrunched in the front seat of the SUV, which had left him with a crick in his neck, a sore back, and a sleepy ass, his body needed more time to recover.

He should have said: *won't sleep*. Because it was a choice. It was the way he was made.

Apparently Lachlan felt the same way.

He beckoned for Gideon and Zara to follow and led them into the cabin. Gideon glanced regretfully down into the white porcelain base of the coffee cup and didn't see even a smear of liquid remaining. He looked back up to notice that the cabin's interior was set up like an office. Desks topped with computer monitors filled the space. There was a quiet hum of electrical equipment and conversation from a couple of people manning computer terminals.

"What's happening?" Lachlan asked.

Harriet closed the door behind herself and bustled into the office. Gideon had half-expected to see an operations center right out of the Pentagon and was a little disappointed by the reality.

It's not like they have spy satellites, he consoled himself.

She pursed her lips. "Gabriel's going to execute them all. It's going down on Sunday."

Lachlan's eyes widened. "You sure about that?"

Harriet made a face. "Sure as we can be. They're building a stage for a rally. Whole ranch has been told where to be on Sunday. But we don't know where the prisoners are being held or how they'll be transported to the stadium."

Gideon raised an eyebrow. "Stadium?"

"It's a sports field with a few rows of bleachers," Lachlan explained, gesturing at the far side of the room. After a moment, Gideon realized he was supposed to follow.

A privacy blind was pulled down over one of the walls. Lachlan bent over and unclipped it, then raised it back up. Gideon had expected to see a window behind it but instead saw a map of New Eden. Different townships were labeled, along with a variety of red and green pins that were mostly found around the ranch's borders. The latter were far more numerous than the former.

Lachlan tapped the largest of the settlements. "This was the first community on the ranch. It's the biggest and most well-established. Population around ten thousand."

Gideon whistled.

"This is where Gabriel and most of the Brotherhood's top echelon live. Plus the main Service Hall and the stadium. It's got seats for a couple of thousand. At big events they build temporary seating. My guess is that that's what they'll do here. They can probably add another five thousand or so spaces."

"What do the pins represent?" Gideon asked.

"The red ones," Lachlan said, his finger drifting toward the nearest of the red dots, "are known Chosen barracks. Some of them are private houses that might just be home to a senior commander. Others are large enough for a quick reaction force.

"The green dots are locations of known checkpoints. They are usually manned by a volunteer police force rather than the Chosen, but that's not always the case."

"They have every road in covered," Gideon noted. "Sometimes with multiple checkpoints that vary at random."

"We found that out the hard way," Lachlan nodded. "We've lost a few good people trying to get in over the years. And more trying to get out."

"How do you know all this?" Gideon asked, gesturing at the location of the stadium. "About the executions, I mean."

"We have sources inside." He turned to Harriet and ran his fingers through his now-limp, greasy hair. Dark bags hung under his eyes, and his cheeks were pockmarked from exhaustion. Even so, a fierce energy crackled off of him. Gideon doubted he knew how to rest.

"What about our people?" Lachlan asked.

"We know at least six of them were captured. We don't know how. Our source inside transmitted a partial list of those arrested. There's no pattern to it. The names just look random."

"That's not an accident," Zara said.

"What do you mean?" Lachlan asked.

"It's a classic move in an authoritarian society. It's better to arrest everyone rather than just cracking down on known troublemakers. That way you keep everybody guessing and you rule through fear."

"The six weren't connected in any way. Comms techniques, handlers, none of it," Harriet said. "I can't rule out a leak, but I don't suspect one either."

Lachlan chewed his bottom lip. "We're going to have to move up the timetable."

"What timetable?" Gideon asked.

"We have to try and get them out."

"How? We don't have time to put your previous plan into action. Sunday's," Gideon checked his watch, "three days away. It'll take us a day just to get to Texas. We're running out of time."

Lachlan's eyes flickered toward Harriet as if looking for permission. She nodded in silent agreement.

"We have a way into the ranch. A tunnel. It's never been used before."

"Do they know about it?"

Lachlan pursed his lips. "No. At least, I don't think so."

"That's not the same thing," Gideon pointed out.

"The alternative's letting fifty innocent people die," Lachlan snapped.

Gideon held up his palms to calm the situation. "I'm not saying we let them die. But we need a plan that amounts to more than just a hit and hope. If we get ourselves killed in the process, then Gabriel wins."

"You're right," Lachlan sighed. "This isn't going to go like we hoped. But if we're smart about it, we have an opportunity to show a lot of people on Sunday that they aren't alone. That somebody out there is fighting for them."

Gideon sighed. He had reservations about the plan—or lack thereof—but Lachlan was right. They couldn't just allow dozens of innocent people to be marched to their deaths. He would never forgive himself for not doing something about it, even if it was hopeless.

"Then we better get started," he said. "Because we're running out of time."

THIRTY-SIX

The crackle of gunfire from the range was practically relentless. The thick logs that made up the walls of the cabin that harbored the compound's main office muffled the noise a little, but only so that it sounded like a high school full of kids had been handed access to an unlimited stockpile of firecrackers.

Harriet, Lachlan, Gideon, and Zara sat facing the wall map of New Eden on chairs they'd pulled up for that purpose. A woman called Ellen was also in the room. She was short and dressed demurely and barely said a word. Still, Gideon couldn't help but notice that when Lachlan had a question about the ranch's terrain, she was whom he directed it to.

"The distance from the tunnel to the stadium is around nine miles. There's no way of knowing exactly where on the roads the checkpoints will be, but we can't bank on avoiding all of them," Lachlan said. "If we don't take each one down silently, our cover will be blown before we even make it to the target."

Gideon stifled a groan. They'd been at this for hours and seemed no closer to figuring out exactly—or even vaguely—how they were going to rescue the prisoners. The Faithless could spare at most thirty trained shooters. Only half that number had ever actually fired a weapon in anger. The remainder made fine camp guards but couldn't be expected to perform a frontal assault.

That left two squads of about eight men who would have to form the spearhead of any assault. Some were ex-Chosen; others had learned their trade since escaping New Eden—often ambushing Brotherhood safe houses used for the cult's trade in narcotics and illegal weapons, which Lachlan explained was how the group generated income.

It's...not exactly an army.

As a result of those raids, the Faithless had weapons, ammunition, and even explosives in abundance. They also had access to plenty of cash and vehicles. But no matter how you cut it, sending two squads of shooters against the entire Chosen on the Brotherhood's home turf was like daubing yourself in blood and then jumping into a shark cage.

What they needed was a ruse. A way of concealing their true intentions until it was too late for their enemy to react. Unfortunately, they didn't have enough time to construct a giant, hollow wooden horse. And their current brainstorming effort was really testing the theory that there was no such thing as a stupid idea.

"I need to clear my head," Gideon said softly to Zara. He gave her hand a quick squeeze. "This is more your area of expertise, anyway."

Zara squeezed his hand back and smiled at him, but her expression was lost in thought. He knew that her quick mind was mostly occupied with analyzing the problem in front of them.

Gideon wished her luck as he climbed out of his chair. None of the others gave him a second look, too occupied by the map and the various scribblings on the flip chart at its side.

He shut the door to the cabin quietly behind him. Hanging off a hook drilled into in one of the logs was a sign that read "Closed," like you might find on the door of any coffee shop in the country. It wasn't exactly a SCIF—Sensitive Compartmented Information Facility—as used by the government and military, but it had kept those in the room undisturbed the last few hours.

The rattle of gunfire was much louder out here. Apart from a handful of parked vehicles—mostly SUVs in different shades of dark paint—the campground in front of him was empty. He started walking with no particular destination in mind and found himself heading toward the sound of the gunshots.

The range was hidden behind a thick section of mostly pine trees. As he passed underneath one of them, Gideon heard a deep rumble and looked upward just in time to see a crow caw loudly. The bird was perched on a sparsely needled branch along with a half dozen others that spotted the same tree.

"I guess you're used to the noise," Gideon said to himself as he rounded a bend in the trail and the forest opened up in front of him.

A sign a few yards ahead read "LIVE RANGE." Gideon figured that he was probably safe from rogue gunfire. He appeared to be walking up to the rear of the range building. Like the rest of the place, it was a wooden structure, but as he got closer, he realized that, unlike the administration and accommodation cabins, the range was built out of concrete and decorated with two-by-sixes, a few of which had come loose to reveal the pale material underneath.

The rear side of the building had a single doorway—a couple of inches ajar—and no windows. Gideon knocked, but when there was no answer, he pushed it open and stepped through.

As he'd expected, there was no outer wall on the opposite side of the building. Instead, half a dozen shooting booths separated by concrete dividers lay to his left. A hallway about as wide as two men standing abreast ran behind the booths. A number of targets of various sizes and shapes were posted at different distances on the range field. At the far end of the range was an earthen berm protected by sandbags.

In the booth directly in front of Gideon, he saw two familiar faces. Well, their frames, anyway. Francis was standing a couple of paces behind Jamie, the man who had initially driven him and Zara from the first Faithless safe house. Both men wore ear defenders, and Jamie held a nine-millimeter pistol in a double-handed grip. Gideon watched the shooting lesson out of one eye as he continued examining the range.

The field itself was divided by a long concrete wall that stood eight feet high. Like the berm, it was protected by several rows of sandbags. The building Gideon had seen from the rear extended as far to his right as it did to his left, but he could only see the latter half. He figured there was another section of shooting booths on the other side. Probably a safety feature.

"Feet a little wider apart," Francis called out so that he could be heard through Jamie's ear protection. To Gideon, it sounded like he was shouting. "That's right. If it helps, keep your right foot a little back. You're right-handed, yeah?"

"Yeah," Jamie said, twisting a little as he tried to look back at his instructor.

"Face front," Francis snapped, his hand jerking upward in case he needed to wrest the pistol from Jamie's grip. "Always keep the barrel pointed downrange. Never aim it at something you're not prepared to kill."

"Sorry," Jimmy replied in a guilty tone.

"We've all been there. Now remember what I told you before: keep those shoulders nice and relaxed. Elbows slightly bent. Just like we practiced."

Jamie stepped his right foot an inch back and wriggled his hips, then his shoulders. The pistol's barrel trembled slightly in his hands.

"Nice deep breath," Francis called out. "Squeeze that trigger, don't jerk it. That's right..."

Gideon heard Jamie's steady exhale and lifted his fingers to his ears just in time to see him squeeze the trigger. The wall divider blocked his view of whatever target Jamie was supposed to be firing at, but he figured from Francis's congratulations that the kid had hit what he was aiming at.

"That'll do for now," Francis said. "I'm gonna reach for the gun, okay?"

"Okay."

Gideon watched Francis eject first the magazine, then the chambered round. He laid both items flat on the tray in front of Jamie.

"Get yourself something to drink. It's been a long day."

Jamie's shoulders hunched forward as he turned in Gideon's direction. His face was pale and he was practically trembling.

"Nice shooting," Gideon said, firing a thumbs-up at him. He had no idea if it had been, but the kid looked like he could use a pick-me-up.

Eyes widening as he saw who was standing in front of him, Jamie just nodded jerkily and brushed past him on his way back out of the range.

"He looks a little nervous," Gideon said to Francis when he judged that enough time had passed for Jamie to be out of earshot.

"A few of them are," Francis replied. A dark bruise had

formed at the base of his chin, and the skin on his forearms was scraped and scabbed. "Don't tell me the brain trust want to send them in? It'll be a massacre."

Gideon shrugged. "Beats me. How you feeling?"

"Better than Evan. And damn sure better than Theo."

"Good," Gideon said without pointing out that feeling better than a dead man was a pretty low bar.

"We keep on trucking, right?"

"Right."

"That was my last 101 refresher course of the day," Francis said. He jerked his thumb at the wall that separated the two halves of the range. "Want to go see the pros?"

Gideon realized for the first time that the most furious gunfire was coming from the direction that Francis had just indicated. This side of the range was mostly single gunshots, spaced deliberately far apart.

He raised an eyebrow, curious about what he was about to see. "Sure."

Francis led him through the door into the other part of the range. On the wall to Gideon's right as he entered, the words "SHOOT HOUSE" were spray-painted in black stenciled letters on the bare concrete.

Right underneath was a small whiteboard, on which somebody had scribbled "Seven days since last fuckup."

Probably just a joke, Gideon decided as he turned to examine the rest of the building.

This side of the range was structured completely differently from the static booths he'd just seen. Instead of individual shooting lanes, rows of old tires had been stacked on top of each other to create walls that reached six feet high. They created hallways and rooms that were easy to shift around.

The entrance to the first of these tire complexes was about ten feet downrange. Muffled gunfire emanated from somewhere deep inside. In front of it was a rack with spaces for both rifles and pistols. A number of each were currently occupied.

Just to Gideon's right, protected from the elements by the overhang of the range's concrete ceiling, was a small relaxation area. It was really just a sofa that was worn through to the springs and a couple of stained and dirty beanbags. Seven men in hiking gear and combat webbing were stretched out on top, about half of whom had their eyes closed.

"This is Bravo squad," Francis said. He jerked his thumb toward the tires. "Looks like my guys are doing a run-through."

As Bravo slowly clambered to their feet for introductions, Gideon noticed a wooden tower just in front of the range building. It was really just a platform with a sunroof and a ladder leading up. A man was currently standing on top of it, cigarette smoke drifting down from his vantage point. In addition to the viewing tower, a small quadcopter drone floated a few feet over the shoot house. One of the men was watching the feed from the belly-mounted camera on an iPad on his lap.

"Good setup you guys got here," Gideon said. It really was.

"Gideon, meet Mick, Aidan, Eli, Mason, Logan, Luke, and Isaac," Francis said, pointing first at a guy with a thick ginger beard and a shaved head, then a lean, swarthy guy with a hiker's physique, then a muscular African American man with acne scars before Gideon lost track.

"Mick, Aidan, Eli, Mason, Logan, Luke, and Isaac," Francis grinned, "meet your Lord and Savior."

"Jackass," Gideon muttered. He shook his head and half-smiled as he shook each man's hand in turn.

"I hear you're a real John Wick," Eli said, his voice a melodic Southern drawl. At least, Gideon thought the voice's owner was named Eli. All seven men shared the same interested but probing expression on their faces. Gideon had seen it before many times at military facilities all across the globe. The men in front of him might not be soldiers. But they were clearly trained and likely not easily impressed.

They want to see what I'm made of.

"That's a shame," Gideon replied quickly.

"How so?"

"I spent most of the last decade attempting not to be heard from at all."

Eli raised an eyebrow. "Well, we heard you, all right."

The muffled report of gunfire inside the tire house faded and a fresh group of armed shooters appeared. Gideon caught a few curious glances coming his way as another group of armed men—who by deduction had to be Alpha squad—emptied their weapons and hung them up on the rack.

Gideon's sensation that he was being sized up only grew more intense as he suffered through a fresh round of introductions—to Finn, Liam, Caleb, Ethan, Owen, Wyatt and Noah—and handshakes. He saw from the creased expression of amusement on Francis's face that his acquaintance knew exactly what he was experiencing. He'd forgotten half of the names already.

"Say, Gideon," Francis called out when Gideon was done shaking his final hand and had to resist the urge to massage his own back to health. Some of these guys seemed to have learned how to greet someone on Wall Street. In the eighties. "You feel up to a little demonstration? Some of these guys could use a primer from a pro like you."

The guy holding the iPad grinned broadly.

Gideon stared daggers at Francis, who could barely hold back his laughter. He had to resist the urge to paint the man's bruised chin a darker shade of purple. He forced a smile, then raised his eyebrow.

"I'm game. Just so long as you are."

THIRTY-SEVEN

"What's wrong with you?" Sheldon McKinney growled from beyond the bathroom door.

The *locked* bathroom door.

If Julia could have risked tipping her head back in frustration, she would have. Sheldon hadn't spoken a word to her all the previous night. At the time, she'd guessed he was licking his wounds. She'd never dared speak back to him that way before.

But that was before she'd seen the true nature of New Eden.

Of her entire life.

But Julia couldn't risk releasing her grasp of the toilet basin. Not even for a second. She'd been here for hours, alternately vomiting and flushing before sitting back against the wall as another wave of nausea rocked her only for the whole cycle to start again.

There was nothing left in her stomach to expel. But that wasn't stopping her brain or whatever part of her body that was prompting this reaction trying again and again.

Despite the nausea, Julia thought of the child growing in

her belly. And despite the nausea, she found she had the energy to resent it. How could something with such pure innocence cause such bitter discomfort?

Worse, she resented the stress the pregnancy was causing her. She'd barely slept in days. Every time her eyelids flickered shut, she pictured the baby's entire life playing out in the darkness. She would have her child for only the briefest of interludes before—boy or girl, nomad or novice—they would be snatched from her and raised by somebody else.

And worst of all, it was *his* baby. In her most private moments, Julia knew that she couldn't bear the thought of not giving birth to the child within her. But she hated that it was his. Her child would never know a father's love.

Sheldon wasn't capable of it.

"You need a doctor," he stated—decided—through the door. She could hear the anger in his voice. This was a burden for him. "I'll arrange for one."

"No!" Julia said immediately. She heard her own voice with a measure of shock. She sounded pained. Terrified. "I'm fine. Just a stomach bug. I just need rest."

"You need fluids. Electrolytes," Sheldon said, sounding as though he was grasping for an unfamiliar word. "You must be dehydrated."

"Since when do you care?" Julia said. She had the energy for that, it seemed.

"Since we're alone here together," he replied. It was probably the first time he'd been honest in their entire relationship.

Relationship, she thought scornfully.

And then she gripped the side of the basin once more and retched. The tiniest trickle of practically clear vomit splattered against the porcelain before sliding down and clouding the water that covered the bottom.

The doorbell chimed. Barely a couple of seconds passed before the noise was accompanied by a firm series of knocks.

"I'll get it," Sheldon muttered.

She listened to his footsteps trailing off into silence and started to tremble. She was barely able to hold herself upright. Her vision was starting to blur. The world began to spin, and she was falling sideways until her head hit the wall and she slid to the floor.

And then nothing. Blackness. Quiet.

"You're all grown up," she said, reaching out to place a palm on the boy's cheeks. "How did it happen so fast?"

"I have to go, Momma. I have to go."

He pulled away from her, and she reached out and tried to hold on. He wasn't strong enough to separate himself from her. Still just a boy. Just a child.

And then a sound like thunder that stole the breath from her chest. Julia looked around, but the world was strangely dark and indistinct. There was no source for the sound. And then there was no boy.

And then nothing.

Julia gasped. A rattling breath filled her lungs and her eyes sparked open. It took several seconds for her vision to focus and for the blur that was the world to fade into a picture. She was staring at the ceiling as a tear trickled down her cheek.

"Julia?" A girl's voice. "Julia, can you hear me? I'm going to get the driver to open the door."

"No," Julia tried to call out. Her mind was filled with horror at the prospect of the Division agent finding her like this. He would send for a doctor. And there would be no hiding her current condition then.

In truth, Julia didn't really know why she felt so driven not to reveal her pregnancy. Even if Father Gabriel reneged on his bargain with Sheldon and condemned her husband to death, he was unlikely to take his vengeance out on either her or her future child. Hadn't she been told for years that children were the future of the Brotherhood? That her role as a woman was to bear the next generation?

And even if she could hide it, how long could that last? Weeks? A few months at best.

But that was enough. It gave her time to think. To find a way to escape.

She rolled onto her front. Her chin grazed the cold tiled floor and her lower row of incisors bit into her lip with the impact. The pain brought yet more tears to her eyes, but she pushed it out of her mind and began to crawl across the floor.

"I'm opening the door," she called out, her voice a husky croak. "Don't go."

Every inch felt like a mile. Her entire body was shaking by the time she pulled herself to the other side of the narrow bathroom. Pushing herself upright drained her last reserves of strength. She twisted the door handle open and fell in the same motion.

"Julia," Rae called out, her voice knotted with concern. She let out a pained breath that she was forced to use all her strength to push not just the door but also Julia's own limp weight. "What's wrong?"

On her side, Julia looked up through a vision blurred by saltwater. Rae's young face filled her field of view. But Sheldon was just behind the girl. His arms were crossed, his eyes narrowed.

"Close the door," she whispered. "Can't see me like this."

Once again, her vision began to blur. She was dehydrated, Julia realized now. Her mouth, lips, the back of her throat, they were all dry.

Water. Need water.

To what surprise Julia was capable of mustering in her

weakened state, Rae didn't obey her instructions. She stood back up and faced Sheldon through a crack in the doorway.

"Bring towels," she said in a commanding voice. "Water, orange juice if you have it. And something she can eat. Best if it's sweet. You can knock when you're back. Just leave the stuff on the other side of the door. I'll take care of things from here."

"What about the driver?"

"Tell him Julia is sick. I'll come out when I can."

The door clicked shut, and an instant later Julia felt Rae's palm on her forehead. The girl's touch was cool against her fevered skin.

"Are you okay?" Rae asked, her voice concerned and yet somehow still in control. "I can send for help—"

Julia reached up and gripped Rae's forearm with a strength she didn't know she possessed. At least, not right now. "Don't. I'm fine."

"You don't look fine," Rae said, pulling away and wetting the hand towel underneath the faucet. The hiss of the water stopped, and a moment later Rae began wiping Julia's face clean.

Despite her fear of what Rae might do—and what would happen then—Julia let her eyes fall shut. Allowed the cooling cloth to wash away the filth that clung to her cheeks.

"You can't," she whispered. "They can't find out."

"Find out what?" Rae asked as she lowered Julia to the ground.

Half delirious now, Julia answered with the truth. "I'm pregnant."

The next few minutes, maybe the next hour went by in a blur. Julia caught the briefest glimpses of herself in the mirror before it was lost in the rolling banks of fog thrown out by the shower that Rae placed her in. It wasn't a pretty sight. Her hair was greasy and stuck to her damp brow. A faint line of something she didn't like to think about had formed around her mouth.

The second she was under the flow of water, she scrubbed that clean first. The hot water was clarifying. It scoured away the sweat and body odor and the general sense of helplessness that had accumulated over the past few hours.

Julia's demeanor improved even further after Rae forced her to sip from a glass of apple juice that Sheldon must've left outside the bathroom door. The girl practically forced a square of banana bread down her throat, despite Julia's protestations that it would only come back up again.

It didn't. Somehow her stomach had settled. The nausea wasn't gone, but it was better than before.

"Thank you," Julia said, matching Rae's gaze as the strength returned to her body. She was swaddled by an enormous white towel, and her hair was still damp. Her skin was red from the heat, her muscles limber. She felt better than she could remember. As if she'd been purged.

Rae, by contrast, looked pale and unwell. For a moment Julia wondered whether her own nausea was entirely unrelated to her pregnancy. Maybe she'd picked up a virus in the cells and passed it along.

The thought dissipated the moment Julia looked into the girl's eyes. She looked haunted. There was none of her usual joy.

"Are you okay?" Julia asked.

Rae shook her head, and as she did so Julia saw the mask she was trying to hold over her face tremble. She was barely holding it together. "No. I don't think I am."

"It's going to be all right," Julia whispered. She stood back up and waited for a second to see whether the world would start swaying again. When it didn't, she dared to walk the couple of steps to the sink and twist the tap on. She let the water flow at full force, bubbling and hissing against the sink, just in case this bathroom was bugged.

"What—" Rae began. "What are they doing in there?"

Julia opened her mouth only to find she had nothing to say. She couldn't lie to the young novice. Her own elders had hidden the truth from her for as long as she could remember.

I can't be part of that cycle.

The decision came in a flash as Julia sank into a crouch at Rae's side on the bathroom tiles. She took no joy in adding to the girl's anguish, but she finally understood that continuing a lie only built up a tension that would inevitably break. Like an elastic band stretched to its limit, it would eventually snap.

And that pain would be far worse to bear.

"Hurting people. Killing people," she whispered, despite the hiss of tap water. "I'm doing what I can to help, but all I'm doing is prolonging their agony."

"We have to stop it!" Rae said loudly, emotion overwhelming the caution that was bred into every member of the Brotherhood from birth. "Father Gabriel needs to know. He'll stop what they're doing."

Julia saw that even as the words came out of Rae's mouth, she didn't believe them. She was holding onto a mirage, a shimmering image of the world that she'd been brought up to know. And the closer she got, the more indistinct it was, until it finally disappeared from view.

"Gabriel knows, Rae. He knows."

"Yeah," Rae said, tears streaking down her cheeks from eyes that were now puffy and red. "I know. But we have to do something about it. We can't be like them! I'd rather die than be part of what they're doing in there."

Julia reached out to comfort the girl before her hand froze in midair. She couldn't contact the man, Marcus, that the Faithless spy had told her about. She was only allowed to leave this house under strict surveillance.

But Rae could.

She's just a child.

"Don't think like that," Julia said softly. "It could get you killed."

"I don't care!" Rae hissed. "Maybe that's better than getting married off to some old man."

She cringed when she realized what she'd said. "Sorry."

"Don't be," Julia said, smiling for the first time in what felt like days. "You're right."

"There must be something we can do," Rae continued. "Maybe somebody from the outside can help. I could...I don't know."

She tensed with frustration and fresh tears spilled from her eyes.

Julia bit her lip. If she did this, she was risking not just Rae's life and not just her own but also that of her unborn child. Her own life she would give gladly. But could she gamble such a precious thing?

But Rae's right. This isn't life. We're caged like birds. Maybe it would be better to taste freedom, if only once.

"There might be a way," she whispered. "But it'll be dangerous. If you do it, you might die."

"I already told you," Rae said. Her jaw was now set firmly. "I don't care."

"There's a man," Julia said, knowing that if Rae got caught doing this for her, it might lead to her death. "His name is Marcus Bennett. He can get a message to the Faithless. Tell him where they're holding the prisoners. They're our only hope."

THIRTY-EIGHT

The Heckler & Koch 416 rifle Gideon had borrowed from one of the Faithless shooters was familiar in his grasp. So was the feeling of resting his right shoulder against a stack of old rubber tires that had been worn to the base of their tread.

But that was about it.

His experience of operating with Francis was confined to a darkened scramble through an abandoned convent and a single scrap with a hardened killer. It wasn't exactly a relationship grooved through years of deliberate practice.

But this was war. Or at least close enough. This was just the way life was. Any Legionnaire like Gideon was used to feeding on scraps. The Legion prided itself on operating in the harshest of conditions, often with little support and carrying weapons that were long past their sell-by date.

"Ready?" Francis asked.

He mirrored Gideon's posture on the other side of the entrance to the black rubber shoot house. He held himself in a relaxed, easy stance that didn't look like that of a man who'd knocked himself cold the night before last.

Gideon inhaled slowly, flooding his lungs with the last dose of easy oxygen they were likely to get. His body and mind were reacting like this was the real thing, not just an exercise. His vision felt sharper, his hearing more distinct. A little hint of adrenaline was hitting his system. Just enough to wake him up.

"You know it."

The sound of a whistle blasted from somewhere behind them. Judging by the direction of the sound, Gideon guessed that the man in the watchtower had blown it. And then he pushed all extraneous thought from his mind.

"Entry in three," he whispered, "two, ONE."

The entrance to the shoot house had no doorway, so Gideon simply stepped inside, bringing his rifle up to cover the space ahead of him. It was only wide enough here for one man to take point, so he did so. The electronic whir of the drone overhead faded considerably the instant he was fully inside the hallway as the sound waves hit the rubber and failed to bounce back.

The same effect held true for the light. It was darker between the two rows of rubber walls. They blocked out a sun that was already sinking toward the horizon, its rays too low to surmount the range building behind him. It took Gideon's eyes a couple of seconds to adjust.

"Clear," he called out in a firm tone. "Hallway left."

Two more quick steps took him to the point where a tire wall faced him and the hallway shifted perpendicularly left. A distant part of Gideon's mind winced at the threat this posed. Corners were kill zones. It was easy for the enemy to cover the entire opening, and the assaulting operator had no idea what lay behind.

Gideon pushed his rifle out an inch, angling his body to see the small sliver of the hallway this movement opened up. His feet followed in tiny steps.

No sign of danger.

He stepped out another few inches, his breath tense but controlled as his body reacted like this was the real thing. More and more of the hallway opened up in front of him. It was twice as wide as the corridor they'd entered by. He sensed Francis twist behind him as his partner covered the rear.

Still good.

He kept slicing the pie until the hallway was completely exposed and he had the space behind it covered. No targets. No hostages, either. This new hallway was about ten feet in length, and there appeared to be openings to both the left and right of where it terminated.

"Corner clear," he called.

He stepped right, allowing Francis to come up alongside him. His partner stayed a pace back, covering the rear as both men moved briskly but steadily toward the end of the second hallway. Gideon's focus grew with every step. He was certain that action lay behind one of those two doorways.

"Taking right," he said in a clear voice as he approached the end.

"I got left," Francis agreed.

The two men swung their rifles outward as though they'd practiced the maneuver a thousand times. This time, both sliced the pie as they cleared the corners a section at a time.

"Hostage, hostage, hostage," Francis called out from behind Gideon.

The man's rifle fired twice. Distinct shots. They were both blanks, but the sound of gunfire so close sent another jolt of adrenaline through Gideon's veins. The body had no real way of distinguishing a drill from true combat. The mind knew, but certain reactions were automatic.

The simulated tire doorway opened into a larger room in

front of Gideon. The section of it that he could see was empty. No hostages, no gunmen.

"Target down," Francis yelled from behind him.

This was where their two paths separated. With only two of them, they couldn't assault the different rooms sequentially due to the risk of an enemy attack from behind. This had to be done in parallel. Alone.

Gideon swung his rifle around the tire to his right. He stepped left, left, left, a couple of inches each time until—

"Target!"

Two shop mannequins had been set up side-by-side. Each had a plastic toy rifle slung across its pink, naked chest. Between them was a metal folding chair with a large stuffed dog tied to it. The faces of the mannequins were covered in paper targets.

Gideon processed the entire scene in a fraction of a second. His rifle jerked an inch to the right before his finger squeezed the trigger. He fired two crisp shots at the chest of the mannequin to the left before shifting his aim farther right and depressing the trigger twice more.

He fired a fifth shot, switching up his aim so that the round —if it was real—would have penetrated the second mannequin's skull right between the eyes. He pivoted back and fired a sixth and final round dead center, right above the mannequin's nostrils.

It was only then that he took in the faces printed on the paper targets.

No, just one face.

His.

Gideon's eyes flared wide at the sight of Father Gabriel. The image had clearly been taken using a long-distance camera lens. It was blown up so that only the man's face was visible on the printed sheets. It had been a long time since he'd seen that man.

But Gideon would never forget him.

Despite the unexpected shock, Gideon didn't slow down. He swung left, clearing the final corner, even though his peripheral vision had already indicated that the space was empty. He swung the muzzle of his rifle over it regardless. Just to its left was another open doorway.

"Moving!" he heard Francis yell out from somewhere beyond it.

Gideon quickly figured from the layout that the doorway probably led into a larger room that linked the complex up with the room Francis had cleared. He didn't hesitate. In room clearance drills—and in real life—speed was of the essence. The goal was to stun the enemy and press the advantage through velocity of action and deliberate brutality.

So that's exactly what he did.

He used the right-hand wall to cover most of his body as he approached the opening. He could see a sliver of the room beyond—a large space, as he'd imagined. There was furniture inside. He thought he could see the end of the couch, but it was difficult in the gloom.

The second he was level with the wall, Gideon pivoted left, clearing that corner to ensure that his entry was clear. He flinched for an instant but relaxed the second his eyes focused on a smashed grandfather clock that had been set up against the wall.

"Entering!"

Once again, Gideon stepped around the doorway, swinging his rifle around steadily and smoothly as he opened up his view of the room.

"Hostage!" he yelled, spotting a life-size inflatable female doll on a threadbare leather couch directly in front of them. It was dressed in a pink miniskirt and lace top. Crude, but darkly funny. The doll's wrists and ankles were bound with rope.

He lifted his rifle and scanned the rest of the room. He saw movement out of the corner of his eye but instinctively discounted it as Francis's arrival as he began stepping around the couch to clear the dead space.

"Target!" Francis called. Before the words were done dying in the air, they were swallowed up by the sound of three rapid gunshots in quick succession. Smoke drifted from the barrel of his weapon and ejected round casings clinked as they hit the floor.

Gideon finished walking around the couch and saw another pink mannequin lying on the ground, its toy rifle pointed directly up at him.

"Clear," he muttered when he was done checking the rest of the room, then he safetied his rifle and pointed it at the floor. He looked up and raised an eyebrow at Francis. "Guess I owe you my life, partner."

"Comes around, goes around," Francis shrugged. He leaned over the mock hostage on the couch and shook his head sadly. "Think she'll ever recover from this?"

Gideon studied the scantily clad doll. Her legs were already patched with duct tape in several places. He snorted. "I don't even want to ask."

Back outside, the Faithless shooters regarded him with a fresh level of professional respect. Not awe. After all, it was just a drill.

"Thirty-seven seconds," Eli said. "Not bad. For a newbie."

Gideon grinned and settled in to watch Bravo squad run the house a few minutes later, after Alpha was done shuffling the targets. The overhead vantage point offered by the drone allowed them to see that they moved with steady professionalism, cutting the corners just like he had.

Francis met his gaze when the sound of shooting died away from inside. "What do you think?"

"Maybe we aren't doomed after all."

THIRTY-NINE

Jamie ran his palms down his face, his knuckles curled as though he was gripped by a spasm. His fingernails raked down the smooth skin of his cheeks, digging in deep enough to leave red marks in their wake.

He stood a few trees deep into the section of woods that surrounded the shooting range, his heart racing. He'd barely been able to walk this far without the panic overtaking him. After seeing him.

"Gideon," he whispered.

He'd come to the range to escape him. To escape the headache pounding between his temples, the fear that gripped his chest every time he tried to inhale. To escape what he knew he had to do.

What he should be doing right now.

And yet he was standing here, alone and paralyzed. He knew and liked these people. Had come to feel almost a part of them, despite the reason for which he had been sent here. After so many months, it was possible to forget that he had a previous life.

"No," he muttered, his voice anguished. Not a previous life. It was still waiting for him. He would go back, had to go back.

Because he knew the consequences if he did not.

"Drew," he whispered. "What the hell should I do?"

He spoke as though his brother could hear him. It was the first time that name had passed his lips in over a year. He'd barely dared even think it. If the Faithless knew who he was, or why he was really here...

They'd kill me.

And he would deserve it, Jamie knew. He was a spy in their ranks. If he fulfilled his duty, the task he'd been sent here to complete, then it was possible—likely, even—that many of these people would die. Perhaps all of them.

He would lose friends in the process. People he'd come to respect.

Would he ever be able to look himself in the mirror again?

Trent had never threatened Drew directly. He didn't need to. It was implied. He never sent spies away from New Eden unless they had relatives. Opportunities to apply pressure.

"He already knows this place exists," Jamie said softly, starting to rationalize what he had to do. The Brotherhood had known for months where the traitors were hiding out. Jamie didn't know how, just that Trent had told him what to expect here.

And what if I'm not the only mole?

In truth, that was the worry that had gripped him all this time. It was hard enough trying to convince the Faithless that he was one of them without the fear deep in his chest that he was doing too good of a job. What if Trent had another spy in the camp? What if that spy sent a message that Jamie had crossed over to the enemy?

Until now, Jamie had been able to justify his actions to himself. Trent already knew where the Faithless training camp was. He knew roughly how many operatives the Faithless had at any one time. He knew their names.

The information Jamie sent wasn't earth-shattering. When he was able to do so, he sent messages outlining new weapons and munitions the Faithless had acquired. Names of new recruits. That kind of thing. Nothing that forced him to confront the stark reality that his actions had consequences.

But that was no longer possible.

Because Gideon was here. And if he didn't report that fact, and another mole did...

A hot tear glistened at the corner of Jamie's eye. He gritted his teeth and tried to push his brother's face out of his mind. Drew was a true believer in a way that even Jamie hadn't been. He certainly wasn't now. His time with the Faithless had shown him there was a world outside of the one he knew.

But it would be Drew who paid, not him.

A sudden rush of noise caught his attention. Not gunfire, but the sound of conversation. He spun toward the range entrance, wiping his eyes with the back of his hand, then inhaling deeply and trying to force the evidence of his conundrum from his face. He'd never been a good poker player.

He tried to slip away from the range without being seen. Before he could disappear toward the main compound, over a dozen men spilled out. They were laughing and joking, digging elbows into one another and calling out jokes.

Gideon was among them. He was grinning, as though he'd been here his entire life.

Jamie envied the man's easy confidence. For a moment he stopped walking and just stared. And, barely a couple of seconds later, he cursed himself for the slip. The wasted time had cost him any chance of getting away unseen.

Not that he had anything to hide.

"Coming for a beer?" Francis called out, clearly aiming his comment at Gideon. "A debrief, I mean."

The shooter grinned. Jamie had always liked the man. He was easygoing and not as cocky as some of the other guys with guns who strode around the place. Lachlan usually kept their egos in line, but men were men. It was a category he'd never really felt comfortable in. As he'd demonstrated earlier, he wasn't exactly proficient with firearms.

And you couldn't fake that.

"I need a piss," Gideon said. "And I'm going to check in on whether the think tank have figured everything out. But I'll meet you after that. Where?"

Francis gestured somewhere out of sight, though Jamie knew the team rec room well enough. It was in a cabin on the other side of the compound. "Look for the 'Don't tread on me' flag and you won't go wrong."

"Real imaginative," Gideon grunted. "See you in a bit."

Francis muttered something in response that Jamie didn't hear and walked off in the direction of the rec room. Gideon turned directly toward him, cutting through the trees and taking the most direct path to the operations office.

There was nothing Jamie could do to get out of sight. And instead of trying, he simply froze. Gideon nearly bumped right into him.

"Sorry," the man said, twisting at the last moment to avoid making physical contact. "Didn't see you there."

He frowned and stared at Jamie intently. The whole while, a single mantra was going through Jamie's head: *Say something. Anything!*

His mouth opened and simply bobbed, displaying all the higher brain function of a catfish.

"Hey, you all right?" Gideon said, reaching out toward him before pulling his hand back. "Jamie, right?"

"Yeah," Jamie answered when his tongue finally started working.

"Everything good? You look a bit, I don't know. Shaken."

"I am," Jamie said, nodding briskly. He jumped onto the explanation without knowing what his mouth was going to say next. "I'm not used to guns. Don't like them."

"You get over it," Gideon shrugged. "I used to find them fun. I'm a decent shot. Now I'd be happy never to pull a trigger ever again. But duty calls, I guess. Anyway, from what I saw you don't have anything to worry about. Just relax. Do what Francis tells you and you'll be fine."

"I guess so."

"So, you okay?"

He nodded again. Too quickly. Again. "I just want all this to be over."

Gideon reached out and squeezed his shoulder. The man looked tired. "Me too. But I guess we have to keep fighting. Do you have family inside?"

Jamie's eyes widened. For an instant, he figured Gideon must know why he was really here. But as his heart raced in his chest, he slowly allowed himself to relax. There was no suspicion in the man's eyes. He was just curious.

Friendly.

"A brother. I haven't seen him in a year."

"What's his name?"

"Andrew. But everybody calls him Drew."

"I left a sister behind," Gideon said. His expression grew pensive, his gaze far away. "She could have killed me, but she didn't. I guess that's what family means. You just have to look after each other as best you can. That's all that matters."

He reached out his hand. Jamie looked at it blankly for a moment before realizing that he was supposed to shake it. A moment too late, he did so.

Gideon grinned and gestured behind him with his chin. "Well, I'm going that way."

"I left something at the range," Jamie lied. Anything to get away from this conversation and the questions it had provoked in his mind.

"Guess I'll see you around."

"Yeah."

Jamie walked quickly toward the range, then turned back when he was sure that Gideon was out of sight. His mouth was dry and his palms moist. His head spun with confusion as he walked to the large dormitory cabin he shared with a couple of others. It was empty when he walked through the door.

"I don't have a choice," he whispered to the silent emptiness of the room, his expression torn with anguish.

He walked quickly yet with jerky and robotic movements to the far side of the room, where old beds, storage trunks, chairs, and other items that weren't in use were kept. Nobody ever ventured this far down the cabin, except occasionally when tossing a baseball back and forth.

The padded envelope was hidden underneath a drawer in an old desk that was covered with stacked wooden chairs and other miscellaneous items. Dust coated the surface and kicked up into mites that swirled in the last rays of the setting sun as Jamie reached back for it. He pulled it out with trembling fingers, barely daring to breathe as he cast occasional glances toward the door.

He'd almost been caught once before.

Jamie slipped the phone out of the envelope. It was an old Nokia with a grayscale display. It took thirty seconds to boot up, and there was no way of silencing the tone it made when it did so, so he pressed the speaker indentations deep into his palm to deaden the sound.

Finally, it was ready. Four bars of battery crept like a vine up the left-hand side of the screen, and three bars of signal on the right. In over a month, he'd only charged the phone once.

He held his breath as he opened the messaging function. He was barely able to keep his eyes open as he typed out just two words.

He's here.

FORTY

"Papa?"

Eduardo Salazar smiled at the sound of his son's voice. It'd been too long since he last heard it. But he couldn't see the boy. Just darkness.

"Papa?" A note of fear in the boy's voice now. It went up an octave. "Are you coming to get me?"

Salazar blinked and ran his right hand across his face. Where the hell was he? He was sitting in the dark on some strange, formless chair. Was he drunk?

"Mateo, where are you?"

"They're going to hurt me, Papa. They are going to kill me unless you do as they say. Promise you'll come for me?"

He tried to bolt upright but couldn't. He was stuck in this chair. He could move his arms and legs, but it was like his torso was pinned. He looked around instead, but all he saw was an impenetrable gloom. What the hell was going on?

"Nobody is going to hurt you, Mateo. Tell me where you are, and I'll come."

"Papa. They're coming..."

The plaintive note in his son's voice shot a dart of terror through Salazar's heart. The sensation was so pure it shocked him. He couldn't remember feeling this much of anything for years. Mostly his emotions were numb. It was better that way.

BANG.

He flinched. What was that sound, a gunshot?

It came again, then once more in quick succession. And finally, he saw Mateo, the light in the boy's eyes fading and a pleading expression on his face. His lips were moving, but no sound escaped them. It didn't matter. Salazar could guess what he was saying.

"Where are you, Papa? Why didn't you come?"

"Hey, buddy, you can't sleep there."

The sound of the man's voice startled Salazar back awake. For a moment as his eyelids flickered open, all he saw was an indistinct blur, as if he was still dreaming. Instinctively he reached down for the gun underneath his seat. But he held back at the last moment, perhaps warned by his subconscious that it would be a bad way to go.

"I'm gonna need you to roll down the window, sir."

And then his vision returned, filled by the face of a Black Atlanta PD officer rocking several days of stubble. The man filled out his uniform—clearly muscular, though probably little use in a foot race.

Salazar switched targets at the last moment. His fingertips closed around a bottle of Gatorade, and he picked it up slowly before raising it to show the officer. Still making no sudden movements, he depressed the window button. When nothing happened, he punched the engine start button and tried again.

It rolled down smoothly, and the cabin of the rented black Chrysler Pacifica minivan immediately filled with thick, humid air tinged with burned gasoline from the nearby highway.

"Sorry, officer," Salazar said. He glanced ostentatiously at the clock on the dashboard. "Shit. My wife's gonna be pissed."

"I need to see some ID, sir," the officer said, his hand resting on his gun belt.

Salazar nodded understandingly but spoke intentionally fast to accentuate the sense of distress. "You gotta do your job. I get it. Crap, Emily's gonna kill me. I promised I'd help her with her luggage. She's bringing a guitar back for me. Is it okay with you if I reach into the glove compartment?"

"Go ahead," the cop motioned.

As he did so, he checked the minivan's rear and wing mirrors. No sign of either the cruiser or the officer's partner. But since the short-stay car park wasn't far from the PD precinct at the Hartsfield-Jackson Atlanta International Airport, it was likely the guy was operating on his own.

Another second of scanning as he clicked open the glove compartment and let it fall open revealed that nobody was close by. If it came to it, he could probably silence the officer and get him inside the vehicle before anybody saw.

Salazar pulled out the car's registration, then reached into his pocket for his wallet. "Car's a rental. Mine's in the shop."

He handed over the registration document, then flicked through his wallet. Each of the credit cards matched the name on his Georgia driving license. The Brotherhood paid attention to the tiny details that most criminal organizations failed to attend to—with predictable consequences.

"Okay, thank you, Mr. Suarez," the officer said after a cursory scan. He handed back both documents. "Like I said, you can't sleep here. This is short stay. Plenty of hotels if you need somewhere to bed down."

"Sure thing, officer," Salazar replied, once again glancing purposefully at the dashboard clock. "I was supposed to meet Emily—my wife—at arrivals twenty minutes ago. One of us is going to be sleeping on the couch tonight, and it ain't going to be her."

"You play guitar?"

"Learning," Salazar shrugged. It was a lie, but he'd found that musicians were generally regarded as unthreatening. "Truth is I'm tone deaf. But she likes it."

The officer gestured toward the terminal. "Don't let me keep you."

Salazar pushed his license back into his wallet and stuffed it into his pocket before climbing out of the car. He kept one eye on the police officer as the man walked away through the parking lot and cursed himself for losing focus. It wasn't his first slip in the last couple of days.

The dreams are back.

Before locking the car—the truth was, he really was late to pick someone up at arrivals—he paused and made a face. Part of him didn't want to stop thinking about his son. The worst part of it was that he couldn't hear his boy's voice anymore. Not awake. Those dreams were his last connection to Mateo.

But he had to.

He reached back into the still-open glove compartment and pulled out the orange pill bottle. He popped the cap and jiggled a single white pill out onto his palm. He paused for a second, then added another.

Just this once.

Salazar tossed them to the back of his mouth and washed them down with sickly warm Gatorade. He only had a dozen or so pills left. He would need to find more soon unless he wanted to sweat his way through withdrawal again. And now really wasn't the time for wild mood swings and a sensation of impending doom.

"Game face, Eduardo," he muttered aloud as he pushed the car door closed and locked it behind him. The men he was here to collect were apex predators. They could sense weakness just as easily as he did.

And that would not be good for anybody involved.

He met them just outside the terminal, standing by a red-and-white crosswalk near the taxi rank. All six of them were Latino, with black hair and tan skin. Three wore Knicks jerseys, and two wore baseball caps with the team's logo. The Knicks were playing the Atlanta Hornets the following evening, so it was a simple cover.

Not that one was needed.

"You're late," the group's leader said. He was the shortest of them by almost half a foot, his torso enveloped in a solid carapace of hard-won muscle. "And supposed to be dead."

"I guess I got lucky," Salazar shrugged.

"We would make a nice bonus by bringing your head back home with us."

"My—," Salazar hesitated before saying the word, "*employer* pays better."

"It's a healthy contract," the leader conceded. "Maybe you'll tell us who you're working for?"

Salazar didn't break eye contact. "Maybe not."

The group's leader grinned and glanced at a couple of his boys for the first time. "He's a cold one, no?"

Salazar extended his hand. "Eduardo."

"Luis," the leader said, jerking his thumb at his chest before pointing at the others: "Bruno, Gus—Gustavo, Diego, Fernando, Juan, and Arturo."

Salazar turned without another word and led them toward the daily parking lot. They traveled light, most carrying only a small backpack, and he knew they would be unarmed. Their representatives had supplied a detailed list of the equipment the former Mexican special forces squad would require. The list was long, and it would be expensive to acquire every item.

But they were the best. So you paid what it took. And besides, it wasn't Salazar's money.

One of the operators snorted as he stopped in front of the Pacifica. "Is your wife going to drive us?"

"No," Salazar said without turning. "She's dead."

FORTY-ONE

"So?" Gideon said as he stepped back into the operations center. "Did you all figure it out?"

"No thanks to you," Zara said sternly before her face cracked and she shot him a wink. "But yes. We have the outline of a plan."

"Lots of details to work out," Harriet pointed out before yawning widely. "But thanks to Zara maybe we at least have a chance."

"Or maybe I'll burn the whole place down," Zara said, her expression once again strained. She rubbed her eyes and slumped back into her chair. It creaked as it accepted her weight.

"I'm lost," Gideon said.

Lachlan gestured for him to come over. He was standing at a desk with a computer, and he turned the screen toward him. A five-day weather forecast for New Eden, was the only thing on the screen. It was supposed to be hot, cloudy, and very, very windy. Gusts would reach forty miles an hour for the next three days.

"Still lost," Gideon said, searching for an explanation in three sets of eyes.

"It's wildfire season," Zara said. "Lachlan said there was one last year, burned five thousand acres in New Eden. They managed to get it under control without outside help. Apparently, it's not uncommon; they have half a dozen fire trucks and frequently run wildfire drills."

"Correct," Lachlan said before he, too, yawned. Gideon flicked the switch on a nearby desk lamp, and the electric glow helped warm the room now that the sunlight was fading fast.

"And there's one burning now?"

Zara shook her head. "But there might be Sunday. Lots of them."

She walked over to the map on the wall and tapped the spot on the northeast edge of the ranch. "The tunnel's here. It's wide enough to wheel a dirt bike through. Not tall enough to ride them, so they'll have to be pre-positioned."

"According to Lachlan," she continued, waving her palm across the entire west and east edges of the ranch, "all this is grassland. It was bone dry at the beginning of June. By now it's practically kindling."

Gideon's eyes widened as the outline of the plan fell into place in his mind. A single inattentive camper with a gas burner could start a wildfire that would swallow tens, even hundreds of thousands of acres. Half a dozen or more of the Faithless—suitably equipped with matches and cans of gasoline—could set half of New Eden ablaze.

"What about collateral damage?" he said. "We can't kill the village to save it."

"That's why I suggest we only set the fires here," Zara said, indicating the areas she'd already pointed out before tapping a contour line that ran down most of the ranch. "This hilly outcropping runs right down the spine of New Eden. It's a natural fire break. It might not stop the fire completely, but it will buy time for people to get out of the way."

"There are a dozen support personnel on this compound who I wouldn't trust in a gunfight," Lachlan said. "But if we deploy them to start fires, they'll be more useful than a hundred extra trained operators. The Chosen have the dual responsibility for managing wildfire season. Every one of them we can pull away is one less guy with a gun we'll have to face."

"And if the wind doesn't blow in the right direction?" Gideon asked.

Lachlan jumped—well, eased himself—to his feet and joined Zara at the map. He tapped a point about fifteen miles west of the tunnel entrance. "Then we set the fire here. It's a riskier play, but we'll make it work."

"The really difficult part will be timing," Zara said. "There are three possible locations where the prisoners are being held, and we won't know which is correct until the transport convoy forms up outside."

"You have spotters inside?"

Lachlan nodded. "We have a handful of remaining assets."

Gideon raised an eyebrow. "And you trust them with our lives? Because if just one of them is compromised, then the whole op is blown before we get going. We'll be walking right into an ambush."

Lachlan and Zara glanced quickly at each other before he responded. "I trust them completely."

"What aren't you telling me?"

Zara's expression softened. "We're staying here, Gideon. This isn't like with my mom. We can't send you into New Eden. It's way too risky. If this plan fails, then you are our only hope at rebuilding a challenge to the Brotherhood."

"The hell I am!" Gideon snapped. He felt his heart rate

kick up into overdrive. "Julia's in there. Alone. I'm not leaving her."

"We'll get her out," Lachlan said. "As soon as we're done here, I'll contact one of my people inside to keep watch on her. She will be a high priority."

"No," Gideon said, shaking his head. He ignored Lachlan and Harriet and stared directly into Zara's eyes. "A man died helping your mom. It could've been worse. I can't let other people keep fighting my battles."

"Don't you think I know that?" Zara said, her gaze flashing —not with anger but guilt. "It's all I can think about. But you're different, Gideon. You're special."

"I'm no different from anybody else. I can't be who you want me to be. I can't just sit here on my hands while other people die. I won't."

"You are different," Lachlan said, his tone gruff. "It doesn't matter whether you think you are or not. It's the truth. No matter what happens, a lot of my guys are going to die on Sunday. I'm sending them to their deaths. And they're prepared for that. We all are. But if you die, Gideon, then Gabriel wins. The Brotherhood wins. And all hope of bringing an end to decades of suffering dies with you."

"There has to be some way I can help," Gideon said, glancing from face to face in a desperate search for support. It would've been easier if he saw hardened hearts staring back at him, but instead there was pity in their eyes. The worst part was he knew they were right. It would have been easier to hate them if they weren't. "At least let me go with the fire starters."

"Still too risky. If a Chosen patrol picks you up, it's game over."

"You can't stop me going in," Gideon said next. His hands formed into fists of their own accord. "What are you going to do, put a gun to my head?"

Lachlan looked at him intently. "Were you just at the range?"

Gideon was taken by surprise by the sudden change in topic. He replied warily. "Yeah."

"I'm guessing you saw my guys. It's taken two years for me to put together an A-team. Two of them, actually. I have fifteen fit and healthy shooters. On Sunday, they are all going in, and me with them. I'll take a detail to extract your sister. The remaining twelve operators will try to hijack the prisoner convoy and hold off the Chosen response long enough to bust them out."

"So you need more guns," Gideon said. "You can't afford for me not to be there."

"No. If you go in, then I'll be forced to put a squad on you to keep you alive. Minimum three guys, but probably four or five. That almost halves my numbers at a stroke."

"Then don't."

"I have to, and you know it. If you insist on going in, I won't stop you. But know this: you'll be putting fifteen lives at risk. And the mission."

Gideon trembled with rage, frustration, and guilt as he stared back at Lachlan. He was so overcome with the maelstrom of emotion in his chest that he was briefly unable to speak. Zara said something, but he didn't even hear the words.

"Nobody's questioning your courage, Gideon. I saw what you did the other night. You probably saved my life, and you definitely saved Francis's."

Lachlan stopped there, but he didn't need to go on. The rushing of blood in Gideon's ears started to fade as he realized that the man was right. He might not agree with the conclusion that the Faithless had drawn about his importance, but he wasn't going to change their minds.

Insisting on going in would be selfish.

His tension fell away in an avalanche, and he might have toppled to the floor if he hadn't bumped against the desk behind him. He reached out and gripped the edge of the desk for support. "When are you going to brief the others?"

To his credit, Lachlan didn't press his victory. "Tomorrow morning. We'll have to move out by lunchtime, but we'll let them blow off some steam tonight. They know something's coming. They don't need the details. Not yet."

FORTY-TWO

It seemed like every living soul on the compound found their way to the shooters' rec room that evening, like they knew a storm was coming and they didn't care. All except Zara.

"I'll catch you up," she said. "I just want to check in on the decryption program. I left it running on the setup at the cabin. I'm guessing it hasn't made any progress, but you never know."

Gideon went ahead. Computers weren't really his thing, and he needed to blow off some steam. Or at least douse the steam billowing inside him with a stiff drink. How was it, he wondered, that a person could understand the logical argument for something and yet his emotions whipped like stormy waves in precisely the opposite direction?

We're just monkeys, he thought. *Monkeys in hairless meat suits.*

The cabin was barely big enough to fit the two squads of Faithless operators. But somehow, with almost twice the number of drinkers the place would usually accommodate, they made it work. There was no bar, either. No rows of neatly arranged spirits or draft beer taps.

Just a fridge rammed to the gunwales with cold bottles of lager and studded on top with half-drunk bottles of amber liquor like spines on a great amphibian's back.

"You made it," Francis grinned as Gideon entered. He was carrying a truly improbable number of beer bottles, at least five in each hand, their necks somehow threaded between the webbing on his fingers—and how he was managing to hold on to the last bottle in each defied the laws of physics.

Gideon mustered a smile in response. It must've been obvious that there was something off about him because Francis half-raised an eyebrow, but the moment was quickly broken by Eli grabbing him by the shoulder and rustling a couple of the bottles from each of his hands.

The kid that Gideon had stumbled across in the woods—Jamie—looked half-drunk already. He was standing on his own at the back of the room, his face red from overconsumption and his eyelids heavy. As Gideon watched, he leaned back against the log wall, only he was a foot too far away and almost collapsed against it.

The scene reminded Gideon of a documentary he'd once watched on the London Blitz, where German bombs and rockets rained down on millions of innocent civilians. Men, women, and even a few children lived in semi-darkness for months at a time, their windows and car headlights draped in dark canvas to avoid giving the enemy a target at night.

Many, to be sure, hid in bomb shelters or underground rail stations as airstrikes pummeled the city, killing hundreds and beating brick tenements into dust. But others partied instead, their bass line the thunder of bombs and their melody the wail of emergency sirens. You had to blow off stress somehow, and for many, simply waiting to die wasn't an appealing option.

It felt like that here. In a couple of days, it was more than likely that everybody in this room could be dead.

But except for the slight glint of madness in their eyes, nobody reflected that knowledge. If they had to die, they were going to go out on their own terms. Gideon could respect that.

Someone pushed into his back, spun him around, and pressed an object into his hands. His fingers gripped the cold cylinder automatically, and it was only when he looked down that he saw it was a bottle of beer.

"Drink!" Eli yelled over the ruckus, grinning from ear to ear. He was clearly half-drunk already.

Before Gideon could thank him for the offering, he spun away into a separate conversation entirely. The cap was still on the bottle, so he fished in his pockets for the only item he was carrying—a brass round casing he'd picked up from the floor of the shoot house earlier that afternoon. He used it to lever the bottle cap off, then tossed both scraps of metal into a nearby garbage can.

He sipped from the bottle as he stood in the center of the chaotic scene, still tense from the earlier confrontation in the operations center. But he forced himself to relax. He was still pissed about Lachlan's decision to ban him from the assault on Sunday.

But he understood it.

An American back in the Legion had been fond of saying, "Shit or get off the pot."

This was one of those situations. He didn't have to like it, but he could damn well suck it up and row in the same direction as the rest of the team. After a couple of minutes with those thoughts ricocheting in his mind, he exhaled a single short, sharp breath and tipped his head back. Half the bottle of beer drained down his throat in a matter of seconds.

"Shit or get off the pot, asshole."

He forced himself to smile, and before he knew it, he didn't need to strain to do so at all. The humor in the room was infectious. He'd only met Francis a couple of days earlier, but it felt like he'd known the guy his entire life. Even a couple of guys from Alpha squad who were nursing soft drinks—presumably because they were pulling a guard shift that night—weren't letting it kill their vibe.

"Why the long face?" Francis called out as Jamie staggered toward the exit, with a distinctly green complexion. As the kid pulled the door open and toppled forward into the darkness, he yelled at him: "Better out than in! When you're done on your hands and knees, come by for a drink."

Gideon snorted. "He'll be out till midday tomorrow. And when he wakes up, he'll wish he hadn't."

Francis turned his head sideways and pointed accusingly at the bottle and Gideon's hand. "Those dregs are looking pretty lonely, soldier."

After flashing a mock salute, Gideon drained the last few droplets from the bottle and thumped it down onto the nearest empty surface. "I'm beat. You guys carry on without me."

"You're not serious?"

Gideon faked a tired smile. The truth was, this wasn't his night. It was theirs. "Drink one for me. I'll leave you to it."

He slipped back to the cabin that he and Zara had been assigned. It was austere but comfortably furnished, with enough space for a double bed pushed up against the wall and a well-creased leather armchair in one corner. That's where he found Zara, her legs folded up beneath her. She was staring intently at her laptop computer and barely noticed his entry.

"Anything?"

"From the program? No."

Gideon let an amused smile onto his lips. "What else?"

She spun the laptop around so that he could see the screen. "We got a warning from Jacques. Apparently the Brotherhood have put a contract out on our heads."

Jacques Leclerc was a former legionnaire, like Gideon, and had once been his agent—in a manner of speaking—hiring him for private security jobs. One of those jobs had landed him in hot water, finally allowing the Brotherhood to track him down after years of trying. Leclerc was still recovering from a stomach wound incurred in Marseille a few weeks earlier in the aftermath of Gideon's escape.

"They've been trying to kill us for weeks," he pointed out.

"But now they're advertising the job to outside contractors," Zara said worriedly. "Why now?"

Gideon shrugged. "I guess we gave their guys the slip one too many times."

"Should we tell Lachlan?"

"It's late," he replied. "I'm sure it can wait till the morning."

FORTY-THREE

Gideon gave up pretending he was going to fall asleep somewhere between 1 a.m. and the heat death of the universe. Leclerc's warning was still reverberating in his mind, a reminder that he—and Zara—might never be safe.

He somehow slipped off the creaking camp bed without waking Zara and shrugged on the pants he'd left at the end of the bed.

"Creepy," he whispered, noticing that she slept with her eyes half open.

Still, at least she was asleep.

He laced up a pair of sneakers but didn't bother pulling anything thicker than a T-shirt over his torso. Despite the late hour, the air in the wooden cabin was thicker than cake mix. Gideon's skin was sticky to the touch, and an experimental sniff at his left armpit revealed only that he shouldn't do that again.

He exited the cabin silently and pulled the door closed behind him, then turned around and stood with his back to the doorframe for almost a minute. A handful of crickets were still operating their buzz saws, and the air was a heady, perfumed mix of pine scent and earth. It was as peaceful as the French château in which Gideon had been nursed back to health several months earlier.

What kind of asshole can't sleep here?

If Gideon looked in the mirror, he knew he'd see one staring back. He shrugged and began wandering through the dark campground. The paths were lit by light bulbs strung on wires, each cone of illumination about twenty feet from the last. They provided just enough light for one to jump from stepping stone to stepping stone but left plenty of cracks of darkness in between.

The other cabins loomed like ships in the night as he wandered through the main parade ground. Hard plastic equipment cases were already stacked in rows close to where most of the Faithless's vehicle fleet was parked—ready for the drive to Texas. A trailer was also pulled up next to one of the pickup trucks, though it wasn't yet loaded.

Gideon stood staring at the two short rows of vehicles for over a minute. The complexity of just transporting two dozen shooters, support personnel, and the equipment required to attempt an assault on New Eden was staggering. Actually pulling off said operation...

"Can't sleep?"

Gideon whirled around, startled by the sudden disturbance. He found himself staring at a man dressed in black fatigues just a couple of feet away. His heart raced in his chest, and he puffed out his cheeks and exhaled in an attempt to slow his breathing.

"Shit, you nearly gave me a heart attack," he said.

The man grinned. Gideon recognized his face—he'd been in the cabin earlier—but they hadn't been introduced yet. He rested his left hand against the rifle clipped to his chest rig and reached out with his right. Gideon shook it.

"Phoenix," he said, taking a step back to open up some space between them. "Yeah, I know, and the answer is I don't know what my parents were thinking either."

Gideon chuckled. "Where did you learn how to move like that?"

"I get around," Phoenix shrugged. He was clearly pleased his trick had worked. "What you doing up?"

Gideon sighed. "Couldn't sleep, like you said."

"I feel you," Phoenix replied, shuffling a bit so they stood companionably side-by-side. He allowed an easy silence to build. "It's why I took the night shift."

"Just you up?"

Phoenix shook his head. "Aidan's in the guard shack and Wyatt's somewhere around. I just walked the perimeter."

"All good?" Gideon asked, his mind once again returning to the cryptic message from Leclerc.

"I wouldn't be here if it wasn't."

"Fair point," Gideon conceded.

"Want to walk with me?" Phoenix suggested. "I'm due to check in at the shack. I could do with a cup of coffee and something sweet. Company wouldn't hurt."

"Sure," Gideon said after a second's consideration. It wasn't like he was going to get any sleep anyway. And this way he could warn them of the potential risk that Leclerc had warned them about.

They walked to the opposite side of the parade ground without saying much. Gideon followed Phoenix's lead since he had no idea where the shack was supposed to be. About halfway across, he yawned wide enough to twist his jaw apart.

"I have that effect on—."

The mortar round whistled half a second before impact. It wasn't like in the movies—more of a vague disturbance in the air before it exploded not fifteen feet behind the two men. The force of the impact tossed both to the ground, and Gideon ate a mouthful of dust as he landed chest first. His ears rang so loud he was sure he'd never hear again, and as he reached up to cover them, his fingertips touched blood.

A second round landed on the roof of one of the larger cabins, this time over a hundred feet away. The flash of the explosion lit up the entire parade ground before it faded in the blink of an eye. Gideon didn't hear it over the ringing.

"Phoenix," he yelled. He knew he was yelling because his throat was already raw, but it sounded like a message through a string telephone, quiet and indistinct. "You good?"

No answer.

Gideon laboriously pushed against the dirt until he was up on his hands and knees. Phoenix was five feet to his right, lying on his back. He wasn't moving.

"Shit," Gideon hissed. Even if his ears weren't fried, the comment would've been lost to yet another mortar round. They were coming in about every ten seconds now. That was the third impact.

He scrambled toward Phoenix. Whatever had happened to his ears, his balance was off, and he found himself pulling to the left. It took conscious effort to correct the sway. As he made it to the man's side, he reached out and grabbed his wrist with his right hand, then placed his left ear over Phoenix's mouth to listen for breathing sounds.

"Stay with me," he said, the words slightly more audible now. He grimaced with frustration as he realized that, despite the improvement, there was no way he would be able to hear Phoenix breathing.

"Okay, pulse," Gideon said, squeezing the man's wrist. It was there. Faint, but present.

BOOM.

Gideon flinched as a fourth mortar round impacted the

camp. It landed somewhere behind him, but it was close enough that he felt the impact of the shockwave buffeting his rear.

"Okay," he muttered—or maybe yelled—as he shook his head to try to clear it. "Let's get you somewhere safe."

He grabbed the straps of Phoenix's chest rig and dragged him in a crab crawl to the side of the nearest cabin. It had a porch out front that was raised on concrete blocks. The space underneath was black as crude oil, but it would be safer than leaving the man out in the open.

Any bleeding?

A fifth round blew off the roof of the nearby cabin and sent splinters showering down like snowfall. Somewhere behind Gideon, the flickering flame light had replaced the sparse starlight speckle of electric illumination in the camp. Something was burning.

As Gideon quickly probed Phoenix's body, head, and torso for any sign of a bleeding wound, he tried to maintain situational awareness. How long had it been since the attack began—thirty seconds? Maybe forty. The first couple of mortar rounds had fallen with minimal spacing. After that, they'd settled into a rhythm.

It's a distraction, Gideon knew.

When he was certain that Phoenix wasn't going to bleed out—shrapnel had maybe nicked his left shoulder, but it was barely bleeding—he unclipped the man's chest rig. Phoenix was also carrying two spare rifle magazines in a thigh pocket, which meant five 30-round magazines in total. Gideon reached out for the pistol strapped to his thigh but decided against it at the last moment. If someone stripped him of every weapon he carried and left him for the enemy to finish off, he'd wait till the afterlife and torment them for eternity.

His thoughts were now running at something approximating their usual pace. Now he was suitably tooled up, he knew he needed to communicate with whoever was in the guard shack. The lights were out, but maybe the cameras and security sensors were still operating. When Phoenix had snuck up on Gideon just a couple of minutes earlier, he'd been holding a radio handset, but that had been lost in the chaos of the initial blast.

"Time to go," he said, grunting as he pushed Phoenix underneath the cabin's porch. He scraped the backs of his hands in the process, but that was the least of his problems.

Another explosion rocked through the camp, much larger than any of the incoming mortar rounds. It was powerful enough to cause Gideon to topple against the side of the cabin as he tried to push himself upright. A flash of light briefly lit the night sky before the flames subsided.

Main entrance, Gideon thought as he spun around and brought the borrowed rifle up to his shoulder. That explosion had definitely come from the camp's main gate. Someone had just knocked it down.

Another mortar round impacted as he swept the rifle's muzzle left and right across the parade ground. The safety was off, and his finger was pressed up against the side of the trigger guard. He was no longer the only soul in sight. Belatedly, cabin doors were beginning to open as their inhabitants realized that this wasn't just a really bad dream. In a couple of cases, men and women in their underwear bolted into the darkness carrying rifles, handguns, even something that looked a hell of a lot like a baseball bat.

Gotta admire the effort...

"This is chaos," Gideon muttered. He had no way of communicating with any of the camp's defenders. Most of them had only met him in the last day, and in the darkness, he was as likely to get filled by lead by any one of them as one of the attackers.

Gunfire was crackling in the distance now. Gideon was pretty sure it was coming from two opposite sides of the camp. There was no way of telling whether both directions were enemy fire—as opposed to friendlies blasting at shadows—but it was a reasonable assumption. Any assault force professional enough to fire mortar rounds downrange as part of their attack was capable of splitting their forces. They were almost certainly equipped with radio headsets, likely night vision too.

Another mortar round. Several seconds later, one more.

And then silence. Despite the chaos of half-naked gun-toting Faithless defenders sprinting across the parade ground, nobody said a word until an alarm siren belatedly began to wail.

"I think we figured it out," Gideon snorted as he finally decided on a course of action. He was much closer to the gunfire coming from the main gate than the other side of the camp.

So that's where he went.

FORTY-FOUR

A pair of heavy black Ford F-250 pickup trucks lurched around the bend in the road that led from the gate to the main campground, stones rattling against their undercarriages as their drivers struggled to maintain control in the dark.

Guess they made it through already.

Gideon slowed his headlong dash to the gate as they came into sight. Neither were operating using headlights, which confirmed his belief that the attackers were using night vision.

"Great," he muttered, grimacing as he brought the rifle butt up to his shoulder. He paused for just a second before squeezing a three-round burst at the first of the two pickups. His gaze narrowed as it started building up speed. There was something wrong with the windshield.

It was too dark to make out exactly what it was, but Gideon instantly switched focus and aimed his bursts of gunfire at the vehicle's engine block. The 5.56mm caliber NATO standard ammunition didn't have the penetrating power of a 50-cal machine gun or even as much stopping power as a 7.62mm round, but it was all he had.

He blew through an entire magazine of tightly aimed bursts in the time it took the trucks to cover twenty yards. They were now only fifty yards distant, and as he dumped the empty magazine, Gideon desperately looked around for cover.

Gideon was alone—the only line of defense on the side of the camp. He could hear footsteps coming from behind him but had no way of knowing how far away backup was. As the first truck loomed out of the darkness, its engine block smoking and a banshee-like scream emanating from beneath the hood, he finally figured out what was wrong with the windshield.

Flak vests.

He seated a second magazine and racked the slide. The instant he had a round in the chamber, he squeezed the trigger again. The incoming pickup truck was so close he couldn't miss. He kept hammering the grille with rifle fire, firing as quickly as he dared. He couldn't avoid missing with even a single round.

A silhouette stumbled out of the darkness behind him. All Gideon saw was a rifle and a bare torso, which he figured was enough confirmation that whoever was holding the gun was friendly.

"Hit the second truck," he yelled over the ringing in his ears and the rat-tat-tat of bullets popping out of his weapon. "First one's just a decoy."

There had to be a driver behind the makeshift wall of flak vests, but he was only there to cover the second pickup. That was the one that would be carrying the main assault team.

Another body appeared at Gideon's side, this time to his right. He thought he recognized Eli's face from the corner of his eye. The man was completely naked. He'd only stopped long enough after leaping out of bed to lash a gun belt to his waist which barely concealed his modesty. He was armed with just a pistol, but he opened fire nonetheless.

"Helluva wake-up call," he yelled as his muzzle flash lit up his face.

"I'm empty," Gideon yelled, just as something popped underneath the hood of the first pickup. There was the groaning wail of something mechanical failing hard and failing quick. The truck skewed off to the left and hit a picnic bench that was mounted on a concrete base. The impact snapped it onto two wheels, and then the vehicle flipped entirely. Gideon was pretty sure he saw the figure of a man flying out of the driver's side window before the darkness swallowed him.

"Loading," he called over the roar of the second pickup's engine revving. It was only ten yards away now. Way too close to stop. Gideon's eyes widened as his brain—way too late—computed his only possible course of action.

He threw himself to his side and landed hard on his shoulder. The magazine he was trying to seat into his weapon fell into the dirt as a flash of pain momentarily wiped out his vision.

"Fuck!"

Whether he yelled the epithet or it was somebody else Gideon would never know. Blood from a cut to the inside of his lip—he must've bitten down when he landed—filled his mouth, the taste warm and metallic.

Gideon rolled onto his back. He desperately patted the ground around him in search of the lost magazine. His chest was heaving, but the adrenaline flowing through his system wiped out any sense that he needed to breathe.

The pickup truck's exhaust cooked Gideon's legs as the vehicle roared past, kicking up a cloud of dust and small pieces of gravel that momentarily blinded him and filled his mouth and lungs with noxious foreign matter. He couldn't be sure, but he thought he felt the truck's tires clip the tips of his sneakers.

And then it was gone, just its rear lights disappearing in the darkness like a pair of cat's eyes as it barreled toward the center of the camp. Muzzle flashes erupted from the truck's bed, but Gideon had no idea where the gunshots were aimed.

Zara.

The realization that he was now on the wrong side of the enemy and the woman he'd come to—what, love?—struck home. He gave up fishing for the lost magazine and pulled another from the chest rig as he pushed himself back to his feet. His eyes widened as he saw the broken, mangled body of a man lying fifteen yards in front of him.

The sight momentarily stunned Gideon. If he hadn't known that it was a person, he might have thought the body belonged to a deer struck by traffic. Six tons of steel and glass traveling at forty miles an hour was enough to destroy any sense that the scattered body parts had once belonged to a functional whole.

"Fucking hell, man," Eli yelled, his tone at first angry before dying in a heartbroken wail. Gideon was close enough to smell the alcohol on the man's breath despite the dirt and filth that coated his nostrils.

But he knew there was nothing fake or overwrought about the emotion. He could see it on the man's face. His eyes were wide with shock, glinting despite the darkness. He began stumbling toward the battered corpse, his pistol tumbling from his grasp.

Gideon reached out and grabbed Eli's bare shoulder. He pulled the man back and twisted him around. Eli stared numbly at him.

"Have to help him," he mumbled. "Mason, shit..."

"Mason's dead," Gideon said, more harshly than he intended. "And a lot more of your friends are going to die unless we do something about it. Can you hear me?"

"I hear you," Eli said, blinking quickly half a dozen times as sense flooded back into him.

He shook his head, blinked again, then looked down and searched for his pistol. His naked body was covered in dirt, and he was bleeding from half a dozen scrapes and cuts. He crouched and scooped up the gun, briefly examining it before presumably concluding it was in working order.

Far ahead of them, the pickup truck skidded to a halt, the brake lights flaring in the dark. Gideon dropped to one knee and raised his rifle. He had no idea whether there were friendlies on the other side, so he confined his aim to the bed of the truck and fired three clipped bursts before pushing himself back upright.

Dark silhouettes jumped off the side of the truck. Behind it was a chaotic backdrop of scattered muzzle flashes and flames licking up the side of buildings. There had been no more mortar rounds since the initial salvo of eight or nine shells that had bookended the charge that took out the main gate, so Gideon figured whoever had fired them was now engaged in the assault.

How many of them are we up against?

"Let's move," he hissed.

The two men sprinted toward danger. As they ran, straight rounds whistled past their ears—friendly fire. There was no way of telling friend from foe in this darkness. But Gideon knew all he had to do was follow one simple rule.

The men in the trucks had to die.

FORTY-FIVE

Salazar's night vision was torched by the first burst of gunfire from the M249 light machine gun. The muzzle flash seemed to reach out for each direction of the compass before collapsing in on itself, only for the next round to start the show all over again.

He lay on his front, his dark fatigues slightly damp from the early-morning condensation that teased the ground. His nostrils drank in the scent of earth and gunpowder, and the machete strapped to his right thigh bit into his flesh. He heard the tinkle of expended shell casings even through the earplugs that protected what was left of his hearing.

Shifting his aim slightly to the left, he squeezed off another measured burst. He fired about fifteen rounds with each practiced squeeze of the trigger. He had no idea if he was hitting anything. That wasn't the point. Like the now-expended stack of mortar rounds just behind him, the purpose of this exercise was to attract the attention of the camp's defenders and distract them from the main offensive.

BOOM.

The breaching charge on the gate detonated with a thunderous force that rocked even the ground Salazar was lying on. The pressure wave knocked against his chest, tightening it further.

Breathe, he reminded himself.

There was something about controlling a weapon of this ferocity that could make a man feel drunk with power. The incandescent white of the muzzle flashes danced on his retinas, and the force of the recoil rocked his entire body despite the fold-out tripod the weapon rested on. Knowing you were sending enough lead downrange to wipe out an entire village could be intoxicating.

Enough to make a man forget to breathe.

But this wasn't that. Salazar had felt the tension in his muscles long before he opened fire. His breathing was shallow and strained. Despite much practice with the weapon he cradled, he was squeezing the trigger in jerky twitches rather than using sustained pressure. The barrel was already hot enough to burn flesh, but that wasn't the cause of the sweat trickling down his temples.

Salazar fired again, and this time the M249 ran dry. For a brief while, he simply lay there, gasping for air. No, it was more than that. He was scared to stand. Scared to push himself forward into combat yet again.

The knife wounds that Gideon had inflicted during their scrap several days earlier ached despite the best efforts of the pain pills he swallowed with reckless abandon. But it wasn't pain he was scared of. No, this injury ran far deeper.

"What are we waiting for?" The lone sicario—Bruno—who had helped him set up this diversion asked. "We need to move."

Salazar's hands trembled as he pulled them away from the machine gun and let the heavy weapon's stock rest on the moist earth. He clenched his fists and dug his nails into the fleshy part of his palm, savoring the hit of pain that resulted.

"Light the fuses," he ordered, hiding his face as he stood. He just needed a moment to steady himself.

Bruno grunted with satisfaction. "On it."

Salazar watched out of the corner of his eye as the hired sicario dragged his thumb down the flint of a cigarette lighter. The flame caught instantly, and as Bruno reached down toward the bundle of prepared fuses, Salazar slipped his own trembling fingers inside his dark jacket. As they closed around the plastic cylinder, he felt a momentary hit of release.

He extracted the pill bottle from his jacket, taking care not to cause the pills to rattle as he popped the cap. He peered into the cylinder despite knowing what he would see staring back at him. It was like staring down the barrel of a telescope—only three white eyes stared back.

Half a dozen fuses hissed into life behind him as he stood, locked into place by the sight of the pills. He was certain now that they were all that was tethering him to sanity. A vice of terror gripped his chest at the realization that he was almost out.

Should have got more. Need to find some.

But there hadn't been the opportunity. Events had moved fast after Trent informed him of Gideon's location. After he picked up the hired team of Mexican assassins, there was no opportunity to drop into a pharmacy.

"Just wait here while I pick up my crazy pills."

The thought cut through Salazar's spiral just long enough for him to snort at the black humor of the situation. The moment unfroze him, and without thinking about it, he knocked two of the pills back and swallowed them dry.

I'm going to regret that.

"They're burning. Let's go," Bruno said tersely.

Salazar subtly pocketed the pill bottle as he reached for his rifle. The name on the label couldn't be traced back to him.

The fingerprints, maybe. But he no longer expected to live long enough for that to pose a problem.

He stared for a moment at the sight of the burning fireworks fuses. The ignition trail was like watching an Olympic sprinter in slow motion, half a dozen of them, in fact, all racing on a track laid out like silly string.

Each of the six fuses was connected to a bundle of firecrackers. They were cut to different lengths, which meant the firecrackers would detonate at slightly different times, giving the defenders the impression that the machine gun he had used to pummel the camp was still firing. It wouldn't take them long to figure out the truth. But he didn't need long, either.

He nodded, and the two men began sprinting along a predetermined path that took them around the edge of the Faithless compound a couple of hundred yards to ensure that the already inaccurate incoming fire would pose them no harm.

Both men skidded to a halt at the same time. Bruno rummaged in a bush and pulled out a pile of precut carpet that he'd left there earlier. The first bundle of firecrackers detonated just as the Mexican hitman threw the carpet over the razor wire that topped the compound's fence.

It took them seconds to clamber over before they were running again—sprinting toward the sound of gunfire. Another bundle of firecrackers went up and was joined by a renewed crackle of return fire from whatever weapons the Faithless had managed to muster.

But they were firing blind at a position that was long-vacated. Dancing to Salazar's tune, not the other way around.

Bruno and Salazar were practically among the main cabins of the camp before they encountered another soul. Most of the action—as they'd expected—was concentrated into knots of gunfire. The first was the one they had provoked, and the other on the opposite side of the camp must have been the battle against the primary assault force.

It was too dark to see the man's face. He was clothed but barefoot and carried a pistol in his hand. He was running in the opposite direction from the two sicarios, toward the rattle of firecrackers. He was too fixated on the imagined threat to notice the immediate danger to his life.

"Quietly," Salazar hissed. He let his rifle fall against its sling and pulled out his machete from its canvas sheath instead. The hilt of the weapon felt like an old friend in his hand. It steadied his still-vibrating nerves. Bruno indicated his understanding as both men slowed.

The man was running across their path. In just a dozen or so steps, they would meet. It was only then, belatedly, that he realized that anything was wrong. His head turned, but it was already too late.

Salazar drew the machete high in the air and chopped it into his enemy's torso. He'd sharpened the blade himself, and it cut easily through both material and flesh before finally bouncing off of bone and coming loose from the body. The man kept running for several more steps before his brain realized what had just happened.

And then he collapsed. Just like that, he was gone.

"Shit," Bruno muttered, shaking his head. He turned to Salazar, who saw a manic gleam in the man's eyes. "You're loco, dude. I like it."

FORTY-SIX

Gideon's eyes were wide with horror as he and Eli approached the spot where the second pickup had run aground. The chassis of the vehicle was pockmarked with bullet holes and smoked from a dozen places. A heady chemical tang of gasoline mixed in with the thick smoke that now hung in the air over the entire compound, stinging his eyes and lungs.

The enemy assault team was already gone. They'd left one of their number behind. A single bullet appeared to have entered the back of his neck right above the top vertebra and exited through his right eyeball. There wasn't much left of his face. The black Kevlar helmet that now hung sideways off its strap couldn't have done anything to save him. It looked almost comical in failure. A smashed set of night vision goggles completed the look.

"Jesus," Eli said simply, before covering his face and nose with his hand in a vain attempt to mask the worst of the smell—whether blood or smoke wasn't clear.

"We got two of them," Gideon said, clenching his fist to stop the trembling in his hand. This was like a nightmare, except there was no waking up from it. No matter where he went or how far he traveled, nowhere was safe.

Should have stayed in the woods.

"Yeah. But how many are left?"

A grenade detonating somewhere in the distance broke the trance that both had settled into. Seeing that the dead Brotherhood fighter carried magazines that were compatible with his own rifle, Gideon picked the man's webbing clean. He tossed a grenade in Eli's direction, not looking to see whether he caught it, then handed back half the scavenged magazines and the dead man's rifle.

"Where the hell am I going to put this?" Eli said when he turned round. He was holding the grenade in midair.

Gideon blinked. He didn't mean to stare at Eli's bare genitals, but it was kind of difficult to look away. He winced. "Point taken."

Eli handed the grenade back, and Gideon pocketed it along with another he'd stolen off the man with the smashed face. It was as though they were standing in the eye of the storm. Gunfire rang out in all directions, echoing off buildings so that even the quiet spots demanded attention. Scattered muzzle flashes lit the trees like the lighting in some kind of dystopian nightclub.

"I counted three," Gideon said, gesturing toward where the rattle of gunfire was most intense. Even though the enemy was using similar rifles, he could distinguish between the two different types with just the naked ear. The assault team was firing in calm, sustained bursts—usually two at a time while the third reloaded.

By contrast, the Faithless defenders were still off-balance and disorganized. There was no center of mass that could resist the enemy thunder run. The good guys were being cut down like a hot poker through cloth.

Cut down.

"Come on," Gideon said. His throat was raw from the smoke and his body was exhausted, but fresh reserves of adrenaline flooded his arteries and veins.

He sprinted toward the sound of combat with Eli at his side. Ahead of them, half a dozen sleeping cabins were aflame like burning oil rigs in the night sky. The orange glow of flames lit pyres of smoke that towered into the heavens. A group of three muzzle flashes up ahead made it easy to pick out where his enemy was. They were only thirty yards away.

But they left a trail of dead and injured underfoot.

"Mick," Eli keened as he hurdled the body of a man whose torso was punctured from pelvis to chin with bullet holes. The Faithless operator squeezed his trigger as he ran, firing madly into the chaos. His bullets sprayed wildly, each spearing his grief into the night.

Gideon watched as another small knot of defenders—seemingly armed with only a single handgun—was cut to pieces by the enemy's smooth efficiency. The horror of the picture scythed through the shock that had started to stop his limbs. These people were the good guys. They were trying to save their friends and family.

And now they were dying for it.

Fifteen yards.

The trio of attackers slowed to reload. Gideon kept running, bringing his rifle up as his enemy grew closer and closer. The rearmost of the three seemed to realize that something was wrong. He turned, bringing his rifle up and ready—but too late.

Gideon squeezed the trigger of his rifle and sent a spray of bullets toward the man. He fired wildly, not sparing ammunition, consumed by a desire for revenge. Some part of his mind knew that he wasn't thinking straight, but he didn't care. The trigger jammed down until the entire magazine ran dry. Almost every round in the second half of the mag missed the target as the force of the recoil progressively skewed his aim farther and farther toward the sky.

It wasn't until his weapon clicked in his hands that Gideon realized he was screaming. Two men lay on the ground in front of him. One was dead, the other nearly so—arterial spray from a wound in his leg reflecting the flames from the burning cabins.

Eli didn't stop.

The naked fighter's magazine was already completely expended. Instead of bothering to reload, he simply reversed the weapon in his hands, ignoring the heat from the barrel as he wielded the rifle like a club. He turned side-on like a baseball batter as the last remaining attacker turned in slow motion to face the assault that had claimed two of his comrades.

The man came face-to-face with fate just in time. The rifle's stock smashed into his chin, sweeping from low to high so that it tipped his skull up and back. He stumbled backward, no doubt already out of the fight. There was no way a man could sustain that kind of damage and keep going.

Before he had tumbled to the ground, Eli brought the rifle down again, this time sweeping low and destroying the man's kneecap. The crack made by the cartilage as it gave way was audible even over the sound of gunfire that still echoed out of the night sky like fireworks.

As Eli brought the rifle up over his head, standing like a mad, naked Viking berserker with his sweat-drenched, gleaming body surrounded by smoke to deliver the final blow, Gideon finally shook himself back to life.

He let his own rifle fall against the sling on his chest rig and rushed toward the grieving Faithless fighter he'd only just met, bear-hugging his torso and holding him tight.

"He's gone, Eli," he yelled. "He's gone."

FORTY-SEVEN

Salazar moved through the camp with vicious purpose, his hands sticky with spilled blood, leaving a trail of death and dismemberment behind him. He'd inflicted so many cuts with the razor-sharp machete that the blade was beginning to dull, forcing him to rely on brute strength to hack through flesh and bone.

Now even that was beginning to fade. And with it came a tempering of the fanatic rage that had carried him this far. With Bruno at his side, he had killed or maimed at least half a dozen men in a couple of minutes, hunting down victims with a furious blood thirst.

And now he stood for a moment in the center of a burning camp, in the midst of columns of smoke coursing into a sky that was lit by the flames of burning cabins. Brief periods of silence punctuated intense bursts of almost unbroken gunfire.

But something was wrong.

"Luis," he transmitted through a radio handset clipped to his webbing. "What's your status?"

He'd worried when Trent hired Luis's team. There was no

doubt that they were the most aggressive of the various freelance Mexican groups of guns for hire. If a cartel boss ordered them to give a suspected mole a sulfuric acid shower, they wouldn't even blink. Salazar knew because, in a different life, he'd watched it happen.

But aggression like that came hand-in-hand with madness. Perhaps the former fed the latter; acting like a corrosive liquid burning away whatever tendrils held a man to sanity. Maybe every application of violence knocked a few more droplets free. Or maybe they'd always been this way.

Like the berserkers of ancient tribal warfare, Luis and his men whipped themselves into a frenzy before an operation. Until tonight, Salazar had never watched it happen. The rumors alone were enough for him to want a different team.

Despite the roar and crackle of entire cabins succumbing to rapacious, parasitic flame, there was no missing the scream that rang out across the camp. It was a man's voice, though whether it was caused by pain, anger, or fear was impossible to say.

"Come in Luis," Salazar hissed.

He clinched the hilt of his machete for comfort. The glow of the fires had made it difficult to find anywhere to hide, but he and Bruno were crouched behind one of the cabins that hadn't yet gone up. It was only a matter of time, though. Fireflies of ash and cinders darted through the air, assisted by superheated jets of air pushed as timbers and roofs collapsed.

"Maybe your radio's out," Bruno muttered. "Let me try."

The sicario's radio was operated through the throat mic that ringed his neck. "Boss, come in," he whispered. "What's your status?"

No answer.

Salazar couldn't help himself. "I told the bastard that a frontal assault was a stupid idea. They got themselves killed."

Bruno shook his head, though his face was creased with doubt. "Must be the radios."

"No," Salazar said, gritting his teeth as a flicker of fear caught in his chest. "Listen."

The sicario cocked his ear but clearly didn't understand what he was being asked to do. Not at first. But the realization slowly dawned on him, as it already had on Salazar.

The sound of gunfire no longer pincered both sides of the camp. The main gate end was now almost silent. Only scattered outbreaks of shots could be heard to their left, where Faithless shooters were still targeting the now-silent position that Salazar and Bruno had long vacated.

"The distraction won't fool them much longer," Salazar said. He could feel the cool kiss of air against his bloodied skin now, despite the warmth of a Georgia summer night and the heat thrown by the fires.

Terror was beginning to kindle in his chest. He tried to stamp it out, but as he focused on it, he only succeeded in making it real.

Twenty yards in front of where the two men were crouched, a woman with a rifle sprinted across open ground. A flaming cabin silhouetted her until she was lost once again to darkness. Her form was imprinted on Salazar's retinas whenever he blinked. She hadn't seen them.

But it was only a matter of time.

"They can't be dead," Bruno muttered, shaking his head. "We've won. Look how many we killed!"

Salazar spun around and slapped the sicario around the face. The blow knocked the man back against the dark cabin. "Pull yourself together. They'll be hunting for us now."

He craned his neck and examined the scene in front of him. Slowly, imperceptibly, the battle lust had faded from him like fine sand through a sieve. He was no longer searching for a way to win.

Just a way *out*.

"We need to move," he said under his breath as his peripheral vision caught a pair of armed men jogging somewhere to his right. "Can't stay here."

He tried to think, tried to concentrate on forming a plan, but his usual calm was nowhere to be found. He dug his fingernails into his palms and rode the pain it caused to clear his thoughts.

The main gate was to the east. If Luis's men were dead, then there had to be a sizable force in that direction. From the west came the occasional ripples of gunshots as the Faithless fired on their initial position. There was nothing but miles of forest to the south. The terrain would slow them down.

That left north as the only workable option. But going that way meant they had to cross the open parade ground at the center of the Faithless compound. It was a risk.

But so was staying here.

"Let's go," Salazar said, grabbing Bruno by the shoulder and hauling him upright. He no longer cared about completing the mission. That hope had died long ago. Now all that was left to do was survive.

And Bruno could either fight at his side or he could be bait.

The two men jogged through the compound, trying to stick to the few dark alleyways that remained. Salazar knew he should sheath the machete and wield the rifle in its place, but the blade was too familiar to discard right now. He dumped his helmet and motioned for Bruno to do the same. None of the Faithless were wearing them. The headgear only made them stick out.

Twice they sprinted past men and women with guns. But Bruno didn't shoot and Salazar didn't slash; they just kept running. Salazar realized that both their faces were covered in soot and dirt, just like the camp's defenders.

Nobody could tell who was who in the chaos.

Shouts rang out now. Even the gunfire to the west had faded. Authoritative voices were beginning to restore order. Half the camp's defenders had to be dead, but the rest were now assembling into search parties.

Salazar reached the bottom edge of the parade ground. There were two options: either he could stick to the edge of the buildings or sprint right across. The first option would allow them to stay hidden. But it would also prolong their stay here. And whether he wanted to admit it to himself or not, that was no longer a fate he was willing to bear.

Without motioning for Bruno, he ran out into the parade ground. Somewhere up ahead and to his right were rows of parked vehicles. To his left was the body of a man. It was impossible to say whether he was friend or foe.

"Who's that?" a voice called from behind him and Bruno, who had belatedly followed. "Hold up!"

Salazar's throat clenched with fear. He could barely think now. He was beginning to panic. Shadows moved in front of him, near the vehicles. He couldn't even tell whether they were real or just a figment of his imagination.

"You in the parade ground—stop or I'll open fire."

"Keep running!" Salazar hissed. They were only ten or fifteen feet from the cars now. "They can't be—"

Before his lips formed around the word "sure," Bruno spun and opened fire. Salazar twisted automatically but continued sprinting forward. Distracted, he didn't realize he was about to collide with something until it was too late to do anything about it. He didn't realize it was a person he'd hit until they were both tumbling to the ground.

Ironically, the fall probably saved both their lives. Bullets chewed through the air where the two men had just been. Maybe some of them were already wet with Bruno's blood.

Salazar hit the ground hard, his fall only partially cushioned by the body of the man he'd collided with. He lost his grip on the machete as he skidded across the earth. The impact buffeted the air from his lungs. But his roadblock suffered worse. The man's head cracked against the dirt with enough force to be audible over the sound of gunshots.

He was out cold.

Salazar scrambled to his hands and knees and raked the earth with his fingertips in search of the machete. They touched the sticky metal of the blade, and he clutched for it with no care for injury. He used the weapon to push himself upright, though he was still on his knees.

His eyes slowly focused on the face of the man on the ground.

"It's you!"

Footsteps sounded from every direction. Urgent cries carried over the crackling of flame and hissing of smoke. But miraculously, Salazar realized that he'd found what he was searching for.

Salvation.

ZARA SKIDDED to a halt at the center of the parade ground just as a voice cried out. She was clutching a pistol she'd taken from a dead man's grasp.

"Back," it cried, hoarse with exertion and strain. "Get the fuck back!"

She didn't recognize the voice, but that wasn't a surprise. They had barely been here long enough to greet all the residents, let alone get to know them.

A loose semicircle had formed around the cluster of vehicles parked in the parade ground. Clouds had swallowed the stars in the sky, and the only light came from the flames swallowing the Faithless's refuge. She pushed her way through so she could see what was happening.

The sight chilled her veins.

A man was dragging Gideon into one of the SUVs. A dropped—*sword?*—glinted on the ground near his feet. He had an object in his left hand. Zara couldn't make out what it was.

"Someone stop him!" she yelled. "Shoot him!"

"Can't," a man said grimly as he grabbed her and pulled her back. "Grenade."

The ring around Gideon and his captor was about ten yards from the two men at the center. Zara tried to do the math in her head. How long between a grenade's lever popping out and it detonating? Three seconds?

The man with the grenade finished stuffing Gideon's prone form into the back seat of the SUV. When he was done, he smashed the back window with the grenade. Zara held her breath at the insanity of the decision.

What the hell's he doing?

The reason for the curious act became clear a moment later. The Brotherhood soldier thrust his hand through the broken window and kept it there as he closed the door around it.

Zara did the same math as everybody else around her. Even if they could shoot Gideon's captor and cross the distance to the vehicle in the three or four seconds before the grenade detonated, it would be almost impossible to open the door and fling it away from danger in time.

The man glanced over his shoulder at the crowd around him. He had a rifle hanging off the webbing on his chest. He switched the grenade to his left hand and kept it inside the vehicle as he gripped the rifle with his right.

"I'm going to take out those other vehicles," he yelled. His voice was pinched. He had a Hispanic accent. Mexican, maybe? "You know what happens if you shoot me."

"We have to do something," Zara whispered. She could see the same thought playing out on a dozen faces. They couldn't just let Gideon be captured by this maniac.

The man raised the rifle and fired wildly into the sides of the vehicles parked around him. In a matter of seconds, his magazine ran dry, and he was left visibly panting from the exertion and the strain. None of the other vehicles went up in smoke or flame. Maybe that was just in the movies. But their windows and windshields were pockmarked with spiderweb cracks.

The man dropped his weapon and moved for the driver's door. He fumbled with it before managing to open it and climb inside. He ostentatiously held the grenade out behind him, dangling it over the passenger seats as he reached with his free hand to close the door.

"I don't care about this fight," he yelled. "Let me out of here and I'll leave him somewhere safe. Try anything stupid, and you can deal with the consequences. You know what happens if you follow me."

For several seconds after the door closed, nothing happened. Zara dared to hope that he didn't have the keys. But then the engine rumbled into life. And then the wheels began to move.

And a dozen eyes stared and watched helplessly as Gideon's kidnapper accelerated out of the parade ground, slewing the vehicle madly around as he headed for the main gate. The back wheels skidded on the dirt. Zara held her breath as she feared the grenade would detonate and—

Kill the man I love.

FORTY-EIGHT

"Eli, go after them. Take two guys. That's all I can spare."

Lachlan's words jolted Zara out of the trance state that had settled over her. "I'm going with them."

He reached out and gripped her by the wrist. "The hell you are. Eli—go!"

Zara tried to pull away as Eli—almost naked, barefoot, and with blood spattered all over his body—grabbed a pair of Faithless shooters. All three men picked a different vehicle to open. Two of the engines were kaput from the kidnapper's strafing. Bullets must've penetrated their engine blocks. The third, however, ran just fine.

Eli climbed in and slammed the driver's side door behind him. Two men jumped in the back as others tossed fresh magazines, rifles, and extra weapons through the rear windows. Eli didn't wait another second before stepping on the gas and skidding away in pursuit. The SUV left a trail of dust in its wake that swirled in the eddies of smoke and heat.

"Get off me," Zara snapped.

Lachlan grimaced. "I don't want to do this, Zara. But right now, I can't lose you too."

"We haven't lost Gideon. Not yet."

The look he shot her back stunned her into silence. It wasn't judgment she saw in his gaze but pain. "Maybe. But look around. I've lost half of my people. At least six of them have gunshot wounds. This attack wiped out most of my best shooters. And if we don't get moving fast, then the rest of us will end up behind bars."

Zara heard it all; she just didn't care. She couldn't just wait here while Gideon's kidnapper was getting away. She had to do something. She'd never be able to look at herself in the mirror again if she didn't.

Lachlan grabbed both of her shoulders. It was as though he could hear her inner monologue as he turned her to face the burning buildings and bodies contorted into the positions they'd fallen into in death. "I only have six people on this compound right now who aren't injured or dead. Harriet—."

His voice broke, and Zara realized for the first time that she hadn't seen his wife since the chaos began. Her gaze fixed on a figure slumped next to a nearby cabin—half underneath it, with only the legs sticking out. Her own legs felt unsteady beneath her.

"—She's been shot in the stomach. I don't know if she's going to make it. I can't have you walking out on me. Not right now."

She felt his grip on her shoulders relinquishing as his strength faded. It was only then that she realized she wasn't the only one suffering. She saw faces that were numb with grief or just plain shock. Men and women clamping bandaged to their injured bodies, even as blood oozed from bullet wounds.

And she knew that she couldn't leave these people to an unknown fate. Gideon would understand.

"Okay," she said, her voice strained from a cocktail of emotion that was only just staying suppressed. "I'm not leaving. What do you need from me?"

The funny thing was that it only took a single decision for her to compartmentalize her feelings. One moment she was in pieces; the next, all thoughts of grief and fear were pushed aside.

"Find gasoline," he said. Zara realized that tears had carved channels down his soot-stained cheeks. "Take it to the ops building. Somehow it's the only damn structure that's not on fire."

"Sure. Why?"

He gritted his teeth. "You'll see."

Zara saw but didn't immediately understand when she stumbled through the doors to the operations building with a five-gallon can of gasoline taken from the stores building in each hand. She stood in the open doorway, her forearms aching from the strain of the weight as her eyes adjusted to the gloom inside. She saw flames dancing every time she blinked.

Six bodies were already laid out side-by-side on the floor. A man pushed her aside as he came through the door carrying two cardboard document boxes stacked on top of each other. He tossed them farther into the room, careful not to disturb the bodies. It was only when he turned back toward her that she saw it was Francis.

"What are we doing here?" Zara asked.

He stared back at her with dead eyes. His clothing was soaked in blood, his hands stained with it, but he didn't appear to be injured.

"It's all evidence," he said, no emotion in his voice. "We're burning it."

Her eyes went wide. "What?"

Francis nodded, his shoulders slumping with exhaustion. "It's protocol. They'd understand."

There was no time for Zara to protest before more Faithless entered carrying yet another body. And then another. Others—walking wounded—carried laptops and boxes of documents that added to the pile. Lachlan was the last to enter. He carried Harriet's broken body as though she weighed no more than a child and laid her gently on the floor. Zara hadn't even known she'd passed.

"Everybody, get to the vehicles," he said quietly, his shoulders hunched with grief. "Load up everything you can and burn the rest. I'll be with you...shortly."

Zara stumbled backward out of the ops building, her vision blurry with tears. The heat from the burning cabins pummeled her from every angle. Most had been reduced to piles of cinders that glowed like fresh-lit charcoal. The smoke was overpowering. It sandpapered her nostrils and lungs and drew fresh moisture from her eyes. She staggered through the chaos, her legs rolling as though she was walking on the deck of a wooden sailboat in the middle of a storm.

She sensed rather than heard the ops building go up behind her. She turned to see Lachlan silhouetted by flame. He stood on the threshold, smoke dancing around his limbs as tongues of fire jetted across the wooden floorboards. For a moment, Zara thought he'd made his choice.

And she didn't blame him.

FORTY-NINE

Zara drove numbly into the budding dawn, her mind blank but her fingers knotted around the steering wheel as her subconscious battled to process the night's events.

The seats behind her were pushed flat so that three of the injured Faithless could lie prone. Two of them were receiving IV fluids from clear bags hanging from the hooks on the roof of the cabin. There was just enough space for Francis to perform basic first aid on the less serious wounds that hadn't been patched in the rush to escape the compound.

Sirens were audible in the distance just as the last Faithless van—one of only four working vehicles remaining—rattled over the debris left after the destruction of the main gate. As soon as practicable, the vans scattered to different back roads. The cops would definitely pay attention to a convoy speeding away from the still-smoking site of a battle. They'd driven alone for two hours before loosely linking up outside of Butler. Eli was in the car behind hers. He'd returned empty-handed.

Gideon could be dead by now...

The radio handset on the passenger seat hissed static for a

moment before Lachlan's voice broke through the universe's backing track. Zara shook the morbid thought off as she listened. "We're stopping. Turn right down the forest track in one mile."

Zara heard the words but didn't process them. It was only when she saw the taillights of the dented van ahead of her disappearing to her right that she finally wrenched the steering wheel to follow it. The SUV jolted over a pothole, and the force of gravity swung her and rattled the injured patients in the back.

"Sorry," she grimaced, holding up her hand in apology.

"Don't sweat it," Francis said. His voice grated with exhaustion. "They are all doped up anyway."

The pathetic convoy slowed as it headed another mile down a rutted dirt track through a section of logging forest. The first rays of sunshine teased sloping shadows out of endless rows of parallel pine trees that towered into the sky. If Zara squinted, she could almost be looking down a Manhattan street as the sun rose out of the East River.

She took her foot almost entirely off the gas pedal, allowing the automatic transmission to creep as slowly as possible over the mountainous potholes and divots. A gap opened up between her vehicle and the van ahead of her, but not for long. Brake lights shone like devil's eyes up ahead, and all three slowed to a stop. Zara tucked in behind them and put the vehicle into park.

Car doors flew open, and people dressed in tattered, blood-stained clothing spilled out. Through the glass, Zara could just hear someone calling for more IV bags, as another sprinted up the side of the column with her arms full of medical supplies. She knew she should get out and help, but her brain seemed to be operating in first gear. Somebody appeared to have chained lead weights to her eyelids. It was all she could do to keep them open.

Eli signaled for her to join him from across the hood of the SUV. The stimulus finally tugged her out of her fugue. She unbuckled her seat belt and turned to look at Francis. "What do you need?"

He was crouching over the man lying parallel to the passenger side and appeared to be finding a fresh vein for a loose IV line. "Coffee, if you can find any. I'm good for medical supplies."

"I'll try," Zara said. "But if I see any, not making any promises it makes it the whole way back."

Francis snorted. "Don't blame you."

"Boss wants you," Eli said as she opened the door, beckoning her to follow. Somewhere he'd found a fresh T-shirt and pants. They were only stained with a watercolor of blood, rather than the full oil palette.

"Where are we going?"

"Hell if I know. Doubt he does, either."

"How's he doing?" Zara asked. It was easier to focus on somebody else's pain right now than think about what was happening to Gideon.

Eli glanced toward her out of the corner of his eye. His face had been a grim mask since he'd returned empty-handed from his pursuit of Gideon's kidnapper. "How do you think?"

Zara had to practically jog at the shooter's side to keep up with him. Her exhausted legs strained at the effort, but thankfully the journey was short. All four doors of Lachlan's white, mud-spattered SUV were wide open. Rather than carrying injured Faithless personnel or even the walking wounded, it was piled high with medical supplies and weaponry.

A blanket had been laid over the pile in a futile attempt to disguise the supplies from any passing cop or busybody with

911 on speed dial. It was pushed out of the way so the medics in the middle two vehicles could restock their bags. Lachlan was still behind the wheel, staring into space.

Eli peeled away and accepted a bottle of water somebody offered him. A couple of the remaining Faithless shooters had fanned out and formed a loose perimeter around the stopped convoy. Two of them knelt with rifles aimed at nothing, probably defending the remaining Faithless from creatures little more dangerous than woodland rodents.

A silhouette of a man stood about ten yards ahead of Lachlan's SUV, facing out. He had a pistol in his right hand, which was aimed at the ground. He stood stock-still, except for his shooting hand, which trembled uncontrollably. As Zara climbed into the passenger seat, the light shifted and she saw that the silhouette was Jamie.

Looks like he's barely holding it together.

Zara couldn't blame him. She wasn't doing much better herself. And plainly, neither was Lachlan. He was still clutching the steering wheel, and it was a tossup as to whether his knuckles or his face were paler.

"You wanted me?"

At first, Zara thought Lachlan didn't hear her. He gave no sign that he'd noticed her presence. She waited in silence for several seconds that stretched into a full minute, unwilling to intrude on the man's grief. She was beginning to wonder whether he'd noticed her at all and was preparing to say something when he finally spoke.

"I've known Harriet ever since we were both kids," he said, his voice leaden and devoid of energy.

"All of this," he continued, gesturing at the vehicles parked along the forest road before snorting in disbelief. "We built it together. I couldn't have done any of it alone. And now it's gone. Harriet's gone."

Another pause developed. Zara didn't know what to say, so she just reached out and squeezed his forearm. She gritted her teeth as she did so, a wave of her own anxiety sweeping across her.

"I'm sorry," Lachlan said, finally releasing his grip on the steering wheel and shaking his head. "I know you're worried about Gideon, too. I just can't think straight. Can't hold it together."

He glanced back at the assorted members of the Faithless, then quickly looked away. "They're all relying on me to make decisions and I can't. Not right now."

His hands began trembling, and he gripped the steering wheel once again just to quell the tremors.

"What can I do?" Zara said. Her own worries for Gideon's safety—and the ever-present question of whether he was even still alive—still felt compartmentalized. She was anxious, sure, but the emotion was strangely distant. She could still function, unlike the man at her side.

"I need you to take charge," he said, nodding to himself. "Just for a while. Until I can get a hold of myself."

"Why me?" Zara asked, startled by the request. "They don't know me. Surely they would trust one of their own better."

And who says I even can?

Lachlan shook his head emphatically. It was the only strong emotion he'd displayed this entire time. "I've got nineteen survivors. Nine of them need medical attention. They're not up to the challenge. The remaining ten are either too young, too inexperienced, or too tactical. I need somebody who can see the whole picture. You're the only one who fits."

Zara swallowed. "What if they don't follow me?"

"They trust me. They'll understand."

Zara's scalp started to itch. Her chest felt a little tight. She wanted to be anywhere other than right here. Then her eyes focused on Jamie through the windshield. The trembling had spread from his gun hand to his entire body. He looked on the verge of a breakdown.

A glance out the window revealed that the rest of the Faithless were in little better shape. Even some of those delivering medical care were wounded themselves. There was lots of action, but no obvious thought. Somebody needed to take charge, or the Brotherhood would catch up to them and find them easy pickings, like an injured antelope trailing its herd on the Serengeti.

And there was no one else.

"Okay," she whispered. "But I need to know where we're going."

"There's a safe house outside Camden, Alabama. It's a few hours' drive. Eli knows where to find it."

Zara grimaced but knew she had to ask the question. "Is it secure?"

"Only Harriet and I knew about it, and a trusted handful of others." A flash of anger crossed Lachlan's face. "The bastards can't know about it."

They found out about the training camp. Zara didn't have to say the words out loud.

She slipped out of the SUV and closed the door quietly behind her. She was about to go looking for Eli when she caught a glimpse of Jamie in her peripheral vision. He was pacing up and down along the track. He seemed to be mumbling something to himself.

Zara turned toward him. She approached with one eye on the pistol. As she grew closer, she saw that his finger was threaded through the trigger guard. She glanced over her shoulder to see if anyone was close enough to help, but nobody was looking. She was on her own.

"Jamie? Everything okay?"

He whipped around sharply, his eyes wide. Zara was shocked by what she saw. A couple days of stubble growth marred his otherwise boyish face. The bags under his eyes were a purplish black that stood out against the absolute lack of any other color.

"I did this," he hissed. He tried to match her gaze but averted his eyes as if ashamed.

"Did what?" Zara said softly. "Why don't you go ahead and put down the gun, okay?"

"You don't understand," he snapped. "They have my brother. I had to do it. Had to tell them he was here."

"Tell who?" Zara asked, even as the pieces fell into place in her mind.

He wasn't Jamie's brother. He was Gideon.

A flash of anger stiffened Zara's back. Assuming Jamie wasn't just crazy, then it was his fault that Gideon had been taken. Was maybe already dead. Her fingers twitched as she wished she'd brought the pistol she'd left in the SUV's glove compartment. If she'd had it on her...

"Jamie, put the gun down," she said, her voice growing more authoritative. "We can talk this out. Whatever you've done, it's okay."

She sensed movement behind her, perhaps attracted by the increased volume of her voice, but she didn't dare turn around. She barely dared to breathe. The moment felt so fraught with tension that even the slightest movement could spell disaster.

"Jamie," a voice called out from behind her. Eli's voice. "What are you doing, kid?"

Shit.

In a flash, Jamie raised the pistol and aimed it at Zara. No, not at her—behind her.

"Stay back!" he yelled. The pistol twitched in his hand as

he shifted his aim from unseen face to unseen face out of her view.

"Put the gun down, Jamie!" Eli yelled. "Don't make me drop you."

Zara closed her eyes. She wished she could take a peek over her shoulder, but that didn't seem sensible. Not right now.

Think.

Eli had to have drawn his weapon. There was no doubt that the Faithless shooter was a crack shot. Gideon had told her that everyone in the Alpha and Bravo squads was. By now, there might even be more than one gun on Jamie. It was likely that all of them were more proficient with firearms than he was.

Part of her wanted them to finish it. Jamie had sold them all out. He'd sacrificed the lives of ten innocent people whose only crime was trying to make the world a better place. Others would bear the scars of his betrayal for the rest of their lives.

And then there was Gideon. Whether he liked to hear it or not, he was the only one who could end the Brotherhood's hold on its adherents. Jamie might have sacrificed that, too.

"But I can't let them kill him," she whispered. She wanted to. Damn, she wanted to. But command wasn't supposed to be easy. It meant making hard choices. And this was one of them.

"Eli," Zara called out. "Don't shoot him. That goes for all of you."

Before they could protest, she stepped to her right—blocking Eli's field of fire. At least where she thought it had to be, given the position of his voice.

"What the hell are you doing, Zara?"

She ignored Eli's hissed protest and took another step, forward this time. Toward Jamie. "Put the gun down. No one's going to hurt you. You did what you had to do to save your brother, right?"

The words burned like stomach acid as she said them, but she needed to win the kid's trust or this would go sideways fast.

"What are you doing?" he said suspiciously.

Zara took another step closer. "Give me the gun, all right?"

He didn't protest this time. His gaze locked on her like a captive cobra on its charmer. Holding her breath, Zara moved closer still. She was almost within touching distance now.

"That's far enough," he said, a note of panic in his voice. He finally aimed the pistol directly at her chest. He couldn't miss. Not at this distance. If he pulled the trigger, even accidentally, then she was dead. "Stay right there. Don't make me kill you."

FIFTY

"I'm sorry, Mateo," the voice mumbled. "I'm sorry. So, so sorry."

Over and over, it repeated in the darkness. There was an almost hypnotic quality about it. He felt himself drifting through an endless vacuum, the only constant being the voice and its endless apology.

The universe trembled. As it settled, a sharp pain jabbed him in the back of the neck. Another twisted through his shoulder blades.

"Forgive me. Please, forgive me."

Another jolt. This time, it felt like an earthquake, and the back of his head cracked against something hard. The blackness was replaced with a white flash that faded as quickly as it had appeared. But not into blackness.

Into gloom.

His eyes were only open a crack. As his eyelids widened, they let more light in. At least, his left did. His right wasn't opening fully. It felt swollen and thick. His eyelashes were crusted together.

Blood?

He shifted his head slowly. He couldn't move it far. His chin was pinned to his chest and there was something heavy against the back of his head.

Where am I?

Once again the world quivered. He tried to reach out and steady himself but found that his arms—his wrists—were pinned together. So were his legs.

Car. I'm in a car.

Gideon's eyes swiveled left and right as the rest of his consciousness returned. He saw that he was in the back seat of a car. The middle seat belt was looped around his waist. His ankles were bound with what looked like a length of rope, and he was lying on his arms and wrists.

They must be tied behind my back.

It took a little longer for the memories of what had happened to filter back. There was so much chaos. He hadn't seen his attacker until it was too late. He must've been knocked cold. Now he was here.

He glanced to his left and saw that a man was sitting in the driver's seat of the car. His fingers were wrapped around a cell phone, but the screen was black. He wasn't talking to anyone.

Just himself.

"Forgive me. Forgive me."

Finally, the driver looked at the phone. The screen burst into life, almost blinding Gideon. He squeezed his eyes into slits, as much to avoid discovery as to shield his eyesight. Only a tiny chink of vision remained. Enough to see the driver typing a phone number into the dial pad. He punched the call button and placed the phone to his ear, still mumbling the same mantra.

"It's me," he said a moment later. In truth, it sounded like another person was speaking entirely. This voice was hard and matter-of-fact. "I have him. I'm bringing him in."

A pause.

"Can't kill him. Won't. I told you, I'm bringing him in!"

Gideon's face crinkled with confusion. It sounded like his kidnapper had been ordered to simply kill him. Then why the hell was he refusing? The man had been part of a team that cut through the Faithless camp without remorse or conscience. How many innocent people had been killed by their hands?

A lump formed in his throat as he remembered the horror and destruction. His memory still wasn't functioning fully after the blow to his head. It reminded him of the weeks—months—of his recovery at the château in France.

What about Zara?

Gideon squeezed his eyes shut as the pain of the thought cut through him. Was she alive? Or just another of the Brotherhood's victims. Another person dead because of the misfortune of his birth.

"I fucking told you," the man up front yelled, the sudden explosion of sound pulling Gideon back to the present. "You kill him. I won't. Now fuck off."

Without pausing, he rolled down the window and tossed the phone onto the road. Warm air buffeted Gideon's thick hair for several seconds before the window mechanism smoothly rolled back up.

And then there was only silence. Gideon tried to shift his position subtly to get a glimpse of his kidnapper's identity, but it was impossible. He was still groggy from the attack that had knocked him unconscious and didn't have the strength to manipulate his bound body.

In the end, it didn't matter.

"I know you're awake," the man said, a familiar accent creeping into his voice. "I can hear you back there."

Gideon's eyes went wide. He'd heard that voice before.

And that time he'd barely escaped with his life.

FIFTY-ONE

For a long time, Zara stayed perfectly still. Every fiber of her being was screaming at her to turn tail and run. Hell, she didn't even have to do that. Just a couple of steps to the left, and Eli would have a clear shot. Jamie would have a bullet through his forehead before he had time to blink.

Nobody on this isolated forest track would lose a second's sleep over his fate. Most would cheer it. He'd betrayed them. Stolen the lives of some of their dearest friends.

And yet Zara couldn't let it happen. This wasn't altruism. She didn't see in Jamie something that could be fixed, or at least that wasn't why she was intervening.

He held the key to New Eden.

Maybe even to saving Gideon.

Zara felt her heart rate slow to the point where she could practically count out the beats. At the same time, her brain seemed to slip into high gear, fueled by the adrenaline pumping through her system.

Jamie's scared. He's guilty. He's responsible for a dozen

deaths. But he didn't actually pull the trigger to kill them. Didn't help the attackers. He doesn't have it in him.

She held her breath. This was one hell of a gamble. If she was wrong, then it was over. But maybe this was her penance for the two dead agents in Marseilles. Two families had lost a son, a father, and a brother because of her.

It was time to pay it forward.

Zara stepped forward with unexpected confidence, bringing her arm up to reach for the gun at the same time. The movement seemed to take Jamie by surprise. He took a step back. Her hyper-focused senses saw his finger twitch on the trigger, braced for the inevitable impact of bullets punching through her flesh.

It didn't come.

Jamie brought the pistol up, his arm trembling. At the last second he switched his aim to his own head. He pressed the muzzle hard against his temple, hard enough that his neck tilted to the left. His finger was twined around the trigger. It wouldn't take more than another ounce, maybe even less than that for the hammer to strike, the powder to ignite, and a few grams of metal to rocket down the barrel and through his skull.

"What's your brother's name, Jamie?" Zara said softly.

"Get away from me," he yelled back.

She closed so they were face-to-face. Made him stare her directly in the eye and showed him that she wasn't going anywhere. If he was going to pull the trigger, then he had to face her as he did it.

"Is this what he would want for you?"

"He'd be ashamed of me," Jamie said, his face contorted with grief and guilt.

"No. He'd understand," Zara said, subtly shifting her balance onto the balls of her feet. She was perfectly poised now. "Can you do something for me, Jamie?"

He replied through gritted teeth. "What?"

"Close your eyes. Picture his face. Ask yourself what he'd really want you to do."

At first, Jamie stared back at her, his eyes wide, a vein popping on his right temple where gunmetal was cutting off the blood flow. Then his eyelids fluttered. Only for a second.

Then a little longer. Zara held her breath.

The second they closed for good, she pitched forward and hooked her fingers around his forearm. The second she felt the warmth of his skin, she tugged back and pulled the pistol away from his temple. It went high above his head, slipped from his grasp entirely, and tumbled into a dark, muddy puddle.

Jamie spun around from the unexpected force of her intervention. Before he'd regained his balance, Eli whipped past Zara and tackled him to the ground. Someone scooped up his discarded weapon before ejecting the chambered round and dumping the magazine onto the ground.

"I need him alive!" she yelled, louder than she would have believed possible as Eli climbed onto Jamie's back and reached for his wrists. More softly, she added, "We all do."

FIFTY-TWO

The safe house was an old farmhouse situated on about ten acres of untilled farmland that had gone to seed many years before. The corrugated iron roof of the adjoining hay barn was rusted through, and there were holes in the wooden slats that formed its walls.

The main building, however, was functional. There was no electricity or heating, but there was a gas range fed by a cylinder that rested against the outside wall.

"Somebody comes by every few months just to check it hasn't fallen down," Eli explained when the Faithless convoy arrived. "And to make sure the cache of weapons in the basement is still right where it's supposed to be."

Lachlan immediately disappeared upstairs. He was lost in his grief. So Zara had Jamie taken to the barn, where he was lashed by the wrists and ankles to a wooden chair. Francis volunteered himself to stand watch.

The prisoner's eyes were wild with madness as he was dragged off, and Zara felt a flicker of discomfort at the psychological damage his treatment was doubtless inflicting on him.

But actions had consequences. All the surviving Faithless had made the trek from Georgia. Many of them were sufficiently fit —and armed—so that even with gunshot wounds, they would be capable of limping across the overgrown field to the barn.

Knotted, thorny undergrowth might slow them down. But loss was a hell of a motivation. And the survivors had that in spades.

"We can patch up most of the gunshot wounds without surgery," Eli said. He pointed toward a woman wearing blue nitrile gloves. "Katy was a med student. She's been our house doc for a couple years. It's not her first rodeo."

"What about medical supplies?"

"We're good," Eli said. "Might run out of IV bags in a couple days, but hopefully we won't need them by then."

Zara ran her hands over her face. She was exhausted. A couple of hours' sleep the previous night wasn't nearly enough to deal with the challenges that today had thrown her way. She exhaled and felt Eli's unblinking gaze on her.

"You want to know why I needed him alive, don't you?"

He nodded.

"Tell me how many combat-effective shooters you have left."

"There's me," Eli said, counting on his fingers. "Francis. Aidan, Finn, Caleb and Isaac."

"I count six," Zara said. "But I never was any good at math."

"That's right."

Zara raised her eyebrows and spoke as plainly as she could. "Then the assault plan's fucked. Nearly fifty innocent people are going to die a couple days from now. There's no way we can bust them out. Not like we intended."

"You want to use him, don't you?"

She nodded. The weight of her newfound responsibilities pushed down on her. It felt like a dump truck had revved up onto her chest and was just sitting there. "His handlers must trust him. Especially now, after—what happened. We can turn that to our advantage."

I'm just not sure how.

Perhaps that final thought was visible on her face because Eli reached out and squeezed her arm. "I'll come with."

Zara nodded but didn't move. The ground floor of the rickety farmhouse was overcome by a kind of semiorganized chaos. The largest room had become a makeshift hospital ward. Folded blankets, towels, and even curtains on the floor served as beds. IV bags were slung over wooden chairs, plastic tubing hanging from them like electric cabling. A man whose name she didn't remember had pulled up a coffee table to the window to the right of the front door. His left leg was swathed in bandages, but he was sitting on the table, keeping watch on the front entrance. A rifle leaned against the wall in front of him.

I should know what's wrong with him.

A flash of emotion overcame her as she slowly turned her neck to take in the entire scene. It was a combination of terror and irritation—the former a natural reaction to being thrust into a position of power. The latter was aimed at Lachlan. It was his fault she was in this place in the first place. Not that she could exactly blame him.

This isn't easy for anyone, she thought. It was as much self-reproach as it was a reminder to give herself some grace.

"Zara?"

For a moment she thought she'd imagined Lachlan's voice. It wouldn't be a surprise if she was borderline hallucinatory from stress, lack of sleep, and the effects of the ball of worry about Gideon's fate that was compressing her lungs.

She turned to see him standing at the base of the creaking wooden stairwell that led to the second floor. He was holding a cell phone in his left hand. His face was still drained of color, but at least he was on his feet.

And talking.

"What is it?"

He beckoned her toward him, then pointed up the stairs. "In private."

She followed him up with a slight frown on her face, half-expecting that he was going to drop another problem onto her plate.

The second story of the farmhouse was as empty as the first. Dust caked the floorboards, a quarter inch thick. Mites of it swirled in the scattered rays of sunshine that broke through the shuttered windows. The clouds grew thicker as they disturbed more and more with every step.

Lachlan guided Zara into a gloomy bedroom and closed the door behind them. He glanced around, though only a poltergeist could have slipped inside without either of them noticing. He turned back to her when he was fully satisfied, but he still spoke in a hushed tone. "I got a call."

"From?"

"One of our last surviving assets inside New Eden. His name is Marcus Bennett. He's reliable. I'd trust him with my life."

Zara raised her eyebrows. This was an interesting development, but she had a thousand larger problems to contend with right now. "And?"

"He was contacted by Gideon's sister. Someone working with Julia, anyway. She wants out."

Frowning, Zara asked, "What changed? A month ago she held a gun to her brother's head."

"She's pregnant."

Zara's mouth formed an O before she closed it again, momentarily lost for words. *That would do it.*

"What does she want from us?" she asked guardedly. After the previous night's events, she was far from ready to rule out the possibility that this was another trap. Lachlan had presumably trusted Jamie, too.

And how did that work out?

"That's exactly it," Lachlan said, speaking quickly now. This was the first time that Zara had seen a spark in his eyes since Harriet's death. Even now it faded quickly, burning as brief and bright as a shooting star. "She didn't ask us to help her get out."

"I don't understand."

"She knows where the prisoners are being held. And she has access to them. This could be the break we've been searching for."

FIFTY-THREE

Gideon stared at the Butcher's eyes in the rearview mirror. His own gaze contained hate and not a little fear. The man in the driver's seat had very nearly killed him. Another inch, and a knife blade could have slipped between his ribs.

Game over.

The Butcher spoke in a vaguely hollow tone. He displayed none of the triumphalism that Gideon had expected. If anything, he sounded almost pleading. "You can talk. I'm not going to hurt you for that. But I may as well tell you my name. It's Eduardo. Eduardo Salazar."

Gideon maintained his stare, attempting to discern what was running through his captor's head through his eyes. Salazar scarcely glanced at the road ahead.

Why does he want me to know who he is?

"Water," he finally croaked. It wasn't an act—or at least it wasn't completely an act. His mouth was gripped by a punishing thirst. His tongue raked like sandpaper against the top of his mouth every time he closed his lips.

A grimace pinched Salazar's face. "Later. We can't stop here."

Gideon let his head fall back against the hard plastic of the car door. He closed his eyes. "Fine," he whispered. "Then no talking."

Salazar clearly suspected that his request was a ruse to give Gideon an opening to try and escape. He wasn't wrong that Gideon harbored such a desire. But as he lay back against the seat, all he could think about was the beginnings of a pulsating headache that felt like it was bouncing between his right and left temples. The sticky coating of dried blood on his cheek was beginning to itch, and the nerves in his bound shoulders and arms had long since gone dead.

The truth was, he was in no shape for a fight. He probably couldn't grapple with a toddler right now, let alone a hardened psychopath like Salazar.

"Say something!" Salazar demanded petulantly. He slapped his palm against the steering wheel and the horn briefly squealed. "Don't just lie there."

A debilitating tiredness gripped Gideon between the pulses of pain. Abstractly, he recognized the symptoms of both dehydration and at least a mild concussion. Each condition was probably increasing the severity of the other.

"Talk to yourself, asshole," Gideon grunted, grimacing from the pain. "It didn't seem to be a problem before I woke up."

A prolonged silence followed this response. Gideon concentrated on his breathing to distract himself from the pain. In, one—two—three—four. Out, one—two—three—four.

In—

Gideon's eyes snapped open as he sensed the car's movement change. It slowed—at first gently, then suddenly, before Salazar turned toward the side of the road. He flinched at the sound of gravel bouncing off the SUV's chassis. In his prone position, it sounded way closer than normal. Then a crunching sound as Salazar braked.

He kept his eyes open but said nothing as Salazar climbed out of the car. Gideon tried to track his kidnapper as best he could, but when Salazar walked around his side of the vehicle, it was impossible to twist his neck enough to follow. He swallowed and once again tested his bound wrists. The slight movement pushed a spearing wave of pain up his spine. It hurt enough to bring tears to his eyes.

There was no way to escape. And even if he could slip his restraints, he was clearly in no fit state to fight. His breathing grew shallow and panicked as Salazar trudged around to the SUV's trunk and popped it. The entire vehicle jolted as the sicario pushed it up to speed its opening.

An alarm signal jangled in Gideon's mind, as if some ancient, primordial section of the brain was taking charge. Electrical signals charged down damaged pathways, making the signal echo louder and louder in his head.

Salazar made rustling sounds as he rummaged through the trunk. He still hadn't spoken since Gideon insulted him. Maybe making the homicidal psychopath mad hadn't exactly been his smartest decision.

Gideon searched through his options. Fight was definitely out. Flight, too. Even if he could get out of the car, could he run with his arms bound behind his back? Definitely not quickly enough to outsprint a bullet.

That left only one: begging for his life.

Fuck that.

It probably wasn't well adjusted of him, but he decided that if he was going to die, he would do it like a man.

The trunk slammed shut. Salazar's soles scrunched against the gravel of the pull-off. The rear door swung open, and Gideon's head fell back into nothing.

"Don't do anything stupid," Salazar muttered.

He reached over Gideon, his crotch unsettlingly close to his face as he unbuckled the metal belt. As the mechanism retracted, he pulled Gideon into an upright, seated position.

Gideon continued to watch his captor warily. The earlier panic still tugged at his chest, but he was no longer getting the sense that he was in immediate danger. If Salazar had wanted to punish him, then a simple punch to the ribs or groin would have worked just as well. This was something else.

The Mexican leaned over and plucked something off the ground outside. Gideon's eyes went wide with longing as he saw that it was a bottle of water. Salazar twisted off the cap and lifted it slowly to Gideon's lips, tipping the transparent cylinder up until a flow of brackish water trickled into his mouth and down his throat.

It tasted as sweet as anything he'd ever drunk.

"Thanks," Gideon said cautiously when he'd had his fill. He worked his way through almost the entire bottle. The liquid sat uneasily in his stomach.

Salazar said nothing. His gaze narrowed as he stared at Gideon for a few seconds, then it returned to normal as if he'd made a decision. He drew a knife from a small sheath at his waist. The blade was only three or four inches in length—a utility tool, not the machete Gideon had seen him wielding before.

"Call that a knife?" Gideon said, still feeling dizzy, almost drunk from the blow to the head.

"Don't make me hurt you," Salazar said. He grabbed him by the shoulder and pulled him forward. Trying to crane his neck to see what was happening was useless. It was only when —his heart pounding in his chest—he heard a slight snick that he realized what was happening.

Salazar was cutting his hands free.

The blade made short work of the rope around his wrists. Gideon barely felt any resistance as it sliced through the final tendrils. He was careful not to jerk his hands away, just in case they got cut.

Not that he had much choice in the matter. The second his wrists parted and the increased movement allowed even a trickle of blood into limbs starved of it, every nerve in his shoulders, arms, and hands seemed to wake up at once. He groaned involuntarily from the agony that followed, but it distracted him from the pain that was still compressing his skull.

"Hands on your lap," Salazar said, backing away a step and gesturing with the knife.

It took a while for Gideon to comply. He didn't have much control over his body right now. When it was done, Salazar cut a new length of rope and knotted it firmly around his wrists, then played a length out and looped it around one of the headrests. Gideon watched curiously as the tingling faded from his arms.

Salazar's plan became clear when he pulled the rope down and tied the end around the restraints that bound Gideon's wrists.

"Try and touch your toes," he ordered.

Gideon did as he was instructed. He was able to reach down about half a foot before the section of rope looped around the headrest went taut. Jackknifing his ankles upward didn't allow him to get anywhere near close enough to try and untie himself, either.

"Neat trick," Gideon muttered.

Salazar tossed another bottle of water onto the back seat, along with a couple of energy bars. Gideon realized that he was able to reach for the bottle, unscrew the lid, and lift it to his lips without the rope preventing him. Any attempt at escape, however, was impossible.

"Now you talk," Salazar said. He eyed Gideon hungrily for several long seconds before slamming the rear door shut and returning to the driver's seat.

Gideon sat for several seconds and just blinked.

What the hell is going on?

Despite his demand, Salazar said nothing for the next ten minutes. The break was long enough for the first wave of fluids to pass through Gideon's large intestine into his blood. The effect was almost instantaneous. The most acute pain—like a rusty saw being dragged deliberately across his gray matter—faded into a dull, manageable ache. Even his exhaustion grew less intense.

Gideon inhaled one of the energy bars. He wanted both, but since he had no idea where his next meal was coming from, he played it safe. The calories flooded his system almost as quickly. The combination of both fluids and energy had him thinking straight for the first time since he opened his eyes.

Finally, Salazar opened his mouth. "Tell me about yourself," he said.

The first thought that crossed Gideon's mind was: *What the hell?*

"Is this a kidnapping or a therapy session?" he asked.

"Either we talk, or I tape your mouth shut. Your choice."

Salazar's tone was unyielding, but Gideon didn't believe he meant it. There was an almost yearning undertone to the man's voice. He wanted to speak to him. Perhaps needed to.

Why?

He decided to play along. "What do you want to know?"

"What were you doing with the traitors?"

"The Faithless?"

"Yes."

"Your buddies tried to kill me." Gideon shrugged. He regretted the motion an instant later as it released a formerly unknown knot of tension between his shoulder blades. "The Faithless helped me escape. I prefer the people who don't try and murder me to the ones who do."

"They're not my friends," Salazar snapped.

"At least you got that going for you," Gideon said. "Your turn."

"What?"

"To tell me something about yourself. Fair's fair." He paused, wondering how far he should push this. "Why don't you start with who you were talking to before?"

Salazar glanced up at the rearview mirror. Now that Gideon was upright, it was easier to match his gaze. Easier to read it, too. He didn't look like a hardened killer right now. He looked...

Lost.

The Mexican blinked rapidly as if processing a wave of thoughts or memories. Maybe both. Once again he fell silent, and Gideon wondered if he was going to reply at all. When he did, it was like a dam had broken inside his skull. He couldn't stop.

"My son," Salazar said, his voice breathy and anguished. "He's been dead a long time. But he's the only one who listens."

Gideon wasn't exactly sure how to play this. When he'd called this a therapy session, he was joking. Now he wasn't so sure.

"How did he die?"

"Murdered," Salazar said. "Because he was my son. A rival cartel took him to make a point. They killed him as easily as snapping a chicken's neck. And they filmed it so that I could watch."

FIFTY-FOUR

Francis jumped to his feet as Zara approached the barn Jamie was being held in. His face was haggard, bearing the effects of too little sleep and too long since his last shave. He was in the valley of death between a handsome five o'clock shadow and a full-on beard.

Still, he wasn't here for his looks.

Zara came alone. Eli was needed elsewhere to prepare the farmhouse's defenses. By the time she left, he had a production line going—filling empty burlap sandbags that somebody with more foresight than Zara knew she possessed had stored in the basement for a time just like this.

There was no sand, exactly, but two of the uninjured Faithless shooters were digging a hole to China as the walking wounded shoveled the moved earth into the actual bags.

"You good?" Francis said by way of greeting.

Zara nodded. Lachlan's revelation that Gideon's sister had —potentially—come over to their side had temporarily washed away her exhaustion. According to Marcus, the source inside New Eden, Julia was helping care for the people who had been arrested. She had access to them and knew where they were being held.

The situation was no longer hopeless. It was still a devilishly tricky puzzle, but at least it had a solution. And Zara liked puzzles.

"How are you holding up?" she asked.

He shrugged. "Tired, but I'll live."

"Yeah," Zara replied softly, her thoughts once again drifting to Gideon's plight, and whether he was even still alive. Francis seemed to notice her reaction and winced, but she waved it away. "What about Jamie?"

"Awake," he replied, his tone now short, visible anger creasing his face. "He's hungry."

Zara was about to ask if he had any food on him when she paused. She wasn't thinking straight. Her position here was tenuous already. She was only in charge because they respected Lachlan. But the whole Faithless group was hurting. That trust would only carry her so far. She needed Francis's help, just like she needed support from Eli and so many others.

She reached up and touched his upper arm. "I know you're hurting. I'm angry, too. I promise you, he'll see justice. But right now we need him."

"I get it," Francis said through gritted teeth. "I just can't like it."

Zara nodded sadly. What else could she say to that?

She gestured toward the barn. "When I walk in there, I need you to cut him loose."

"No way," he replied instantly, already shaking his head. "Out of the question."

"Is he armed?"

"No. I searched him myself. That's not the point."

Zara changed tack. She gestured at the holstered pistol in Francis's thigh rig. "How's your aim?"

He replied guardedly, as if knowing she was trying to trip him up. "Good..."

"If Jamie tries anything, you have my permission to shoot him. Unload that whole magazine if you have to. But he's not going to run. And he's not going to try and hurt me."

Francis maintained eye contact but didn't protest any further. He gave Zara a peremptory nod, then turned toward the barn. He shouldered through the barn door, which creaked on rusted hinges as it swung inward. Little shards of oxidized iron coursed to the dirt floor.

As Zara followed, she caught a glimpse of their prisoner. His ankles were lashed to the front legs of a wooden chair that sat in the center of the gloomy barn. His wrists appeared to be tied behind his back. His expression was pinched, as if his restraints were causing him pain. Other than that, though, he appeared unharmed. Francis was angry, like the others, but he wasn't vindictive.

He knew his job.

Francis drew a penknife out of his right pocket and flicked it open. Jamie flinched at the sight of the blade. He pinned his lips together and closed his eyes but said nothing.

"We're not going to hurt you," Zara called out over the dull scrape of Francis sawing through the knots that bound him. "I just want to talk."

Jamie rubbed his reddened wrists but stayed seated as Francis stalked menacingly behind him. His eyes flickered left and right, but he didn't commit to actually looking around, perhaps scared of what he would see.

"Come on," Zara said from where she was standing in the open doorway. She gestured at the grassy meadow beyond. Sunlight dappled the gently swaying stalks of grass. "Let's walk together."

Jamie rose cautiously and walked toward her with an

unsteady, stiff gait. His eyes were puffy, and she guessed he'd been silently crying, a suspicion that was confirmed when he drew close enough for her to see the wet stains on his T-shirt. Mostly he stared down at the ground as if unwilling to meet her gaze.

Francis trailed at a safe distance—well within range of the pistol his fingertips now grazed, far enough away to be out of earshot.

Zara waited until the two of them were a few feet into the meadow, seed heads tickling their thighs before she spoke. "Has anybody hurt you?"

Jamie shook his head.

"Good. That's the way it's going to stay."

"What are you going to do with me?" he muttered. Zara had to strain to hear him over the gentle whisper of the breeze.

She held her tongue before answering. The truth was, she didn't know. They couldn't exactly hand him over to the police, though he surely deserved to spend the rest of his life in jail. He was an accessory before the fact to a dozen murders. And the fate of many more prisoners was directly downstream of the decision he'd taken to betray the location of the Faithless compound. She saw him glance toward her in her peripheral vision. He was nervous.

Good.

"That's up to you," she finally said.

"I don't understand."

"Are you a good person, Jamie?"

She saw him flinch at the question. It was his turn to delay his answer. Finally, "I don't think so."

"Do you believe that Gabriel is a good person?"

Jamie shook his head.

"So you didn't betray your friends because you believe in him?"

"No!"

"That's right. You did it out of love."

"Yes..." he said, his wretched, anguished tone drawing a flicker of sympathy from Zara.

"I don't think that makes you a bad person, Jamie," she said, choosing her words carefully. "It makes you an ordinary human being placed in a terrible situation with no good choices."

"Would you have sold out thirty people to save one?" Jamie hissed. His hands formed into fists. Zara sensed Francis stir behind them, and she discreetly signaled for him to relax.

"When we write our stories, nobody ever makes themselves the bad guy," she said. "But we've all done things we're not proud of."

"You've done nothing like this, have you?"

Zara closed her eyes. Once again—what was this, the ten thousandth time—she saw the scene in Marseille play out in her mind's eye. Heard the bullets puncturing the car's chassis and the two French agents falling, falling, their blood staining the sidewalk.

"You'd be surprised," she said, her voice breathy now. "Not long ago, two men died because I valued my career over doing the right thing. I promised myself I wouldn't rest until I'd done everything in my power to make amends. I don't know if anything I ever do will be enough. But I have to try."

Jamie finally looked up and matched her gaze. There was an emotion in his eyes that she couldn't quite read. Hunger?

"You want that, don't you?" she asked. "To make things right."

"Of course," he moaned, clutching his chest.

"Even if it hurts? Or hurts somebody you care for?"

His hands fell to his sides. "What are you asking from me?"

"To make amends. To help us save lives. For you to repay your debt."

Tears formed in Jamie's eyes. "You want to use me as a double agent, don't you?"

Zara nodded.

"Trent will know. And when he figures it out, he'll come for Drew. I've seen it happen before. You're asking me to sign my own brother's death warrant."

She met his gaze and dared him to look away. "No, Jamie. I'm asking you to think about what Drew would want you to do. That's all."

FIFTY-FIVE

"Mateo was a good kid, man," Salazar said, looking up at the rearview mirror for—what—reassurance? Gideon wasn't sure. Maybe it was simpler than that. Maybe Salazar had finally found someone who was willing to listen.

Not that Gideon had any other choice.

Still, the further they drove, the more he was warming to his kidnapper.

Is this how Stockholm syndrom starts? he wondered.

Salazar was an evil man; there was no doubt about that. He had probably killed more people than most of the famous American serial killers of the twentieth century. And that was before his employer became the Brotherhood.

By his telling, at least, he'd never killed innocent women and children. He had his own moral code. Only the guilty died by his hand. It's just that the definition of "guilty" was extremely flexible. When he was younger, guilt was usually determined by the highest bidder.

"Everything changed after he died, right?" Gideon said. He'd given up working his restraints with his fingers. The skin between them was rubbed raw from trying. Salazar knew how to tie a knot. You didn't survive as long in his line of work as he had by being sloppy.

"Yeah. Shit, I don't know why I am telling you any of this."

Gideon did. He'd seen this kind of thing before with men who'd faced combat. You could only push the human mind so far before it broke. Some people retreated in on themselves, became shells of what they once were. Others just wanted to talk. And talk. And talk.

Salazar clearly belonged to the latter camp. The brakes restraining his train of thought had long since failed. And he had a lifetime of pain to get off his chest.

"Because you're done," Gideon said. "I heard you on the phone. You're done killing. Done sacrificing yourself for people who don't give a shit about you. Done setting yourself on fire to keep others warm."

Gideon maintained eye contact with Salazar in the rearview mirror. His own face was a mask, unlike his driver's. He felt pity for what the man had experienced in his life. Given where he was born, the only two paths that lay open to him were to become either predator or prey. Could Gideon blame him for choosing the former?

The way Salazar told it, all the killing back in his hometown was for a purpose. He didn't go in for muscle cars or gold jewelry. Definitely didn't dabble in the cartel's product. Other young men did, and they usually didn't live to see their twenty-fifth birthday. He had a different head on his shoulders. He saved every penny he earned from every contract he fulfilled. He was going to get himself out.

And then men came for his son in the middle of the night. And everything changed.

"If I do that," Salazar asked. "What am I?"

After that he fell silent. His gaze returned to the road, and even his breathing steadied and became even and rhythmic. It was as if he was lost deep in thought.

At least, Gideon hoped he was. Because the alternative was far darker. If Salazar was just a mindless killer, then there was nothing holding him back from doing to his passenger what he did best.

He tried to look at the fuel gauge. They'd been driving for hours. He guessed that the SUV was probably fully topped up with gasoline when they left the burning compound. But it had to be running low by now. He could just make out the needle, but it was too dark to see which direction it pointed in.

Gideon gave up. He closed his own eyes and replayed the story he'd been told.

After Mateo died, Salazar washed his hands of the cartels. He traveled north, crossing the Rio Grande under his own steam. Nobody stopped him, so he kept on going.

He'd saved a lot of money while doing his bosses' dirty work. But for the first time in his life, he started to drink. And then he didn't stop. Not until he'd drained every cent in his bank account and every nickel in his pockets. After that, he did what he had to do to fuel his addiction. Even untrained, carrying thirty pounds of alcohol weight, few people resisted handing over their wallets and phones when he came knocking. And then he drank their savings too and didn't stop until he hit rock bottom.

That was where a Brotherhood missionary had found him. They picked him up out of the gutter like dozens of other broken things each year and drove him to Texas with the promise of a new life. Of forgiveness.

"I see it now," Salazar had hissed before he fell silent. *"He never gave a shit about helping me. He's just like the narcos back home. All that matters to him is money and power. No matter who gets hurt on the way."*

A man like Father Gabriel was never going to allow Eduardo Salazar to heal. For an organization like the Brotherhood, his appearance must have been like a gift from heaven. Why simply forgive his sins when you could wield him as a weapon of your own?

Why not make him work for his salvation?

But Salazar had hit rock bottom once before. Then it was grief and alcohol and whatever drugs he could get his hands on. This time was far more serious. His mind was beginning to rebel. To break.

And there was no turning back from this.

Gideon felt pity for his driver. Felt sorrow for the tale he'd spun. He'd lived a life more horrible than most could even imagine. But that didn't mean he would hesitate to take the man's life if he was given the chance. Maybe it wasn't Gideon's responsibility to give all of Salazar's victims justice. Maybe it would be better if he was arrested, charged, and tried, and spent the rest of his life in jail.

At least that way, the families of his victims would know that justice had been served.

But that outcome wasn't on offer. Gideon could only play the cards he was dealt, and all he knew was that his captor was teetering on the very edge of sanity. The only question remaining was which way he'd fall.

And which of them would survive when he did.

FIFTY-SIX

"We need gas," Salazar said. It was about half an hour since he'd last said anything.

Gideon was growing increasingly concerned that Salazar was on the verge of passing out. It was difficult to catch a glimpse of the man's face in any of the reflections he could see, but on every occasion he did, it looked like his eyes were half-closed. His yawns were growing louder and longer, and twice he veered into the oncoming lane before jerking the wheel back to center.

A mile farther up the road a gas station's sign loomed. As they turned in to fill up, Gideon saw that the lot also housed a single-story motel.

"You need rest," he said.

"Just gas. We keep going."

"Lock me in the trunk if you have to," Gideon said, raising his wrists so that Salazar could see his bound hands in the rearview mirror. "Tape my mouth like you threatened. I'm not going anywhere. But if you don't get some sleep, you're going to drive us both off the road. I don't want to burn to death in this tin can because you lashed my ankles to the headrest."

The strength of the statement seemed to sway Salazar. Perhaps Gideon's argument benefited from the fact that even as he was speaking, Salazar's hand covered yet another yawn.

The sicario brought the car to a near-stop. The motel was to their left, the gas pumps straight ahead. Gideon held his breath but said nothing.

Has to be his decision.

Unlike his captor, Gideon was wired with nervous energy. Perhaps it had something to do with the fact that he was the prey in this equation. Salazar's hunger was already sated. But just because Gideon was frozen in place didn't mean his legs weren't primed to run the second he got the opportunity.

He faked a yawn of his own. Didn't dogs do that to demonstrate they didn't pose a threat? The evolutionary psychology made sense to him. Sleepy people didn't usually beat one another to death.

Salazar's lips briefly pursed and made a kissing sound before he twisted the wheel to the left and guided the SUV into a parking bay. He put the vehicle into park but didn't kill the engine as he thoroughly studied their surroundings, checking all three mirrors and twisting in his seat to look out of every window.

Gideon consciously avoided doing the same, though as far as he could see through his peripheral vision, there were no pedestrians in sight. Just a couple of cars at the gas pumps thirty yards away. He faked another yawn and rubbed his head injury. The wince that followed was anything but fake.

"I'm going to get us a room," Salazar said over the low rumble of the engine as he fixed Gideon with a cold stare. Gideon felt a chill run down his spine at the sight. His captor might be wavering, but the devil in him was still there.

Gideon raised his eyebrows. "Guess I'll just sit tight."

Salazar looked down at his own clothes and muttered, "Shit."

He unbuckled his belt and unclipped the chest rig before tossing it in the passenger footwell. The pistol holster followed, though he stuffed the weapon into his belt loop. When he was done, he twisted and checked their surroundings once again before climbing out of the car.

Instead of heading for the motel's front office, he walked around to the SUV's trunk and popped it. Gideon watched him pull off his bloodstained fatigue jacket and toss it into the back. He leaned forward and rummaged through the supplies. A moment later, he unfurled an army-green military surplus rain poncho and slipped it over his head.

Salazar closed the trunk, then opened the door next to Gideon. His outfit looked ridiculous in the blazing Georgia sunshine. Bloodstains were still visible on his pants, but only because Gideon knew what they were. He lifted the poncho up above his belt line and flashed the pistol's grip to his prisoner.

"Do you know what will happen if you try and call for help?"

"I won't."

"I'll put a bullet between the eyes of the front desk clerk. Then I'll kill anyone I see you talking to. And then it's your turn."

"Noted," Gideon said with as much equanimity as he could muster. He'd met a lot of dangerous men in his life, but this one was head and shoulders above the rest. And this was the kinder, gentler version of Eduardo Salazar. The one who said he didn't want to kill anymore.

Guess there's nothing rational about a mental breakdown.

Salazar nodded peremptorily, then closed and locked the door. The SUV's windows were tinted, so a casual observer would have to get pretty close to notice Gideon's restraints, and there were no other cars parked within view.

He returned after a delay of about five minutes and unlocked the door, room keys in hand. He was smiling now, as if mentally relishing the break. His earlier threats seemed to have disappeared like clouds in a summer squall.

"Room twelve," he said as he leaned over Gideon and loosened the knots around his ankles. "Don't worry, I got us twin beds."

Gideon couldn't help sighing as the tension that had forced his ankle joints to grind against each other faded. He wanted to laugh at Salazar's comment. This was fast becoming a buddy comedy.

Except Salazar really would kill him.

Salazar pulled back, and Gideon gestured at his bound wrists. "What are we going to do about these?"

The hitman chewed his lip, then pulled the poncho up and over his head. "Put this on."

Gideon did as he was told. The process of pulling the thick canvas material over his head and shoulders with his hands lashed together was unwieldy, but he managed in the end. After he climbed out of the vehicle, he saw that the poncho dipped past his waist, covering his hands entirely.

"Pull up the loose rope," Salazar instructed.

"Got it," Gideon replied. He took several deep breaths to flood his lungs and bloodstream with oxygen. Salazar was starting to look demob happy, like this was the end of the road. He was more distracted than Gideon had seen him before.

I'm only going to get one shot at this, Gideon realized. Once this break was over, Salazar wouldn't stop again. And then it was New Eden and certain death—unless he could talk him out of it. But that was a whole lot of trust to place in a psychopath's spiral ending up in the wrong place.

He stretched tense muscles as he climbed out of the car.

"Two yards ahead of me," Salazar instructed. "Walk slowly."

He didn't flash the pistol again, but Gideon knew it was there. Knew that he'd be able to draw it quicker than he could turn and knock him down.

So Gideon walked exactly as expected, pausing only long enough to scan for the arrow that pointed to rooms 6 to 12. On the surface, he was anything but a threat, dragging his feet and hunching forward to emphasize his exhaustion.

Underneath the poncho, he fashioned a length of the rope into a noose. He held the end of the loop in his left.

"Stop there," Salazar said when they reached the room. "Where I can see you."

Gideon nodded. He leaned against the wall to the right-hand side of the door. It hinged on the left and would swing inward. He shifted his weight onto the balls of his feet and turned his knees and hips just an inch. Subtle enough to remain unnoticed but sufficient to buy him a fraction of a second.

Salazar inserted the old-school key into the lock. The tumblers clicked as he twisted and pushed the door, taking a half-step forward as he did so to maintain his balance. He turned his head to beckon Gideon in.

And that's when he pounced.

Gideon drove all of his weight and power through his right foot, pushing himself up and into the air. At the same time, he brought his hands up, pushing the canvas poncho aside. Salazar's eyes widened, and he threw up his arms in a defensive posture.

But not quickly enough. Gideon looped the length of rope around the hitman's neck, and the second his toes touched back down to earth, he twisted around Salazar and darted into the motel room. The sudden attack clearly took his captor by surprise. He was still looking the wrong way when Gideon was already beyond him.

Salazar gutturally gasped for air as the makeshift noose tightened around his windpipe. Gideon glanced over his shoulder for just a second as he brought his hands up and rested them above his left pectoral. He saw the rope cutting into his captor's Adam's apple. The man's eyes bulged wide as a combination of shock and fear smashed into him.

Gideon didn't hesitate to press his advantage. He drove forward, his body angled like an Olympic sprinter powering out of the blocks, both hands clenched around the rope in his hands. The entwined fibers burned the skin of his palms, but the unexpected forward movement dragged Salazar off his feet.

"Ungh," Gideon grunted as the man's full weight pulled the noose taut. He kept sprinting forward, though the anchor he was pulling meant that he was actually moving in slow motion.

Salazar's feet scrabbled for purchase on the floor. Gideon felt the man's hands reach for his neck, then bat ineffectually at the back of his head. Fingernails scratched down the side of his cheeks as Gideon dove for the bathroom door.

The floor underneath his feet was a wood-effect vinyl covered in a cheap Persian-pattern rug. The rug slipped underneath him and sent him crashing to the ground, face first. The momentary relaxation of tension might have bought Salazar a second to react if he'd fallen in any other direction, but falling forward meant he maintained his pressure on the rope.

Gideon punched the floor with his nose. Despite the white flash of pain that followed and the smear of blood that trickled down his chin, he didn't stop. He rolled onto his back, twisted underneath the rope, and kicked out so the soles of his sneakers rested on Salazar's shoulders.

The man lay on his front, jerking spasmodically like a dying rat. His eyes were bulging from their sockets and his face was beet-read. One hand scrabbled uselessly at the noose. Gideon raised himself up into a rowing position, pulling at the rope for leverage and causing it to tighten even further around Salazar's neck. He could see the man's eyes beginning to close as his brain grew starved of oxygen. His hands, his biceps, his back, everything burned.

Just another few seconds...

But Gideon didn't have them. Salazar's other hand—his left—appeared out of nowhere. Gideon's eyes tracked on the muzzle of the pistol he was holding.

"Shit," he swore. For an instant, he failed to react, eyes locked onto the weapon that was about to end his life.

And then he chose the only path open to him. He relaxed his grip on Salazar's neck so that the noose went slack around his throat. The man's autonomic nervous system took over, and he sucked in a deep, wheezing gasp of desperately needed air. The arm with the pistol twitched in midair.

Gideon tightened the noose once again and pulled with all his strength, pushing through his left foot and his left foot alone. Salazar's gun hand swayed in the air like a balloon on a string as he tried to take aim. Gideon's eyes fixated on the weapon. He was only going to get one shot at this.

Now!

Gideon collapsed his load-bearing left knee and dragged himself toward Salazar with the rope. The rug slipped easily underneath him and sped him along. He kicked out with the toe of his right sneaker, twisting and angling his hip like a soccer player in a last-minute defensive challenge and drove the kick forward with all his strength.

His foot collided with the pistol, and the force of the blow broke it free from Salazar's grip. It skittered along the ground but thankfully didn't misfire. Gideon last saw it disappearing under the left of the two promised twin beds.

His ass was now only half a foot from Salazar's head, which meant he no longer had the man's shoulders to use as a convenient shelf to push off from. His heels and toes scrabbled for purchase but slipped uselessly off Salazar's front.

Uh oh.

The noose was still tight around Salazar's neck, but not like it was before. It was loose enough for him to breathe. Not freely, but enough. And the combination of adrenaline and fresh reserves of energy that now had to be flooding through the hitman's body began to tell.

Salazar lashed wildly out and landed a blow into Gideon's side. From his prone position, it was difficult to generate much momentum, but even so, the force of the strike winded Gideon slightly. The hitman switched up strategies and grabbed hold of the rope with both hands. It had just enough slack in it to turn this from an execution into a tug-of-war.

And it was one Gideon was certain he wasn't going to win. He was on his side now, rather than his back, awkwardly straddling the rope. He no longer had either purchase or leverage.

And Salazar was stronger.

The two men grunted and hissed as they wrestled silently on the floor of the motel room. Warm air gusted into the cool room, and car engines rumbled on the road outside. Still, nobody appeared to have noticed the commotion just a few feet away from the gas station.

Gideon quickly understood that he was going to lose this battle. Salazar was heavier, and he no longer had the advantage of surprise. In about thirty seconds or so, the man's greater bulk would start to tell. It was time for Plan B.

For a second time, Gideon relinquished his grip on the rope. He scrambled forward, toward the bed, toward the little black silhouette he could see in the three-inch gap between the base and the floor. He thrust his hand inside, and his fingers closed around the grip of the pistol.

Any second now, Salazar was going to yank him back, use the other end of the rope that was still lashed around his wrists to throw off his aim. He needed to pull the trigger before the hitman had the chance.

Gideon twisted onto his back, holding the pistol in a double-handed grip and tugging against the rope to buy himself a little slack as he took aim. Just enough to—

He blinked. Instead of seeing Salazar lurching toward him, he saw the opposite. His opponent was instead slowly, ponderously pulling himself up onto his knees. As Gideon watched, he interlocked his fingers behind his head.

"Do it," he muttered. "Get it over with."

FIFTY-SEVEN

Gideon's chest heaved from the intensity of the wrestling bout he'd just engaged in. He eyed Salazar warily as he kicked out his feet to push his back up the side of the bed. Getting into a seated position without being able to use his hands was awkward, but he really didn't want to lose his grip on the pistol right now.

He glanced at the open doorway for a fraction of a second before returning his attention to Salazar's still-red face. A deep purple welt had already formed into a necklace around his throat. He wheezed as he breathed, perhaps as a result of damage to his windpipe.

"What are you doing?" Gideon asked, his own brain only running at half speed as he replaced the oxygen he'd burned through in the fight. This had to be a trick, right?

"I'm done," Salazar said. His voice was empty, his posture slumped. "Pull the trigger already."

Gideon calculated the distance between him and his opponent. Almost five feet. Too far for him to launch a fresh attack from his kneeling position. The reassurance allowed Gideon to reach out with his left hand and push himself upright. He sidestepped toward the door, trailing several feet of rope, and kicked it closed. Either none of the adjoining rooms were occupied or their occupants were deaf.

Salazar didn't bother tracking Gideon's movement. He just stared down at the floor. He gave every sign that he was a beaten man. But then, Gideon had played exactly the same card, hadn't he? And how had that ended for Salazar?

"Reach for the knife," Gideon instructed. "Two fingers only."

"Don't you get it?" Salazar said. "It's over. I'm done."

"Toss it over to me," Gideon repeated. "Two fingers only."

Salazar didn't move for several seconds. Finally, slowly, he reached for the small sheath on his belt—the stocky blade he'd used earlier to cut the rope—and plucked it out. He tossed it carelessly toward Gideon, who scooped it up.

"Over to the bathroom," Gideon said next, gesturing with the pistol. "On your knees."

Salazar complied with all the fight of a broken dog. His strange kneeling gait resembled a trudge more than a stride.

"Face the wall," Gideon called out. There was no mirror, so he would be out of the man's sight.

Salazar was now as far away from him as the cramped room allowed. Gideon pressed his back against the corner where the door met the wall and dropped into a crouch. He placed the gun on the floor within easy reach and twisted the knife toward his wrists so that he could slice at the rope that bound them. He kept one eye on Salazar's back the entire time, but he didn't move.

Gideon's fingers ached by the time the job was done, and two sections of rope dropped to the floor. He snapped the gun back up and massaged his right wrist with his free hand.

He slowly approached Salazar but hung back far enough to

stay clear of any surprise attack. Finally, he gave voice to the question that was at the front of his mind. "Why?"

Salazar's chin dropped to his chest. He spoke so quietly that Gideon had to cock his ear to hear the words. "Because it's time. I want to go to Mateo."

Gideon returned to the discarded rope and formed a figure-eight double-loop knot, which resembled a hanging noose with two loops instead of one. He tossed the loop end toward his new captive and instructed him to place his wrists between them, then lie flat on the floor with his bound wrists extended over his head.

"Stay still," he said as he tightened the knots around Salazar's wrists, still expecting an attack at any moment.

But none came. Salazar lay with his right cheek pressed against the vinyl floor. His eyes were closed. He was barely breathing.

Gideon backed away, playing out the main length of rope over his palm until he held the very end. He maintained a slight pressure—not enough to cut the blood flow through Salazar's wrists but sufficient that his prisoner would be incapable of surreptitiously loosening his restraints.

Not that he tried.

He kept his eyes on Salazar's prone form and didn't stop until the back of his exhausted legs bumped up against a cheap, dented table that sat between the two beds. A corded phone rested on the surface. He scooped up the handset and nestled it between his left shoulder and ear as he dialed 1 for the motel office.

It rang six times before anybody answered. When he finally heard a voice, Gideon was pretty sure the speaker was covering a yawn. "Reception?"

"Can I make an international call on this thing?"

"Yes sir. All charges will be placed on the credit card you

left on file. Just dial 9 for an outside line. Want me to advise you on our fees?"

"I'm good, thanks," Gideon said.

He pressed the handset's earpiece against the hook switch just long enough to end the call and summon a fresh dial tone. As soon as the line was active, he punched in +33—the country code for France—and a number he'd memorized weeks earlier.

This time the phone rang just twice before a familiar voice answered. "Who is this?"

"Jacques," Gideon said, closing his eyes as a wave of relief washed over him. "It's me."

"Gideon!" Jacques Leclerc's tone instantly switched from guarded to emotional. "What took you so long? I've been trying to contact you for hours. You're in danger."

Gideon's eyes flickered open as he remembered Zara mentioning that Leclerc had left them a message just before the attack on the compound. "That's right. You knew."

"GIDEON, listen to me very carefully. A contract's being advertised for immediate execution. I am not certain, but you may be in grave danger."

He snorted. "It's a bit late for that."

Leclerc said nothing for a long time. "They came for you already?"

"I'm alive. Just," Gideon answered. "Listen, Jacques, I need you to do something for me."

"What about Zara?" Leclerc said quickly, his tone anguished. "Is she well?"

Gideon's stomach clenched. He squeezed his eyes shut and tried to remember those last few chaotic seconds. Salazar and another man had sprinted toward him as he tried to hand out weapons and ammunition with which to prepare the compound's defense. Dozens of others had surrounded him, but Zara wasn't among them.

"I don't know."

Leclerc's voice steadied. He was an old pro. Business came first. "Where are you?"

"In a motel off Interstate 20, right out of Livingston, Alabama. We got separated. I need you to try and get her a message. Everything's gone to hell, but there might be a way of rescuing it. Can you do that?"

"I'll try."

FIFTY-EIGHT

Gideon's hand twitched toward the phone as a ring sounded, only to arrest the movement when he realized it was coming from another of the motel rooms. He grimaced and looked away, only to sense Salazar's close attention on him from the other side of the room.

"What?" he asked tetchily.

"Why are you doing this?"

"Doing what?"

"Keeping me alive."

Gideon frowned. He couldn't get a read on his captive. The man had risked his life to capture him, only to then refuse a direct order to kill him. He could have kept fighting in this very room, but instead he meekly surrendered.

"Why do you want to die?"

Salazar shrugged. His left eye was beginning to swell. It must have been hit during their fight. The band around his neck was a purple mass bracketed by raw, red rope burns. He looked like he'd been pulled out of some Vietcong jungle prison. "I have nothing to live for."

"So what changed?" Gideon asked.

The broken hitman slumped against the wall. He didn't reply for several seconds. "You could say the veil slipped from my eyes."

"That you were lied to?"

Salazar's lips formed a thin line. "I lied to myself. I told myself that my work for the Brotherhood would save my soul. But even then, I knew it wasn't true. It was just easier to pretend."

"And now?"

"You showed me death today. I realized it doesn't scare me." He raised his bound hands and hunched his head at the same time to tap his left temple. It was an awkward, ungainly movement, but he straightened with a visible sense of pride. "I'm ready to meet my judgment."

Gideon's grip tightened around the warm metal of the pistol. His palm was sweaty from stress and exhaustion. "And you want me to do it?"

Salazar bowed his head. "If you wish."

Gideon raised the pistol in midair and leveled it at the hitman's head. Even an amateur would make this shot ninety-nine times in a hundred. There was no wind. They were only separated by a few yards. Salazar was doing the decent thing and remaining still. He wasn't even looking up.

His finger brushed the trigger. A slow, burning rage at all the death this man had caused curdled the meager contents of his stomach. "Don't you think that's the coward's way out?"

Salazar looked up. For the first time since he'd submitted, Gideon saw a flash of emotion in his eyes. Anger? Or maybe hurt? "You don't think I should pay for what I've done?"

A muscle under Gideon's left eye twitched. "I don't have a problem with you dying. I just think you should make your death count."

"FATHER GABRIEL WILL SEE YOU NOW." One of Gabriel's private secretaries gestured down the marble-floored hallway.

Trent Riley flinched at the reminder of why he was here. He sat perched on the lip of a three-sided window seat that ran around the interior of a bay window looking out onto the villa's verdant gardens. He did not see the scenery outside, nor did he smell the rich perfume of the rows of carefully manicured flowers.

The secretary waited without saying another word. He was used to the anxiety engendered by even an expected meeting with his master.

"Sure," Trent said breathlessly as he tented his fingers on the couch cushion to push himself to his feet. "Thanks," he added.

He was perfectly aware of the ridiculous nature of his current position. He was feared by thousands of the Brotherhood's faithful. By everybody, in fact, except those who lived or worked in this one villa.

Gabriel's minions controlled access to the man himself. Insofar as he accepted counsel from anyone, he listened to the men who managed his diary, prepared his food, and attended to his personal needs. And they knew that Gabriel's protection was extended to them. Trent couldn't touch them. Not without a direct order from the boss himself.

The secretary cleared his throat. "He's waiting."

Trent nodded and smoothed his clothing. He used the moment to inhale deeply to steady his nerves. He was bringing good news. But then, he was also bringing probably the only news that would allow him to keep on living. Gabriel didn't just reward those who followed him; he punished those who failed.

But that wasn't him. Not today.

He followed the man down the hallway. As always, the heels of his shoes clicked against the polished flagstones before the noise was swallowed up by the villa's opulent furnishing.

"It's late," Gabriel said by way of greeting.

He was standing on the far side of his dressing room—a space that was larger than the master bedroom in Trent's own home—and faced a floor-to-ceiling trifold vanity mirror. His arms were extended in the shape of a cross as a diminutive young teenager stretched to lift the sash off his neck. Another stood just to his left carrying a polished silver tray, from the very center of which rose a single crystal champagne flute.

"I'm sorry for disturbing you," Trent said, his throat tight. "But I thought you'd want to know. Salazar just checked in. He'll be here tomorrow."

Gabriel whipped around with such alacrity; he almost knocked the champagne glass from the tray. The teenager untying the sash that secured his robe stepped back and flattened his back against a nearby wall. He wore a blank mask that was clearly intended to convey a simple message.

I see nothing. I hear nothing. I'll say nothing.

"What took so long?" Gabriel asked, his eyes narrowed beneath a dark frown.

"Surveillance detection routine," Trent said, embellishing slightly to cover the fact that he didn't know why Salazar had gone dark after sending that text. "It's standard practice. And Salazar is an old pro. That's why I picked him."

"You're sure it's not a trap?"

"Certain," Trent nodded. "He used the correct passwords. If he was under duress, he would've told me."

Gabriel clicked the thumb and middle finger of his right hand together. "Pour another glass."

Trent felt his shoulders hunch forward with relief as a broad smile crossed Gabriel's face. Sometimes being part of the Brotherhood's inner circle felt like being the pilot of a hurricane-hunting plane. You were never more than one wrong move away from disaster. But the adrenaline rush of success—in his case, praise—couldn't be beat.

It's a sentence delayed, not commuted...

"What time?" Gabriel said, striding toward him with a second glass of champagne that seemed to have appeared from nowhere.

"Midday," Trent said, his heart racing. "An hour before the sermon."

"Bring him straight there," Gabriel said, drinking giddily from the pale-yellow glass. His eyes were half-closed as if in exultation. "It'll be the ideal finale."

"There's more."

Gabriel's eyes flashed open. He stared directly at Trent, then raised one eyebrow slowly. "Oh?"

"My asset with the Faith—," he caught himself, "—the traitors. He just checked in."

"He's alive?"

Trent nodded. "It seems they think we followed Gideon to their camp. They don't suspect him. The survivors fled to a safe house after escaping the attack. There are fewer than a dozen of them left. Half of them can barely walk."

Gabriel held out his glass. Trent reached out with his own and clinked the two glasses together. His mind was filled with daydreams of where this victory would take him. He'd brought Gabriel the thing he'd wanted most. Safety. Security.

That had to be worth something.

"You've done well, Trent. It seems I was right to invest so much belief into you."

"Thank you, Father," Trent said, bowing his head.

"What do you want from me?" Gabriel asked, his gaze piercing when Trent looked back up.

"Want?" he asked, his heart skipping a beat. "Nothing. Only ever to serve."

"Of course," Gabriel said, his face expressionless until it softened into a cold smile. "But it would be ungracious of me not to thank you, wouldn't it?"

"Not at all."

The temperature in the room dropped several degrees. The two servants froze into ice statues. "Are you calling me a liar? Or is it that you don't value my gratitude?"

"Neither," Trent choked. "I'll accept anything, everything you think me worthy of. It's just that I don't serve you for earthly rewards. Our purpose is enough."

He wished he could close his eyes. Do anything to look away from his master. But all he could do was match the man's stare until, finally, the squall passed.

Gabriel smiled. He raised the champagne glass in salute, then sipped from it. "I judged you correctly, Trent. I'll find you something."

"Yes, Father. Thank you, Father," Trent said, resisting the urge to tremble. He sensed that his audience was drawing to a close, that Gabriel was losing interest as the man's eyes flickered away from him. He almost sagged with relief. "What about the traitors?"

"Eliminate them," Gabriel said. "And this time, don't let any escape."

"Yes, Father."

"One last thing, Trent. The sister, Julia. You've been watching her. Is she reliable?"

Trent hadn't expected the question. It took him a couple of moments to rally his thoughts. "I believe so," he said. "She's done everything asked of her with the prisoners."

"Make sure she's at the sermon tomorrow," Gabriel said, his eyes sparkling with the mirth of some hidden joke. "Let's find out."

FIFTY-NINE

Zara slumped onto a chair left unattended on the farmhouse's front porch. The exertions of the day—and the previous night's terrifying escape—had finally caught up to her. As did thoughts of Gideon.

She'd been trying to avoid dwelling on what was happening to him—whether he was even still alive. But the brief lull between frenetic bursts of activity had finally given her time to think.

How could you let him be taken?

Zara knew, rationally, that there was little she could have done to prevent Gideon's kidnapping. But there was nothing rational about the way she felt. She might only have known him for a month, but in that time he'd come to know her better than almost anyone in her entire life.

A career as a CIA case officer didn't exactly allow for much personal time. Even when she found herself on the occasional date, there was little she could share about her life or career.

There were only so many times you could answer the question of what you did for work with the joke, *"I could tell you, but then I'd have to kill you..."* Eventually it wore thin.

Besides, in her experience most men didn't like the idea that their girlfriend was a secret agent, not them. Even if that wasn't an accurate description of her job. Plus, ironically enough, secrecy didn't exactly go hand-in-hand with trust. And without a foundation of trust, pretty much every relationship she'd started had failed.

Until Gideon.

The peculiar circumstances of their meeting had acted like a pressure cooker: forcing years of relationship development into as many weeks. She might not know the litany of personal details and memories a longer courtship would have unveiled—his favorite color, meal, that kind of thing— but she knew in her bones that she could trust him through thick and thin.

Zara's gaze narrowed, her attention caught by a couple of figures in the distance. As she squinted, she realized one belonged to Eli. He was digging up the dirt track that led to the farmhouse. She vaguely remembered him mentioning that he was going to prepare some surprises for anyone who came knocking. It looked like he'd decided to lay down an IED.

She knew he was also preparing a squad to take to New Eden to try and rescue the hostages. Before, the plan had been an insane gamble. Now, with so many dead, it was surely a suicide mission.

"What's on your mind?"

She flinched at the unexpected sound, then turned to see Lachlan leaning against the front door's frame. His face was gray, and speckled with a haggard stubble, and he was fidgeting with his cell phone. But at least he was up.

"Gideon. I just—"

"—Wish you knew what was happening to him?"

"Yeah," Zara muttered, her shoulders hunching forward with exhaustion.

"I doubt they killed him already. Gabriel's the vindictive type. He'll want to see it happen himself."

Zara's stomach turned at the image of a public execution that this thought generated in her mind. "Thanks."

"It's a good thing," Lachlan said.

"I'm not sure I buy that idea."

"It means we still have a chance."

Zara whipped her head around and fixed Lachlan with a hard stare. "Are you hiding an army somewhere that you forgot to tell me about?"

He gestured around the farm. "Nope. What you see is what you get."

She gritted her teeth. "I read my Sun Tzu. 'Appear weak when you're strong, and strong when you are weak'. Well, we're not just pretending. There's no way we can pull off this rescue with half a dozen guys. Believe me, I've been racking my brain to figure out how. We can use Jamie to misdirect them. Even kill a lot of them when they come here to find us. Then what?"

A flash of pain crossed Lachlan's face. "I don't know. Maybe it's time we went to the authorities."

"Before, you said that would lead to Waco on steroids. What changed?"

"Everything did!" Lachlan snapped. "It took us decades to build the organization you saw last night. Now it's all gone. Eli and the others, they'd give their lives if there was even a chance of saving those hostages—or Gideon. But without him, there's no hope for the future. Getting the cops involved was never the optimal plan. But maybe it's all that's left."

Zara closed her eyes, which now felt so leaden from exhaustion she doubted she'd ever be able to open them again. She sagged back into the chair.

But only for a second. Her eyes snapped open. "Give me your phone."

"Why?"

She gestured hurriedly for him to hand it over. She didn't have time to explain why. Lachlan did so reluctantly.

Zara waited impatiently for the burner to power back up. The second the signal bars climbed up the side of the screen, she dialed in Leclerc's number. With so much on her mind, she'd completely forgotten that Jacques had been trying to get in touch before the attack on the Faithless farmhouse. If there was anyone who could help, it was him. She pressed the phone to her ear.

Leclerc answered on the first ring. "Who is this?"

"Jacques, it's me. Zara."

"I've been trying to call you all day. You—"

"—We're in danger," Zara laughed bleakly. "I know. It's a bit late for that."

"No. It's Gideon."

"What about him?"

"He's alive. And he has a plan."

SIXTY

The SUV and a work van rolled into the pool of light thrown by the vehicle Gideon and Salazar were sitting in. Right on time.

"They're here," Gideon murmured with relief. He and Salazar had driven cross-country, sharing the driving so that the other could sleep. The first time Gideon handed over the wheel, it had felt unnatural. After all, just a handful of hours before, this man had tried to kill him.

The second time was easier. But it was still a little like trying to nap on a crocodile's back.

"I hope it's your friends," Salazar said gruffly in response. "Or we're both about to die."

Gideon flashed the headlights three times. There was a short pause before the SUV flashed four times in response. It was a simple code to establish that each party was who they claimed to be. There hadn't been time to establish secure comms, so until now all information had been exchanged through Leclerc. Which meant it was low bandwidth.

He shrugged and pulled the SUV's door handle open. "Guess we may as well find out."

Salazar followed, though not eagerly. Gideon supposed that wasn't a surprise. After all, Eli and the others had every reason to want him dead. In truth, so did Gideon. No matter what happened to him, Salazar had inflicted more harm on the world than almost anybody he'd ever met.

It was time for him to pay his dues.

On the other side of the clearing, four sets of doors swung open and dark silhouettes jumped out. Tiny piles of dust wafted in the glow of battling headlights before disappearing. The night air smelled hot and humid.

"Gideon?" A voice rang out. "That you?"

Eli's voice.

Gideon exhaled with relief. He walked briskly toward the center of the clearing. Eli and the others did the same. None of them were carrying rifles, but he knew that all were armed. Likely to the teeth. All except Eli watched Salazar suspiciously.

"You trust this motherfucker?" Eli said after the two men shook hands.

Glancing back, Gideon shrugged. "I think he wants to make amends."

"Why now?"

Salazar answered first, his voice low and tired. "I have no answer that will make you happy. Perhaps he showed me the way."

Gideon interrupted, gesturing at the work van behind Eli's SUV. "It's ready?"

"Prepped and ready to blow," Eli nodded, thin-lipped. "Not sure there's an OSHA regulation we didn't break driving this a thousand miles while rigging it up en route."

"You made it."

"Guess so." Eli reached into his pocket and pulled out a cell phone. "Somebody wants to talk to you. Last number dialed."

Gideon nodded his thanks and stepped away. He wanted to do this privately, though he kept one eye on Salazar and Eli's guys. There was a lot of bad blood between them that wouldn't go away just because a serial killer said he wanted to do the right thing.

Zara answered on the second ring.

"It's me," he said before she had a chance to speak.

"Gideon," she said breathlessly. "Are you really okay?"

"More or less," he said. "Though after driving across half the country in the last few days, I'm not exactly sure."

"Never do that to me again."

"I'll try," he replied, touched by the genuine anguish he heard in Zara's voice. "You okay?"

"I am now." She paused, and he heard several deep breaths whistling through the phone. "Do you think this is going to work?"

It was Gideon's turn to hesitate. The plan was simple, mostly because it had to be. There were too few good guys left for anything more elaborate. They were going to try and draw as many Brotherhood shooters away from the prisoners as possible.

Some of that was Salazar's role. They also hoped that Gabriel would take the bait Zara had fed him through Jamie, and send a team to the safe house, which she, Francis, and a handful of the Faithless's walking wounded had spent the last day turning into a deathtrap. If it worked then New Eden's defenses might be threadbare enough for Gideon and a hand-picked group of fighters to simply walk on in.

That's the theory, anyway.

"It has to," he said at last. He wanted to ask—beg—her to get to safety when the shooting started. But he had no right to, and he knew she wouldn't listen anyway. "Please, just be careful, okay?"

"I'll try. We'll take that vacation when this is all over?" Zara asked. She meant it as a joke, but Gideon could tell how exhausted she was.

He smiled. "I promise."

SIXTY-ONE

Gideon ran with his head bowed and his back stooped. Sweat soaked the elastic band that held the flashlight in place around the crown of his head. He held one hand out ahead of him despite the feeble cone of light it cast to feel for obstructions in his way.

His harried breaths echoed in the narrow, cramped tunnel, competing with five others. They were on the clock, all weighed down by bags heavy with weapons and ammo. The other flashlight beams bounced in every direction. It was like a chaotic underground rave.

Not that he had much experience with those. He glanced at his watch. The green digital face gleamed back at him. It was 11:44.

"We're a minute behind," he called out. "Pick it up!"

They should've hit the end of the tunnel by now. One of the last remaining Faithless operatives on the inside at New Eden would be excavating the exit at this very moment. Dirt bikes were waiting for them, painstakingly rolled into place the previous night. The plan was to have duffel bags of weapons waiting alongside them as well, but there hadn't been time, so each man carried one on his back. The additional weight was what was slowing them down.

So many dominoes had to fall in exactly the right path for this plan to succeed. If any of a dozen individual components failed to work precisely the way they were supposed to, it was all over.

Gideon's boots thudded against the soft dirt floor of the tunnel. The walls were reinforced with concrete blocks and wooden pillars. It must have taken months to dig and construct —all by hand to avoid detection. Electricity wiring dangled from the ceiling but wasn't connected to anything. The tunnel wasn't complete. It wasn't ready. Nobody was.

But it reached the other end. And that end was almost in sight. Gideon could see a crack of illumination now that wasn't thrown by the flashlight he was wearing. The realization spurred his already laboring muscles on to fresh effort. He felt his pace increase, and then all of a sudden, he pumped the brakes. He only just avoided bumping into the back of the man ahead of him who had slowed almost to a halt to avoid a cave-in that had blocked half the tunnel since the previous night.

"Shit," someone muttered.

"Come on, over," Eli grunted. "We're almost there.

Gideon checked his watch again. 11:46. He didn't have time for this.

All six men scrambled over the obstruction, coating their clothing in dirt. Their movement kicked up clouds of dust. Gideon was bringing up the rear, so he had it the worst. He unshouldered the duffel bag, coughing as he thrust it over the dirt bank, then clasped onto a filthy forearm that poked back through the haze. Whoever it belonged to hauled him through, and then the tight formation was moving again.

Gideon barely had time to hoist the bag of rifles and ammunition back onto his shoulder before they reached the end of the line. A row of six powerful dirt bikes rested along the left side of the wall, cramping the space even further. Cracks of light glimmered above them. A wooden ladder lay on its side along the right wall. All six men—possibly the best and definitely the last of the Faithless fighting force—crouched, steeling themselves for what came next.

11:48. Time was running out.

Up ahead, a man whistled. Gideon couldn't see his face, but he knew that task was Eli's. He held his breath. None of them had voiced the possibility that the Faithless operative waiting for them had been turned by the Brotherhood. But the truth was, they had no way of knowing what was waiting for them on the other side. It would only take a single grenade in this cramped space to cut their entire column apart.

Pained, heavy breathing filled the space. Despite the tension, none of them could hold their breath.

Eli whistled again.

"Come on," someone whispered, his tone heavy with frustration.

Trickles of dust began coursing down from above. At first light and tentative, then in a flood that once again filled the tunnel, coating faces and making breathing difficult. Gideon blinked away the filth and found that his eyes were streaming with tears.

In an instant, light replaced darkness as the wooden screen that capped the tunnel was pulled away. Now, Gideon held his breath. What would it be? A dozen rifles pumping lead into them? Gasoline and a single match?

Just a head.

The light flooding in from above made it impossible to make out the man's face. He spoke in a low voice. "Send up the ladder."

Eli did so immediately, grasping the side of the ladder and pushing it upward hand over hand. He was first up and was soon joined by three of his men. Gideon stayed with the last and began pulling the bikes closer to the base of the ladder.

"We're ready," he called up.

It took four painstaking, backbreaking minutes of labor to carry all six bikes up the ladder. The last was the hardest because Gideon had to hold onto the handlebars as his forearms screamed for mercy and two other men pulled him up to sea level.

When he reached the surface, he saw that the other five bikes were lying flat on the ground, as were all of those who had made it up before him, plus one fresh face.

11:53.

As soon as Gideon was up, all six men around him leapt to their feet, pushed a bike upright, and pulled a bag of weapons over their shoulders. There was no time to wait for introductions. The Faithless operative looked worried, as if he'd just marked himself for death.

One by one, the bike engines grumbled into life. Gideon grabbed one for himself, and the second he was on the saddle, he revved the engine. Their target was five miles away. They didn't have much time.

"That way," Eli pointed, pausing long enough to check that each of them understood, and not a second longer.

The second Gideon nodded, Eli twisted his bike's throttle. A puff of black smoke coughed out of the exhaust, followed by a cloud of dust kicked up by the rear tire. And then he was off.

The roar of the six dirt bikes was deafening. Despite the expensive-looking suspension, the ride was punishing. The saddle kicked up into Gideon's groin with every bump in the uneven terrain, and jolts of pain radiated up through his forearms, meeting the ones sparking up his spine. The bag of rifles on his shoulder bumped painfully against his hip bone and his rib cage.

Gideon shook off the discomfort, dropped his knuckles, and fed more gas into the engine. The odometer hit seventy-four miles per hour. Any faster, and he would have no chance of staying in control of this bucking bronco. The line of bikes was now strung out across about fifty yards. The cloud of dust behind them would probably be visible for miles.

The question was: Was anyone watching?

There was no time to wonder. Gideon reached into his pants pocket and gingerly pulled out a cheap Nokia cell phone. The device was easily sturdy enough to survive a fall from this speed. But if he dropped it, he'd never find it in time.

The text message was already queued up. The screen vibrated in front of him as he held it aloft, backing off the throttle only enough for his vision to stabilize. The message was there. It was ready to send.

So he did.

SIXTY-TWO

"Is this how the first astronauts felt?" Eduardo Salazar wondered out loud to himself in the otherwise meditative silence of the front cabin of the Chevrolet Express van. The rear panels were opaque fiberglass, and he'd personally taped cardboard over the windows in the rear doors. The contents of the cargo compartment would be a mystery to anybody looking in.

He decided not. The astronauts would've had a hope, if not exactly an expectation, of survival. He no longer did. In fact, he was looking forward to death, tired of lugging this burden around with him every single day. He was used up. Couldn't do it any longer.

Didn't want to.

Salazar toyed with the orange medicine bottle in his hand as he waited, hearing the lonely rattle of the last remaining pill inside. Considered swallowing it. But for the first time in weeks, he decided he shouldn't. It wasn't right.

Go out like a man.

The sun streaming through the windshield was at odds

with the darkness of his thoughts. The sky overhead was a rich Caribbean blue. Only a single wisp of cloud dared to obscure its face. Perhaps it was the world's parting gift.

The black flip phone in the center console buzzed, causing the loose assortment of coins it was sitting on to vibrate and clink together. He reached for it slowly. There was no point hurrying. He knew what it would say.

Salazar flipped open the phone. A notification icon on the pixelated home screen told him he had a message. He navigated to open it using the four-way arrow button.

It's time.

Though Salazar understood intellectually that he was reading his death warrant, he felt relief at the sight of the words. It was almost over. There was also gratitude. Gideon could simply have shot him in that motel room. Just an ounce more pressure on the trigger, and he would have been dead before he knew it was coming.

Instead, Gideon had offered him a chance. Not of a fresh start or a new life, but redemption for the one he'd already lived. A decade ago, perhaps even a *month* ago, he would have mocked the idea. Probably tried to drink or smoke or fuck through the mental discordance of the judgment the offer implied.

But no longer. He was exhausted. And Gideon was right about something.

It really is time.

His vision blurred as he reached for the engine start button. As he tried to blink it away, warm droplets fell onto his cheeks, and he realized he was crying. Perhaps for the first time since he was a boy.

I didn't even cry after Mateo died, Salazar thought.

Mateo's face replaced the blurry outline of the steering wheel and dashboard and the sapphire sky beyond. He watched his son sprint and laugh and cry and simply be in memories that he hadn't allowed himself to replay in years.

Salazar closed his eyes and felt his heart break with a mixture of happiness and grief. It was as though he was reliving the pain all over again. Perhaps in truth, he was experiencing it for the first time, at least the first time unburdened by anger or alcohol.

"Will you judge me?" he whispered, focusing on a single image of his son's face, a memory of the boy's third birthday party. He was wearing a paper crown, his eyes scrunched up as he pursed his lips and prepared to blow out the candles of his cake. His cheeks puffed out, and he blew and blew and the flame flickered and finally puffed into smoke.

Mateo's eyes popped open, and he sought his father's approving gaze. There was no judgment in the memory. And Salazar clung to that, even as he knew that he deserved whatever fate awaited him in the world after this.

The phone buzzed again. He wiped his eyes and found that his T-shirt was stained with fallen tears. He blinked away the last of them and glanced at the clock in the center of the dashboard. It shimmered in his still-moist gaze, but the digits were clear enough. It was 11:55.

He pushed the engine start button, for real this time. Nothing happened. Bolts of pure panic shot through him. His insides felt white. There was no other way of explaining it. Every muscle in his body was instantly knotted and sinewy.

"Come on," he said, any peace he'd felt a moment ago already gone.

He stabbed the button again with his index finger. Again, nothing happened. The engine didn't even cough. Instead of the dashboard screen flickering into life, the van remained as dark and lifeless as an Egyptian pyramid.

"I'll roll you there if I have to, you piece of shit," he grunted, punching the button a third time. To the same result.

Salazar thumped the dashboard with frustration. His eyes were wide, a vein in his temple throbbing fit to burst. He searched the dashboard in the center console for inspiration. Came up empty.

"Dammit."

Closed his eyes. Thought hard. Then it hit him. "You dumb fuck."

He reached out with his right foot for the brake pedal. Depressed it, then gingerly pressed the engine start button one last time. The vehicle was only four or five years old, but it had been used hard in that short time. The base of the cargo compartment was coated in plaster dust, and the suspension sagged.

Fourth time lucky.

The van's engine grumbled agreeably into life. Every light on the dashboard flickered on, then darkened, except for one warning icon that would never be investigated. The rev counter hung on one. The air conditioning rumbled into life, throwing out a chill breeze that wafted the hairs on Salazar's arms.

He shook his head with disbelief. That was a pure rookie mistake. He must've started a car the same way ten thousand times. How could he forget something so basic?

Because this time it counts.

Salazar inhaled a pure, clean breath of air that filled his lungs to the brim. He held onto it as oxygen flooded into his bloodstream, then exhaled slowly. He was ready.

He put the car into drive, and his eyes once again automatically searched out the dashboard clock. His screwup had only cost him a minute. He had the time.

The van's wheels spun as he hit the gas and eased the vehicle out of the pull-off he'd parked in. A cloud of dust formed behind him, but it disappeared the second he hit the paved road that led to the east gate of New Eden. Dried-out grass clung to the parched ground on either side of the road. It was fixing to go up in flames. Only needed a spark.

11:57. The odometer hit sixty-three miles an hour. The bones of the battered van couldn't handle going much faster. The whole chassis vibrated in the wind. He felt the creaking movement through the steering wheel. Didn't help that it was carrying so heavy a load.

He could smell it now. Hadn't noticed before. The diesel fumes made his eyes sting. He rolled down the passenger side window. Just long enough to let fresh air waft through the cargo compartment and wash out the scent.

11:58. The van rounded a corner, and the fence that bordered New Eden grew visible in the distance. It was just a line in the grass, but it grew larger and more distinct with every hundred yards he traveled.

A minute later, he could see the gate. He was early, but so were they. More than a dozen vehicles were clustered around the ordinarily sleepy checkpoint. He could only make out a couple of figures, but that would be by design. The others would be hidden away in the vans and trucks.

Salazar took his foot off the gas pedal but didn't hit the brake. He let the engine slow the van's speed and watched it tick down on the dashboard in front of him, mile by mile. The needle hung on thirty for what felt like an age, and then the collapse was sudden. Ten. five.

Two.

The van stopped a couple of inches in front of the gate. Salazar never even touched the brake pedal. He stared out through the windshield looking directly ahead. The guard at the gate signaled for his attention, and he gestured irritably for the man to open the gate instead.

There was a pause for a moment as the guard tried to figure out what to do next. Indecision. Concern.

Salazar looked through the windshield but saw his son's face instead. Whispered a prayer for redemption under his breath.

The gate rolled open.

The second it was wide enough for the van to pass through, Salazar tapped the gas pedal. The rev counter jerked up as he guided the vehicle forward, into the cluster of trucks and vans. And then he stopped. His right hand reached down for the phone, and he flipped open the screen. Three bars of signal.

Was somebody watching him from a distance, he wondered? An unseen pair of eyes glued to the lenses of a set of binoculars drilled on the very vehicle he was driving, waiting for him to inch forward just a couple more feet? Did Gideon really trust him to fulfill this final task on his own? He hoped so. But in truth, he wouldn't blame the man for making other arrangements.

Salazar's thumb rested on the first button on the keypad. A trickle of sweat rolled down his temple despite the blasting air conditioning. He breathed in short, jerky rasping inhalations. He needed to hold it together. Just for a few more seconds.

Movement ahead of him. He blinked, and the movement caused a stinging bead of sweat to fall into his eye. He winced as he dragged his forearm across his face to clear his vision. Couldn't spare the distraction. Not right now.

Men with guns appeared. Half of them wore tan fatigues, the other half gray hiking pants and brown safari shirts. The men in fatigues were the Chosen. The others were his own colleagues. Trent's boys.

Internal Security. The Division.

The two groups streamed out of their respective vehicles. The Chosen shooters lugged heavy automatic rifles, the internal security men walked with hands resting lightly on holstered pistols. At first, they walked, then they practically ran.

Salazar's eyes widened as he saw why. Trent himself headed the group from internal security. The reason was obvious: Morgan Baker, the Chosen's leader, trotted in front of the phalanx of a dozen of his own men.

I have the prize. And they both want to claim credit.

For a moment, Salazar's features wrinkled into a grim smile. This had worked out better than he dared hope. It was only a pity that Gabriel himself wasn't present. Well, if he couldn't cut off the head of the snake, then he could at least take its neck.

Trent and Morgan exchanged sideways glances as each approached the Chevrolet. Trent was on the left, Morgan the right. They were as close to running as they possibly could be while maintaining even a shred of dignity. Trent got there first. He rapped his knuckles impatiently on the driver's side window.

"Open up," he said brusquely.

Salazar waited as almost twenty security personnel of various stripes approached and fanned out around the van. The farthest was only a dozen footsteps away. Almost close enough to smell the heady mixture of plastic explosive, fertilizer, and diesel that the Faithless had supplied him with. Maybe they already could.

He keyed the window button with his index finger but said nothing as the glass pane disappeared. The van rocked slightly behind him as an unseen hand tried the rear door handle only to discover that it was locked.

"Where is he?" Trent asked, sweat glinting on his forehead and a wild light in his eyes. He raised his voice over the sound of Morgan hammering against the passenger window. They were like siblings fighting over a prized toy. "In the back?"

Salazar nodded. He raised his chin slowly to match Trent's gaze. He allowed his face to curl with the distaste he'd concealed for so long.

"What's that in your hand?" Trent asked suspiciously.

Salazar glanced at the cell phone out of the corner of his eye. He heard his boy's laughter in the distance, smelled the sweet soapy scent of the top of the infant's head when he was just a few days old. And then he closed his eyes so that it was his son's features, not this charlatan's, that would be his last sight in this world.

"Open the fucking doors," Trent yelled, a nervous tightness in his voice. "Drop the phone."

Salazar ignored both instructions. He breathed in deeply and held his thumb down on the first and only speed dial programmed into his phone.

"He's got—"

Whatever the distant voice was going to say was lost to the energy of a fresh sun being born in the grasslands of Texas. It burned for only a second before exploding in a catastrophic fashion, first sending out a shock wave that buffeted the swaying grass for over a mile in every direction.

Then a wave of ball bearings and chunks of scrap metal and pieces of the van itself thundered forth ahead a chariot of flame and heat.

And then only silence. It had begun.

SIXTY-THREE

Gideon's eyes still stung from the dust and sweat that had assaulted them over the course of the five-mile race. He was covered in grime, and even without the mask that covered his face he probably wasn't recognizable even to anybody who knew him well.

That's a short list.

They'd driven the last mile slowly to avoid detection and sprinted the final half as quickly as they could on foot. He was grateful now for the punishing fitness regime he'd put himself through in the woods of West Virginia. Without it, his heart would probably have given out already. His throat was parched, and he was desperate for a drink. But as soon as he saw the prize laid out in front of him, it was as though all his personal discomfort had faded away.

A gleaming office building rose out of the dry ranchland ahead of them, surrounded by parking spaces and rows of neatly tended hedges and vegetation. If Gideon didn't know he was looking at the headquarters of the Brotherhood's internal security arm, he might have figured they were lost.

But it was kind of hard to miss the line of men and women clad in orange jumpsuits shuffling toward a pair of yellow school buses. The two vehicles were parked nose to tail, bracketed by two pairs of black pickup trucks at the front and rear of the column. Several armed guards in hiking pants and tan shirts sat on benches in the lead truck, paying attention to their colleagues driving the procession of prisoners into the transport buses.

"Nine guards, six drivers," Eli whispered. "Somebody check my math."

Another voice confirmed what Gideon already knew. He'd seen one of the pickup truck's drivers climb into his vehicle and clocked the pistol the man had holstered. That made fifteen armed tangos.

He checked his watch. 11:59.

All six men were lying on their bellies in a ditch that bordered the internal security complex spaced several feet apart. Surveillance cameras dotted the building's exterior, and others were raised on lampposts, but nobody appeared to have noticed they had company.

It was far from a perfect shooting position, but it was the best they had open to them.

"I'll take the lead pickup," Eli whispered. "Share the rest out among yourselves. We go right after the boom."

12:00 hit a moment later. But the boom was late.

Gideon felt his heart racing in his chest as he stared down through his rifle's scope. The center of a set of crosshairs rested just a fraction of an inch to the left of his chosen target's skull. He glanced around for Julia, but there was no sign of her, then exhaled slowly, trying to ignore the questions racing through his mind and focus only on the here and now.

What if I misjudged Salazar?

This gunfight was going to happen whether or not Salazar's

car bomb—in military terms VBIED, or Vehicle Borne Improvised Explosive Device—detonated or not. But it was almost certainly the case that many of the Brotherhood's finest fighters had been sent to the east gate to meet Salazar and his supposed prisoner.

"Me," Gideon whispered.

The crosshairs jerked left once again. He was breathing too hard, his muscles too tense for optimal aim. He needed to calm down. The element of surprise didn't tend to stick around once lead started flying. There were a hell of a lot of innocent prisoners down there. And if he missed his shot and his target started shooting instead...

The shock wave rocked the dirt, chasing the sound wave that had already temporarily deafened Gideon, even at this range. He resisted the natural human urge to turn and goggle at the smoke cloud that had to already be rising into the air.

And he squeezed the rifle's trigger.

He saw his target crumple, a single puff of blood or brain matter glinting in the sunlight before the man's destroyed face collapsed out of view. It was a perfect shot. All his prior tension had faded away. It was like dust in the wind.

Gideon twisted, his barrel slaving in the same direction as the sight. Acquired a second target. This one was moving—unlike some of the other Division goons who had reacted to their curiosity instead of instinct. He attempted to duck behind the nearest of the commandeered school buses just as Gideon fired for a second time.

The single round kicked a burst of dust and debris up off the asphalt. *Miss.*

"Dammit," he grunted over the ringing in his ears and gunfire as steady and intense as a hailstorm on a tin roof echoing all around him.

Gideon inhaled slowly and fired three rounds in quick

succession as his target tripped, perhaps overcome by the stress of coming under unexpected gunfire as his comrades died one after another all around him. The road was already painted with blood and unmoving corpses.

The shooter rolled onto his back and brought his pistol up, firing blindly as he kicked his feet back to push himself toward cover. Gideon blocked out the sight of muzzle flashes and the fear—evident even at this distance—on his target's face.

He fired two more shots. Both punctured center mass. He watched the man's posture change instantly. It was as though his strings had been cut, leaving him slumped back against the road, jerking spasmodically.

Artery, Gideon knew at once. The knowledge filled him with no joy. He didn't like killing. Especially not people whose main crime was to have been brainwashed. If he was here, at internal security's HQ, then the guard was probably responsible for too many crimes to count. But he was also just another victim.

Only he would never get to be rescued.

"Got a problem," one of the strike team called out, his voice tense.

Since both of Gideon's targets were already down, he looked up from his scope to check out the situation. He took it in immediately. Almost all of the guards were already dead. One of the three survivors fell to a burst of gunfire even as he watched.

A second who had thrown down his primary weapon was trying to run. He wouldn't get far.

But the problem was the third. Somehow, he'd got his hands on one of the prisoners and had a pistol lodged at the woman's temple as he pulled her backward. Her cries of terror were audible even at this distance.

"Shit," Gideon whispered. The original sin of their tactical position immediately became apparent: the need to stick to cover meant they only had shooters on one side. That meant the hostage taker could back away from them using a hostage as a human shield.

Which was exactly what he was doing.

Gideon bit down hard as he tried to block out the terrified hostage's screams. It was cold-hearted, but the distraction could end up costing the hostage her life. Twice he got a fix on the hostage taker's head through the rifle's scope, but it wasn't long enough to be sure of making the shot without collateral damage.

"Anybody got a shot?"

The silence spoke volumes.

Every heartbeat felt like somebody was thumping Gideon's chest. They'd all known going into this that innocent people would probably lose their lives. But it was different seeing it.

A flicker of movement in Gideon's peripheral vision caught his attention. A woman—no, a girl—was moving in a crouched scramble across the ground. She didn't seem to notice the gunfire all around her. Unlike the prisoners, she was dressed in a light gray tunic. She paused over one of the guards' corpses just long enough to grasp something, then darted behind one of the buses.

"What's she doing?" somebody muttered.

The girl appeared on the other side of the bus. She'd used it to cover her approach so that she was now behind the hostage taker. His eyes were focused on the action in front of him, so he hadn't noticed the movement.

Still didn't notice.

Gideon saw a glimmer of reflected sunlight in her hands. The realization of what was about to happen hit him immediately.

Focus on me, buddy.

He aimed at the ground about fifteen feet ahead of the hostage taker. Fired half a dozen shots, each spaced a second apart. The girl crept closer to the retreating guard with every second as puffs of dust exploded around the man's feet.

Ten feet.

Gideon fired again, just as the guard's head started to twitch around. It jerked back before the recoil kicked his shoulder.

Five...

He squeezed the trigger twice more. The hostage's screams had given way to muffled sobs. She was giving up.

The guard must've sensed movement behind him. He whipped his head around, despite Gideon firing half a dozen more rounds in quick succession.

But it was too late.

The blade in the girl's hands glinted once again in the sunlight. And then it disappeared from view as she buried it into the guard's back.

The pistol pulled away from the prisoner's temple just long enough for Gideon to fire one last, decisive round. The weapon dropped to the dirt about a second before the now-dead body of its former owner.

"Hold fire, hold fire," Eli called out at the top of his voice, just as a final gunshot rang out and the runner fell to the ground.

"Everybody make their targets?"

One by one, the small strike cell checked in to confirm what each of them could already see. Every single one of the guards was dead. A couple of them were spreadeagled on the ground, face down in the direction of the prisoner transports. They'd tried to make it there even in the face of certain death.

To what end? Gideon wondered. Would they have tried to

execute the prisoners, fulfilling their orders even in the face of certain death?

"Everybody up," Eli yelled.

Gideon caught a glance over his shoulder as he pushed himself to his feet. He dumped the half-spent mag from his rifle and caught it with his left hand, sliding it into his rear pants pocket in case it came in useful later. His eyes widened as he fed a fresh magazine into the weapon, then he crouched to grab the duffel bag from the ditch.

A top-heavy black cloud rose like a funeral pyre in the distance. The wind was pushing it west.

"Ain't nobody surviving that," one of Eli's men snorted. He punched Gideon lightly in the arm. "Guess your boy came good."

SIXTY-FOUR

"We've got incoming," Francis's voice crackled through the radio handset just to Zara's left. There was one in each of the four machine gun nests that they had dug—and extensively camouflaged—over the previous day. "Three vehicles on the road. Driving fast."

Zara felt her mouth go dry. She didn't acknowledge receipt of the message, even though the sound was unlikely to travel through the wooden roof of her fighting position, and especially not through the thick layers of earth and foliage that made it look like a part of the forest floor.

Camouflage netting obscured the view of the farmhouse ahead of her. All of the wounded had been moved to a nearby motel. Anybody left who could pull a trigger was manning one of the fighting positions.

"Here we go," a voice whispered to her side. It belonged to a man called Phoenix. She had barely spoken to him, but Francis had told her that Gideon was with him when the shooting at the camp in Georgia started. In an ideal world he would probably be in hospital.

But there was nothing ideal about today.

Zara felt a vibration through the earth beneath her several seconds before she heard the sound of car engines growling in the distance. The breath caught in her throat, but she forced herself to say, "Good luck."

She swallowed and dropped her head so that her cheek rested against the stock of the rifle Francis had given her. She was far from a crack shot, but the barrel of the weapon rested on a length of wood that had been driven into the ground with a sledgehammer at the perfect height to prop it up.

They'd made every preparation possible.

Now it was up to fate.

She heard Phoenix's nervous breathing at her side. Tried to force thoughts of Gideon out of her mind, until droplets of stinging sweat trickled into her eyes and gave her no choice in the matter.

Zara wiped her eyes, deeply aware of how loud her own breathing was.

CRACK.

She froze. It sounded like a twig snapping extremely close by. She didn't allow herself to breathe even as anxious scenarios ran through her mind, each more fanciful than the last.

Footsteps. I can hear footsteps.

Zara slowed her breathing until her lungs screamed for oxygen. Someone was nearby. And that someone was definitely not friendly.

"Vehicles parked around the cabin," a voice spoke from just a few feet away. "I don't see any movement. No guards."

Was it a spotter? Whoever it was definitely wanted to do her harm.

If there was an answer to what Zara assumed was a radio transmission, she couldn't hear it. The roar of vehicle engines grew louder, but so did the sound of footsteps nearby. Her eyes widened as a figure in dark combat fatigues stopped only four or five feet ahead of her concealed position. The man took a knee and aimed his rifle at the farmhouse, peering through the scope that sat on top of the barrel.

"Still nothing," he said. "Hit it."

Barely a heartbeat elapsed between those words being spoken and three SUVs spinning around the last corner on the dirt road that led to the farmhouse, riding a column of smoke as they accelerated toward their destination.

No sooner had the vehicles appeared than Zara saw more figures emerging from the woods and fields that surrounded the Faithless safe house. She realized that at least half a dozen fighters had approached on foot in addition to the ones in the vehicles. There were probably more on the far side of the farmhouse that she couldn't see. These fighters were setting up shooting positions on the high ground, such as it was.

Definitely not friendly.

It took all of her willpower to resist squeezing the trigger and emptying her entire magazine into the enemy in front of her. They had to wait. Had to lure their opponents into the trap they had set, or all this would be for nothing.

The first of the three SUVs rocketed over the spot at which Eli had laid an IED. Then the second.

By the time the third was safely across, the head of the convoy had almost reached the farmhouse. It skidded to a halt, and all four doors swung open almost before it came to a complete stop.

Wait, Zara reminded herself, so loud she feared the enemy shooter ahead of her might hear. Wait!

The second SUV stopped. Then the third.

When Francis's voice echoed through the handset, the release was almost cathartic. "Now!"

Zara swiveled the barrel of her rifle toward the man

standing in front of her. There was no way of telling whether she or Phoenix squeezed the trigger first. Either way, he was cut down in a cloud of blood that hung thick in the air as his body slumped to the turf.

"Push them into the house," Francis yelled as waves of gunfire from the hidden positions rattled down into the Brotherhood SUVs, puncturing tires and shattering glass.

The enemy reacted professionally, going to ground as they returned fire. But the four Faithless fighting positions were well-dug into the earth. As the men who had approached through the trees and fields were riddled with gunfire, one by one, the leader of the enemy party bowed to the inevitable. Their position outside was too exposed.

The farmhouse was at least defensible.

Low calls carried somehow through the rattle of death that echoed from every direction. Brotherhood shooters lay down covering fire to allow their comrades to retreat. Then the ones who'd made it to the house sent tongues of flame and metal spitting out into the tree line.

Zara reached for the radio handset when the last of them made it inside. She hated death. Hoped that one day soon she would never have to give an order like this again. But she also remembered two men in France, Florian and Marwan, who would no longer live to see their children grow up.

She squeezed the transmit button. She knew that Francis's finger was probably already poised over the detonator. But she had to be the one to say it.

"Francis—take them down."

SIXTY-FIVE

"Let's cut 'em loose," Eli called out, his southern drawl pronounced from the adrenaline of the abrupt gunfight.

The small team had taken down almost a dozen enemy combatants without incurring a single loss. The worst injury any of them had sustained was a slight scratch caused by debris being kicked up as incoming rounds ate dirt.

Gideon let his rifle fall against its sling and held his hand out in midair. It shook a little, and he clenched his fist to quell the motion.

"Shit," Isaac gasped as he trotted alongside Gideon. "My stomach's doing back flips."

Gideon merely nodded, his lips pursed tight. He didn't trust his vocal cords to accurately convey his own thoughts without squeaking. So far, the assault had gone better than they could have dared to hope. The girl's intervention had come like a gift from God, but it meant they'd successfully pulled off the first stage of the prisoner rescue without incurring a single friendly casualty.

He crouched by the first of the Brotherhood dead just long

enough to check the man's pulse. A bullet wound had punctured the shooter's right lung, and since the wound wasn't sucking, he was pretty sure what he would find before his fingers pressed against still-warm skin.

"Dead," he called out as he stood and used the underside of his right foot to send the corpse's pistol skittering away from trouble.

Similar cries rang out from the other Faithless operators. They'd spared no mercy and offered no quarter. There wasn't time for that. And, bluntly, the Brotherhood couldn't be trusted to abide by an old-fashioned concept like honor.

Gideon checked one more Brotherhood corpse for signs of life as he made his way over to the girl who'd cut down the last of the enemy shooters. She sat on the ground several feet from her victim, arms cocooning her knees, her light gray dress marked with dust and stained with blood. Her eyes were open in a faraway stare, and her right hand wore a crown of dried blood.

The knife she'd used to stab the hostage taker was nowhere in proximity. A quick glance at the nearest body told Gideon that it had dug deep foundations.

"Hey," he said in a soft voice as he approached the girl. "Are you okay?"

No response. She kept looking past him as though he wasn't there.

Gideon gently waved his arm in front of her face. He didn't want to reach out and touch her right now. She'd probably had enough trouble with unfriendly men to last a lifetime, despite her tender age.

"You're going to be okay," he said, continuing to talk but knowing that his tone was much more important than the words that passed his lips. "We're going to get you out of here."

Still she didn't react. She just stared past Gideon, her only movement being to shift her gaze slightly when he threatened to block her view.

He glanced over his shoulder to check what she was looking at and saw the line of bound prisoners being cut free by the other members of the Faithless team. One by one prisoners rose to their feet, tossing cut zip ties to the ground with looks of disgust and relief battling on their faces. One of them threw her head back and let out a piercing scream, then rushed over to the nearest corpse and delivered a powerful kick to the body's rib cage.

Gideon winced, then turned back to the girl. He couldn't blame the woman for her reaction. Not after the horrors she must have experienced down there.

"Can I give you a hand up?" he asked, extending his arm toward her and hoping she didn't sense the hint of urgency in his voice. The car bomb would have distracted the camp's defenders, but there was no way they wouldn't react to the sound of a prolonged gun battle inside New Eden's borders.

It's only a matter of time before they come hunting.

And when they arrived, Gideon wanted to be long gone.

Still the girl said nothing. Gideon grimaced and tapped her on the shoulder, walking a fine line between attempting to remain unthreatening and also wanting to tap her hard enough to break her out of her trance.

It worked.

Kind of.

The girl's eyes widened in shock. Gideon retreated a couple of inches on instinct. He wanted to provoke a reaction, but not like this. He could easily drag the young teenager to one of the buses and put her on the road to safety, but that would only deepen the wounds of trauma that had already cut into her.

Figuring he was the cause of her response, Gideon was

slow to react himself. Slow to realize that the shouts behind him were of alarm. That the girl wasn't looking at him at all.

He twisted awkwardly in his crouched position. "What the hell—? Shit!"

One of the prisoners was standing over the body of a dead Brotherhood shooter, fumbling with a fallen rifle. He was in his late forties or early fifties, judging by the gray incursions at his temples and the sparseness of the hair on the crown of his head.

Gideon stumbled, off balance as he reached for his own rifle and tried to twist toward this fresh threat at the same time. He fell back, costing himself precious moments as the orange-clad former prisoner began bringing the rifle up into a firing position.

"Drop it!" Eli yelled.

A quick glance through his peripheral vision at his team leader told Gideon that Eli—like most of the Faithless shooters —was on the wrong side of the line of prisoners. Maybe two dozen silhouettes in orange clothing began to react in alarm at this fresh threat, sprinting in every direction. The chaos further muddied the picture.

For the briefest of instants, the muzzle of the rifle rose, aimed at the corpse of its former owner on the ground. Gideon almost breathed a sigh of relief, figuring that the man was just looking for a moment of catharsis.

But the emotion on his face told a different story. It was a rictus of pure rage. Of hatred.

Of relief.

Gideon's back crunched against the ground beneath him. The impact caused him to exhale sharply with discomfort. But he didn't let the distraction stop him from bringing his rifle up.

Too late.

The freed prisoner opened fire. He held the weapon out in front of him, almost as if he was carrying a priceless Ming vase.

The rifle's stock was easily a foot away from his shoulder. He jerked at the trigger instead of squeezing it like somebody experienced with firearms.

And none of it mattered.

The first crack of gunfire hung for a moment, cutting through the sound of screams and terror before it was lost in all the others. Gideon's eyes widened with shock of his own. The muzzle flashed as the rifle bucked wildly in its wielder's hands, the recoil and the unsteady firing position causing it to lurch in midair like a garden hose on full blast.

And then came the sight of blood mist hanging in the air. Of orange uniforms crumbling to the ground, the cloth now daubed in much darker stains.

Muzzle flashes. Exhaust gases condensing. The rifle lurching wildly in the man's feeble grip.

Gideon finally brought his own weapon up. The delay had cost him only a couple of seconds. But they were vital seconds. He was the only Faithless shooter with a clean shot.

He fired twice. Both bullets hit center mass, and the man's body crumpled from the bottom to the top, like a tower being dropped in a controlled demolition. His knees gave out first, holding for just a second before he crumpled at the waist and collapsed onto the body underneath him.

Gideon was up on his feet in an instant. Almost all of the prisoners had been cut loose. The meager line of a dozen or so who were still bound to each other cringed on the ground, some covering their faces in the crooks of their arms.

"Everybody okay?" he called out, pivoting his rifle left and right in search of any more trouble. "Talk to me!"

He could already see the answer. At least three of the Brotherhood prisoners had been cut down by the man's wild gunfire in a matter of seconds. One was clearly dead. A bullet had clipped his forehead, taking off most of the crown of his skull.

Two of the others had bullet wounds. It was impossible to judge their severity at this distance. Gideon didn't stop moving, now painfully aware that any one of the freed prisoners might pose a similar danger.

His throat was tight. Acid bubbled in his stomach like detergent in a washing machine. He scanned face after face, searching each time for any sign that he was looking at a wolf in sheep's clothing.

And he was sickened by the need to do so.

Unzipped duffel bags lay all around. He could see muzzles and stocks of rifles poking out, even the occasional flash of green metal that indicated a grenade. They'd brought the extra weapons to hand out to any of the prisoners who had military experience, knowing that if their escape came down to a shootout—as it probably would—then five guns weren't nearly enough to guarantee success.

Almost a dozen of the freed prisoners had already armed themselves. Most looked familiar and comfortable with the weapons they now held.

But even as they watched, the men and women who'd picked up rifles, pistols, and grenades began lowering them to the ground. Two even interlaced their fingers behind their heads, resignation filling their expressions.

Gideon realized that they expected the Faithless to cut them down. Expected a wave of vindictive revenge to cut through them.

"Everybody hold fire," he yelled as loud as he could. "Don't fucking shoot!"

He liked the Faithless team he'd inserted with. Liked Eli. Knew that all of them were better men than the Brotherhood prison guards they'd just cut down. They wouldn't open fire, wouldn't intentionally execute the prisoners they'd come here to save.

But another stray gunshot, even a car backfiring could have horrific consequences with everybody so on edge.

"Put down the weapons," Eli called out, taking his cue. "We're here to get you out, not hurt you. But we can't do that until we know it's going to be safe."

Gideon grimaced at the sight of crushed hopes on the faces of men and women—even a few teenagers—all around him. They'd believed themselves saved. And now they were following orders all over again. It had to be this way, he knew.

But I don't have to like it.

"I should've known," said a man with blond hair that was frosting white.

He was in his late fifties, if Gideon had to guess. He thrust himself through the crowd. It took Gideon a moment to realize that, unlike all the others, he wasn't wearing an orange jumpsuit. He was dressed instead in dark jeans and a brown shirt. It wasn't exactly the same uniform as those worn by the internal security goons. But it was close enough that he wouldn't attract immediate attention.

"Who are you?"

"Marcus," the man whispered, his expression vacant as he stared at the body of the prisoner Gideon had just gunned down. "I'm the one who told you where to come. He was called Leroy. A true believer. I should have known that even torture wouldn't dent his faith."

Gideon spun as he felt something tugging the cloth around his arm. The surge of adrenaline flooded through his system, and he began raising his weapon, only to lower it a moment later when he saw the girl's alarmed face staring back up at him.

"Sorry," he muttered. "Startled me."

"You're Gideon, aren't you?"

He nodded. He didn't have it in him to be annoyed by recognition. Not right now. Anyway, she didn't seem to be overawed by his presence. Instead, a different emotion glimmered in her eyes. Anxiety bordering on panic.

"Are you okay?"

"It's about your sister," she said.

Gideon looked around, realizing for the first time that Julia was nowhere to be seen. Apparently, the girl's anxiety was contagious because he felt his heart rate kick up by fifty beats a minute in a matter of seconds. "Where is she?"

"I'm Rae, her...friend," the girl said. She still appeared to be in shock but was somehow getting the words out, like she'd run through them in her head a hundred times. "She told me to come here. Said I had to tell you to leave without her. She made me promise."

Gideon flinched at this unexpected assault on his mental picture of how this day would play out. His stomach clenched. "Where's Julia?"

Rae's eyes glistened with tears. "Gabriel took her. She's at the stadium. She said we had to leave her behind."

"What are y'all talking about?" Eli asked, his voice gravelly from the dust that coated all their throats. Still stunned by what the girl had just said, Gideon hadn't heard the man approach. "Leave who behind?"

"My sister," Gideon answered through a jaw that was ground tight together. "And I'm not leaving Julia. I'm going to go get her."

He pivoted, the sole of his boot audibly scraping the asphalt underneath his feet. For a moment, he was spun around, couldn't remember where they'd dumped the bikes before sprinting to the ditch at the edge of the internal security office complex. Once he finally oriented himself, he strode in that direction only to be pulled up short by Eli's hand on his shoulder.

"Don't try and stop me, Eli," Gideon snapped, roughly brushing the man's fingers off of him.

"Wouldn't dare," the Faithless team leader grinned. "But the way I see it, you're gonna need some help."

SIXTY-SIX

Julia couldn't take her eyes off the black mushroom cloud that hung over the top of the stadium's bleachers. It was lopsided now, only the center of the pyre holding as the wind pulled it along—clearly blowing faster higher up than it was down below.

"Father, we need to get you out of here," a male voice said, his tone hushed but just barely audible from where Julia was sitting at the back of the temporary stage. A couple of thousand faces stared back at her—well, at Father Gabriel—from the cheap seats.

Breathe.

It didn't matter how hard Julia tried to obey her mind's conscious commands because her body was in no mood to comply. She could feel the sweat beading on her forehead and trickling down her face. Knew she was hunching forward due to her stomach muscles clenching tight with fear and worry.

Felt her heart racing in her chest, pumping blood around her veins way too fast for her lungs to keep up with short, sharp, panicked breaths.

Breathe!

She concentrated on inhaling slowly, stretching each breath out for three, four, five seconds before holding it for just as long. As her heart rate began to decrease, she slowly straightened her back. Her hands were already primly crossed on her lap, just like she'd been taught to do as a girl. Her face was a mask. That was another lesson learned long ago.

Julia only allowed her eyes to move, flickering left and right while the rest of her body remained in statuesque form. You wouldn't be able to tell from looking at her that her thoughts were racing in her head, that she was itching to find a way out of here.

Or so she hoped.

Several members of Gabriel's private security detail were arrayed around him in an outward-facing circle a few steps back from the podium at the front of the stage. He hadn't even begun his sermon when the explosion happened. She knew it had to be miles away, but she swore she felt the ground vibrate underneath her feet. The temporary wooden structure beneath her was like the skin of a drum, funneling the sensations through the legs of her chair and into her frame.

For a moment she'd thought that panic might ensue. She grew certain of it when the gunfire began in the distance. Some of the congregation arrayed for this extraordinary sermon had risen from their seats as fear whipped through the crowd like wildfire. A few began to scurry toward the exits.

And then the men with guns fanned out. In the congregation, people remembered they were more scared of Father Gabriel than they were of the sound of distant terror.

"Please, let her be okay," Julia whispered without moving her lips, her mind filled with images of Rae. The girl was too sweet to die in a place like this.

She sensed Lady Miranda's gaze on her, the attention hot

and uncomfortable on her skin. The woman was always present at such events. Julia didn't react. She stared expressionlessly out into the crowd, only daring to observe the security detail's frantic discussion with their principal through her peripheral vision.

"—sixteen dead at the front gate," a voice said. "Don't know how many attackers. We need to move."

"How many men do you have here?" Gabriel said, his face turned away from the crowd—and thus toward Julia.

"Approximately ninety. But half of them are just mouth-breathers here to keep the livestock in line," the head of his detail replied.

Gabriel paused for a moment, his eyes closed. When they snapped back open, he said, "We stay here."

"Sir—"

"I won't leave my people," Gabriel snapped. This time, his voice was designed to carry across the crowd.

Julia saw spines stiffen among them. A fervent, almost hungry light gleamed out of the eyes of those faces she was close enough to see. They wanted to believe.

At least, some of them did. Others wore blank stares. They were here in body but not spirit.

Like me.

More gunshots rattled in the distance, breaking a brief lull. The short snaps and cracks of the first wave had blended into a drum track of gunfire that mixed with the sounds of engines growling in seemingly every direction.

Someone will hear this, she thought. *The authorities will come.*

But her hopes rang false almost immediately. New Eden was just too far from civilization. How far could the sound of a gunshot carry? A couple of miles? Five?

Even if it was twice that, or three times, then the only living beings that would hear the sound of the raging battle would be grazing cows and other members of the faithful. There was no escaping this. And the cavalry weren't coming to save her.

Or her child.

The thought of failing the living soul growing steadily within her sent an icy chill down Julia's spine. She'd failed the child once already by returning to New Eden. But then she didn't know she was carrying new life.

There has to be a way.

She watched as Father Gabriel strode toward the podium, all but one member of his security detail turning to stare at the crowd. The last faced away, toward the row of chairs on which she, Lady Miranda, and a handful of other Brotherhood dignitaries were seated.

All of them were armed. They usually carried only handguns, but after the explosion, a stack of automatic rifles had been handed out.

Julia's gaze narrowed. The man standing to the right of Father Gabriel had a pistol in a thigh holster. The clasp that held it in was unfastened.

How far away was he? Ten feet?

Her eyes flicked back to the sole member of the detail facing her as she tried desperately to conceal the torrent of adrenaline and fear that flooded her system. Every five seconds or so, his gaze passed over her. But the rest of that time, his neck turned left and right, moving in a strange pattern, almost like a grid search.

Julia held her breath and watched, counting the seconds out in her head.

It's more like nine, she thought when she was done.

If she sprinted out of her chair when the man's neck was at the apex of its turn away from her, she might have just enough time to get to the gun and get hold of it before anybody reacted.

And then what?

"Are you afraid?" Gabriel said, grasping one edge of the podium with each of his hands. He spoke in a quiet voice. Despite the audio speakers positioned on either side of the stage and throughout the crowd, Julia had to strain to hear him.

The choice was intentional, she saw. Hundreds of people leaned forward slightly to hear him better. Bought into his message just slightly with their body language without even realizing it.

She considered the question. The answer was simple.

Yes.

Julia was certain now that she would be able to make it to the guard before anybody could stop her. She would wrestle free the weapon. But what happened after that was left to fate.

Would they just shoot her here, on the stage?

Probably.

"I said: *Are you afraid?*"

This time, Father Gabriel practically bellowed the question. She couldn't see his face, but she could picture it, having watched this scene play out a hundred, perhaps a thousand times before. His face was growing red, his eyes narrow, seeming to pick out every single person in the crowd individually.

"No," a voice rang out from one of the bleachers.

As it died away, so did every other sound except the rattle of gunfire in the distance. The crowd sat perfectly still, barely even daring to breathe.

"Well, you should be," Gabriel said, his voice lower again. He stopped to survey the gathering, letting the tension build. "Didn't I tell you that today would come?"

A scattering of voices sounded this time. "Yes!"

"Perhaps some of you wanted not to believe me. After all, why would anyone try and harm our community? All we've ever wanted is to live in peace. To raise our children in peace. To grow old in peace. Isn't that right?"

Individuals in the crowd rose to their feet. Then pairs and small groups, until finally entire rows and sections snapped upright at once. Nobody wanted to be the last to stand. "Yes! Yes!"

"Well, now the evil is here. Just like I promised. Should we surrender to it? Let our wives be raped and our children tortured?"

"No!"

Julia began to tremble as she watched a master whip fear into rage. Peaceful faces, men and women she'd never known to harbor even an ounce of hatred in their hearts were now torn into vicious scowls.

The answer to her question of what to do with the gun came to her simply. If there was no hope of engineering a physical escape, then only one other choice remained.

If somebody's going to pull the trigger, at least let it be me.

Gabriel thumped the podium. "So what are we going to do about it?"

"Fight!"

SIXTY-SEVEN

"Where the hell do you think you're going?" Gideon said. He had one hand on the handlebar of the dirt bike he'd just hoisted back upright. Eli had already climbed up onto his.

The trio of rescued prisoners, still clad in their orange jumpsuits, had just skidded to a halt by the three remaining bikes. Each was armed with a rifle taken from one of the duffel bags they'd carried into New Eden.

The oldest of the three, a tall, fit-looking kid in his late teens or early twenties had one of the bags slung over his shoulder. It resembled a sock weighed down with baseballs. Gideon figured it was probably stacked with spare magazines since the jumpsuits didn't come with pockets.

"We're coming with you," he said.

"The hell you are," Gideon snapped. "Head to the buses and get out of here. This is too dangerous."

"You know what they did to my brother?" the kid fired back.

Gideon glanced helplessly in the direction of the makeshift arena. They were running out of time. He cast an apologetic look at Eli for what he was about to say, then tried a different tack. "This is a suicide mission. I'm probably going to get myself killed doing it. You don't want to be by my side."

"They tied his wrists behind his back and hoisted them up with a rope to the ceiling. Left him there for three days without food or water. He's probably never going to raise his arms above his head again. I don't give a shit about dying. None of us do. We want to help."

"You can't—" Gideon began.

The kid cut him off. "What are you going to do, shoot us?"

It was a good point.

"Can't stop 'em," Eli grunted, revving his bike's engine. "And we could use the numbers."

Gideon puffed out his cheeks. He made a snap decision. "Fine. At least tell me your name."

"Cassius."

Eli grinned. "Hope they don't run out of S's by the time they get to your tombstone."

Cassius grabbed a bike and gestured for the two men he was with to follow. "You're getting ideas above your station. My bet is all five of us get dumped in unmarked dirt graves."

"So you're an optimist," Eli yelled over the sound of now five revving engines. "Guess you'd have to be to join this club."

This time, Gideon led the procession. As before, they stuck to dirt tracks and farm roads through the ranch, avoiding the paved main roads where they were more likely to encounter Chosen patrols.

The bike's powerful engine throbbed between his thighs. The air stank of burned gasoline, smoke, and body odor. Trickles of sweat ran down his cheeks, only for the wind to whip them back into his hair. A quick glance into his rear mirrors revealed that the small group of riders had fanned out behind him in the shape of an arrow, with him at the head and a cloud of dust trailing behind like a comet's tail. The roar of five engines being gunned to full power over uneven ground was almost overpowering. It felt like sitting on top of a rocket beginning its thundering ascent into the clouds. Or else riding at the head of a medieval cavalry charge.

Gideon had never felt anything like it. Adrenaline combined with desperation to save Julia's life, mixing like fuel and oxygen and combusting to scour away any residual fear.

"Contact!" he yelled as his bike crested a small rise at the end of a dirt track. A pickup truck was parked dead center, almost—but not quite—blocking the road. Two men with rifles sat in its bed.

Despite the noise of the bike engines, they were somehow—impossibly—looking the wrong way. Gideon threw his body to the left and gunned the bike's throttle at the same time, coaxing more power out of the beast, more downforce and friction as he guided the dirt bike through the narrow gap at the side of the road.

Dried amber-colored grass disappeared from his peripheral vision to the left, a solid body of metal and rubber and glass to the right. He screamed his warning again, knowing there was no way the group following him would be able to hear.

At the very last second, just as the front wheel of his bike drew level with the rear of the pickup truck, he saw two faces turned toward him, their eyes wide with shock and surprise. Gideon closed his eyes.

He'd done all he could.

All that was left now was to pray.

Just let me get to her.

The front tire of his motorcycle bounced up out of a pothole and momentarily threw the entire bike into the air. His stomach dropped away beneath him, and he opened his eyes again just as rubber met road.

He was through.

Alive!

Gideon was already thirty yards down the road by the time he twisted around and peered over his shoulder. All five bikes had made it through the gap. The two armed patrol guards on the truck had only just finished turning toward the sound of approaching vehicles when they were forced to twist back.

He saw one of them raise his rifle. Steady it. Flinched as compressed gas chased the muzzle flash out of the barrel.

Heard, or perhaps imagined, a bullet whistling past his left ear.

And then they were gone. Out of sight. And on the valley floor beneath them, Gabriel's makeshift arena loomed into view.

THE PLAN WAS SIMPLE. It had to be. There was no time to devise anything else. The small group split into two parts a mile from the arena: one containing Gideon and Eli, the other Cassius and the two other freed prisoners.

Their job was to mount a diversion: to attack the guards at the main entrance to the arena and make as much noise doing so as possible. Gideon and Eli would attempt to use the distraction to sneak into the rear of the structure. Now that they were this close, they could see that most of the bleachers were temporary. The fence that ringed the arena was made of steel barriers that only rose to waist height—easy to hurdle.

"I guess New Eden runs on trust," Eli said.

"Yeah," Gideon agreed. "That and fear."

"Don't worry, I'm an optimist," Cassius yelled as he rode away to the right, accelerating so fast he almost lost control.

"Guess you'd have to be to survive in a place like this," Eli muttered. "Glad I got out when I did."

The two men slowed down until they were creeping over the ground at a jogging pace. Somehow the ride became bumpier than it had at high speed.

In the distance, a furious gun battle raged. Both Gideon and Eli knew that the sound of gunshots was echoing from the edge of the ranch—where the rest of the Faithless team were trying to get the prisoners out. But neither man gave voice to their concerns.

There was nothing they could do to help.

Barely a minute had passed since they'd separated from Cassius when a far closer gun battle broke out. Gideon imagined the three prisoners dressed in orange firing their rifles into the sky to attract attention like Afghan warlords or Mongol warriors dropped into the twenty-first century.

It sounded like dozens of weapons were firing. It was impossible to pick out individual gunshots. They were lost in a rolling wave of thunder.

By unspoken agreement, Eli and Gideon dumped the two bikes on the ground and continued on foot as they approached a parking lot at the rear of the converted sports field. Dozens of cars and passenger vans were lined up. If he hadn't known better, Gideon might've thought he was arriving at a youth baseball game.

He dropped into a crouch as Eli held up a fist.

"I see three sentries," the other man whispered, gesturing at where they were located.

Gideon popped up slowly before he nodded his agreement. "I'll take left, you take right. Whoever finishes first gets dibs on the third guy."

Rationally, he knew that it was inhumane to talk about taking human life this casually. But the part of his mind that thought like that was locked up. Boxed away while his animal spirits ran the asylum.

"On three," Eli agreed.

Two.

One.

Both men darted up above the trunk of an aging red Toyota sedan. Gideon steadied himself for a second as he lined up the shot. His rifle had no silencer, but he doubted anybody would hear one more gunshot over all this chaos.

A man's head hovered between his rifle's crosshairs.

Gideon exhaled.

He squeezed the trigger and the face snapped back. He probably imagined the spray of blood that hung in the air.

Twisting, he pivoted his rifle toward the second target.

"Too late," Eli called out. He let the muzzle of his rifle drop toward the ground, still smoking, his chest heaving from exertion and adrenaline in equal measure.

"Don't think we're getting off that easy," Gideon said, his eyes going as wide as saucers.

"Huh?" Eli grunted. It took him a moment to clock the party of almost a dozen armed shooters pouring out of one of the arena's exits. His response was remarkably restrained, given the circumstances. "Shit."

SIXTY-EIGHT

"Guess they spotted us," Gideon yelled, ducking behind a black SUV in the final row of vehicles in the parking lot just as half a dozen bullets thudded into it.

"What gave you that idea?" Eli called back. He popped up and let off two quick shots before dropping back behind cover just in time to avoid another wave of gunshots whipping in like yellowjackets. "Got one."

They'd managed to close within twenty yards of the escaping group of shooters before they were noticed. There was only one explanation for the group's purpose. It had to be Gabriel's security detail beating a hasty retreat.

Didn't want to go down with the ship. Big surprise.

Gideon crawled to the far side of the SUV, steadied the stock of his rifle in the crook of his shoulder, then popped out just long enough to squeeze off a shot.

Except he didn't.

"Hold fire," he hissed. "It's Julia. They have her."

GABRIEL'S SECURITY detail was caught in no man's land when the first of his bodyguards spotted danger. Julia threw herself to the ground, scraping the skin off her forearms in the process and bloodying the front of her dress.

Make it stop!

She didn't know whether she was screaming or just thinking as she belly-crawled somewhere, anywhere, in search of safety. Of cover.

But there was none to be found.

Julia pressed her face to the ground and screamed over the sound of gunshots as bullets chewed up the asphalt all around her. She squeezed her palms to her ears in a desperate, hopeless attempt to block out the din of violence.

"Kill them," Gabriel screamed, his voice hoarse with fear. "Get me out of here!"

Julia didn't know how or why she'd been caught up in his security detail. He'd used the commotion of the attack as an opportunity to slip away without being noticed, belying all his brave words. She found herself bundled in the middle of his guards, pushed down stairs and out of the sports field, only able to stay upright when she stumbled because the bodies were hemmed too closely all around for her to fall.

A bullet hit home close by. Julia knew because the side of her face that wasn't covered with her hand was suddenly wet with blood. She wiped her arm against her face, looked at her bloodied fingers in shock, and saw out of the corner of her eye just in time that the unfortunate victim was about to crumple on top of her.

She rolled, but not quickly enough to avoid him collapsing over the back of her legs. It took several seconds for her to kick herself free. She was definitely screaming now. Louder still when two more bullets kicked up into the corpse in front of her, causing it to jerk spasmodically like somebody undergoing an epileptic fit.

And then she fell silent. It was as if a clarity came over her. She pushed herself up off the ground, almost seal-like, just long enough to take a good look around. Roughly a third of Gabriel's security detail was already dead. The other six were either kneeling or lying prone as they fired relentlessly into the rows of cars.

Gabriel had a pistol in his hand, but he was sheltering behind yet another corpse, using the body as a shield. His guards weren't facing him—they were too occupied by the danger to the front.

Julia's stomach clenched as a realization swept over her. *I could end this.*

The dead bodyguard who'd collapsed on her was holding a rifle when he went down. He'd dropped it just a couple of feet away.

She could hear yelling from the direction of the SUVs, but her ears were ringing too loudly to make out the words being said. The roar of nearby gunfire didn't help. Julia pulled her legs up into a crouch, then popped upright. Her heart raced in her chest.

Bullets snapped in the air all around her. She should have cringed, ducked from the near-certain death, but somehow, she knew that they weren't aimed in her direction. Or maybe the adrenaline was just blocking out the fear.

She took a step toward the gun.

"What are you doing?" Gabriel hissed. He seemed to have momentarily forgotten his narcissism and appeared genuinely concerned for her safety.

Julia scooped up the rifle. She had no idea whether or not it was loaded, but a glance at the safety switch on the side showed that it was definitely ready to fire. She brought it up to her shoulder and stared icily at the man who had ruined her life and that of so many others.

Felt her finger brush the trigger. Her mouth curled up into a snarl.

And she heard her voice as she'd never heard it before. "Tell them to drop their fucking guns!"

"What are you doing, Julia?" Gabriel hissed.

She realized with a start that she could hear him despite his quiet tone and the ringing in her ears. All the gunfire around her had ceased. Gabriel's remaining bodyguards were frozen, most of them with their weapons facing out. They didn't dare turn their aim on her for fear of what she might do.

"This ends now," Julia snapped.

"You can't be serious," Gabriel said, blinking rapidly. "There's no way out of here."

"Yes, there is," she said forcefully, gesturing at Gabriel to drop the pistol in his hand. "Because you're going to make it happen. I'm taking you with me."

SIXTY-NINE

"What's the plan, Gideon?" Eli hissed as the eye of the storm crept over them. Gunfire raged in the distance, but an eerie calm had silenced the gunfight they'd just been embroiled in. Eli's trigger was half-depressed, as if he'd caught himself in the action of firing as Gabriel's bodyguards had spun inward.

Toward Julia.

She was only twenty or thirty yards away, a black rifle stock held up to her right shoulder. The sling hung loosely underneath it, shivering every time she trembled. Half a dozen weapons were trained on her.

But none of Gideon's men could shoot. Not with their leader in the crosshairs of an automatic weapon.

The punishing storm of lead that had chewed through the vehicles Eli and Gideon were sheltering behind had abruptly ceased. The risk they posed was no longer the prime concern. Julia was the enemy within.

"Gideon?" Eli repeated.

Gideon started moving toward the circle of firearms before he knew why. He saw Eli grimace with frustration out of the corner of his eye, but the man didn't hesitate before stepping out from behind cover and keeping pace with him. Gideon strode toward Gabriel's protective detail.

And Julia at the center of it.

More armed men were now running out of the makeshift stadium, making a beeline for Gabriel. There was even a woman among them, older, wearing gray robes. She moved gracefully despite the chaos around her.

But Gideon was closer.

He pushed through the outer circle of Gabriel's guards before they even realized who he was. One of them twitched and brought his weapon up, but the man visibly shirked away from opening fire. The risk of setting off a storm of bullets that might gut his own leader was too great.

Eli followed close behind, his pistol constantly roving left and right as he covered a dozen different enemy shooters, all close enough to stick a blade through their ribs, let alone pull a trigger.

"Julia..." Gideon said softly.

His sister's cheeks were red with rage. Her dress was dusty and speckled with droplets of blood. He couldn't tell whether it was her own, though she didn't seem visibly injured. Though her entire frame trembled with some combination of rage and fear and whatever other emotions were roiling through her, the rifle remained completely steady.

"Nobody shoot," Father Gabriel snapped out loud. "We're going to talk this out."

A few sideways glances were exchanged by members of his protective detail, but nobody disobeyed his order.

"Julia?" Gideon said, ignoring the cult leader's attempts to attract his attention. "Can you hear me?"

At first, his sister didn't even flinch. It was like talking to a stone wall. But a shadow passed from her eyes, and she glanced slightly toward him, if only for an instant.

"He has to die, Gideon," she said, her voice flat. "You were right. I should have listened."

Her finger tightened on the trigger, sending another fraction of an ounce of pressure through it. Gideon hid a wince. There was no way of knowing how much more it would take. He had no idea how practiced she was with firearms, but he guessed not very. It would be easy to accidentally put a bullet through Gabriel's chest.

And then they were all dead.

A dozen more armed men ran to the circle of Chosen bodyguards. Then more. Gabriel shouted out another command for calm, his voice tight in his throat.

"He's evil, Gideon," Julia said, still in a conversational tone of voice. "He's like a cancer. He needs to be excised."

"Lower your weapon and I'll let you all live," Gabriel said, clearly attempting to wrestle back control of the situation.

"It's not up to you!" Julia yelled, the sudden fury shocking compared to her previous calm. "Don't you get it? It's over!"

Gideon walked toward his sister. He felt the weight of a dozen barrels trained on his head, but he knew that nobody would open fire.

Not yet.

"I can't bring up a baby in a world he gets to live in," Julia said softly. "I'd rather die."

Gideon felt as though he'd been punched in the gut. "You're pregnant?"

The question came out in a whisper. Gabriel squinted as though he hadn't heard, opened his mouth, but closed it again. Maybe it was because of the expression on Julia's face.

Julia didn't answer. Silent tears streamed down her face

now. Gideon sensed that she was losing control. That any second now she would either pull the trigger—or collapse.

Do something!

He slowly raised his pistol and leveled it at Gabriel's forehead. An audible rustle of clothing and the clicking of metal rang out as more weapons were trained on him, but he didn't flinch.

"Does that offer still stand?" he asked, fixing his gaze on Gabriel's. "We live?"

"That's right," Gabriel said, nodding slowly. "Just get her to drop the gun."

Gideon took a step closer to him, then another. One more brought him close enough to grab the man's shoulder and spin him around so that his pistol's muzzle was pressed against Gabriel's rib cage. He held his breath as he waited for a bullet, a dozen bullets to slam into him and take both of them down.

But other than a sharp intake of breath, nobody fired.

"What are you doing?" Gabriel hissed, momentarily affronted by his temerity rather than just afraid. Gideon wondered how long it had been since somebody had dared to touch him without permission.

"You're coming with us," Gideon said, maneuvering his body so that it was in between Gabriel's weapon and the rifle Julia held. He hoped that she wouldn't pull the trigger anyway.

"That's not happening," a gruff male voice snapped from somewhere behind.

"The hell it isn't," Gideon snapped. "Either you come with us, or you die. I don't trust you to keep your word. Not without leverage."

He felt Gabriel stiffen at his side. The man's breath audibly slowed in his chest. It was as though he was relaxing despite the chaos.

"I can take him," the same guard said from somewhere behind Gideon. "Just give me the word, sir."

"You better be sure about that," Gideon whispered into Gabriel's ear. "It's a hell of a gamble."

"I told you not to shoot," Gabriel snapped. "Where's Miranda?"

Gideon frowned with confusion at the question before he realized it wasn't aimed at him. Heads turned and murmured voices carried a message outward through the circle. It took almost a minute before Miranda—the woman in gray he'd seen before—approached.

She bowed her head.

"Do you trust me, Miranda?" Gabriel asked.

"Of course..."

"I need to go with these people."

A murmur of shock ran around the gathering.

"Not for long," he added sharply. "You will take command in my absence."

"What if they don't bring you back?" Miranda asked.

"Would you sacrifice yourself for me, Miranda?"

"You know I would."

"What about you, Ronan?" Gabriel asked loudly. Gideon twisted his head to see who he was talking to.

Ronan, it seemed, was the bodyguard who had spoken earlier. He was a powerful man, not tall but with a bodybuilder's frame. He had a pistol aimed at Julia's chest. "Anytime, sir."

"Do it," Gabriel ordered.

"Sir?"

"I gave you a command, Ronan. Don't make me ask twice."

Gideon watched in silent horror as the realization of what he was being asked to do hit home on Ronan's face. For the first time, his pistol hand trembled. The weapon began to droop toward the ground.

It steadied halfway there. Held in the air for several seconds. Then Ronan brought the muzzle up to the underside of his chin. He hesitated for an instant, drew in a deep breath, then squeezed the trigger.

The sound of the single gunshot made Gideon flinch. He felt a coldness grow in his stomach and chest at the callousness of Gabriel's order. He looked away from the body now slumped in a heap on the ground when he saw that the back of Ronan's skull was missing.

"Miranda," Gabriel said casually, as if he hadn't noticed the violence, "if I am not returned to this place, you know what to do."

Even Julia seemed shaken from her trance at Ronan's death. Gabriel's message was clear. He would give them safe passage out of the ranch. But hundreds, perhaps thousands would die if they didn't let him come back.

"We'll need a car," Gideon said, knowing he had to seize control of this opening.

"Get them one," Gabriel said flatly.

"Julia," Gideon continued as somebody scurried off on the edge of the circle. He flashed a look at Eli, who had sidled closer to his sister. "Your baby can still live. They can grow up far away from all this. Come with me."

"How do you know that?"

"I promise you, Julia. I won't let anybody hurt you again."

He watched as the fight went out of his sister. The instant she relaxed, Eli worked the rifle from her hands. He trained it on Gabriel while his other hand reached for Julia's.

Gideon began to push the cult leader through the circle of his stunned bodyguards.

"Eli?" he said quietly.

"Yeah?"

"It's time to go."

EPILOGUE

Zara forced her way inside the second the motel door cracked open and wrapped her arms around Gideon. He motioned for Eli to relax, and the Faithless shooter lowered the pistol he'd snatched up. Julia was sitting on one of the room's two beds. She awkwardly hugged her knees to her chest but said nothing.

"You're okay," Zara whispered into his right ear. "Thank God."

Gideon pushed the door closed with his foot. "Safe and sound," he said, disguising a wince as the movement sent a jab of pain up through his abused frame. He'd somehow avoided being shot or killed in the rescue attempt, but smaller scrapes, cuts, and bruises covered almost every inch of his body.

She squeezed him harder before finally, reluctantly letting go. Eli pulled the curtain back and peered out the window.

"I came alone," Zara said firmly. "I wasn't followed."

Eli let the curtain fall back. "Just checking."

Gideon reached for Zara's hand. "What about you?"

She gave him a thin-lipped smile, still visibly strained by

the events of the previous week. It softened as he met her gaze and held it there. "Getting by."

"How's Lachlan?"

Zara shrugged. "Surviving. I guess we all are. He's doing better than he was. I think the shock of Harriet's death is fading. He's thrown his energies into sorting this whole mess out. It's distracting him for now, but he'll have to deal with his grief sooner than later."

"Maybe not," Gideon said softly.

The Faithless were scattered. Almost every single one of their safehouses had been either destroyed in the last few days or compromised by Jamie's betrayal. Lachlan had tapped every last cent of the group's financial holdings to buy a few weeks of runway, but it wouldn't stretch much longer than that.

Small groups had been formed from the remaining Faithless, including those rescued from inside New Eden and the freed members of the Brotherhood. After sustaining so many casualties, the latter group now outnumbered the former. From what little Gideon had gleaned over the past few days from the limited communications he'd shared with Zara, some of them were almost catatonic. Their entire worldview had been shattered.

Lachlan had shared out the money with each of the groups. None of them knew the locations of the others, in case any true believers remained among the escaped Brotherhood members.

"We'll have to figure out a plan fast," Zara said. "Before the money runs out."

Her eyes settled on the bound prisoner who lay on the floor between the motel room's twin beds. His wrists and ankles were bound with duct tape, and another piece had been slapped over his lips. A ripped-up T-shirt had been wrapped around his eyes to block out his vision. Her jaw tightened as she saw his face.

"I wish we could kill him," she said, almost baring her teeth. "It's what he deserves."

"That's what I keep saying," Julia agreed, opening her mouth for the first time. She'd spoken only occasionally over the past two days, and her voice was hoarse from lack of use.

Zara walked slowly over to Gideon's sister. She stopped a couple of feet away, clearly being careful not to crowd her. "He'll see justice, Julia," she said. "I promise you."

"When?" Julia hissed.

Gideon joined the two women. "Right now, he's leverage. He's more valuable alive than dead. But he won't be forever. And I'll make him pay for everything he's done."

AUTHOR'S NOTE

Hi,

Thanks so much for reading *Test of Faith*. As I guess you know, I'm two books deep into the Ryker series now, and I'm loving writing every word. I hope that comes through the pages!

Book 3, *Proof of Life*, should be out early January (2025, if you're reading this in the future), so there's not long to wait. Before then you can expect a Trapp installment, and the fourth book in the *Blake Larsen* series. Some of this work has been completed a while, but due to the vagaries of publishers and publishing dates and preorder slots it's all going to come out in the space of about three months!

I'll keep things short, since this was quite a long book. Thanks as always for reading. If you enjoyed, please consider leaving a review or a rating on Amazon. It's make-or-break for independent authors like myself.

Thanks,

Jack.

FOR ALL THE LATEST NEWS

I hope you enjoyed *Test of Faith.* If you did, and don't fancy sifting through thousands of books on Amazon and leaving your next great read to chance, then sign up to my mailing list and be the first to hear when I release a new book.

Visit - www.jack-slater.com/updates

You can also visit Amazon to leave a review on *Test of Faith*, for which as ever I would be most grateful.

Thanks so much for reading!

Jack.

Printed in Great Britain
by Amazon

60384313R00255